# BREAK NO BONES

As a forensic anthropologist to the province of Quebec, Canada, Kathy Reichs has often said that she works *with* the dead, but *for* the living.

Forensics are an integral part of her world, with cases constantly coming in to her lab. And yet her chosen profession is, she says, like any other job. However, though you may get used to what's happening around you, and to the sounds and smells and sights of death, this doesn't mean you become immune to it.

Each of her books is based loosely on the cases she's worked on, or an experience she's had. She believes that her stories remain fresh because they originate from her being enmeshed and engaged in forensic work on a regular basis.

Kathy Reichs is one of only eighty-two forensic anthropologists ever certified by the American Board of Forensic Anthropology. She served on the Board of Directors and as Vice President of both the American Academy of Forensic Sciences and the American Board of Forensic Anthropology, and is currently a member of the National Police Services Advisory Council in Canada. She is a Professor in the Department at the University of North Carolina-Charlotte. She is a native of Chicago, where she received her PhD. at Northwestern. She now divides her time between Charlotte, NC and Montreal, Quebec.

www.kathyreichs.com
www.facebook.com/kathyreichsbooks
twitter.com/kathyreichs

**Praise for Kathy Reichs**

'Reichs' real-life expertise gives her novels an authenticity that most other crime novelists would kill for'
*Daily Express*

'Reichs is the queen of pathology thrillers'
*Independent*

'Completely engrossing ... drags the reader into a different world where dialogue is tense, dead men tell the best tales and the ice will freeze the bones. Read this and you'll know why the word "thriller" was invented'
Frances Fyfield

'Reichs has proved that she is now up there with the best'
Marcel Berlins, *The Times*

'The forensic detail is harrowing, the pace relentless and the prose assured. Kathy Reichs just gets better and better and is now the Alpha female of the genre'
*Irish Independent*

'A long way from your standard forensic thriller: all the excitement you crave, indefatigably expert. But conscience-generated and compassionate too'
*Literary Review*

'A brilliant novel ... fascinating science and dead-on psychological portrayals, not to mention a whirlwind of a plot ... a must-read'
Jeffrey Deaver

Tempe Brennan ... is smart, resourceful and likeable ... an investigator to follow'
*Daily Telegraph*

'It's becoming apparent that Reichs is not just "as good as" Cornwell, she has become the finer writer ... the ever-accelerating unfolding of the plot has all the élan of Kathy Reichs at her most adroit'
*Daily Express*

'Inevitably compared to Patricia Cornwell, Reichs is actually in a different league. Tempe Brennan is already ... a much more rounded character than Cornwell's heroine Scarpetta: more human, less driven and much better company during the time it takes her to untangle these complex crimes'
*Sunday Times*

'Kathy Reichs is some kind of writer! Deep in Patricia Cornwell territory, she outdoes the queen of slice 'em and dice 'em fiction ... Terrific'
*Independent on Sunday*

'Better than Patricia Cornwell'
*Sunday Express*

'Reichs is in real life a highly experienced forensic anthropologist. But her leading character, Temperance Brennan, is a fictional creation and a tough and gutsy heroine she makes'
*Scotland on Sunday*

'[Kathy Reichs's] novels keep a tight grip on the plot, move along at a ferocious pace and manage to frighten and intrigue the reader in equal measure'
*Irish Independent*

'Tough, exciting stuff ... you are in for a good, chilling time'
*Daily Express*

'Reichs gets better with every book, her heroine, forensic anthropologist Temperance Brennan, more feisty ... Gritty detail, chilling atmosphere, engrossing plot'
*Woman & Home*

'Reichs ... expertly directs a busy plot that moves with electrical force in the final quarter. She capitalises on the morbid, yet captivating aspects of the forensic trenchwork, yet never lets it overwhelm her story. But it is Reichs's ongoing development of Tempe, a woman ... with a mature understanding of human nature, and a self-deprecating sense of humour that truly lifts the book above many of its peers'
*Publishers Weekly*

Also available by Kathy Reichs

# Kathy
# REICHS

# BREAK NO BONES

arrow books

Published by arrangement with the original publisher, Scribner,
an imprint of Simon & Schuster, Inc.

First published in Great Britain in 2006 by William Heinemann

First published in paperback in 2007 by
Arrow Books
The Random House Group Limited
20 Vauxhall Bridge Road, London, SW1V 2SA

www.randomhouse.co.uk

Addresses for companies within The Random House Group Limited
can be found at: www.randomhouse.co.uk/offices.htm

The Random House Group Limited Reg. No. 954009

A CIP catalogue record for this book is available from the British Library

Typeset by SX Composing DTP, Rayleigh, Essex SS6 7XF

Penguin Random House is committed to a sustainable future for
our business, our readers and our planet. This book is made from
Forest Stewardship Council® certified paper.

Printed and bound in Great Britain by Clays Ltd, St Ives plc

In loving memory of
Arvils Reichs
February 9, 1949–February 23, 2006
*Dusi Saldi*

# Acknowledgments

For their willingness to help, and for the knowledge and support they provided, I owe thanks to many.

Ted Rathbun, Ph.D., University of South Carolina, Columbia (retired), provided information on South Carolina archaeology. Robert Dillon, Ph.D., College of Charleston, gave guidance on malacology. Lee Goff, Ph.D., Chaminade University, is, and will always be, the guru of bugs.

Detective Chris Dozier, Charlotte-Mecklenburg Police Department, coached me on the use of AFIS. Detective John Appel, Guilford County, North Carolina, Sheriff's Department (retired), and Detective Investigator Joseph P. Noya, Jr., NYPD Crime Scene Unit, helped with police minutiae.

Linda Kramer, R.N., Michelle Skipper, M.B.A., and Eric Skipper, M.D., helped with the non-Hodgkins lymphoma scenario.

Kerry Reichs kept me accurate on Charleston geography. Paul Reichs provided information on legal proceedings and offered useful comments on early versions of the manuscript.

Others helped but prefer to remain anonymous. You know who you are. Thanks a million.

J. Lawrence Angel was one of the grand old men of

forensic anthropology. His chapter on the Spanish windlass and vertebral fracture really does exist: Angel, J. L., and P. C. Caldwell, "Death by strangulation: a forensic anthropological case from Wilmington, Delaware," in *Human Identification: Case Studies in Forensic Anthropology*, eds. T. A. Rathbun and J. E. Buikstra (Springfield, Ill.: Charles C. Thomas, 1986).

Heartfelt thanks to my editor, Nan Graham. *Break No Bones* benefited greatly from your advice. Thanks also to Nan's assistant, Anna deVries. And thanks to Susan Sandon, my editor across the pond.

Last, but far from least, thanks to my agent, Jennifer Rudolph-Walsh, who always has time for a word of encouragement. And who always makes me feel smart. And pretty.

Though *Break No Bones* is a work of fiction, I have tried to keep details of the story honest. If there are mistakes, I own them. Don't blame the folks acknowledged above.

# BREAK
# NO
# BONES

# 1

Never fails. You're wrapping up the operation when someone blunders onto the season's big score.

OK. I'm exaggerating. But it's damn close to what happened. And the final outcome was far more disturbing than any last-minute discovery of a potsherd or hearth.

It was May 18, the *second*-to-the-last day of the archaeological field school. I had twenty students digging a site on Dewees, a barrier island north of Charleston, South Carolina.

I also had a journalist. With the IQ of plankton.

"Sixteen bodies?" Plankton pulled a spiral notebook as his brain strobed visions of Dahmer and Bundy. "Vics ID'd?"

"The graves are prehistoric."

Two eyes rolled up, narrowed under puffy lids. "Old Indians?"

"Native Americans."

1

"They got me covering dead Indians?" No political correctness prize for this guy.

"They?" Icy.

"The *Moultrie News*. The East Cooper community paper."

Charleston, as Rhett told Scarlett, is a city marked by the genial grace of days gone by. Its heart is the Peninsula, a district of antebellum homes, cobbled streets, and outdoor markets bounded by the Ashley and Cooper rivers. Charlestonians define their turf by these waterways. Neighborhoods are referred to as "West Ashley" or "East Cooper," the latter including Mount Pleasant, and three islands, Sullivan's, the Isle of Palms, and Dewees. I assumed plankton's paper covered that beat.

"And you are?" I asked.

"Homer Winborne."

With his five-o'clock shadow and fast food paunch, the guy looked more like Homer Simpson.

"We're busy here, Mr. Winborne."

Winborne ignored that. "Isn't it illegal?"

"We have a permit. The island's being developed, and this little patch is slated for home sites."

"Why bother?" Sweat soaked Winborne's hairline. When he reached for a hanky, I noticed a tick cruising his collar.

"I'm an anthropologist on faculty at the University of North Carolina at Charlotte. My students and I are here at the request of the state."

Though the first bit was true, the back end was a stretch. Actually, it happened like this.

UNCC's New World archaeologist normally conducted a student excavation during the short presummer term each May. In late March of this year, the lady had announced her acceptance of a position at Purdue. Busy sending out résumés throughout the winter, she'd ignored the field school. Sayonara. No instructor. No site.

Though my specialty is forensics, and I now work with the dead sent to coroners and medical examiners, my graduate training and early professional career were devoted to the not so recently deceased. For my doctoral research I'd examined thousands of prehistoric skeletons recovered from North American burial mounds.

The field school is one of the Anthropology Department's most popular courses, and, as usual, was enrolled to capacity. My colleague's unexpected departure sent the chair into a panic. He begged that I take over. The students were counting on it! A return to my roots! Two weeks at the beach! Extra pay! I thought he was going to throw in a Buick.

I'd suggested Dan Jaffer, a bioarchaeologist and my professional counterpart with the medical examiner/coroner system in the great Palmetto State to our south. I pleaded possible cases at the ME office in Charlotte, or at the Laboratoire de sciences judiciaires et de médecine légale in Montreal, the two agencies for which I regularly consult.

The chair gave it a shot. Good idea, bad timing. Dan Jaffer was on his way to Iraq.

I'd contacted Jaffer and he'd suggested Dewees

as an excavation possibility. A burial ground was slated for destruction, and he'd been trying to forestall the bulldozers until the site's significance could be ascertained. Predictably, the developer was ignoring his requests.

I'd contacted the Office of the State Archaeologist in Columbia, and on Dan's recommendation they'd accepted my offer to dig some test trenches, thereby greatly displeasing the developer.

And here I was. With twenty undergraduates. And, on our thirteenth and penultimate day, plankton-brain.

My patience was fraying like an overused rope.

"Name?" Winborne might have been asking about grass seed.

I fought back the urge to walk away. Give him what he wants, I told myself. He'll leave. Or, with luck, die from the heat.

"Temperance Brennan."

"Temperance?" Amused.

"Yes, *Homer*."

Winborne shrugged. "Don't hear that name so much."

"I'm called Tempe."

"Like the town in Utah."

"Arizona."

"Right. What kind of Indians?"

"Probably Sewee."

"How'd you know stuff was here?"

"Through a colleague at USC-Columbia."

"How'd he know?"

4

"He spotted small mounds while doing a survey after the news of an impending development was announced."

Winborne took a moment to make notes in his spiral. Or maybe he was buying time to come up with his idea of an insightful question. In the distance I could hear student chatter and the clatter of buckets. Overhead, a gull cawed and another answered.

"Mounds?" No one was going to short-list this guy for a Pulitzer.

"Following closure of the graves, shells and sand were heaped on top."

"What's the point in digging them up?"

That was it. I hit the little cretin with the interview terminator. Jargon.

"Burial customs aren't well known for aboriginal Southeastern coastal populations, and this site could substantiate or refute ethnohistoric accounts. Many anthropologists believe the Sewee were part of the Cusabo group. According to some sources, Cusabo funerary practices involved defleshing of the corpse, then placement of the bones in bundles or boxes. Others describe the scaffolding of bodies to allow decomposition prior to burial in common graves."

"Holy crap. That's gross."

"More so than draining the blood from a corpse and replacing it with chemical preservatives, injecting waxes and perfumes and applying makeup to simulate life, then interring in airtight coffins and vaults to forestall decay?"

Winborne looked at me as though I'd spoken Sanskrit. "Who does that?"

"We do."

"So what are you finding?"

"Bones."

"Just bones?" The tick was now crawling up Winborne's neck. Give a heads-up? Screw it. The guy was irritating as hell.

I launched into my standard cop and coroner spiel. "The skeleton paints a story of an individual. Sex. Age. Height. Ancestry. In certain cases, medical history or manner of death." Pointedly glancing at my watch, I followed with my archaeological shtick. "Ancient bones are a source of information on extinct populations. How people lived, how they died, what they ate, what diseases they suffered—"

Winborne's gaze drifted over my shoulder. I turned.

Topher Burgess was approaching, various forms of organic and inorganic debris pasted to his sunburned torso. Short and plump, with knit cap, wire rims, and muttonchop sideburns, the kid reminded me of an undergraduate Smee.

"Odd one intruding into three-east."

I waited, but Topher didn't elaborate. Not surprising. On exams, Topher's essays often consisted of single-sentence answers. Illustrated.

"Odd?" I coaxed.

"It's articulated."

A complete sentence. Gratifying, but not

6

enlightening. I curled my fingers in a "give me more" gesture.

"We're thinking intrusive." Topher shifted his weight from one bare foot to another. It was a lot to shift.

"I'll check it out in a minute."

Topher nodded, turned, and trudged back to the excavation.

"What's that mean, 'articulated'?" The tick had reached Winborne's ear and appeared to be considering alternate routes.

"In proper anatomical alignment. It's uncommon with secondary burials, corpses put into the ground after loss of the flesh. The bones are usually jumbled, sometimes in clumps. Occasionally in these communal graves one or two skeletons will be articulated."

"Why?"

"Could be a lot of reasons. Maybe someone died immediately before closure of a common pit. Maybe the group was moving on, didn't have time to wait out decomposition."

A full ten seconds of scribbling, during which the tick moved out of sight.

"Intrusive. What's that mean?"

"A body was placed in the grave later. Would you like a closer look?"

"It's what I'm living for." Putting hanky to forehead, Winborne sighed as if he were onstage.

I crumbled. "There's a tick in your collar."

Winborne moved faster than it seemed possible

for a man of his bulk to move, yanking his collar, doubling over, and batting his neck in one jerk. The tick flew to the sand and righted itself, apparently used to rejection.

I set off, skirting clusters of sea oats, their tasseled heads motionless in the heavy air. Only May, and already the mercury was hitting ninety. Though I love the Lowcountry, I was glad I wouldn't be digging here into the summer.

I moved quickly, knowing Winborne wouldn't keep up. Mean? Yes. But time was short. I had none to waste on a dullard reporter.

And I was conscience-clear on the tick.

Some student's boom-box pounded out a tune I didn't recognize by a group whose name I didn't know and wouldn't remember if told. I'd have preferred seabirds and surf, though today's selections were better than the heavy metal the kids usually blasted.

Waiting for Winborne, I scanned the excavation. Two test trenches had already been dug and refilled. The first had yielded nothing but sterile soil. The second had produced human bone, early vindication of Jaffer's suspicions.

Three other trenches were still open. At each, students worked trowels, hauled buckets, and sifted earth through mesh screens resting on sawhorse supports.

Topher was shooting pictures at the easternmost trench. The rest of his team sat cross-legged, eyeing the focus of his interest.

Winborne joined me on the cusp between

panting and gasping. Mopping his forehead, he fought for breath.

"Hot day," I said.

Winborne nodded, face the color of raspberry sherbet.

"You OK?"

"Peachy."

I was moving toward Topher when Winborne's voice stopped me.

"We got company."

Turning, I saw a man in a pink Polo shirt and khaki pants hurrying across, not around, the dunes. He was small, almost child-size, with silver-gray hair buzzed to the scalp. I recognized him instantly. Richard L. "Dickie" Dupree, entrepreneur, developer, and all-around sleaze.

Dupree was accompanied by a basset whose tongue and belly barely cleared the ground.

First a journalist, now Dupree. This day was definitely heading for the scrap heap.

Ignoring Winborne, Dupree bore down on me with the determined self-righteousness of a Taliban mullah. The basset hung back to squirt a clump of sea oats.

We've all heard of personal space, that blanket of nothing we need between ourselves and others. For me, the zone is eighteen inches. Break in, I get edgy.

Some strangers crowd up close because of vision or hearing. Others, because of differing cultural mores. Not Dickie. Dupree believed nearness lent him greater force of expression.

Stopping a foot from my face, Dupree crossed his arms and squinted up into my eyes.

"Y'all be finishing tomorrow, I expect." More statement than question.

"We will." I stepped back.

"And then?" Dupree's face was birdlike, the bones sharp under pink, translucent skin.

"I'll file a preliminary report with the Office of the State Archaeologist next week."

The basset wandered over and started sniffing my leg. It looked to be at least eighty years old.

"Colonel, don't be rude with the little lady." To me. "Colonel's getting on. Forgets his manners."

The little lady scratched Colonel behind one mangy ear.

"Shame to disappoint folks because of a buncha ole Indians." Dupree smiled what he no doubt considered his "Southern gentleman" smile. Probably practiced it in the mirror while clipping his nose hairs.

"Many view this country's heritage as something valuable," I said.

"Can't let these things stop progress, though, can we?"

I did not reply.

"You do understand my position, ma'am?"

"Yes, sir. I do."

I abhorred Dupree's position. His goal was money, earned by any means that wouldn't get him indicted. Screw the rain forest, the wetlands, the seashore, the dunes, the culture that was here when the English arrived. Dickie Dupree would implode the Temple of Artemis if it stood where he wanted to slap up condos.

Behind us, Winborne had gone still. I knew he was listening.

"And what might this fine document say?" Another Sheriff of Mayberry smile.

"That this area is underlain by a pre-Columbian burial ground."

Dupree's smile wavered, held. Sensing tension, or perhaps bored, Colonel abandoned me for Winborne. I wiped my hand on my cutoffs.

"You know those folks up in Columbia well as I do. A report of that nature will shut me down for some time. That delay will cost me money."

"An archaeological site is a nonrenewable cultural resource. Once it's gone, it's gone forever. I can't in good conscience allow your needs to influence my findings, Mr. Dupree."

The smile dissolved, and Dupree eyed me coldly.

"We'll just have to see about that." The veiled threat was little softened by the gentle, Lowcountry drawl.

"Yes, sir. We will."

Pulling a pack of Kools from his pocket, Dupree cupped a hand and lit up. Chucking the match, he drew deeply, nodded, and started back toward the dunes, Colonel waddling at his heels.

"Mr. Dupree," I called after him.

Dupree stopped, but didn't turn to face me.

"It's environmentally irresponsible to walk on dunes."

Flicking a wave, Dupree continued on his way.

Anger and loathing rose in my chest.

"Dickie not your choice for Man of the Year?"

I turned. Winborne was unwrapping a stick of Juicy Fruit. I watched him put the gum in his mouth, daring with my eyes that he toss the paper as Dupree had tossed his match.

He got the message.

Wordlessly, I hooked a one-eighty and walked to three-east. I could hear Winborne scrabbling along behind me.

The students fell silent when I joined them. Eight eyes followed as I hopped down into the trench. Topher handed me a trowel. I squatted, and was enveloped by the smell of freshly turned earth.

And something else. Sweet. Fetid. Faint, but undeniable.

An odor that shouldn't be there.

My stomach tightened.

Dropping to all fours, I examined Topher's oddity, a segment of vertebral column curving outward from halfway up the western wall.

Above me, students threw out explanations.

"We were cleaning up the sides, you know, so we could, like, take photos of the stratigraphy."

"We spotted stained soil."

Topher added some brief detail.

I wasn't listening. I was troweling, creating a profile view of the burial lying to the west of the trench. With each scrape my apprehension was heading north.

12

Thirty minutes of work revealed a spine and upper pelvic rim.

I sat back, a tingle of dread crawling my scalp.

The bones were connected by muscle and ligament.

As I stared, the first fly buzzed in, sun iridescent on its emerald body.

Sweet Jesus.

Rising, I brushed dirt from my knees. I had to get to a phone.

Dickie Dupree had a lot more to worry about than the ancient Sewee.

# 2

Dewees Islanders are rigidly smug about the ecological purity of living "across the way." Sixty-five percent of their little kingdom is given over to a conservation easement. Ninety percent is undeveloped. Residents prefer things, as they say, wild on the vine. No grooming, no pruning.

No bridge. Access to Dewees is by private ferry or boat. Roads are sand-based, and internal combustion transport is tolerated solely for construction service and deliveries. Oh, yeah. The island has an ambulance, a fire engine, and an all-terrain brushfire-fighting vehicle. Though fond of serenity, the homeowners aren't totally naive.

Ask me? Nature's great when on vacation. It's a pain in the ass when trying to report a suspicious death.

Dewees is only twelve hundred acres, and my crew was digging in the far southeastern corner, in a stand of maritime forest between Lake Timicau and the Atlantic Ocean. Not a chance of scoring a cell phone signal.

Leaving Topher in charge of the site, I hiked up the beach to a wooden boardwalk, used it to cross the dunes, and hopped into one of our half dozen golf carts. I was turning the key when a pack hit the seat beside me, followed by Winborne's polyester-clad buttocks. Intent on finding a working phone, I hadn't heard him trailing behind.

OK. Better than leaving the twit to snoop unsupervised.

Wordlessly, I gunned it, or whatever one does with electric carts. Winborne braced one hand on the dash and wrapped the other around an upright roof support.

I paralleled the ocean on Pelican Flight, made a right onto Dewees Inlet, passed the picnic pavilion, the pool, the tennis courts, and the nature center, and, at the top of the lagoon, hung a left toward the water. Pulling up at the ferry dock, I turned to Winborne.

"End of the line."

"What?"

"How did you get out here?"

"Ferry."

"And by ferry thou shalt return."

"No way."

"Suit yourself."

Mistaking my meaning, Winborne settled back.

"Swim," I clarified.

"You can't jus—"

15

"Out."

"I left a cart at your site."

"A student will return it."

Winborne slid to the ground, features crimped into a mask of poached displeasure.

"Have a good day, Mr. Winborne."

Shooting east on Old House Lane, I passed through wrought iron gates decorated with free-form shells, and into the island's public works area. Fire station. Water treatment facility. Administrative office. Island manager's residence.

I felt like a first responder after an explosion of one of those neutron bombs. Buildings intact, but not a soul to be found.

Frustrated, I recircled the lagoon and pulled in behind a two-winged structure wrapped by an enormous porch. With its four guest suites and tiny restaurant, Huyler House was Dewees's only concession to outsiders needing a bed or a beer. It was also home to the island's community center. Bounding from the cart, I hurried toward it.

Though preoccupied with the grisly find in three-east, I had to appreciate the structure I was approaching. The designers of Huyler House wanted to give the impression of decades of sun and salt air. Weathered wood. Natural staining. Though standing fewer than ten years, the place resembled a heritage building.

Quite the reverse for the woman emerging through a side door. Althea Hunneycut "Honey" Youngblood looked old, but was probably ancient.

Local lore had it Honey had witnessed the granting of Dewees to Thomas Cary by King William III in 1696.

Honey's history was the topic of ongoing speculation, but islanders agreed on certain points. Honey had first visited Dewees as a guest of the Coulter Huyler family prior to World War II. The Huylers had been roughing it on Dewees since purchasing the island in '25. No electricity. No phone. Windmill-powered well. Not my idea of beach ease.

Honey had arrived with a husband, though opinions vary as to the gentleman's rank in the roll of spouses. When this hubby died Honey kept coming back, eventually marrying into the R. S. Reynolds family, to whom the Huylers sold their holdings in '56. Yep. The aluminum folks. After that, Honey could do as she chose. She chose to remain on Dewees.

The Reynolds family sold their acreage to an investment partnership in '72, and, within a decade, the first private homes went up. Honey's was number one, a compact little bungalow overlooking Dewees Inlet. With the formation of the Island Preservation Partnership, or IPP, in '91, Honey hired on as the island naturalist.

No one knew her age. Honey wasn't sharing.

"Gonna be a hot one." Honey's conversations invariably opened with references to the weather.

"Yes, Miss Honey. It surely will."

"I expect we'll hit ninety today." Honey's "I"s came out "Ah"s, and many of her syllables took on lives of their own. Via our many conversations, I'd learned that the old gal could work vowels like no one I knew.

"I expect we will." Smiling, I tried hurrying past.

"Thank God and all his angels and saints for air-conditioning."

"Yes, ma'am."

"Y'all are digging by the old tower?"

"Not far from there." The tower had been built to spot submarines during World War II.

"Finding anything?"

"Yes, ma'am."

"That's grand. We could use some new specimens in our nature center."

Not these specimens.

I smiled, and again tried moving on.

"I'll be coming by one of these days." Sun sparked the blue-white curls. "Gal's gotta keep up with island events. Did I ever tell—"

"Please excuse me, but I'm in a bit of a hurry, Miss Honey." I hated to brush her off, but I had to get to a phone.

"'Course you are. Where are my manners?" Honey patted my arm. "Soon's you get free, we'll go fishing. My nephew's living here now and he's got a dandy of a boat."

"Does he?"

"He surely does, gave it to him myself. Can't take the helm like I once did, but I still love to fish. I'll give him a holler, we'll go out."

With that, Honey strode down the path, backbone straight as a loblolly pine.

Taking the stairs two at a time, I bounded onto the porch and into the community center. Like the public works area, it was deserted.

Did the locals know something I didn't? Where the hell was everyone?

Letting myself into the office, I crossed to the desk, dialed Information, then punched a number. A voice answered on the second ring.

"Charleston County Coroner's Office."

"This is Temperance Brennan. I called about a week ago. Is the coroner back?"

"One moment, please."

I'd phoned Emma Rousseau shortly after arriving in Charleston, but had been disappointed to learn that my friend was in Florida, taking her first vacation in five years. Poor planning on my part. I should have e-mailed before I came down. But our friendship had never worked like that. When at a distance, we communicated infrequently. When reunited, we jumped in as if we'd parted only hours before.

"She'll be with you shortly," the operator updated me.

On hold, I recalled my first encounter with Emma Rousseau.

Eight years back. I was a guest lecturer at the College of Charleston. Emma, a nurse by training, had just been elected Charleston County coroner. A family was questioning her finding of "undetermined" as the manner of death in a skeletal case. Needing a consult, but afraid I'd refuse, and determined to have mine as an outside

19

opinion, Emma hauled the bones to my lecture in a large plastic container. Impressed with such moxie, I'd agreed to help.

"Emma Rousseau."

"Got a man in a tub who's dying to meet you." Bad joke, but we used it over and over.

"Hell's bells, Tempe. You in Charleston?" Emma's vowels weren't up to Honey's, but they came damn close.

"You'll find a phone message somewhere in your mail stack. I'm running an archaeological field school out on Dewees. How was Florida?"

"Hot and sticky. You should have let me know you were coming. I could have rescheduled."

"If you actually took time off, I'm sure you needed the break."

Emma didn't reply to that. "Dan Jaffer still out of the loop?"

"He's been deployed to Iraq until sometime next month."

"You met Miss Honey?"

"Oh, yeah."

"Love that old lady. Brimming with piss and vinegar."

"She is that. Listen, Emma. I may have a problem."

"Shoot."

"Jaffer put me on to the site, thought it might be a Sewee burial ground. He was right. We've been getting bone since day one, but it's typical pre-Columbian stuff. Dry, bleached, lots of postmortem deterioration."

Emma didn't interrupt with questions or comments.

"This morning my students spotted a fresh burial about eighteen inches down. The bone looks solid, and the vertebrae are connected by soft tissue. I cleared what I felt was safe without contaminating the scene, then figured I'd better give someone a heads-up. Not sure who handles Dewees."

"Sheriff's got jurisdiction for criminal matters. For suspicious death evaluation, the winner would be me. Got any hypotheses?"

"None involving the ancient Sewee."

"You think the burial is recent?"

"Flies were opening a soup kitchen as I was scraping dirt."

There was a pause. I could picture Emma checking her watch.

"I'll be there in about an hour and a half. Need anything?"

"Body bag."

I was waiting on the pier when Emma arrived in a twin-engine Sea Ray. Her hair was tucked under a baseball cap, and her face seemed thinner than I remembered. She wore Dolce & Gabbana shades, jeans, and a yellow T with *Charleston County Coroner* lettered in black.

I watched Emma drop fenders, maneuver to the dock, and tie up. When I reached the boat, she handed out a body bag, grabbed camera equipment, and stepped over the side.

In the cart I explained that, following our phone conversation, I'd returned to the site, staked out a simple ten-by-ten square, and shot a series of photographs. I described in more detail what I'd seen in the ground. And gave warning that my students were totally jazzed.

Emma spoke little as I drove. She seemed moody, distracted. Or maybe she trusted that I'd told her all she needed to know. All I knew.

Now and then I stole a sideways glance. Emma's sunglasses made it impossible to know her expression. As we moved in and out of sunlight, shadows threw patterns across her features.

I didn't share that I was feeling uneasy, anxious that I might be wrong and wasting Emma's time.

More accurately, anxious that I might be right.

A shallow grave off a lonely beach. A decomposing corpse. I could think of few explanations. All of them involved suspicious death and body disposal.

Emma looked outwardly calm. Like me, she'd worked dozens, perhaps hundreds of scenes. Incinerated bodies, severed heads, mummified infants, plastic-wrapped body parts. For me, it was never easy. I wondered if Emma's adrenaline was pumping like mine.

"That guy an undergrad?" Emma's question broke into my thoughts.

I followed her line of vision.

Homer Winborne. Each time Topher turned his back, the creep was snapping photos with a pocket-size digital.

"Sonovabitch."

"I take that as a negative."

"He's a reporter."

"Shouldn't be shooting."

"Shouldn't be here at all."

Flying from the cart, I confronted Winborne. "What the hell are you doing?"

My students turned into a frozen tableau.

"Missed the ferry." Winborne's right shoulder hunched as his arm slid behind his back.

"Fork over the Nikon." Razor tone.

"You've got no right to take my property."

"Your ass is out of here. Now. Or I'm calling the sheriff to haul it to the bag."

"Dr. Brennan."

Emma had come up behind me. Winborne's eyes narrowed as they read her T.

"Perhaps the gentleman could observe from a distance." Emma, the voice of reason.

I turned my glare from Winborne to Emma. I was so peeved I couldn't think of a suitable reply. "No way" lacked style, and "in a pig's eye" seemed low in originality.

Emma nodded almost imperceptibly, indicating I should go along. Winborne was right, of course. I had no authority to confiscate his property or to give him orders. Emma was right, too. Better to control the press than to turn it away angry.

Or was the coroner thinking ahead to her next election?

"Whatever." My reply was no better than the ones I'd rejected.

"Providing we hold the camera for safekeeping."
Emma held out a hand.

With a self-satisfied smile in my direction,
Winborne placed the Nikon in it.

"This is puppy shit," I muttered.

"How far back would you like Mr. Winborne to
stand?"

"How about the mainland?"

As things turned out, Winborne's presence made
little difference.

Within hours we'd crossed an event horizon that
changed my dig, my summer, and my views on
human nature.

# 3

Topher and a kid named Joe Horne started in with long-handled spades, gently slicing topsoil inside my ten-foot square. Six inches down we spotted discoloration.

Send in the A team.

Emma shot videos and stills, then she and I troweled, teasing away earth from around the stain. Topher worked the screen. The kid might be goofy, but he was a world-class sifter. Throughout the afternoon, students dropped by for progress checks, their *CSI* zeal wilting in inverse relation to the blossoming fly population.

By four, we'd uncovered a barely articulated torso, limb bones, a skull, and a jaw. The remains were encased in rotted fabric and topped by wisps of pale, blond hair.

Emma repeatedly radioed Junius Gullet, sheriff of Charleston County. Each time she was told that

Gullett was unavailable, handling a domestic disturbance.

Winborne stayed on us like a hound on a cottontail. With the ratcheting heat and odor, his face morphed into something resembling splatter on a sidewalk.

At five, my students piled into carts and split for the ferry. Topher alone seemed open to working for as long as it took. He, Emma, and I kept moving dirt, sweating, and shooing *Calliphoridae*.

Winborne disappeared as we were transferring the last bones into a body bag. I didn't see his departure. One time I glanced over, and he was gone.

I assumed Winborne was scurrying to his editor and then his keyboard. Emma wasn't concerned. A body wasn't big news in Charleston County, which chalked up twenty-six homicides a year with a mere three hundred thousand citizens working at it.

We'd kept our voices low, our actions discreet, Emma argued. Winborne had gotten nothing that could compromise an investigation. Coverage might be a plus, draw reports of missing persons, ultimately help with an ID. I remained skeptical, but said nothing. It was her patch.

Emma and I had our first real exchange on the way to the dock. The sun was low, slashing crimson through the trees and across the road. Even though we were moving, the salty pine smell of woods and marsh was tainted by the bouquet drifting from our backseat passenger.

Or maybe it was us. I couldn't wait to shower, shampoo, and burn my clothes.

"First impressions?" Emma asked.

"Bone's well preserved, but there's less soft tissue than I'd anticipated based on eyeballing those first vertebrae. Ligament, some muscle fiber deep in the joints, that's about it. Most of the smell is coming from the clothes."

"Body was wrapped in them, not wearing them, right?"

"Right."

"PMI?" Emma was asking how much time had elapsed since the victim's death.

"For postmortem interval you'll need to study the insect inclusions."

"I'll get an entomologist. Rough estimate?"

I shrugged. "In this climate, shallow burial, I'd say minimum of two years, maximum of five."

"We got a lot of teeth." Emma's thoughts were slip-streaming ahead to the ID.

"Damn right we did. Eighteen in the sockets, eight in the ground, three in the screen."

"And hair," Emma added.

"Yes."

"Long."

"Meaningless, if you're thinking gender. Look at Tom Wolfe. Willie Nelson."

"Fabio."

I definitely liked this woman.

"Where are you taking the remains?" I asked.

"Everything under my jurisdiction goes to the morgue at MUSC." The Medical University of South Carolina. "The pathologists there perform all our autopsies. My forensic anthropologist and dentist work there, too. Guess I won't be requesting a pathologist in this case."

"Brain and organs are long gone. The autopsy will be skeletal only. You'll need Jaffer."

"He's in Iraq."

"He'll be back next month," I said.

"Can't wait that long."

"I'm committed to this field school."

"It's finished tomorrow."

"I have to haul equipment back to UNCC. Write a report. Turn in grades."

Emma didn't reply.

"I may have cases at my lab in Charlotte."

Emma continued to not reply.

"Or in Montreal."

We rode in silence awhile, listening to the peeping of tree frogs and the hum of the cart. When Emma spoke again her voice was different, softer, yet quietly insistent.

"Someone's probably missing this guy."

I thought of the solitary grave we'd just unearthed.

I thought of my long-ago lecture and the guy in the tub.

I stopped trying to beg off.

We talked again as we loaded the boat and cast off, fell silent when we left the no-wake zone. Once Emma opened throttle, our words were lost to the wind, the motor, and the slap of water on the bow.

My car was at the marina on Isle of Palms, a narrow tongue of real estate lying between

Sullivan's and Dewees. So was a coroner's van. It took only minutes to transfer our sad cargo.

Before cutting out into the intracoastal waterway, Emma left me with two words.

"I'll call."

I didn't argue. I was tired and hungry. And cranky. I wanted to go home, shower, and eat the cold shrimp and she-crab soup I'd left in the fridge.

Walking up the dock, I noticed Topher Burgess stepping from the ferry. He was listening to his iPod, and didn't seem to see or hear me.

I watched my student cross to his Jeep. Funny kid, I thought. Smart, though far from a brilliant performer. Accepted by his peers, but always apart.

Like me at that age.

I clicked on the roof light in my Mazda, dug my mobile from my pack, and checked for a signal. Four bars.

Three messages. I recognized none of the numbers.

It was now 8:45.

Disappointed, I replaced the phone, pulled from the lot, cut across the island, and turned right onto Palm Boulevard. Traffic was light, though that wouldn't last. Two weeks and cars would be clogging these roads like silt in a storm drain.

I was staying at a friend's beach house. When Anne had upgraded from Sullivan's two years earlier, she hadn't messed around. Her new getaway had five bedrooms, six baths, and enough square footage to host the World Cup.

Taking a couple of feeder streets, I maneuvered

toward the beach, pulled into Anne's drive, and parked under the house. Ocean Boulevard. No second row for oceanfront Annie.

Every window was dark since I had planned on a predusk return. Without turning on lights, I went straight to the outdoor shower, stripped, and cranked up the hot water. Twenty minutes with rosemary, mint, and a lot of lather, and I felt reasonably restored.

Leaving the stall, I bundled my clothing into a plastic sack and trashed it. No way I'd subject Annie's Maytag to that.

Wearing only a towel, I entered the house through the back veranda and climbed to my room. Panties and a T. Brush through my hair. Gorgeous.

While zapping my soup, I again checked my messages. Nothing. Where was Ryan? Taking my mobile and my dinner to the porch, I settled in a rocker.

Anne called her place "Sea for Miles." No kidding. The horizon spread from Havana to Halifax.

There's something about the ocean. One minute I was eating. The next I was jolted awake by the sound of my cell. My plate and bowl sat empty. I had no recollection of closing my eyes.

The voice wasn't the one I was hoping to hear.

"Yo."

Only frat boys and my estranged husband still said "yo."

"Dude." I was too tired to be clever.

"How goes the dig?"

I pictured the bones now lying in the MUSC morgue. I pictured Emma's face as she had pulled away from the dock. I didn't want to go into it.

"Fine."

"Wrapping up tomorrow?"

"Some loose ends may take longer than I'd expected. How's Birdie?"

"Doing twenty-four/seven surveillance on Boyd. Your cat thinks my dog's been conjured up from the dark side to pollute his life. Chow thinks the cat's some kind of fluffy wind-up toy."

"Who's in control?"

"Bird's definitely alpha. So, when are you back to Charlotte?" Too casual. Something was up.

"I'm not sure. Why?" Wary.

"Gentleman came to my office yesterday. He has financial issues with Aubrey Herron, and it seems his daughter's hooked up with Herron as well."

The Reverend Aubrey Herron was a tele-vangelist with a small but ardent following throughout the Southeast, known as God's Mercy Church. In addition to its headquarters and TV studio, GMC operated a number of Third World orphanages and several free medical clinics in the Carolinas and Georgia.

"God Means Charity." Herron closed every broadcast with the slogan.

"Give Mucho Cash." Pete quoted a popular variation.

"What's the problem?" I asked.

"Financial reports have not been forthcoming, the kid's gone incommunicado, and the Reverend

Herron is being less than cooperative on either issue."

"Shouldn't Daddy hire a private investigator?"

"Daddy did. The guy went missing."

"You're thinking Bermuda Triangle?"

"Aliens."

"You're a lawyer, Pete. Not a gumshoe."

"There's money involved."

"No!"

Pete ignored that.

"Daddy's really worried?" I asked.

"Daddy's beyond worried and out the other side."

"About the money or the daughter?"

"Perceptive question. Flynn's really hiring me to look into the books. Wants me to bring pressure on GMC. If I can scare up something on the daughter, that's a bonus. I offered to drop in on the reverend."

"And scare the wingtips off him."

"With my legal acumen."

Comprehension sprang into focus.

"GMC is headquartered in Charleston," I said.

"I talked to Anne. She offered the house, if it's cool with you."

"When?" I gave a sigh that would have made Homer Winborne proud.

"Sunday?"

"Why not." Only a billion reasons.

A beep indicated an incoming call. When I lowered the phone, the LCD panel glowed the digits I'd been hoping to see. Montreal exchange.

"Gotta go, Pete."

I clicked over.

"Phoning too late?"

"Never." I smiled my first smile since uncovering the skeleton in three-east.

"Lonely?"

"I posted my number in the men's room at Hyman's Seafood."

"I love it when you go all mushy missing me."

Andrew Ryan is a detective with the Major Crimes Division of the Quebec Provincial Police. You get the picture: Brennan, anthropologist, Laboratoire de sciences judiciaires et de médecine légale; Ryan, cop, Section de crimes contre la personne, Sûrété du Québec. We've worked homicides together for more than a decade.

Recently, Ryan and I had started working other things, as well. Personal things.

One of them did a wee flip at the sound of his voice.

"Good day digging?"

I drew a breath, stopped. Share? Wait?

Ryan picked up on my hesitation.

"What?" he encouraged.

"We found an intrusive burial. A complete skeleton with vestiges of soft tissue and associated clothing."

"Recent?"

"Yes. I called the coroner. She and I exhumed it together. It's now at the morgue."

While Ryan is charming, thoughtful, and witty, he can also be annoying as hell. I knew his response before it left his lips.

"How do you get yourself into these situations, Brennan?"

"I submit well-written résumés."

"Will you do the consult?"

"I have my students to think about."

Wind ruffled the palmetto fronds. Across the dunes, surf pounded sand.

"You'll take the case."

I didn't agree or disagree.

"How's Lily?" I asked.

"Only three door-slamming incidents today. Minor league. No broken glass or splintered wood. I take that as a sign the visit's going well."

Lily was new to Ryan's life. And vice versa. For almost two decades father and daughter knew nothing of each other. Then Lily's mother made contact.

Nineteen and pregnant, though not sharing that biological reality with her weekend pal-in-the-dark Ryan, Lutetia had fled Canada for her family home in the Bahamas. She'd married in the islands, divorced when Lily was twelve, and returned to Nova Scotia. Once Lily was out of high school, she'd begun running with a fast crowd. She'd taken to staying out nights, had been busted for possession. Lutetia knew the signs. She'd tried the outlaw life herself. That's where she'd met Ryan, during his own personal undergraduate counter-culture insurrection. Knowing her long-ago lover was now a cop, Lutetia had decided he should participate in the effort to salvage his young-adult daughter.

34

Though the news had hit Ryan in the old solar plexus, he'd embraced fatherhood and was trying hard. This visit to Nova Scotia was his latest foray into his daughter's world. But Lily wasn't making her old man's task easy.

"One word," I said. "Patience."

"Roger that, wise one." Ryan knew I'd had runins with my own daughter, Katy.

"How long will you stay in Halifax?"

"We'll see how it goes. I haven't given up on that idea of joining you if you're still willing to hang there awhile."

Oh, boy.

"That could be complicated. Pete just called. He may be here for a day or two."

Ryan waited.

"He has business in Charleston, so Anne invited him. What could I say? It's Anne's house and the place has enough beds to accommodate the College of Cardinals."

"Beds or bedrooms?"

At times Ryan had the tact of a wrecking ball.

"Call me tomorrow?" I closed the topic.

"Scrub your number from that men's-room wall?"

"You bet, sailor."

I was wired after talking to Pete and Ryan. Or maybe it was the unplanned power nap. I knew I wouldn't sleep.

Pulling on shorts, I padded barefoot across the boardwalk. The tide was out, and the beach yawned fifty yards to the water's edge. A gazillion stars winked overhead. Walking the surf, I let my thoughts roam.

Pete, my first love. My only love for over two decades.

Ryan, my first gamble since Pete's betrayal.

Katy, my wonderful, flighty, finally-about-to-be-a-college-graduate daughter.

But mostly, I pondered that sad grave on Dewees. Violent death is my job. I see it often, yet I never get used to it.

I have come to think of violence as a self-perpetuating mania of the power of the aggressive over those less strong. Friends ask how I can bear to do the work that I do. It is simple. I am committed to demolishing the maniacs before they demolish more innocents.

Violence wounds the body and it wounds the soul. Of the predator. Of the prey. Of the mourners. Of collective humanity. It diminishes us all.

In my view, death in anonymity is the ultimate insult to human dignity. To spend eternity under a Jane Doe plaque. To disappear nameless into an unmarked grave without those who care about you knowing that you have gone. That offends. While I cannot make the dead live again, I can reunite victims with their names, and give those left behind some measure of closure. In that way, I help the dead to speak, to say a final good-bye, and, sometimes, to say what took their lives.

I knew I would do what Emma was asking. Because of who I am. Because of what I feel. I would not walk away.

# 4

The next morning, I lay in bed staring into the breach of the opening day. I had failed to lower the blinds, so I watched dawn tint the ocean, the dunes, and the deck outside Anne's sliding glass doors.

Closing my eyes, I thought about Ryan. His reaction had been predictable, meant to amuse. But I wondered what he'd say if he were here. If he'd seen the grave. And I regretted my annoyance with him. I missed him. We'd been apart for over a month.

I thought about Pete. Endearing, charming, adulterous Pete. I told myself I'd forgiven him. But had I? If not, why didn't I file for divorce and cut myself loose?

Lawyers and paperwork. But was that really it?

I turned on my side and pulled the quilt to my chin.

I thought about Emma. She'd be calling soon. What would I tell her?

I had no reason to refuse Emma's request. Sure, Charleston wasn't my turf. But Dan Jaffer would be out of the country for several more weeks. Anne was offering "Sea for Miles" for as long as I wanted. Ryan was in Nova Scotia, but had talked of possibly coming to Charleston. Katy was in Chile, doing a four-week course on Spanish literature.

I smiled. "Cervantes and Cerveza," my daughter had dubbed her summer program. Whatever the project, those last three credits would close out a BA six years in the making. Yes!

Back to Emma. Emma dilemma.

My students could transport the equipment to UNCC. I could complete their evaluations here and e-mail the grades. I could do the same with my site report for the state archaeologist.

Were cases piling up in Montreal? I could call and find out.

What to do?

Easy one. Bagel and coffee.

Throwing back the covers, I dressed.

Quick toilette. Hair in a pony. Done.

That's probably what attracted me to archaeology. No makeup, no fluffing or mousseing. Every day is casual Friday. Less than casual.

While I worked the toaster, Mr. Coffee brewed. By now the sun was up, and the day was warming. Again, I headed outside.

I'm a news junkie. Gotta have it. When home, my morning begins with CNN and a paper. *Observer* in Charlotte. *Gazette* in Montreal. *NY*

*Times* e-mail edition. When traveling, I fall back on *USA Today,* the local press, even tabloids if desperate.

There was no home delivery at "Sea for Miles." While eating, I perused a *Post and Courier* I'd purchased on Thursday but barely skimmed.

A family had died in a tenement blaze. Faulty wiring was being blamed.

A man was suing after finding an ear in his coleslaw at a fried chicken franchise. Police and health officials had discovered no missing ears among the workers involved in the restaurant's coleslaw supply chain. DNA testing was being done.

A man was missing, and authorities were seeking help from the public. Jimmie Ray Teal, forty-seven, left his brother's Jackson Street apartment around three on Monday, May 8, heading for a medical appointment. Teal hadn't been seen since.

My brain cells hoisted that little flag. Dewees Island?

No way. Teal had been breathing eleven days ago. The victim in our body bag hadn't drawn oxygen in at least two years.

I was down to the weekly neighborhood section when my mobile sounded. I checked the caller ID. Showtime.

Emma was a street fighter. She went straight for the kidneys.

"Do you want *them* to win?"

My beach-walk lecture to myself.

"When?" I asked.

"Nine tomorrow morning?"

"What's the address?"

I wrote it down.

Ten yards offshore, a pair of porpoises arced in and out of the sea, the morning sun glistening their backs a shiny blue-gray porcelain. I watched them nose up, then plunge, vanishing into a world I didn't know.

Draining my coffee, I wondered.

What unknown world was I about to enter?

The remainder of the day passed uneventfully.

At the site, I explained to my students what had taken place following their departure the previous day. Then, while I logged last-minute photos and notes, they refilled open trenches. Together we cleaned shovels, trowels, brushes, and screens, returned our carts to the landings building, and boarded the *Aggie Gray* for her six o'clock crossing.

That evening, the group ate shrimp and oysters at the Boat House at Breach Inlet. After dinner, we reconvened on Anne's veranda for one final class meeting. The students reviewed what they'd done, and double-checked cataloging on all artifacts and bones. Around nine, they redistributed equipment among their vehicles, exchanged hugs, and were gone.

I suffered the usual post–collective experience letdown. Sure, I was relieved. Field school was concluded without any disasters of note, and now I could focus on Emma's skeleton. But the students' departure also left me feeling dismally empty.

The kids could be exasperating, no question. The unending hubbub. The clowning. The inattention. But my students were also energizing, bursting with enthusiasm, and lousy with youth.

I sat a few moments, enveloped by the silence in Anne's million-dollar home. Irrationally, I felt the stillness as ominous, not calming.

Moving through the house, I extinguished lights, then climbed the stairs to my room. Opening the glass doors, I welcomed the sound of waves on sand.

By eight thirty the next morning, I was roller-coastering the Cooper River Bridge, a soaring postmodern structure linking Mount Pleasant and the offshore islands with Charleston proper. With its colossal struts and arching backbone, the thing always makes me think of an impressionistic triceratops, frozen in steel. The bridge rises so high above terra firma, Anne still white-knuckles it every time she crosses.

MUSC is in the northwestern part of the Peninsula, halfway between the Citadel and the historic district. Continuing on Highway 17, I found Rutledge Avenue, then wound through campus to the parking deck Emma had indicated.

The sun warmed my neck and hair as I angled across Sabin Street to a massive brick building known simply as the main hospital. Following Emma's directions, I located the morgue entrance, climbed the ramp, and pressed a buzzer beside a rectangular speaker. In seconds a motor hummed, and one of two gray metal doors rolled up.

Emma looked awful.

Her face was pale, her outfit rumpled. The bags under her eyes looked big enough to hold several changes of clothing.

"Hey," she said quietly.

"Hey." OK. It sounds odd. But that's how we Southerners greet.

"Are you all right?" I asked, taking one of Emma's hands in mine.

"Migraine."

"This can wait."

"I'm fine now."

Emma hit a button and the door ground down behind me.

"I'm not leaving town," I said. "We can do this when you feel better."

"I'm fine." Soft, but allowing not an inch of wiggle room.

Emma led me up another concrete ramp. Where the floor leveled, I could see two stainless steel compression doors that I guessed led to coolers. Ahead was a normal door, probably giving access to the more populated side of the hospital. ER. OB-GYN. ICU. Those working for life. We were on the flip side. The death side.

Emma chin-cocked one of the metal doors. "We're in here."

We crossed to it, and Emma pulled the handle. Cold air whooshed over us, carrying the smell of refrigerated flesh and putrefaction.

The room measured approximately sixteen by twenty, and held a dozen gurneys with removable trays. On six were body bags, some bulging, some barely humped.

Emma chose a bag that looked piteously flat. Toeing the brake release, she wheeled the cart into the corridor as I held open the door of the room she had selected.

An elevator took us to an upper floor. Autopsy suites. Locker room. Doors leading to places I couldn't identify. Emma said little. I didn't bother her with questions.

As Emma and I changed from street clothes to scrubs, she explained that today would be my show. I was the anthropologist. She was the coroner. I would give orders. She would assist me. Later, she would incorporate my findings into a central case file with those of all other experts, and make a ruling.

Returning to the autopsy room, Emma double-checked paperwork, wrote the case number on an ID card, and shot photos of the unopened body bag. I booted my laptop and arranged work sheets on a clipboard.

"Case number?" I would use the Charleston County coroner's labeling system.

Emma held up the ID card. "I coded it 02, undetermined. It's coroner death two seventy-seven this year."

I entered CCC-2006020277 into my case form.

Emma spread a sheet over the autopsy table and set a screen over the sink. Then we tied plastic aprons behind our necks and waists, secured masks over our mouths, and gloved.

Emma unzipped the bag.

The hair was in one small plastic container, the isolated teeth in another. I set them on the counter.

The skeleton was as I remembered, largely intact, with only a few vertebrae and the left tibia and femur connected by remnants of desiccated tissue. The disarticulated bones had been jumbled in transport.

We began by extracting all visible insect inclusions and placing them in vials. Then Emma and I cleaned the dirt as best we could from every bone, collecting it for later inspection. As we progressed, I arranged elements in anatomical order on the sheet.

By noon the painstaking process was done. Two tubs and four vials sat on the counter, and a skeleton lay on the table, hand and toe bones fanned like those of a specimen in a biosupply catalog.

We broke for a quick cafeteria lunch. Emma had a large Coke and Jell-O. I had chips and a very questionable tuna sandwich. We were back in the autopsy suite by one.

While I inventoried, identifying bones and separating right and left sides, Emma shot more photos. Then she disappeared with the skull, jaw, and isolated teeth to make dental X-rays.

I was turning my attention to gender when Emma reappeared. I suspected the victim was male, since most bones were large and carried robust muscle attachments.

"Ready for sex?" I asked.

"Got a headache."

Yep. I liked this woman.

Picking up a pelvic half, I pointed to the front.

"Pubic bone is chunky, its lower branch is thick, and the subpubic angle is more V than U." I turned the bone and ran my finger inside a hollow below the broad pelvic blade. "Sciatic notch is narrow."

"You're thinking Y chromosome."

I nodded. "Let's see the cranium."

Emma handed it to me.

"Large brow ridges, blunt orbital borders." I rotated the skull. It had a large bump at the midline in back. "Occipital protuberance is large enough to require a zip code."

"All boy."

"Oh, yeah." I noted "male" on my case form.

"Age?" Emma asked.

Generally, the last of the molars appear during the late teens or early twenties, about the same time the skeleton is wrapping up its act. The final skeletal growth center to fuse is a little cap at the throat end of the collarbone. Combined, clavicular fusion and wisdom tooth eruption are good indicators of adulthood.

"All the molars out?" I asked.

Emma nodded.

I picked up the collarbone.

"Medial epiphysis is fused." I lay the bone on the table. "So he's no kid."

I returned to the pelvis. Again, I was interested in the belly side, this time the face that had kissed the face of the other pelvic half during life. In young adults, these faces have topography like the Shenandoah, all mountains and valleys. With age, the mountains wear down and the valleys fill in.

"Pubic symphysis is smooth," I said. "With a raised rim around the perimeter. Let's look at the dental X-rays."

Emma flipped the switch on a light box, then dumped ten black rectangles from a small brown envelope. I arranged the films into two rows, uppers and lowers, with each tooth in proper alignment.

Throughout life, pulp chambers and root canals fill with secondary dentin. The older a tooth, the more opaque its image on X-ray. These babies shouted young to middle-aged adult. In addition, all molar roots were complete to their tips, and crown wear was minimal.

"The teeth are consistent with the bones," I said.

"Meaning?"

"Forties. But keep in mind, males are variable."

"That's being generous," Emma said. "Race?"

I returned to the skull.

Evaluating racial identifiers is usually a bitch. Not with this guy.

The lower face showed no forward projection when viewed from the side. The nasal bones met at a church-steeple angle along the midline. The nasal opening was constricted, with a sharp lower border sporting a bony spike at its center.

"Narrow, prominent nose. Flat facial profile."

Emma watched as I shined a flashlight into the ear canal.

"Oval opening to the inner ear is visible."

When I looked up, Emma's eyes were closed and she was rubbing slow circles on her temples.

"I'll run measurements through Fordisc 3.0. But this guy looks like a page from the Caucasoid picture book."

"A forty-something white male."

"To be safe, I'd go with thirty-five to fifty."

"Time frame?"

I indicated the plastic vials on the counter. "Lots of empty puparial cases, some dead beetles and shed beetle skins. Your entomologist should be able to provide a solid PMI."

"Bugs take time. I want to shoot this right into NCIC."

Emma was referring to the FBI's National Crime Information Center, a computerized index of information on criminal records, fugitives, stolen properties, and missing and unidentified persons. With such a huge database, the narrower the time frame the better.

"I originally said two to five, but to be certain you don't exclude any possibles, I'd broaden the interval to one to five years."

Emma nodded. "If nothing pops with NCIC, I'll start working local missing persons reports."

"The dentals will help," I said. "This guy had some metal in his mouth."

"Our odontologist will chart him on Monday." Again Emma rubbed her temples. Though trying hard, she was fading.

"I'll measure the leg bones and calculate height," I said.

Weak nod. "Any other identifiers?"

I shook my head. I'd seen no healed trauma, no congenital anomaly, not a single unique skeletal feature.

"Cause of death?"

"Nothing obvious. No fractures, no bullet entrances or exits, no sharp instrument cuts. I'd like to view the bones under magnification when they've been fully cleaned, but for now, nada."

"Full-body X-rays?"

"Can't hurt."

As I began measuring a femur, Emma's mobile sounded. I heard her walk to the counter and flip the cover.

"Emma Rousseau."

She listened.

"I can live with it." Guarded.

Pause.

"How bad?"

Longer pause.

"Now what?" Taut.

I looked up.

Emma had turned her back to me. Though her face was hidden, her voice told me something was very wrong.

# 5

Emma tossed her mobile onto the counter, closed her eyes, and went still. I watched, knowing she was trying to quell the pounding in her head.

I've traveled the migraine trail. I'm familiar with the pain. I knew, even for Emma, sheer willpower wouldn't prevail. Nothing pacifies dilating cranial vessels but time and sleep. And drugs.

I refocused on my measurements. Best to finish estimating stature so Emma could go home and crash. If she wanted to discuss the phone call, she would.

I heard the door open, click shut.

I'd moved from the osteometric board to my laptop when the door opened again. Footsteps crossed the tile as I entered the last figure and asked the program to calculate.

"I went over the clothes." Emma was at my shoulder. "No belt, no shoes, no jewelry or personal effects. Nothing in the pockets. Fabric's rotten and the labels are barely legible, but I think the pants were a thirty-eight long. Assuming they're his, the guy wasn't short."

"Five-ten to six-one." I shifted to allow her a better view of the screen.

Emma eyeballed the height estimate, then stepped to the table. Reaching out, she stroked the skull.

"Who are you, tall white man in your forties?" Emma's voice was soft, as intimate as the caress. "We need a name, big guy."

The moment was so personal, I felt like a voyeur.

But I knew what Emma meant.

Thanks to some less than meticulously researched TV crime shows, the public now views DNA as the shining Excalibur of modern justice. Hollywood has spawned the myth that the double helix solves all riddles, unlocks all doors, rights all wrongs. Got bones? No problem. Extract and let the little molecule do its magic.

Unfortunately, it doesn't work that way in the nameless-body business. A Jane or John Doe exists in a vacuum, stripped of everything that links it to life. Anonymity means no family, no dentist, no home to search for a toothbrush or chewing gum.

No name.

With our profile, Emma could now send CCC-2006020277 into the system, looking for missing persons matches. If the matches produced a manageable number of names, she could request medical and dental records, and contact relatives for DNA comparison samples.

Rolling the edge of a glove, I checked my watch. Four forty-five.

"We've been at this eight hours," I said. "Here's a plan. We reconvene Monday. You order full-body X-rays. I view the films and scope the bones while your dentist charts the teeth. Then you shoot the whole enchilada through NCIC."

Emma turned. The fluorescents made her face look like autopsy flesh.

"I'm perky as a hellcat," she said dully.

"What's a hellcat?" I asked.

"Not sure."

"You're going home."

She didn't argue.

Outside, the afternoon felt heavy and damp. Rush hour was in full swing, and exhaust rode the salt-air cocktail coming off the harbor. Though it was May, the city already smelled like summer.

Emma and I walked side by side down the ramp. Before parting, she hesitated, then opened her lips to speak. I thought she was going to explain the phone call. Instead, she wished me a pleasant weekend, and trudged off down the sidewalk.

The car was an oven. Lowering the windows, I popped in a Sam Fisher CD. *People Living.* Melancholy. Volatile. A perfect fit for my mood.

Crossing the Cooper River, I could see thunderheads elbowing for position on the eastern horizon. A storm was gathering. I decided on a quick stop at Simmons's Seafood, then dinner chez moi.

The store was deserted. Steel cases offered the remains of the day's catch on crushed ice.

Every cell in my hypothalamus sat up at the sight of the swordfish.

So did the conscience guys. *Overfishing! Population decline! Noncompliance!*

Fine. Wasn't swordfish supposed to be mercury-laden, anyway?

I looked at the mahimahi.

No protest from the bully pulpit in my forebrain.

As usual, I dined al fresco, watching nature perform a light show in three acts. I imagined the playbill.

Scene I, sunlight dissolves and night slowly edges out day. Scene II, veined lightning sparks a fandango in black-green clouds. Scene III, fade to gray as rain pounds the dunes and wind thrashes the palms.

I slept like a baby.

And awoke to sun lighting the blinds. And banging.

I sat up, trying to pinpoint the noise. Had one of the hurricane shutters torn loose in the storm? Was someone in the house?

I looked at the clock. Eight forty.

Slipping on a robe, I tiptoed to the stairs, descended three treads, and crouched so I could see the front door. A head and shoulders were silhouetted in the frosted oval window.

As I watched, the head pressed its nose to the glass, then drew back. The banging resumed.

Eschewing theatrics, I reverse-tiptoed up the stairs, padded to a front bedroom, brushed the curtain aside, and looked down onto the driveway.

Sure enough, Pete's latest road toy was nosed up to my Mazda.

Returning to the bedroom, I yanked on yesterday's outfit and hurried downstairs.

As I approached the door, the banging gave way to scratching.

I flipped the dead bolt. The scratching grew frenzied.

I turned the knob.

The door flew in. Boyd went upright and landed two paws on my chest. As I struggled for balance, the chow dropped and raced circles around my ankles, tangling us both in his leash.

Unnerved by the commotion, Birdie shot from Pete's chest. Paws spread and ears aerodynamically flat, the cat cleared the foyer and streaked toward the back of the house.

Confused, or just wildly happy to be out of the car, Boyd took chase, leash fishtailing behind as he skidded through the foyer, the dining room, then the kitchen doors.

"Good morning, Charleston!" Pete crushed me with a hug as he did his Robin Williams imitation.

I did a two-palm chest push. "Jesus, Pete, how early did you leave Charlotte?"

"Time waits for no man, sugar britches."

"Don't call me that."

"Butter bean."

Something crashed somewhere out of sight.

"Close the door." I headed for the kitchen.

Pete followed.

Boyd was investigating the contents of a

shattered cookie jar. Bird was watching from the safety of the refrigerator top.

"That's the first item you're buying for Anne," I said.

"It's on the list."

Boyd looked up, snout speckled with crumbs, then went back to licking broken Lorna Doones.

"You couldn't find a kennel?" I asked, filling a water bowl.

"Boyd loves the beach," Pete said.

"Boyd would love the Gulag if they fed him."

I set the bowl on the floor. Boyd began lapping, tongue darting like a long, purple eel.

While I made breakfast, Pete unloaded his car. Cat pan and litter, canine and feline chow, eleven supermarket sacks, a large briefcase, one garment bag, and one small duffel.

Typical Pete. Big league on cuisine, bush league on wardrobe.

With a neck two sizes too large for his torso, my estranged husband can never find shirts to fit. No worries. Pete's three-tiered fashion system hadn't changed since I met him in the seventies. Shorts or jeans when possible; sport jacket when styling; suit and tie when going to court.

Today Pete wore an argyle Rosasen golf shirt, knee-length khakis, loafers, no socks.

"Think you bought enough groceries?" I asked, extracting a carton of eggs from a bag.

"So much food. So little time."

"You're doing your best."

"I am." Big Janis "Pete" Petersons grin. "I

figured you might not be expecting me for breakfast."

I'd been expecting him in the evening.

"Almost kept motoring when I saw the other car." Big Janis "Pete" Petersons wink.

I stopped cracking eggs and turned. "What other car?"

"Parked out front. Pulled away, so I came on in."

"What kind of car?"

Pete shrugged. "Dark. Large. Four-door. Where do you want the Birdster?"

I flapped an arm toward the utility room. Pete disappeared with the cat pan.

Puzzled, I started scrambling the eggs. Who would have been here so early on a Sunday morning?

"Probably some tourist looking for his beach house." Pete was back and ladling ground coffee. "A lot of places rent Sunday to Sunday."

"But check-in is never before noon." I removed bread from the toaster, put two more in.

"OK. Someone leaving. Stopped to program his OnStar before motoring to Toledo."

I handed Pete mats and utensils. He distributed them, then settled at the table.

Boyd walked over and laid his chin on Pete's knee. Pete reached down and scratched the chow's ear.

"So the field school's history. Planning to hit the beach today?"

I told him about the Dewees skeleton.

"No shit."

I filled coffee mugs, handed Pete a plate, and took the chair opposite his. Boyd switched from Pete's knee to mine.

"White male in his forties. No signs of foul play."

"Except that the guy was in a clandestine grave."

"Except for that. You remember Emma Rousseau?"

Pete's chewing slowed. He raised a fork. "Long brown hair. Tits that could—"

"She's the Charleston County coroner. A dentist is going to chart the unknown's teeth on Monday, then Emma will send the descriptors through NCIC."

Boyd snorted, chin-tapped my knee to let me know he was still there. And interested in eggs.

"How long are you staying down here?" Pete asked.

"As long as it takes to help Emma out with these bones. The local forensic anthropologist is away. Tell me about this Herron thing."

"Client came in Wednesday. Patrick Bertolds Flynn. Friends call him Buck."

Pete finished his eggs.

"Tight-assed little wanker. I offer coffee, Flynn tells me he doesn't use stimulants. Acts as though I've suggested we snort a few lines."

Pete pushed his plate away. Hearing the scrape, Boyd recircled the table. Pete gave the chow a triangle of toast.

"Posture to make a drill sergeant proud, though. Good eye contact."

"Impressive character analysis. Is Flynn an old client?"

Pete shook his head. "Wasn't before now. Flynn's mother is Latvian. Dagnija Kalniņš. He picked me because I'm one of the tribe."

"What did he want?"

"Took forever to get to the point. Went on and on about the Bible and the less fortunate and Christian responsibility. I actually started making hash marks on my tablet every time I heard the word 'obligation' or 'duty.' Gave up when I hit a million."

There seemed nowhere to go with that, so I said nothing. Pete took my silence as reproach.

"Flynn thought I was taking notes. More coffee?"

I nodded. Pete refilled our mugs, sat down, and tipped back his chair.

"To make the story short, Flynn and a gaggle of Biblemates have been funding Herron and his God's Mercy Church. Lately, the money boys have grown disenchanted over what they view to be lack of financial reporting."

Paws *thupped* the counter, then the floor. Moving fast, Birdie slithered from the room. Boyd's gaze never left Pete's plate.

"Also, Flynn's daughter hooked up with Herron a little over three years ago. Helene, that's her name, bounced around working at one or another of the poverty clinics the reverend bankrolls. According to Flynn, at first she called regularly to tell him what a bad-ass job GMC was doing for the poor, and how fulfilling it was to be helping in the effort."

Pete blew across his coffee, then sipped.

"Then contact grew infrequent. When Helene did call, she was always frustrated, complained that the clinic she was at never had enough supplies, maintenance sucked, patients were getting short-changed. She thought GMC might be cooking the books. Or the doctor who ran the place might be skimming off the top."

More coffee.

"Flynn admitted that he was unsympathetic, thought Helene was on another of her defender-of-the-poor crusades. Apparently she took that posture frequently. Besides, Flynn wanted the kid to get on a more traditional career path. As a result, things became less than warm and fuzzy between Helene and the old man. But then, Buck's not a warm and fuzzy guy."

"So now Flynn and his pals want an accounting of how their money's been spent. Why the change of heart?"

"For whatever reason, communication break-down, too busy recruiting lost souls, GMC dragged their collective feet in responding to Flynn's initial inquiry."

"And Flynn doesn't take kindly to being ignored."

"Bingo. So the money is my primary mission. But there's a sideline. Helene's dropped out of sight, and Herron has made no effort to provide Flynn with any explanation of that, either. I think

Flynn's interest in Herron may grow partly out of arrogance and wounded pride, partly out of guilt."

"How long has Helene been missing?"

"Flynn hasn't heard from his daughter in over six months."

"What about Mrs. Flynn?"

"Died years ago. And there are no siblings."

"Flynn's just now starting to search for Helene?"

"Their last conversation ended in a fight. Helene said she never wanted him to call her again, so he discontinued attempts at contact. The only reason he's bringing up the Helene issue now is that he's decided to launch a financial investigation and apparently feels I could learn more about Helene's departure at the same time. Or so he says."

I raised my brows in surprise.

"Flynn's a very rigid guy."

"He asked Herron about Helene?"

"Yes. But getting to see the rev is like getting an audience with the pope. Herron's *people* told Flynn that before Helene left she'd mentioned to some of the GMC staff that she had inquired about a position with a free clinic in Los Angeles. Said it was a larger operation."

"That's it?"

"Flynn managed to harangue the cops into checking with the kid's landlord. She said Helene had mailed her a note stating she was moving on. The envelope contained the key and the last rent owed. Helene had left some things, but nothing of value. Place was just a tiny studio, utilities included."

"What about bank accounts? Credit cards? Cell phone records?"

"Helene didn't believe in worldly possessions."

"Maybe there's nothing more to it. Maybe Helene split for the other coast and hasn't reported in."

"Maybe."

I thought a moment. The whole tale didn't seem to hang true.

"If Flynn was such a big donor, wouldn't Herron have met with him personally?"

"Million and a half smackers big enough? I agree with you. Herron should be falling all over himself helping to locate Helene. Something's weird, and Flynn should have been on top of this before now. But my main job is the money."

Pete drained his cup, then set it on the table.

"In the words of that great humanitarian Jerry McGuire, 'Show me the money.' "

# 6

After breakfast, Pete left to fly his first sortie over GMC. I settled on the veranda, Boyd at my feet, twenty blue books in my lap.

Maybe it was the ocean. Maybe the quality of the take-home exams. I found it hard to concentrate. I kept seeing the grave on Dewees. The bones on the autopsy table. Emma's pained face.

Emma had started to speak outside the hospital, then changed her mind. Was she about to explain what she'd learned on the phone? The call had obviously upset her. Why?

Was she about to say something concerning the skeleton? Was she withholding information? Improbable.

I stuck with grading until I could bear it no longer. Just past one I checked a tide chart, then laced on my Nikes and did a couple of miles on the beach with Boyd. It was not high season, so the "unleashed dog" hours weren't strictly enforced.

The chow darted in and out of the surf while I pounded the hardpack left by its retreat. The sandpipers weren't thrilled with either of us.

On the return loop I cut over to Ocean Boulevard and picked up Sunday papers. A quick shower, then Boyd and I inventoried Pete's contributions to the pantry.

Six varieties of cold cuts, four cheeses, sweet and dill pickles, wheat, rye, and onion bread. Coleslaw, potato salad, and more chips than a Frito-Lay factory.

Pete had a lot of shortcomings, but the man could stock a larder.

After constructing an artwork of pastrami, Swiss, and slaw on rye, I popped a Diet Coke and lugged the newspapers out to the veranda.

I spent a blissful hour and a half with *The New York Times*. And that's not counting the crossword. All the news that's fit to print. You gotta love it.

Having eaten my crusts and whatever pastrami I was willing to share, Boyd dozed at my feet.

Ten minutes into the *Post and Courier* I nearly lost my sandwich.

Local section. Fifth page, below the fold. Headline pure alliterative art.

### Buried Body on Barrier Beach

*Charleston, SC. Archaeology students excavating a Dewees Island site dug up more than dead Indians this week. The group, led by Dr.*

*Temperance Brennan of UNC-Charlotte's Anthropology Department, stumbled upon a recent grave occupied by a very modern corpse.*

*Brennan refused comment on the grisly discovery, but the remains appeared to be those of an adult. According to student excavator Topher Burgess, the body had been bundled in clothing and buried less than two feet below the ground surface. Burgess estimates the grave had been dug sometime during the past five years.*

*Though police were not called to the scene, Charleston County Coroner Emma Rousseau deemed the discovery significant enough to personally oversee excavation of the grave. A two-term electee, Rousseau has come under criticism recently for the role of the coroner's office in the mishandling of a cruise ship death last year.*

*Following recovery, the unidentified remains were transported from Dewees to the MUSC morgue. Morgue personnel refused comment on the case.*

*—Special to the* Post and Courier *by Homer Winborne*

A grainy black-and-white showed my face and Emma's south end. We were on our hands and knees on Dewees.

I flew into the house, Boyd at my heels. Grabbing the first phone in reach, I punched in a number. My actions were so jerky, it took two tries.

Emma's voice mail answered.

"Sonovabitch!"

I waited out the message, moving pointlessly from room to room.

*Beep.*

"Have you seen today's paper? Happy day! We made the news!"

I hit the sunroom, threw myself onto the couch. Got up. Birdie dropped to the floor and slunk out of sight.

"Forget the *Moultrie News*. Winborne hit the big time! *Charleston Post and Courier*. The boy's on the way up!"

I knew I was ranting at a machine. I couldn't stop myself.

"No wonde—"

"I'm here." Emma sounded sluggish, as though I'd awakened her.

"No wonder the little worm forked over his Nikon. He had a backup camera. Probably a whole stash!"

"Tempe."

"An SLR in his shorts! A wide-angle in his ballpoint! A miniature camcorder strapped to his dick! Who knows? We might make *Court TV*!"

"Are you finished?" Emma asked.

"Have you seen it?"

"Yes."

"And?" I considered crushing the handset.

"And what?"

"You're not furious?"

"Sure I'm furious. My butt looks huge. Are you done venting?"

That's what it was, of course. Venting.

"Our goal is to get the skeleton identified." Emma's voice sounded dull. "Exposure could help."

"That was your line on Friday."

"It still is."

"Winborne's article could tip the killer."

"If there *is* a killer. Maybe this guy died of an overdose. Maybe his buddies panicked and dumped his body where they thought it wouldn't be found. Maybe we have nothing more serious than a Chapter Seventeen violation."

"I'll bite."

"Improper disposal of a corpse. Look. Someone's probably missing this guy. If that someone is local, he or she may read the piece and make a call. Admit it. You're just pissed that Winborne outwitted us."

I threw up a hand in an "I'm not believing this" gesture.

When puzzled, Boyd twirls his eyebrow hairs. He did that now, from the safety of the doorway.

"I'll see you tomorrow morning," Emma said.

Climbing the stairs, I went to my bathroom and rested my forehead on the mirror. The glass felt cool against my flushed skin.

*Goddamn nosy, interfering reporters! Goddamn Winborne!*

I breathed deeply and let it out slowly.

I have a temper. I admit that. Occasionally, that temper triggers overreaction. I admit that, too. I despise such lapses. And I resent those able to trip that switch in my head.

Emma was right. The article was benign. Winborne was doing his job and he'd out-maneuvered us.

I took another deep breath.

I wasn't angry at Winborne. I was angry at myself for being outsmarted by plankton.

I straightened and stared at myself in the mirror, assessing.

Hazel eyes, bright, some would say intense. Crow's-feet at the corners, but still my best feature.

High cheekbones, nose a bit on the small side. Jaw holding firm. A few gray hairs, but the honey-brown still in charge.

I stepped back for a full body view.

Five-five. One twenty.

Overall, not bad for an odometer reading forty plus.

I locked on to the hazel gaze in the glass. A familiar voice sounded in my brain. *Do your job, Brennan. Ignore the distractions and focus. Get it done. That's what you do. Get it done.*

Boyd padded over and nudged my knee. I directed my next comment to him.

"Screw Winborne." The eyebrow hairs went crazy. "And the byline he rode in on."

Boyd shot his snout skyward in full agreement. I patted his head.

After splashing water on my face, I applied makeup, twisted my hair into a topknot, and hurried downstairs. I was filling pet dishes when the front door slammed.

"Honey! I'm home!"

Pete appeared with yet more groceries.

"Planning a reunion of your entire Marine unit?"

Pete snapped a salute and replied with the Marine Corps motto. *"Semper Fi."*

"How did it go with Herron?" I extracted a jar of pickled herring from Pete's bag and placed it in the fridge.

Reaching around me, Pete grabbed a Sam Adams and popped the cap on a drawer handle.

I bit back a rebuke. Pete's annoying habits were no longer my problem.

"Spent my time doing recon," Pete said.

"You couldn't get anywhere near Herron," I translated.

"No."

"What did you do?"

"Watched a whole lot of prayin' and making joyful sounds unto the Lord. When the show let out, I floated Helene's picture to a few of the faithful."

"And?"

"They are a spectacularly unobservant flock."

"No one remembered her?"

Pete drew a snapshot from his pocket and laid it on the table. I crossed to study it.

The image was blurry, a blowup of a driver's license or passport photo. A young woman stared, unsmiling, into the camera.

Helene wasn't pretty, though her features were even in a bland sort of way. Her hair was middle-parted and drawn back at the nape of her neck.

I had to admit. Helene Flynn had little to

distinguish her from a thousand other women her age.

"Afterward I had a chat with Helene's landlady," Pete said. "Didn't learn much. Helene was polite, paid her rent on time, had no visitors. She did volunteer that the kid seemed agitated toward the end. But Helene's leaving took her by surprise. Until the envelope with the final rent showed up, she had no idea Helene was leaving."

I looked again at the face in the photo. So forgettable. Witnesses would give unusable descriptions. Medium height. Medium weight. No recall of the face.

"Flynn had no other photos of his daughter?" I asked.

"None post-dating high school."

"Odd."

"Flynn's an odd bird."

"You said he hired an investigator."

Pete nodded. "Former Charlotte-Mecklenburg cop named Noble Cruikshank."

"Cruikshank simply vanished?"

"Stopped sending reports and returning phone calls. I did a little digging. Cruikshank wasn't in the running to be CMPD poster boy. Got invited off the force in ninety-four for substance abuse."

"Cocktail of choice?"

"Jimmy B neat. Cruikshank's also a non-nominee for PI of the Year. Seems he's pulled his disappearing act on other clients. Takes a job, collects an upfront fee, goes on a bender."

"Wouldn't a PI lose his license for that?"

"Apparently Cruikshank doesn't believe in paperwork. That was also a problem with the CMPD."

"Flynn didn't know Cruikshank drank and wasn't licensed?"

"Flynn hired him off the Net."

"Risky."

"Cruikshank's ad said he specialized in missing persons. That's the skill set Flynn needed. He also liked the idea that Cruikshank worked Charlotte and Charleston."

"When did Flynn hire him?"

"Last January. Couple months after Helene dropped out of sight. Flynn thinks their last conversation was in late March. Cruikshank said the investigation was moving forward, but provided no detail. Then nothing."

"Where did Cruikshank go on his other benders?"

"Once to Atlantic City. Once to Vegas. But not all Cruikshank's clients were unhappy. Most that I contacted thought they'd gotten their money's worth."

"How did you find them?"

"Cruikshank gave Flynn a list of references. I started with those, picked up new names as I worked my way backward."

"What do you know about Cruikshank's final activities?"

"Cruikshank never cashed the last check Flynn sent him. That was the February payment. There's been no activity on his credit card or bank account since March. He owed over twenty-four hundred on the former, had four fifty-two in the latter. The last phone bill was paid in February. Account's since been cut off."

"He must have had a car."

"Whereabouts unknown."

"Cell phone?"

"Terminated in early December for nonpayment. Wasn't the first time Cruikshank had been dropped."

"A PI without a mobile these days?"

Pete shrugged. "Maybe the guy worked alone, did all his phoning from home."

"Family?"

"Divorced. No kids. The split wasn't amicable. The wife's remarried and hasn't heard from him in years."

"Brothers? Sisters?"

Pete shook his head. "Cruikshank was an only child and the parents are dead. Toward the end of his stint with the Charlotte PD he'd become pretty much a loner, and wasn't close to anyone."

I looped back to GMC.

"If you can't get to Herron, what's your next step?"

Pete pointed a finger heavenward. "Fear not, fair lady. The Latvian Savant has just entered the footrace."

Pete was a law student when we met. He'd already adopted the nickname back then. I never learned who coined it. I suspected it was Pete.

Rolling my eyes, I returned to the groceries and

put a package of feta into the fridge.

Pete tipped back his chair and rested his heels on the table edge.

I started to object. Not my problem. Anne's? She invited him here.

"And how was your day, sugar britches?"

I retrieved the *Post and Courier,* dropped it on the table, and pointed.

Pete read Winborne's article.

"Hey, nice use of alliteration. 'Buried Body Barrier Beach.' "

"Pure poetry."

"I take it you're not pleased this kid talked to the press."

"I'm not pleased with any of it."

I hadn't even thought about Topher. When had Winborne buttonholed him? How had he persuaded Topher to give a statement?

"The photo's not bad."

I shot Pete a look.

"What's this cruise ship thing your friend screwed up?"

"I don't know."

"Gonna ask her?"

"Definitely not."

Roast peppers, salmon spread, and Ben & Jerry's into the fridge and freezer. Chocolate chips and pistachios into the cabinet. Then I turned back to Pete.

"A man is dead. His family doesn't know that yet. I view Winborne's story as an invasion of that family's privacy. Am I way off base?"

71

Pete shrugged, then drained his beer.

"News is news. Know what you need?"

"What?" Wary.

"Picnic."

"I had a sandwich at three."

Dropping his chair to the floor, Pete stood, turned me by the shoulders, and gently pushed me from the kitchen.

"Go grade a paper or something. Meet me at the gazebo at eight."

"I don't know, Pete."

I did know. And every cell in my hindbrain was running up a warning flag.

Pete and I had been married for twenty years, separated for only a few. Though our marriage had posed many challenges, sexual attraction had never been one of them. We'd rocked when we were newlyweds. We could still rock.

If Pete hadn't rocked off the reservation.

My libido's view of Pete worried me. Things were going well with Ryan. I didn't want to do something that might compromise that. And the last time Pete and I spent an evening together we'd ended up like kids in the back of a Chevy.

"I do know," Pete said. "Go."

"Pete—"

"You've got to eat. I've got to eat. We'll do it together and include a little sand."

There's something deep in my psyche that links food with human interaction. When home alone, I live on carry-out or frozen dinners. When solo on the road, I order room service and dine with

Letterman or Raymond or Oprah.

Company did sound nice. And Pete was a good cook.

"This isn't a date, Pete."

"Of course not."

# 7

I got through three more exams before drifting off. Slumped sideways on my bed pillows, I floated in that limbo between waking and sleep, dreaming meaningless snatches. Running on a beach. Arranging bones with Emma.

In one fragment, I was sitting in a circle at an AA meeting. Ryan was there. Pete. A tall, blond man. The three were talking, but I couldn't hear the conversation. Their faces were in shadow so I couldn't read their expressions.

I awoke to a room bathed in orange and a breeze clattering the palmettos against the outside deck. The clock said eight ten.

I walked to the bathroom and rehabbed the top-knot. While I'd been dozing, my bangs had decided to go for that spiky thing. I wet them, grabbed a brush, and began blow-drying. Halfway through, I stopped. Why? And why had I bothered earlier with makeup? Tossing the brush, I hurried downstairs.

Anne's house is connected to the beach by a long wooden boardwalk. A gazebo occupies a deck at the walkway's highest point in its trajectory over the dunes. Pete was there, drinking wine, the last glow of sunset warming his hair.

Katy's hair. The genetic echo was so strong I could never look at one without seeing the other.

I was barefoot, so Pete didn't hear me approach. He'd found a tablecloth, silver candles, a bud vase, and an ice bucket. Two places were set, and a cooler rested on the gazebo floor.

I pulled up short, clotheslined by an unexpected sense of loss.

I don't buy into the "there's but one soul mate" philosophy, but when I met Pete the attraction had been nuclear fusion. The flipping gut when our arms brushed. The thumping heart when I spotted his face in a crowd. I'd known from the start Pete was the guy I was going to marry.

I looked at Pete's face now, lined and tanned, the forehead creeping a little to the north. I'd awakened to that face for more than two decades. Those eyes watched in awe as my daughter was born. My fingers had traced that skin a thousand times. I knew every pore, every muscle, every bone.

Every excuse those lips had constructed.

Every time the truth had shredded my heart.

No way. Done.

"Hey, dude."

Pete rose and turned at the sound of my voice. "Thought I'd been stood up."

"Sorry. I fell asleep."

"Table by the window, madam?"

I took a seat. Towel-draping his arm, Pete pulled a Diet Coke from the ice bucket and laid it on his wrist for my inspection.

"Excellent year," I said.

Pete poured, then began spreading food. Cold spiced shrimp. Smoked trout. Lobster salad. Marinated asparagus. Brie. Pumpernickel squares. Tapenade.

I doubt my estranged husband could survive in a world without a good deli.

We ate, watching fingers of sunlight change from yellow to orange to gray. The ocean was calm, a background symphony of swells rolling gently to shore. Now and then a seabird called out and another answered.

We finished with key lime pie as the gray turned to black.

Pete cleared the table, then we both put our feet on the railing.

"The beach suits you, Tempe. You're lookin' good."

Pete looked good, too, in his rumpled, tousled Pete Petersons way.

I repeated my earlier warning. "This isn't a date, Pete."

"I can't mention the fact that you look nice?" All innocence.

Muted yellow lights were appearing in the houses lining the shore. Another day was checking out. Pete and I watched in silence, the salt breeze playing with our hair.

When Pete spoke again his voice had taken on a deeper tone.

"What I'm having a hard time remembering is why we split up."

"Because you're annoying as hell and spectacularly unfaithful."

"People change, Tempe."

All responses to that seemed dumb, so I didn't make one.

"You ever think—"

At that moment my cell phone sounded. I dug it from my pocket and clicked on.

"How's the most beautiful woman on the planet?" Ryan.

"Good." I dropped my feet and did a half turn in my chair.

"Busy day?"

"Not bad."

"Any word on your skeleton?"

"No."

Pete served himself more of the Chardonnay, then waggled another Coke in my direction. I shook my head no.

Sounds slipped over the line. Or Ryan picked up on my reticence. "Is this a bad time?"

"I'm finishing dinner." A gull screamed overhead.

"On the beach?"

"It's a beautiful night." Dumb. Ryan knew my attitude toward dining solo. "Pete made a picnic."

Ryan didn't answer for a full five seconds. Then, "OK."

"How's Lily?"

"Good." After another long pause, "I'll talk to you later, Tempe."

I was listening to dead air.

"Problem?" Pete asked.

I shook my head. "I'm going to turn in." I rose. "Thanks for dinner. It really was nice."

"My pleasure."

I started up the boardwalk.

"Tempe."

I turned.

"When you're ready to listen, I'd like to talk."

I walked toward the house, feeling Pete's eyes on my back.

My late afternoon nap kept me up until well past three.

Or was it agitation over Ryan's displeasure? Though I phoned several times, my calls went unanswered.

*Was* Ryan displeased? Was I being paranoid? He's the one who'd gone to Nova Scotia to visit Lily. Wasn't Lily's mother in Nova Scotia?

Whatever.

And what was bothering Emma? Saturday's caller had obviously not delivered good news. Was she in trouble over this cruise ship case?

Who was parked outside Anne's house early this morning? Dickie Dupree? He'd threatened me, but I hadn't taken him seriously. Would Dupree stoop to physical intimidation? No, but he might send somebody.

Could Dupree have something to do with the skeleton buried on Dewees? That seemed a stretch.

Had bacteria really contaminated the iceman's bones? Five thousand years in the Alps and now he's snack food for microbes?

Why two spellings for ketchup? Catsup? And where did that name come from, anyway?

I tossed and turned for hours, then slept later than I'd planned on Monday.

By the time I got to the hospital it was after ten. Emma was there. So was the forensic dentist, a behemoth in a sweatsuit he must have picked up at a Kmart closeout. Emma introduced him as Bernie Grimes.

Grimes's handshake was one of those you don't know quite how to handle. Too weak to grasp. Too clingy to slip.

Freeing my hand, I smiled at Grimes. He smiled back, looking like a silo in blue velour.

Emma had already wheeled the skeleton from the cooler. It lay on the same gurney it had occupied on Saturday, a large brown envelope covering the ribs. The dental X-rays were again spread on the light box.

Grimes led us through a point-by-point description of the morphological characteristics, oral hygiene, and entire dental history of CCC-2006020277. Smoker. Negligent brusher. Non-flosser. Fillings. Untreated cavities and massive tartar buildup, hadn't seen a dentist in several years preceding death. I hardly listened. I was anxious to get to the bones.

Finally, Grimes finished, and he and Emma left to begin filling out an NCIC case form. One by one, I examined the full-body films. Skull. Upper limbs. Lower limbs. Pelvis.

Zip. That didn't surprise me. I'd noticed nothing obvious while handling the bones.

I moved on to the torso.

Since no flesh remained to hold the ribs in place, the technician had spread them flat and shot from above. I saw nothing suspicious in the right arcade. I was finishing with the left when I spotted a dark crescent near the vertebral end of the twelfth rib.

Moving to the gurney, I selected that rib and took it to a scope. Under magnification the imperfection appeared as a tiny gash bordered by a curl of bone on the rib's lower edge. Though small, the defect was real.

Had the gash been caused by a knife blade? Had our unknown been stabbed? Or was the nick a postmortem artifact? From a trowel? A snail or crustacean? No matter how much I angled and reangled the rib, no matter how high I kicked the magnification or adjusted the fiber optic light, I just couldn't tell.

Returning to the X-rays, I inspected the breast- and collarbones, the shoulder blades, then the rest of the ribs. Nothing looked amiss.

I moved on to the spine. The vertebrae had been filmed separated and placed flat, like the ribs, then articulated and lying on their sides.

In a stabbing, it's often the posterior arch or the back of the vertebral body that takes the hit. I moved through the vertebral films. None gave a clear view of these surfaces.

Returning to the skeleton, I began a bone-by-bone inspection, rotating and scrutinizing every element under a magnifying lens surrounded by a fluorescent bulb.

I found nothing until I started on the spine.

Every one's a specialist. Even the vertebrae. The seven cervicals support the head and allow for neck mobility. The twelve thoracics anchor the rib cage. The five lumbars throw in a lower-back curve. The five sacrals form the tail side of the pelvic girdle. Different jobs. Different shapes.

It was the sixth cervical that got my attention.

But I oversimplify. The neck vertebrae have tasks other than head support. One of their jobs is to provide safe passage for arteries traveling to the back of the brain. The transit route involves a small hole, or foramen, in the transverse process, a tiny bone platform between the body of the vertebra and its arch. CCC-2006020277 had a vertical hinge fracture snaking across the left transverse process, on the body side of the hole.

I brought the bone closer to the lens. And found a hairline fracture on the arch side of the hole.

No signs of healing. Hinging. No question here. Both fractures had involved trauma to fresh bone. The injury had occurred around the time of death.

I sat back, considering.

C-6. Lower neck.

Fall? Falls cause sudden excessive impaction. Such impaction can lead to vertebral fracture. But fractures due to falls are generally compressive in nature, and usually involve the vertebral body. This was a hinge fracture. Of the transverse process.

Strangulation? Strangulation most often affects the hyoid, a small bone in the front of the throat.

Whiplash? Not likely.

Blow to the chin? Head?

I could think of no scenario that fit the pattern I was seeing.

Frustrated, I moved on.

And found more.

The twelfth thoracic vertebra sported a pair of nicks similar to the one I'd spotted on the twelfth rib. The first and third lumbar vertebrae had a single nick each.

Like the neck fracture, the pattern of the nicks was confusing. All were located on the belly side.

Knife marks? To penetrate to the front of a lumbar vertebra you'd have to thrust hard enough to pass through the entire abdomen. That's a mighty big thrust.

And these were very small nicks. Made with a very sharp tool.

What the hell had gone on?

I was still speculating when Emma returned.

"Grimes gone?" I asked.

Emma nodded. What color she'd shown earlier had ebbed from her face, accentuating the dark circles under her eyes. "Form's done. Now it will be up to the sheriff."

Though NCIC is operational 24/7, year-round,

only members of federal, state, and local law enforcement can input data.

"Gullet will shoot it through right away?"

Emma raised both hands in a "who knows" gesture. Pulling a chair from the wall, she dropped and leaned her elbows on her thighs.

"What's wrong?" I asked.

Emma shrugged. "Sometimes it just seems so hopeless."

I waited.

"Gullett's not going to slap this case with a priority sticker. And when he does enter our guy into the system, what are the chances we'll get a hit? To submit a missing adult into the database under the new regs, the person's got to be disabled, a disaster victim, abducted or kidnapped, endangered—"

"What does that mean?"

"Missing in the company of another under circumstances suggesting his or her physical safety is in danger."

"So a lot of MP's never get entered? Our guy may not have made it into the computer when he vanished?"

"The thinking is that most missing adults take off on their own. Husbands skipping town with their mistresses. Smothered wives looking for something more. Deadbeats cutting out on debt."

"The runaway bride." I referred to a case wrung dry in a recent media frenzy.

"It's head cases like that one that nurture the mind-set." Emma threw out her feet and leaned back. "But it's true. The vast majority of missing adults are people just trying to escape their lives. There's no law against that, and entering them all overloads the system."

Emma closed her eyes and tipped her head back against the wall.

"I doubt this guy simply went missing," I said, turning back to the gurney. "Take a look at this."

I was lining up the vertebrae when I heard movement, then a heart-stopping crack.

I whipped around.

Emma lay crumpled on the tile floor.

# 8

Emma had landed on the crown of her head. Her back was humped and her neck and limbs were in-kinked like the legs of a sun-fried spider.

I rushed over and pressed two fingers to her throat. The pulse was steady, but weak.

"Emma!"

She didn't respond.

Lowering Emma, I gently eased her cheek to the tile. Then I bolted to the corridor.

"Help! I need medical help!"

A door opened and a face appeared.

"Emma Rousseau's collapsed. Call the ER."

The brows rocketed and the mouth went round.

"Now!"

The face withdrew. I raced back to Emma. Seconds later two paramedics blasted into the room. They fired questions as they loaded Emma onto a gurney.

"What happened?"

"She collapsed."

"Did you move her?"

"I rolled her to clear the windpipe."

"Medical problems?"

I blinked and looked at him.

"Was she taking medication?"

I felt helpless. I hadn't a clue.

"Out of the way, please."

I heard the whine of rubber wheels on tile. A soft squeaking.

Then the autopsy room door clicked shut.

Emma's eyes were closed. A tube ran from her left arm to an IV bag above her head. The tube was taped with white adhesive. Its color was little different from that of Emma's skin.

This woman had always been a firestorm of energy, a force of nature. Not now. In her hospital bed she looked small and fragile.

I tiptoed across the cubicle and took my friend's hand.

Emma's eyes opened.

"I'm sorry, Tempe."

Her words surprised me. Wasn't it I who should be apologizing? Wasn't it I who had ignored the signs of distress?

"Rest, Emma. We'll talk later."

"Non-Hodgkin's lymphoma."

"What?" Reflex. Denial. I knew what Emma was saying.

"I have non-Hodgkin's lymphoma. NHL. And I'm not talking hockey." Weak smile.

"How long?" Something cold started to congeal in my chest.

"Awhile."

"How long is awhile?"

"A couple of years."

"What type?" Stupid. I knew next to nothing about lymphoma.

"Nothing exotic. Diffuse large B-cell lymphoma." Rote, as though she'd heard or read the words a thousand times. Dear God, she probably had.

I swallowed hard. "You're in treatment?"

Emma nodded. "I was in remission, but I've relapsed. I'm getting the CHOP regime on an outpatient basis. Vincristine, prednisolone, doxorubicin, and cyclophosphamide. My biggest worry is infection. The cytotoxic drugs leave me wide open to infection. One good staph offensive could lay me flat."

I wanted to close my eyes, to make this all go away. I kept them open.

"You're a hellcat." Forced smile. "You'll be fine."

"I learned Saturday that I'm not responding as well as my doctor had hoped."

The bad-news phone call. Was that what Emma had started to share outside the hospital? Had I been too preoccupied with the skeleton to listen? Had I done something to discourage her confidence?

"Have you told anyone?"

Emma shook her head.

"That wasn't a migraine on Saturday."

"No."

"You should have leveled with me, Emma. You could have trusted me."

Emma shrugged. "You can't help. Why worry you?"

"Does your staff know?"

A look flared in Emma's eyes. "I've lost some weight and some hair, but I can still do my job."

"Of course you can."

I stroked Emma's hand. I understood my friend. But only in part.

Emma cared fiercely about her duties, and would let nothing interfere with her performance of them. She and I were clones in that way.

But something else drove Emma Rousseau. Something I'd never fully grasped. A desire for power? Recognition? Some manic need to out-shine? Emma marched to drumbeats I didn't hear.

"They're having a lot of success with lymphoma these days." Lousy at nurturing, I fell back on cliché.

"Damn right."

Emma raised a palm. I high-fived it. Her hand dropped back to the bed.

Diffuse large B-cell. A high-grade lymphoma. The cancer was destructive and moving fast.

I felt burning behind my eyes. Again, I managed to keep them open. To keep my lips smiling.

The muffled sound of "Bad Boys" floated from a bedside locker.

"My cell," Emma said.

"Is that the *COPS* theme?"

Emma gestured impatiently. "It's in the plastic bag with my clothes."

By the time I extracted the phone the music had ended. Emma checked the caller ID and hit redial.

I knew I should protest, should advise rest and stress avoidance, but it was pointless. Emma would do what Emma would do. In that, we were also clones.

"Emma Rousseau."

I heard a tinny voice on the other end of the line.

"I've been tied up," Emma said.

Tied up? I mouthed.

Emma shushed me with a hand.

I rolled my eyes. Emma pointed a warning finger.

"Who phoned it in?"

The tinny voice answered, but I couldn't make out the words.

"Where?"

Emma pantomimed writing. I dug a pen and tablet from my purse. The IV tubing rattled as Emma scribbled.

"Who's on it?"

The tinny voice spoke at length.

"Give me the particulars."

Emma shifted the phone and the voice was cut off. As she listened, her eyes flicked to her watch. It wasn't there. She pointed at mine. I held out my wrist.

"Don't touch the body. I'll be there in an hour."

Clicking off, Emma threw back the blanket and swung her legs over the side of the bed.

"No way," I said, placing a hand on each of her knees. "Unless I'm mistaken, you lost consciousness a few hours back."

"The ER doc says it's fatigue brought on by the meds. All my vitals are good."

"Fatigue?" Even for Emma, this was a stretch. "You collapsed and nearly left your brains on the floor."

"I'm OK now." Emma stood, took a step, and her knees buckled. Bracing against the headboard, she closed her eyes, willing her body to work.

"I'm fine," she whispered.

I didn't bother to argue. Prying loose her fingers, I eased Emma back onto the bed, and pulled the blanket to her waist.

"I have too much to do," she resisted weakly.

"You're not going anywhere until a doctor releases you," I said.

Emma's eye roll left mine in the dust.

I looked at my friend. She had no husband or children. No lover that I knew of. She'd spoken once of an estranged sister, but that had been years ago. As far as I knew Emma had no one close in her life.

"Do you have friends who can look in on you?"

"Whole squadrons." Emma flicked at a nonexistent something on the blanket. "I'm not the freakoid loner you think I am."

"I don't think that at all," I lied.

At that moment, an ER resident stepped into the

90

cubicle. He had greasy black hair and looked like he'd been up since Reagan held the White House. A plastic rectangle on his scrubs said his name was Bliss.

Or was the badge some sort of subliminal greeting? *I wish you bliss.*

Bliss began flipping through the pages of Emma's chart.

"Tell her you're not eyeing me as today's organ donor," Emma said.

Bliss looked up. "You're fine."

"Two hours ago she was passed out cold," I said.

"The treatment she's undergoing can be debilitating." Bliss turned to Emma. "You shouldn't run a marathon, but otherwise you're good to go. Assuming you contact your regular physician."

Emma gave a thumbs-up.

"She's planning to go straight back to work," I said.

"That's not a great idea," Bliss said. "Go home. Take some time to recover your strength."

"It's not like I play tackle for the Carolina Panthers," Emma said.

"What do you do?" Weary, making notes in the chart.

"She's the coroner," I said.

Bliss stopped writing and looked at Emma. "That's why the name seemed familiar."

A nurse appeared. Bliss instructed her to disconnect Emma's IV.

"Your friend's right." Bliss flipped back the pages of the chart. "Take the day off. If you don't get rest there could be a repeat performance."

Seconds after Bliss's departure, Emma was on the phone to Gullet. The sheriff was out. Emma said she would personally drop off the NCIC forms.

Disconnecting, she dressed and strode from the cubicle. I trailed behind, determined to talk her into going home. Or, failing that, to stay close in the event she took another header.

Together, we zipped CCC-2006020277 into his body bag and asked a tech to return him to the cooler. Then we stored his X-rays and gathered his paperwork. Throughout, I pushed my plan for bed rest.

Throughout, Emma repeated, "I'm OK."

Leaving the hospital felt like walking into a vat of warm honey. Emma fired down the ramp, as though trying to put space between us.

Catching up, I tried one last salvo.

"Emma." Sharper than I'd intended. I was frustrated and out of arguments. "It's ninety-five. You're exhausted. No case is so important it can't wait until tomorrow."

Emma let out her breath in annoyance.

"The call I just took was from one of my investigators. Couple of boys found a body in the woods this afternoon."

"Let your investigator handle it."

"The case could be sensitive."

"Every death is sensitive."

"Damn, Tempe. First two, three thousand cases I've worked, I guess I didn't see that."

I just looked at her.

"Sorry." Emma pushed the hair from her forehead. "About three months back an eighteen-year-old kid vanished. History of depression, no money, passport, or possessions missing."

"The cops suspected suicide?"

Emma nodded. "No note or body was ever found. My investigator thinks this could be him."

"Let your investigator handle the recovery."

"There's no margin for error on this one. Daddy's a local politico. Guy's angry, vocal, and hangs with the power boys. That's a dangerous combination."

I wondered again if blowback from the cruise ship incident was affecting Emma more than I knew.

"What tipped your investigator?"

"The remains are hanging from a tree. The tree's less than a mile from the kid's last known address."

I pictured the scene. That picture was all too familiar.

"Has Daddy been told?"

Emma shook her head.

Plan B.

"How about this?" I proposed. "Tell Daddy that his son's disappearance is being given top priority. A body has been found, but three months' exposure complicates analysis. Outside expertise is needed to make an identification."

As usual, Emma got it right off. "The coroner's office wants the best, and cost is no obstacle."

"I like the way you think."

Emma smiled a weak smile. "You'll really do it?"

"You have the authority to bring me into the case?"

"Yes."

"I'll do it if you promise to go straight home to bed."

"How about this?" Emma counterproposed. "I deliver the NCIC forms to the sheriff, get him working on the Dewees skeleton. You supervise recovery of my hanging victim. We keep in touch by phone."

"After your nap."

"Yeah, yeah."

"Sounds like a plan."

# 9

This is what Emma knew.

Matthew Summerfield IV was a troubled kid from a family that didn't tolerate imperfection. Mama was Sally, née Middleton, of the First Continental Congress Middletons. Daddy was a Citadel grad and reigning monarch on the Charleston City Council.

Matthew IV tried foot-stepping Matthew III, but got bounced for smoking pot as a plebe. Deciding on tough love, Daddy booted Sonny from the family homestead.

Matthew IV bunked in with friends, made spare change by buying rice and dried beans at the Piggly Wiggly and repackaging them as thirteen-bean soup and hoppin' John mix for the tourists. On February 28, young Matt left his stall at the Old City Market near East Bay Street, walked to Meeting Street, and vanished. He was eighteen.

Emma's directions sent me over the Wando

River and north to the Francis Marion National Forest, a quarter-million-acre triangle of coastal plain bordered on the north by the Santee River, on the east by the intracoastal waterway, and on the west by Lake Moultrie. Slammed hard in '89 by Hurricane Hugo, the flora in the Francis Marion had rebounded with all the vigor of a Brazilian jungle. The whole drive I worried about finding the action.

I needn't have. Vehicles lined the shoulder. Cruisers with their lights flashing. A coroner's van. A park ranger's Jeep. A battered Chevy Nova. Two SUVs, their occupants bumper-leaning in tanks and cutoffs, faces bearing identical expressions of eager curiosity, already telling the story in their heads.

I was pleased to see no media trucks, but, given the crowd, doubted that would last.

Besides the gawkers, the only people visible were a uniform and two black kids. Grabbing my pack, I climbed from the car and headed toward them.

The boys had shaved heads and looked about sixteen. Both were gangstered up in enormous basketball jerseys and butt-hanger jeans. From Emma's report, I guessed this was the lucky pair that had blundered upon the body.

The cop was a small man with brown-black eyes. His name tag said H. Tybee. Despite the oppressive heat and humidity, Deputy Tybee's creases were razors and his hat sat perfectly squared to his brows.

Hearing me approach, Tybee stopped his

interview and looked up. His nose was pointy with a high, narrow bridge. I imagined his buddies calling him "Hawk."

The kids regarded me with arms crossed, heads canted so their ears almost touched their shoulders. Tybee kept his expression neutral so I could read it any way I chose. I read it as arrogant.

Three boys acting tough.

I introduced myself and explained my connection to the coroner.

Tybee crooked his head toward the woods.

"DOA's yonder."

Yonder?

"These homeboys claim they don't know squat."

The homeboys shifted their slouches to smirk at each other.

I spoke to the taller of the two. "What's your name?"

"Jamal."

"What happened, Jamal?"

"We already tole him."

"Tell me."

Jamal shrugged. "We seen something hanging from a tree. That's it."

"Did you recognize the person hanging from the tree?"

"Dude's messed up."

"Why were you in the woods?"

"Enjoying nature." Traded smirks.

Hearing a motor, we all checked the road.

A white Ford Explorer with a blue star on the side panel was rounding the curve. We watched it pull to a stop behind one of the cruisers. A man got out, followed by a dog.

The man was tall, maybe six-two, and broad-chested, like a boxer. He wore pressed khakis and aviator shades. The dog was brown and had retriever somewhere in its parentage.

I was beginning to feel underdressed. Next outing, I'd bring Boyd.

The man strode toward us, carrying himself like someone who might speed-dial the governor. The words "Sheriff Junius Gullet" were embroidered on the left of his crisp white shirt.

Jamal uncrossed his arms and shoved his hands downward. Only the fingertips went low enough to take cover in the pockets.

"Afternoon, sir." Tybee touched his brim. "Lady says she's with the coroner."

"Spoke to Miz Rousseau." Gullet pronounced the name "Roosa." "And such would appear to be the case."

The dog moved to the edge of the woods and lifted a leg at each of several trees.

Gullet's eyes flicked me up and down. Then he thrust out an arm, and his hand swallowed mine in a ball-breaker grip.

"You're the lady doc from Charlotte." Gullet spoke without intonation.

"Anthropologist."

"Miz Rousseau usually uses Jaffer."

"I'm sure she told you, he's out of the country."

"Bit out of the ordinary, but it's Miz Rousseau's call. She give you background?"

I nodded.

"Kid lived less than a mile from here with a houseful of baseheads." OK. The sheriff wasn't one for gushy intros. "Seen the body?" Flat.

"I just arrived."

"Dude's worm food." Jamal's smirk went wider than his face.

Gullet's face came around slowly. It was without expression, almost bored. There was a long, uncomfortable silence, then, "You get off on disrespecting the dead, son?"

Jamal shrugged. "Man, that dude's head—"

Gullet hit him in the sternum with one beefy finger. "You want to shut your mouth long enough to listen? That 'worm food' is one of the Lord's own souls, just like the rest of us." Gullet withdrew his finger. "Maybe even you, son."

Both boys developed an intense interest in their sneakers.

To me: "Yonder's a trail leading to swampland. This part of the park isn't a hot spot for locals or tourists. Nothing much to fish. Too buggy to camp."

I nodded.

"Hope you're ready for this."

I nodded again.

"Nothin' shocks this old boy anymore."

The dog scampered ahead. I followed Gullet.

Walking into the woods, I channeled my mind into death scene mode. From this point on I would tune out the extraneous and focus only on the relevant. I would notice every overly lush plant, every bent twig, every odor, every insect. The human melee around me would become white noise.

Here the forest was a mixture of loblolly pine, sweet gum, hemlock, and beech. Dogwood, witch hazel, and sweet shrub packed the understory, tinting the air with sun-baked sweetness.

Gullet set a swift pace. Sun slipped through the lattice overhead, creating a wild geometry of light and shadow. Now and then leaves rustled, tattling on some startled creature. Underfoot, the soil felt soft and moist.

Twenty yards in, the trees yielded to a small clearing. On the right lay a bog, its black glass surface disturbed only occasionally by a dragonfly or some water-striding insect.

Pond pine and loblolly bay rimmed the water. The trees looked stunted, primordial, their trunks disappearing into inky darkness, their roots gnarled and mossy green.

Five yards from the water's edge stood a single white oak. A body dangled from the oak's lowest branch, toes barely clearing the ground.

Closing in on the gruesome tableau, I wondered what black vision had led to such an end. What tortured state of mind drove this anguished soul to fashion a noose, tie a rope, and jump?

Men in uniform and civvies stood talking, shooing flies, slapping mosquitoes. Every shirt was limp, every armpit rimmed with a dark sweat crescent.

A woman shot video. Two still cameras hung

from her neck. The Charleston County coroner logo decorated her shirt.

I crossed the clearing and introduced myself. The woman's name was Lee Ann Miller. She was built like a lumberjack, with copper-red curls that came straight from a bottle.

"Mind if I check the body?"

"Jump right in, darlin'." Lifting her hair, Miller beamed a smile as wide as Charleston Harbor.

"I don't mind waiting until you've finished shooting."

"I can't work around your skinny little butt, I'm in the wrong line of work." Miller fanned her neck and again flashed the harbor smile.

Despite the circumstances, I grinned back. Lee Ann Miller looked like a woman folks went to when seeking comfort. Or advice. Or just a good laugh.

As I moved to the tree, Gullet spoke to one of the other players. I paid little attention. I was taking in detail.

The body was hung with a yellow three-strand polypropylene rope. The noose was embedded deep in the neck, around the level of the third and fourth cervical vertebrae. Above it, the head and top two cervical vertebrae were missing.

The bones were overlain by fried and putrefied connective tissue. The clothing looked flat, as though hung on a scarecrow. Black pants. A denim jacket, suggesting the hanging had occurred during cooler weather. Brown socks. Scuffed boots.

Boot.

I looked around. The right leg bones lay ten feet

east of the body, marked with a small yellow flag.

I walked over. The foot bones and the distal ends of the tibia and fibula remained firmly in the boot. The proximal ends were missing, and the shafts were cracked and splintered. A piece of the femur showed similar damage.

"Explain that." Gullet was at my elbow.

"Animals are opportunists. Most will scavenge if given the opportunity."

A mosquito drilled my arm. Slapping it, I moved on.

The skull lay six feet downslope from the tree, nestled against one of the roots snaking from its trunk. It, too, had been flagged.

It, too, had been scavenged.

"No animal climbed up and chucked that down." Gullet was staying with me.

"In hangings, exposure often causes the head to fall off." I heard flapping overhead, looked up to see a crow settle onto a branch. "Birds might have helped. And scavengers yanking on the legs."

As I spoke, I scanned for the mandible.

"Jaw's missing," I said.

"I'm on it." Matter-of-fact.

While Gullet questioned Miller, I squatted for a closer look at the head. For reasons of his own, Gullet's dog joined me. No way I'd have tolerated a canine compromising "my" crime scene, but this was Gullet's baby. I knew better than to challenge Sheriff Shockproof.

Gloving my right hand, I made mental notes. Little hair remained. The bone was sun-bleached, but subtly variegated where rootlets had clung to the surface. Tiny beetles still roamed the geography of the empty features.

Using one finger, I gently rolled the skull.

Patches of tissue clung to the left cheek and temple, mottled by the ground cover on which it had lain. One eye remained, a black raisin in a socket packed with dirt and moss.

As I allowed the skull to settle back into its original position, a lone cloud slipped over the sun. The day dimmed, and the temperature dropped. I felt a chill. I was staring into the remains of overpowering despair.

Returning to the body, I inspected the soil directly below the feet. No maggots, but puparial casings attested to their passing. Pulling a plastic vial from my pack, I collected a sample.

Gullet's dog watched, tongue drooping from the side of its mouth.

"No jaw." Gullet was back.

I got to my feet.

"How about having some searchers fan out and check the woods."

While Gullet gave the order, I stored more detail.

No animal scat. Yellow jackets, flies, beetles, ants. Nicks on the tree trunk, abrasions on the limb. Rope frayed on the ends. Noose knot at the back of the neck.

"Miller wants to know how much more time you'll need."

"I'm finished," I said.

Gullet's voice boomed, and he circled a hand in the air. "Good to go."

Giving a thumbs-up, Miller crossed to the point at which we'd entered the clearing and spoke to one of those watching. The man disappeared.

With the aid of another watcher, Miller carried a gurney to the tree. Then she unbuckled and dropped the security straps over the sides, unzipped a body bag, and laid back the flap.

The first watcher joined us with a collapsible ladder. Gullet gestured him up the tree.

Spreading the ladder as wide as possible, the man climbed the treads, steadied himself with his arms, and straddled the branch. Gullet moved in to act as spotter.

The others watched from afar, their eyes silently fixed on the corpse.

Miller handed up a pair of long-handled pruning shears. Then, with her helper, she repositioned the gurney, gingerly eased the victim's leg into one end of the bag, and raised the other end so it paralleled the hanging body as closely as possible.

The climber looked a question at Gullet.

"Cut him down." Gullet's face remained neutral. "Gently."

"As far from the knot as you can," I said.

Bending forward, the climber snared the rope between the short, curved blades and compressed the handles.

I stepped in, prepared to direct the body into the bag.

On the second try, the shears severed the rope.

Miller raised her end of the bag as her helper lowered his. I held my arms up, preventing the body from sliding in my direction.

The corpse slithered into place. Sweating and grunting, the two lowered the bag from above their heads to the gurney.

"You've done this before," I said.

Miller nodded, wiped sweat from her face with a forearm.

As Miller moved off to collect the head and leg bones, Gullet began searching the clothing for ID.

Nothing in the pants. Nothing in the shirt.

Then, "Hell-o."

Gullet pulled a wallet from one of the jacket pockets. The leather was degraded due to runoff from decomposition that had penetrated the cloth.

Using a thumbnail, Gullet pried the front cover open. The wallet's insides were sodden and congealed.

Using the same nail, the sheriff scraped dirt from the face of the first plastic compartment.

His cheeks may have crimped a fraction of a hair.

"Well. Well."

# 10

"Driving permit issued by the great state of South Carolina." Gullet thumb-scraped the plastic some more, raised his shades to his head, and tilted the wallet this way and that.

"No way this poor fella's Matthew Summerfield." Gullet thrust the wallet at Miller.

The coroner's investigator angled the plastic as the sheriff had done. "You got that right." Miller offered the wallet to me. "Print's too small for these old eyes."

Though the photo was badly deteriorated, it was clear the man pictured was no kid. He had flabby features, black-rimmed glasses, and wispy hair slicked into a comb-over. I strained to make out the lettering to the right of the photo.

"The name looks like Chester something Pinney. Maybe Pickney. Or Pinckney. The rest is too damaged," I said.

Miller produced a ziplock and I dropped the

wallet into it. She handed the baggie to Gullet.

"If you've got no objection, we'll deliver this gentleman's mortal remains to the morgue. Miss Rousseau will want to find out who he is and make next-of-kin notification as soon as possible."

Miller looked at her watch. We all followed suit, Pavlovian pups.

"Going on seven," Gullet said. "Nothing more going to happen tonight."

Nodding to Miller and me, the sheriff repositioned his shades on the bridge of his nose, whistled to the dog, and set off toward the road.

While her colleague cut free and bagged the remaining segment of rope, Miller and I satisfied ourselves that no further information could be wrung from the site. Vines and moss whispered overhead. Mosquitoes whined. Amphibians chanted from the murky gloom of the bog.

The sky was bleeding into a Lowcountry dusk as Miller slammed the double doors on the coroner's van. Her face was splotchy with insect bites, and perspiration darkened her back and chest.

"I'll be calling Emma shortly," I said. "I can fill her in."

"Thank ya, sweetie. That's one less chore to worry my mind."

I dialed from the road. Emma answered after three rings, her voice sounding thin and edgy. I explained what had taken place.

"I don't know how to thank you."

"No need," I said.

"The Summerfields will be relieved."

"Yes," I said, with little enthusiasm. A common scenario. One family gets good news, another gets bad.

I heard an intake of air, then nothing.

"What?"

"You've done so much."

"Not really."

"I hate to ask."

"Ask."

A hitch, then, "I have a treatment tomorrow. I—"

"What time?"

"The appointment is at seven."

"I'll pick you up at six thirty."

"Thanks, Tempe." The relief in her voice almost made me cry.

Again, I arrived home steeped in the smell of death. Again, I went straight to the outdoor shower and stood under water as hot as I could stand, soaping and lathering over and over.

Boyd greeted me with his usual enthusiasm, going upright, then working figure eights around my legs. Birdie watched with disapproval. Or maybe scorn. It's hard to tell with cats.

After throwing on clothes, I filled pet bowls, then checked the house phone. Ryan hadn't called. Nor had he left a message on my cell.

Pete's car was not in the drive. Except for Bird and the chow, the place was empty.

When I unpegged his leash, Boyd flew into a frenzy, racing circles around the kitchen, ending with forepaws down, rump pointed skyward. I took him for a long walk on the beach.

Returning home, I again checked both phones. Nada.

"Call Ryan?" I asked Boyd.

The chow twirled his eyebrow hairs and canted his head.

"You're right. If he's pouting, we'll give him space. If he's busy, he'll phone when he can."

Climbing to my room, I slid open the glass door and fell into bed. Boyd settled on the floor. For a long time I lay awake, listening to the surf and smelling the ocean.

At some point, Birdie hopped up and curled at my side. I was thinking about eating something when I drifted off.

Gullet was right. Nothing more happened that night.


"Pinckney?"

At shortly after eleven the next morning, Emma and I were in a treatment room at a clinic two blocks east of the main hospital. She wore a hospital smock. An IV ran from her left arm. With her right she held a mobile to her ear. Coroner perk. Dispensation from the no cell phone rule.

"Landline?" Emma asked.

Pause.

"What's the address?"

Pause.

"I know it. I'll swing by there in about an hour."

Emma clicked off and spoke to me.

"Chester Tyrus Pinckney."

"I was close," I said.

"The phone's been cut off, but the address isn't too far from Rockville."

"Isn't that way south? Down by Kiawah and Seabrook?"

"Wadmalaw Island. The area's pretty rural."

I thought about that.

"Mr. Pinckney traveled a long way to hang himself."

Before Emma could reply a woman entered the room. She wore a white coat and held a chart in one hand. Her face was friendly but neutral.

Emma introduced the woman as Dr. Nadja Lee Russell. Despite the bravado she'd been showing all morning, her voice belied nervousness.

"I understand you had an episode," Russell said.

"Just fatigue," Emma said.

"You lost consciousness?"

"Yes," Emma admitted.

"Has that happened before?"

"No."

"Any fever? Nausea? Night sweats?"

"Some."

"Which?"

"All of the above."

Russell made notes, then flipped pages in the chart. The room hummed with the sound of the overhead fluorescents.

Russell read on. The silence grew ominous. I felt cold bands squeezing my chest. It was like waiting out a verdict. You will live. You will die. You are better. You are not. I forced myself to smile.

Finally, Russell spoke.

"I'm afraid I don't have good news, Emma. Your counts still have not improved as much as I would have liked."

"They're down?"

"Let's just say I'm not seeing the level of progress I was hoping for."

The room seemed to compress around me. I reached out and took Emma's hand.

"What now?" Emma's voice was devoid of emotion. Her face had gone rigid.

"We continue," Russell said. "Every patient is different. For some, the treatment takes longer to kick in."

Emma nodded.

"You're young, you're still strong. Continue to work if you feel up to it."

"I will."

Emma's eyes followed Russell's retreat out the door. In them I saw fear and sadness. But most of all, I saw defiance.

"You bet your sweet ass I'll keep working."

The travel brochures describe Wadmalaw as the most unspoiled of Charleston's islands. In this case, also the least alluring.

Technically, Wadmalaw is an island, carved off from the mainland by the Bohicket and North Edisto rivers. But Wadmalaw is blocked from the ocean by its upscale "barrier" neighbors to the south and east, Kiawah and Seabrook. The good news: Wadmalaw is stable, and rarely suffers the full-frontal blast of a hurricane. The bad news: no sandy beaches. Wadmalaw's acreage is a hodge-podge of woodland and wetland, ecozones hardly packing in tourists and vacation home buyers.

Though a few upscale houses have recently gone up on Wadmalaw, the area's residents remain mostly farmers, fishers, crabbers, and shrimpers. The island's one attraction is the Charleston Tea Plantation. Begun in 1799, the plantation lays claim to the title of oldest tea farm in America. But then, it's perhaps the only tea farm in America.

But who knows? If skinks and cooters ever catch the imagination of ecotourists, Wadmalaw will be golden.

The small town of Rockville lies at Wadmalaw's southern tip. It was in the general direction of this metropolis that Emma and I pointed ourselves after leaving the clinic.

On the walk to my car I tried broaching the subject of NHL. Emma made it clear that the topic was off-limits. Initially, her attitude annoyed me. Why ask for my company then close me out? But then, wasn't that exactly how I'd behave? Nullify weakness by refusing to grant it the validation of the spoken word? I wasn't sure, but I yielded to Emma's wishes. Her illness, her call.

I drove, Emma rode shotgun. Her directions took us southwest across James and Johns islands, onto the Maybank Highway, then onto Bears Bluff Road. Except for navigational commands, and a few exchanges concerning road signs, we rode in silence, listening to the air conditioner and to bugs slapping the windshield.

Eventually, Emma directed me to turn onto a small road lined with live oaks dripping Spanish moss. Shortly, she ordered another right, then, a quarter mile later, a left onto a rutted dirt lane.

Ancient trees leaned inward from both sides, drawn through decades to the ribbon of sunlight created by the lane's passage. Beyond the trees were trenches, black-green with moss and brackish water.

Here and there, a battered mailbox marked the opening to a driveway snaking off from one shoulder or the other. Otherwise, the narrow track was so overhung with vegetation, I felt like I was piloting through a leafy green wormhole in space.

"There."

Emma pointed to a mailbox. I pulled up beside it.

Metallic letters formed an uneven row, the kind you buy at Home Depot and paste on. PINCKNEY.

On the ground, a homemade sign leaned against the box's upright. Rabbits for Sale. Good bait.

"What do you catch with rabbits?" I asked.

"Tularemia," Emma answered. "Turn here."

Thirty yards in, the trees yielded to tangled scrub. Ten more and the scrub dissolved into a small dirt clearing.

No developer's dream had reworked this place. No condos. No tennis courts. No Dickie Dupree.

A small clapboard house occupied the center of the clearing, surrounded by the usual piled tires, auto parts, broken lawn furniture, and rusted

113

appliances. The house was single story, raised above the ground on crumbling brick pilings. The front door was open, but I could see nothing through the outer screening.

A steel cable ran between two uprights on the clearing's right side. A leash hung from the cable, a choke-chain collar clipped to its lower end.

An unpainted wooden shed stood at the clearing's left. Barely. I assumed this was home to the unfortunate rabbits.

I watched Emma draw a long, deep breath. I knew she hated what she was about to do. She got out. I followed. The air was hot and heavy with moisture and the smell of rotting vegetation.

I waited at the foot of the steps while Emma climbed to the porch. I kept my eyes roving, alert for a pit bull or rottweiler. I'm a dog lover, but a realist. Rural canines and strangers spell stitches and shots.

Emma knocked.

A large black bird cawed and darted low over the shed. I watched it spiral upward, then disappear into the loblolly pines behind the clearing.

Emma called out and knocked again.

I heard a male voice, then the *thrup* of rusty hinges.

I glanced back toward the house.

And saw the very last person I expected to see.

# 11

Emma's knock had been answered by a man in baggy yellow pants, homemade tire-tread sandals, and an apricot T that said: Go home. Earth is full. The man had black-rimmed glasses and hair greased into the worst comb-over I'd ever seen.

"Who's banging on my damn door?"

I froze, mouth open, staring at Chester Pinckney.

Emma had not seen Pinckney's license, and had no idea she was addressing the man pictured on it. She proceeded, unaware of my reaction.

"How do you do, sir. May I ask if you're a member of the Pinckney family?"

"Last I looked, this was my damn house."

"Yes, sir. And you would be?"

"You ladies needing crawlers?"

"No, sir. I'd like to talk to you about Chester Tyrus Pinckney."

Pinckney's eyes slithered to me.

"This some kinda joke?"

"No, sir," Emma said.

"Emma," I whispered.

Emma shushed me with a low backward wave of one hand.

A smile crawled Pinckney's lips, revealing teeth browned by smoking and years of neglect.

"Harlan send you?" Pinckney asked.

"No, sir. I'm the Charleston County coroner."

"We got a girl coroner?"

Emma badged him.

Pinckney ignored it.

"Emma," I tried again.

"That's dead bodies, right, like I seen on TV?"

"Yes, sir. Do you know Chester Pinckney?"

Maybe Emma's question confused him. Or maybe Pinckney was working on his idea of clever riposte. He gave her a blank stare.

"Mr. Pinckney," I jumped in.

Emma and Pinckney both looked at me.

"Any chance you've lost your wallet?"

Emma's brows dipped, rose, then her eyes rolled skyward. Giving a small head shake, she turned back to Pinckney.

"That what this is about?" Pinckney asked.

"You are Chester Tyrus Pinckney?" Emma's tone was somewhat more relaxed.

"I look like Hillary damn Clinton?"

"You don't, sir."

"You finally nail the little pissant what fingered my wallet? Am I getting my money back?"

"When did you lose your billfold, sir?"

"Didn't lose the damn thing. It was stole."

"When was that?"

"Been so long I hardly remember."

"Please try."

Pinckney gave the question some thought.

"Afore the truck got drove into the ditch. Didn't sweat the license none after that."

We waited for Pinckney to continue. He didn't.

"The date?" Emma prompted.

"February. March. It was cold. Nearly froze my ass walking home."

"Did you file a police report?"

"Weren't worth spit. Sold it for scrap."

"I'm referring to your wallet."

"Damn right I filed a report." It came out "ree-port." "Sixty-four bucks is sixty-four bucks."

"Where did the loss take place?" Emma was now scribbling notes.

"It weren't no loss. I was robbed."

"You're certain?"

"I look like some kinda damn bonehead can't retain his own belongings?" Ree-tain.

"No, sir. Please describe the incident."

"We was out looking to meet some ladies."

"We?"

"Me and my buddy Alf."

"Tell me what happened."

"Not much to tell. Alf and me had us some barbecue, knocked back some beers and shots. I woke up the next morning, I got no wallet."

"Did you inquire at each of the establishments you'd visited?"

"Ones as we could remember."

"Where were you?"

"Think for a while we was at the Double L." Pinckney shrugged. "Alf and me was drinking pretty heavy."

Emma slid her notepad into a shirt pocket.

"Your property has been located, Mr. Pinckney."

Pinckney hooted. "Already kissed that sixty-four smackers good-bye. Don't need the license. Got no truck."

"I'm sorry, sir."

Pinckney's eyes narrowed. "Why's a coroner come calling to tell me this?"

Emma regarded Pinckney, considering, I suspected, how much to disclose about the recovery of his billfold.

"Just lending the sheriff a hand," Emma said.

Thanking Pinckney for his time, Emma descended the steps. When she joined me, we both turned to cross the yard.

Blocking our path was a mangy gray poodle in a studded pink collar. Between its forepaws lay a dead squirrel.

The poodle regarded us with curiosity. We reciprocated.

"Douglas." Pinckney gave a short, sharp whistle. "Get in here."

Douglas rose, clamped the squirrel in his teeth, and circled us.

I heard a *thrup*, then a bang as Emma and I continued toward the car.

"Nice old coot," Emma said.

"Douglas?"

"Pinckney."

"Travels with Squirrely."

Emma shot me a look.

I started the car, made a U-ey, and plowed up the drive.

"Douglas?" Emma asked.

"Collar's a bit of a fashion risk, but Doug makes it work. Color highlights his eyes."

"What are the chances the old coot was robbed?" Emma asked.

"What are the chances I'll be this year's American Idol?" I replied.

"And then there were two," Emma said when we'd reached the blacktop.

"The man in the trees. The man on Dewees."

"Nice rhyme."

"Irish blood. By the way, how's yours today?"

"I'm a little tired, but OK."

"Honestly?"

She nodded.

"Good."

Emma didn't ask if I'd help with the skeletal analysis of the man in the trees. We both knew the answer. We also knew that Gullet would be doing some legwork, and that he'd be skeptical of my involvement in yet another case.

Imagining the conversation he and Emma would have, I drove straight to the morgue.

After Emma called Gullet to give him the news,

Tuesday afternoon was a replay of Saturday morning. Same morgue cooler. Same tile and stainless steel autopsy room. Same smell of disinfected death.

Miller had logged the hanging victim as CCC-2006020285.

After changing into scrubs, Emma and I transferred CCC-2006020285 from his bag to the autopsy table. First the articulated portions, next the skull, finally the body parts that had fallen or been yanked free and dragged off by scavengers.

The brain and internal organs were gone. The torso, arms, and upper leg bones remained encased in muscle and ligament, at some points putrefied, at others browned and toughened by sun and wind. Though inconvenient for skeletal analysis, the flesh was a potential bonus for a quick ID. Tissue means skin. Skin means prints.

A jacket sleeve had protected the right hand, sparing it full-out mummification. But decomposition had rendered the tissue extremely fragile.

"Got TES?" I asked Emma. Tissue Enhancing Solution, a citric acid–buffered salt solution useful for restoring dried or damaged tissue.

"Courtesy of my favorite embalmer."

"Warm it to about fifty Celsius, please." As with the Dewees case, Emma had made me head honcho during examination of these bones. I wasn't sure how long she'd get away with it, but I was determined to do the job until someone pulled the plug.

"Microwave?"

120

"Fine."

While Emma was gone, I removed each of the right digits at the level of the first interphalangeal joint. When she returned, I placed the severed fingers in the solution and set them aside to soak.

"Mind if I slide out for a while? There's a construction site death needs my attention. When the prints are ready, give them to the tech and he'll shoot them to Gullet."

"No problem."

The skeletal exam was straightforward enough. And, save for the tedium of cutting and stripping tissue, somewhat reminiscent of Saturday's analysis of the Dewees unknown.

The vertebral column was the most difficult to separate into component parts. While it soaked, I began with those bones less tenaciously imprisoned in flesh.

Skull and pelvic shape said this vic was male.

Dental, rib, and pubic symphyseal indicators said he'd lived thirty-five to fifty years.

Cranial and facial architecture said his ancestors came from Europe.

Another white guy in his forties.

There the physical similarities ended.

While the man from Dewees was tall, long-bone measurements said the man from the trees stood only five-six to five-eight.

The former had long blond hair. This guy sported short brown curls.

Unlike the man from Dewees, the man from the trees had no dental work, and was, in fact, missing three upper molars and an upper bicuspid. The lowers were a mystery since I had no jaw. Tongue-side staining suggested the deceased had enjoyed cigarettes.

When I'd completed the biological profile, I began my search for skeletal abnormalities. As usual, I was looking for congenital oddities, bony remodeling due to repetitive activities, healed injuries, and evidence of medical history.

The man from the trees had taken his lumps, including a broken right fibula, fractured cheekbones, and some type of injury to his left shoulder blade, all healed. The X-rays showed an abnormal opacity on the left collarbone, suggesting the possibility of another old fracture.

The guy wasn't big, but he was a scrapper. And a great mender.

Straightening, I rolled my shoulders, then my head. My back felt like the Panthers had run scrimmages on my spine.

The wall clock said four forty. Time to check the digits.

The tissue had softened nicely. Using a small syringe, I injected TES beneath the dermal pads. The fingertips plumped. I wiped each with alcohol, blotted, ink-rolled, then printed. The ridge detail came out reasonably clear.

I called the tech. He collected the prints and I went back to the bones.

Postmortem damage was limited to the lower legs. Gnawing and splintering, coupled with the presence of small circular puncture wounds, suggested the culprits were probably dogs.

I found no evidence of perimortem injury, nothing to suggest that death had resulted from anything but the obvious: asphyxiation due to compression of the neck structures. In laymen's terms, hanging.

Emma called at seven. I updated her. She said she planned to swing by the sheriff's office shortly to "goose" Gullet. Her words.

Reminded of my hunger by the reference to fowl, I hit the cafeteria. After an exquisite repast of undersauced lasagna and overdressed salad, I returned to the autopsy room.

Though some segments were still insufficiently rehydrated, I was able to free most of the spine from its sleeve of putrefied muscle. Leaving one obstinate chunk to soak, I placed the newly liberated cervical and thoracic vertebrae on a tray with the two neck vertebrae I'd detached from the skull base.

Moving to the scope, I started with C-1, then, slowly, worked my way south. I found no surprises until I got to C-6.

Then it was Saturday all over again.

There was the vertebral body. There was the arch. There were the transverse processes with their small holes for the passage of cranial vessels.

There, on the left, was the hinge fracture.

I adjusted focus and repositioned the light.

No question. A hairline crack kinked across the left transverse process, radiating from opposite sides of the foramen.

It was the exact pattern I'd seen on the Dewees skeleton. The hinging and lack of bony reaction told me that this fracture had also resulted from force applied to fresh bone. This injury had also been sustained around the time of death.

But how?

C-6. Lower neck. Too far down to have resulted from hanging. Though the head had fallen off, probably dislodged by yanking scavengers, the noose had remained, embedded between C-3 and C-4.

Sudden wrenching when the victim jumped from the branch? If he had jumped from the branch, how had he gotten up there? Shinnied six feet up the trunk? Maybe.

Closing my eyes, I conjured a picture of the body hanging from the tree. The knot had been at the back of the neck, not at the side. That seemed inconsistent with unilateral fracturing. I made a mental note to check Miller's scene photos.

Could hanging explain the Dewees victim's neck injury? Had he, too, committed suicide?

Maybe. But the guy sure hadn't dug his own grave.

Could Emma be on the right track? Might the Dewees man have killed himself, then been buried by a friend or family member? Why? Shame? Reluctance to pony up funeral expenses? Fear that insurance payments might be denied? That seemed unlikely. It took years to have a missing person declared dead.

Might the Dewees case turn out to be nothing

more than improper disposal of a human corpse?

I ran through alternative explanations for the unilateral neck trauma I was seeing on the man in the trees. The same explanations I'd considered for the man from Dewees.

Fall? Strangulation? Whiplash? Blow to the head?

Nothing made sense, given the type of fracture and its location.

I was still pondering when Emma burst through the door.

"We've got him!"

I turned from the scope.

Emma waved a printout at the skeleton. "Gullet ran the prints through AFIS." The Automated Fingerprint Identification System. "Our boy popped right up."

The name she announced blew vertebral fractures right off my radar.

# 12

"Noble Cruikshank."

"Sweet Jesus."

If my reaction surprised Emma, she let it go.

"Cruikshank's a retired Charlotte-Mecklenburg cop. But that's not why he was in the system. CMPD rookies are printed at their academy, of course, but the prints are kept in-house. Cruikshank was arrested in ninety-two for DWI. That's when he was entered."

"You're certain it's Cruikshank?" Stupid. I knew the answer to that.

"Twelve-point match."

I took the printout and read Cruikshank's descriptors. Male. White. Five foot six. DOB put his age at forty-seven.

My skeletal profile fit. Body condition was consistent with two months' exposure. Of course it was Cruikshank.

Noble Cruikshank. Buck Flynn's missing detective.

I studied the photo. Though grainy black-and-white, it gave a sense of the man.

Cruikshank's skin was pockmarked, his nose humped, his hair combed straight back and curled up on the ends. The flesh was starting to sag along his jawline and cheekbones, and he was probably carrying less poundage than he would have liked. Still, the expression was pure macho tough guy.

"Noble Cruikshank. I'll be damned."

"You know him?"

"Not personally. Cruikshank got booted from the force in ninety-four for getting in bed with Jimmy B. He was working private when he went missing last March."

"And we're privy to this because . . . ?"

"You remember Pete?"

"Your husband."

"*Estranged* husband. Pete's been retained to investigate some financial dealings at GMC and also look into the whereabouts of the client's missing daughter, who was involved with the organization. Before he hired Pete, Buck Flynn, that's the client, hired Cruikshank. While conducting his inquiry, Cruikshank vanished."

"Pete's a lawyer."

"That was my reaction. Pete's Latvian. Flynn's mother was Latvian. Flynn trusts him because he's one of the clan."

"Flynn's kid disappeared here?"

"Presumably. Cruikshank's specialty was

missing persons and his patch was Charleston and Charlotte. Helene Flynn, that's the daughter, was a member of GMC, where Buck was a major donor."

"Aubrey Herron. There's a piece of work. Flynn didn't get curious when his investigator stopped reporting?"

"Apparently Cruikshank had a history of binge drinking."

"Flynn hired a drunk?"

"He didn't know that until after he hired him. Found Cruikshank on the Internet. Thus his subsequent preference for a member of his own Baltic gene pool."

Emma voiced the question I'd been asking myself.

"What was Cruikshank doing with Pinckney's wallet?"

"Found it?" I threw out.

"Stole it?"

"Got it from someone who found or stole it?"

"Pinckney said the wallet disappeared in February or March, right around the time Cruikshank killed himself."

"Presumably," I said.

"Presumably. Maybe someone found the body hanging in the woods and planted the wallet on it."

"Why?" I asked.

"Practical joke?"

"That would take a pretty morbid sense of humor."

"To create confusion when it came time to ID the deceased?"

"The wallet was in the jacket pocket, right? Maybe Cruikshank borrowed, found, or swiped the jacket and never knew the wallet was there. Did Pinckney say anything about losing a jacket?"

Emma shook her head.

"And why wasn't Cruikshank carrying any of his own personal effects?"

"The truly suicidal often leave their belongings behind." Emma thought a moment. "But why the Francis Marion forest? And how did Cruikshank get out there?"

"Astute questions, Madam Coroner," I said.

Neither Emma nor I had any astute answers.

I held up the AFIS printout. "Can I keep this?"

"That's your copy." As I laid the paper on the counter, Emma said, "So your Mr. Cruikshank has hanged himself."

"*Pete's* Mr. Cruikshank," I corrected.

"Is Pete here in Charleston?"

"Oh, yeah."

Emma cocked a lascivious brow.

My response would have made the cut for the U.S. Open of eye rolls.

It was close to nine when I got back to "Sea for Miles." Two kitchen counters were covered with peaches and tomatoes. Tuesday. I assumed Pete had stumbled onto the Mount Pleasant farmer's market.

Pete and Boyd were in the den watching baseball. The Twins were whupping Pete's beloved White Sox 10–4. The Sox had been the team of Pete's

Chicago boyhood, and when they placed their AAA farm team in Charlotte, Pete was resmitten.

"Cruikshank's dead," I said, without preamble.

Pete sat up and gave me his full attention. Boyd kept his eyes on a half-empty popcorn bowl.

"No shit?"

"Hanged himself."

"You're sure it's Cruikshank?"

"Twelve-point AFIS match."

Pete moved a pillow and I dropped to the couch. As I described my adventures with Pinckney and then with the man in the trees, Boyd oozed toward the snack food, one body hair at a time.

"How did Cruikshank get this other guy's billfold?"

"Who knows?"

"Emma intends to have another heart-to-heart with Pinckney?"

"I'm sure she does."

Eyes on Pete, Boyd tipped his head sideways and brushed his tongue across the popcorn. Pete relocated the bowl to a table behind our heads.

Ever the optimist, Boyd hopped onto the couch and pressed his weight against my side. Absently, I rubbed his ear.

"No question Cruikshank offed himself?" Pete asked.

I hesitated, remembering Emma's and my lack of astute answers. And the sixth cervical vertebrae.

"What?"

"It's probably nothing."

Pete chugged the remains of his Heineken, set

down the bottle, and assumed a listening posture.

I described the hinge fracture on the vertebra's left transverse process.

"What's so odd about that?"

"The injury is inconsistent with hanging, especially given the fact that the noose was positioned behind, not to the side of the skull. But it's more than that. The Dewees skeleton has an identical fracture in the same location."

"Is that a big deal?"

"I've never seen this trauma pattern before. Then I find two instances in one week. Don't you find that suspicious?"

"Explanation?"

"I have several, none persuasive."

"Indecision is the key to flexibility."

Boyd placed his chin on my shoulder, positioning his nose inches from the popcorn. I eased him sideways. He lay down across my lap.

"How was your day?" I asked.

"Isn't this great?" Big Pete grin. "Just like real married people."

"We were real married people. It wasn't great."

"We're still real married people."

I nudged Boyd. The chow moved across our laps and pressed against Pete. I started to rise.

"OK. OK." Pete held up both hands. "I poked around up at GMC today."

I settled back. "Did you talk to Herron?"

Pete shook his head. "Dropped a lot of scary words. Litigation. Mismanagement of charitable funds. Pot to piss in."

131

"Chilling."

"Apparently. I have an appointment with Herron on Thursday morning."

At that moment my cell phone sounded. I checked the little screen. Emma.

"Gullet tracked down an address for Cruikshank. Place is off Calhoun, not far from the MUSC complex. He dropped by, managed to pry the landlord loose from his *Rocky* DVD long enough to learn that Cruikshank had been a tenant for about two years, but hadn't set foot in his apartment since March. Landlord's name is Harold Parrot, a real humanitarian. When Cruikshank fell thirty days behind in the rent, Parrot stuffed his belongings into cartons, changed the locks, and recycled the unit."

"What happened to the cartons?"

Pete raised questioning brows and mouthed the word "Cruikshank." I nodded.

"Parrot stacked them in the basement. He assumed Cruikshank had skipped town, but didn't want trouble if the guy showed up wanting his stuff. Gullet got the sense Cruikshank scared the nappies off Parrot. Gullet and I are going back in the morning, thought you might like to join us."

"Where?"

Emma read the address and I wrote it down.

"What time?"

Pete pointed a finger at his chest.

"Nine."

"Shall I meet you there?"

"Sounds like a plan."

Pete's pointing became, well, more pointed.

"Mind if Pete rides along?"

"Sounds like a stunningly more entertaining plan."

The day began badly and went downslope from there.

Emma rang shortly before eight to say she'd had a rough night. Would I mind meeting with Gullet and Parrot on my own? She'd explained to the sheriff that I was officially consulting on the case, and requested full cooperation from his office.

I heard the bitterness in Emma's voice, knew what it was costing my friend to admit that her body was failing. I assured Emma I'd be fine, and that I'd touch base as soon as I left Parrot's.

Pete was flipping shut his mobile when I entered the kitchen. He'd called Flynn. Though dismayed by the circumstances, Buck was pleased to hear that Cruikshank had been located. Buck was even more pleased over the upcoming Herron meeting and the possibility of some answers to his several questions.

Pete had also phoned a buddy at the Charlotte-Mecklenburg PD. The man was not surprised to learn of his former colleague's death. He'd known Cruikshank during the PI's days on the force. In his words, Cruikshank was a barrel in the mouth waiting for the pull of a trigger.

Gullet's Explorer was already at the curb when Pete and I turned from Calhoun onto a dead-end side street. Though once lush and residential, the avenue's oleander-and-elderberry-wine charm had long ago been boot-heeled by modern redevelopment. Offices and commercial buildings stood brick to petticoat with grand old belles hanging on by their Confederate nails.

Emma's address brought us to an antebellum survivor with an archetypically Charlestonian design: narrow across the front, deep down the lot, side verandas upstairs and down.

Pete and I got out and started up the walk. Though cloud cover kept the temperature down, humidity ruled the day. Within seconds my clothes felt limp against my skin.

Approaching the building, I took in more detail. Rotting wood, faded paint, more trim than Brighton's Royal Pavilion. An ornate plaque above the door said MAGNOLIA MANOR.

No magnolias. No blossoms. Side yard a tangle of kudzu-clad scrub.

The front was unlocked. Passing through the door, Pete and I stepped from syrupy warmth into slightly cooler syrupy warmth.

What was once an elegant foyer now served as a lobby, complete with bannistered staircase, sconced walls, and chandeliered ceiling. The sparse furnishings exuded all the charm of a dental office. Laminated wood sideboard. Vinyl couch. Plastic plant. Plastic runner. Plastic wastebasket filled with discarded ads.

Two rows of nameplates suggested the house had been divided into six units. Below and to the right of the buzzers, a hand-scrawled card provided the number of the resident manager.

I dialed. Parrot answered on the third ring.

I identified myself. Parrot said he and Gullet were in the basement, and directed me down the central hallway to the back of the building. The stairs were through a door on the left.

I gestured Pete to follow me.

The cellar door was located where promised. And wide open.

"Cruikshank didn't choose the old manor for its security system," I said in a low voice.

"Must have been attracted by the cutting-edge interior design," Pete said.

From below, I could hear Gullet and Parrot speaking.

"And the name," Pete added. "The name's got a certain panache."

As Pete and I clomped down wooden stairs, the temperature plummeted at least half a degree. At bottom, the air smelled of decades of mildew and mold. I was unsure whether to breathe through my nose or my mouth.

The cellar was as expected. Dirt floor. Low ceiling. Brick walls with crumbling mortar. The few concessions to the twentieth century included an ancient washer and dryer, a water heater, and low-wattage bulbs hanging from badly frayed wires.

Junk was crammed everywhere. Stacked newspapers. Wooden crates. Broken lamps. Garden tools. A brass headboard.

Gullet and Parrot were on the far side of the room, an open carton on a workbench between them. Gullet was holding a manila folder in one hand, rifling its contents with the other.

Both men turned at the sound of our footsteps.

"Seems you're becoming a regular fixture with our coroner." Gullet really did have a way with openings. "I've got no problem with that, long as everyone understands borders and terrain."

"Of course." I introduced Pete, and gave the briefest explanation of his interest in Parrot's former tenant.

"Your Mr. Cruikshank was one busy fella, Counselor."

"I'm only indirectly concerned with Cruikshank—"

Gullet cut him off. "The man killed himself in my town. That makes him my problem. You're free to tag along with the doc, here. But you get any ideas about freelancing, you keep that train in the station."

Pete said nothing.

"Miz Rousseau says you're looking for a young lady name of Helene Flynn." The usual flat tone.

"I am," Pete said.

"May I ask why, sir?"

"Helene's father is concerned because she broke off contact."

"And when you find this young lady?"

"I'll tell Daddy."

Gullet regarded Pete for so long I thought he was going to send him packing. Then, "No harm in that. My child dropped out of sight, I'd want to know why."

The sheriff closed and waggled the manila folder.

"This should make for some fascinating reading."

# 13

Gullet reversed the file so we could see the handwritten name on the tab. Flynn, Helene. The date matched the time of Buck Flynn's initial contact with Cruikshank.

Handing the folder to Pete, Gullet turned back to the carton and resumed rummaging, pulling out a folder, reading its tab, sliding it back among the others.

Pete scanned the contents of Helene Flynn's file.

I observed Parrot. He was an elderly black man with kinky hair side-parted and slicked down hard. Nat King Cole in a tank undershirt. Right now he looked jumpy as someone expecting a kidney punch.

After pulling a few more random files, Gullet turned to Parrot.

"You packed all these boxes, sir?"

"Not the files. They's exactly as Cruikshank left them. I done those uns over there." Parrot pointed to a stack of cardboard boxes.

"You did collect every last one of Mr. Cruikshank's possessions, now didn't you, Mr. Parrot? Nothing got misplaced or lost or anything along those lines?"

"'Course I did." Parrot's gaze hopped from Gullet to me, then dived to the floor. "I didn't make no list, if that's what you're asking. I just boxed the stuff."

"Uh-huh." Gullet skewered the landlord with a look.

Parrot ran a hand across the top of his head. Not a hair budged. The stuff was more glazed than a Krispy Kreme doughnut.

Seconds passed. A full minute. Somewhere out of sight, a faucet dripped.

Parrot repeated the hair thing. Folded his arms. Dropped them. The sheriff's eyes remained glued to Parrot's face.

Finally, Gullet broke the silence. "You don't mind if I take Mr. Cruikshank's things along for safekeeping, now do you, sir?"

"Don't you need a warrant or some kinda official paper?"

Not a muscle fiber flickered in Gullet's face.

Parrot's hands flew up. "OK. OK. No problem, Sheriff. I was just trying to be legal. You know. Tenants' rights and all."

There were eight boxes. I took the file carton. Pete and Gullet started with two boxes each. While the men made a second trip to the basement, I phoned Emma from the Explorer. Though she sounded better, her voice was still weak.

I reported that we were heading to the sheriff's office. Emma thanked me, and asked that I keep her informed.

Twenty minutes after leaving Magnolia Manor, Pete and I turned behind Gullet into the lot at the Charleston County Sheriff's Office, a low-rise brick and stucco affair on Pinehaven Drive in North Charleston. Two trips relocated the boxes to a small conference room.

While Gullet called the Charleston City Police, Pete and I began with Cruikshank's belongings. Pete took the Flynn file. I started with the boxes.

The first yielded bathroom towels and toiletries. Toothpaste. Plastic razors. Shaving cream. Shampoo. Foot powder.

The second contained kitchenware. Plastic cups and dishes. A few glasses. Cheap utensils.

Box three held the larder. Frosted Flakes. Froot Loops. Dried spaghetti and macaroni dinners. Cans of Campbell's soup, baked beans, Beenie Weenies.

"The guy wasn't into gourmet cooking," I said, folding in and overlapping box flaps.

Focused on the file, Pete gave a noncommittal grunt.

Box four contained an alarm clock, bed linens, and blankets.

Box five was stuffed with pillows.

Box six held clothing.

"Finding anything?" Pete asked, his attention on notes he was scribbling.

"A lot of bad shirts."

"Yeah?" Pete wasn't listening.

"The guy liked brown."

"Mm." Pete wrote something, scratched it out.

"And Dale Evans swimsuits. Those are tough to get these days."

"Mm."

"And garter belts."

Pete's head came up. "What?"

I displayed a brown work shirt.

"You're a laugh riot, sugar buns."

"Are you learning anything useful?" I asked.

"He used some sort of shorthand system."

Crossing the room, I glanced at one of Cruikshank's handwritten pages. The notes were composed of combinations of numbers, letters, and short phrases.

2/20
LM
Cl-9-6
Ho-6-2
AB Cl-8-4
CD Cl-9-4
mp no
No F
23 i/o

2/21
LM
Cl 2-4
Ok stops
Ho 7-2

AB Cl-8-5
CD Cl-8-1
???
No F
31 i/o


2/22
LM
No Cl
???
AB Cl-8-4
CD Cl-12-4
No F
Cl 9-6
28 i/27 o
si/so rec! photos


"Probably a date," I said, pointing to the first line of each entry. "February twentieth, February twenty-first, and so on."

"Rejewski's got nothing on you, babe." Pete smiled up at me.

I waited.

"Enigma?"

I shook my head.

"During World War Two the Germans used an electromechanical rotor-based cipher system known as Enigma. Rejewski cracked the code using theoretical mathematics."

"You're on your own, Latvian Savant." I returned to the boxes.

And made my discovery in the second to last.

The contents of box seven suggested a desk or workstation. Packets of paper. Envelopes. Blank notepads. Pens. Scissors. Tape. Staple gun. Paper clips, rubber bands, staples.

A cylinder of CDs.

Removing the outer casing, I slid the discs free from the center spool. Six. I checked each label.

Five blank. One with writing.

I felt a buzz of adrenaline.

Written in black marker was the name Flynn, Helene.

The buzz ebbed slightly. Why? Disappointment? What did I think the label would say? "Unmarked grave on Dewees Island"?

"Pete."

"Mm."

"Pete!"

Pete's head snapped up.

I held out the disc.

Pete's brows shot toward his hairline. He was about to speak when Gullet appeared. I showed him the CD.

"Do you have a computer we can use to view this?"

"Follow me."

Leading us to his office, Gullet took a leather chair behind a desk just a few inches smaller than a basketball court. After typing some commands, he held out a hand. I gave him the disc and he entered more keystrokes.

The computer hummed as it sniffed out Cruikshank's CD. Gullet hit a few more keys, then gestured that we should move around behind him.

Pete and I circled the desk and peered over Gullet's shoulders. The screen was covered with tiny squares: JPEG files.

Gullet double-clicked the first square and an image filled the screen.

The scene showed a two-story brick building with a center door and picture windows to either side. Neither the door nor the window glass had lettering or a symbol of any kind. There were no street signs or address plaques with which to pinpoint the building's location. Any view of its interior was blocked by closed venetian blinds.

"Minimal depth of field," I said. "Pretty grainy. Must have been taken from a distance with a zoom lens."

"Good eye," Pete said.

"Recognize the place?" I asked Gullet.

"It's not Rainbow Row, that's for sure. But otherwise, it could be anywhere."

The next several images showed the same structure from differing vantage points. None included a neighboring building or identifiable landmark.

"Go to that one," I said, indicating an image with a man exiting the building.

Gullet double-clicked the file.

The man was of average height but robust build. He had dark hair, and wore a belted raincoat and muffler. He was not looking at or acknowledging the camera.

The next image showed another man making his exit. He, too, had dark hair, but was taller and more muscular than the first, probably younger. This man wore jeans and a windbreaker. Like the first, he did not look into the lens.

In the next photo was a woman. Black. Blond hair. Big. Very big.

The disc held a total of forty-two images. Except for the first few, each showed someone entering or leaving the brick building. A kid with one arm in a sling. An old man in a Tilly hat. A woman with an infant strapped to her chest.

"Change the view," I suggested, pointing to an icon on the toolbar.

Gullet clicked on the arrow to the right of the tiny blue screen, hesitated.

"Try the detail view," I instructed, trying not to sound overly bossy.

Gullet double-clicked the last option, and the screen changed to columns of print. The fourth column provided the date and time of exposure for each JPEG file.

Pete stated the obvious: "The pictures were all taken on March fourth, between eight A.M. and four P.M."

"Hotline to Rejewski?" I asked under my breath.

The Latvian Savant ignored my jibe.

Gullet returned to thumbnail view and opened the first image. "So Cruikshank was still alive on March fourth." Monotone. "And he was sur-veilling this place."

"Or someone else was, and that someone gave Cruikshank the disc."

"But in the end, it doesn't much matter. The

man killed himself." Gullet sent a questioning look over one shoulder. "This is a suicide, now, isn't it, ma'am?"

"Manner of death could be"—I searched for a word—"complicated."

Gullet swiveled to face me full on. Pete rested one haunch on the credenza. I had the floor.

I described the trauma on Cruikshank's sixth cervical vertebra. Gullet listened without interrupting. I then explained that identical trauma was present on the skeleton Emma and I had recovered from the shallow grave on Dewees.

"Both were white males in their forties," Gullet said, not excited so much as interested.

I nodded.

"Could be coincidence."

"Could be." A coincidence the size of the Serengeti.

Gullet swiveled back to the computer screen. "If Cruikshank didn't die by his own hand, then the question becomes, who helped him? And why? And what's the significance of the place in these photos?"

"Could be the place is incidental," I suggested. "Maybe the subject of interest was one of the people."

"Only one disc is labeled," Pete said. "With Helene Flynn's name."

"Let's check the others," I said.

We did. All were blank.

"You search every box?" Gullet asked.

"Except one."

We trooped back to the conference room. The

last box had once held jars of Hellman's mayo. Pete and Gullet watched as I pulled back the flaps.

Books. Framed photos. An album. A trophy. Police memorabilia.

No discs.

"Let's back up a few trots," Gullet said when I'd resecured the flaps. "Could have been Cruikshank staking out that building, could have been someone else. If it was someone else, who? And why? And what's Cruikshank's interest in the pictures?"

"And how did he get them?" Pete asked.

I thought a moment.

"There are several possibilities." I ticked them off on my fingers. "One, Cruikshank took the shots himself. Two, he was given the disc. Three, he was given a camera smart card or photo chip. Four, he received the images electronically."

"Meaning, we haven't a clue," Pete said.

"But we do know one significant thing."

Both men looked at me.

"To download from a camera, smart card, or Web site? To receive e-mail? To save files to disc? To view images on a CD?"

Pete and Gullet spoke simultaneously.

"Cruikshank had a computer."

"I'd say there's a good possibility. Maybe a digital camera, too."

Gullet's eyes narrowed in anger. Maybe. Maybe I imagined it.

"Time to revisit the good landlord Parrot."

I made a gesture that took in the files and box eight. "In the meantime, may we take this?"

147

Gullet thumb-hooked his belt and pooched out his lower lip. As seconds passed, I was unsure if he was ignoring or considering my request. Then he hitched his pants and let out a long breath.

"Truth is, I'm short a deputy right now. Miz Rousseau trusts you enough to take you on, I guess your poking through some boxes can't hurt. Make sure every item's inventoried and logged, then sign for the lot. And mind the security." Gullet didn't finish the admonition. No point in stating the obvious.

We were entering Mount Pleasant when my mobile rang. Pete was driving.

I dug the phone from my purse. The screen showed a local number I didn't recognize. I started to ignore the call, changed my mind. What if it concerned Emma?

I should have gone with my first instinct.

# 14

"How's it going, Doc?"

It took a nanosecond to recognize the voice. Plankton.

"How did you get this number?"

"Pretty good, eh?"

"I don't do interviews, Mr. Winborne."

"Did you see my piece in the *Post and Courier*? The one on the Dewees stiff?"

I said nothing.

"Editor went batshit. Green-lighted me for a follow-up."

I said nothing again.

"So I've got a few questions."

I used my steely voice, the one I'd learned from cops and customs officials. "I. Don't. Do. Interviews."

"It'll take only a minute."

"No." Impermeable.

"It's in your interest to—"

"I'm going to hang up now. Don't call me again."

"I advise you not to do that."

"Do you still have that Nikon, Mr. Winborne?"

"Sure do."

"*I* advise *you* to take that camera and shove it where the sun don't shi—"

"I'm hip to the body you cut down in the Francis Marion."

That worked. I didn't disconnect.

"The guy's name is Noble Cruikshank, and he was a Charlotte cop."

So Plankton had a mole.

"Where did you get this information?" I asked, my voice pure ice.

"Doc." Mock disappointment. "You know my sources are confidential. But my facts are solid, right?"

"I'm confirming nothing."

Pete was throwing quizzical glances my way. I gestured that he should keep his eyes on the road.

"But something is bothering me." Slow. Ponderous. Winborne sounded like he'd watched way too many *Columbo* episodes. "Cruikshank was a PI, a former cop. He was probably on a case when he died. What could be so mind-blowing that it would cause a guy like that to string himself up?"

Silence hummed across the line.

"And the demographic." He pronounced it "dee-mographic." "Male, white, forty-something. Sound familiar?"

"Keanu Reeves."

150

Winborne ignored that. Or didn't get it. "So I'm checking out what Cruikshank was working when he hanged himself. You got any insight into that?"

"No comment."

"And I'm looking for links between Cruikshank and your bones on Dewees."

"For multiple reasons, I advise you to print nothing."

"Yeah? Gimme one."

"First, if the body from the Francis Marion is that of Noble Cruikshank, a man committing suicide is hardly a scoop. Second, as you know, Cruikshank was a cop. His former colleagues might not appreciate you dragging his name through the mud. And third, whoever the victim turns out to be, it is unethical to reveal information about a death before notification of next of kin."

"I'll think about it."

"I'm going to disconnect now, Mr. Winborne. If you take my picture again I will sue you."

I clicked off.

"Sonovabitch!" I came close to hurling the handset through the windshield.

"Lunch?" Pete asked.

Too angry to speak, I nodded my head.

Just past Shem Creek, Pete turned right from Coleman Boulevard onto Live Oak Drive, a residential side street lined with bungalows and shaded by, yep, you guessed it, live oaks wrapped with Spanish moss. Pete went left onto Haddrell, curved left, then turned into a gravel parking area.

Across the lot, between the Wando Seafood

Company and Magwood & Sons Seafoods, stood a ramshackle structure that looked like it had been hammered together by a committee sharing no common language. The Wreck of the Richard and Charlene is known to locals as "the Wreck." Unmarked and unadvertised, the restaurant may be Charleston's best-kept secret.

The story goes something like this. During Hurricane Hugo, a fishing boat named the *Richard and Charlene* was tossed onto the restaurant owners' property. Seeing it as an omen, the restaurant owner's wife christened her establishment in honor of the wreck.

*Just sit right back and you'll hear a tale. . . .*

That was 1989. The wreck is still there, and the Wreck is still there, its owners disdaining all forms of marketing and publicity. Even signs.

Concrete floors. Ceiling fans. Screened porches. An honor system for help-yourself beers in a deck cooler should you have to wait for a table. The formula works, and the place is always packed.

At four thirty in the afternoon things were uncharacteristically quiet. Service didn't start until five thirty, but we were seated. What the hell? The Wreck is that kind of place.

The Wreck's ordering system is as simple as its menu. With the crayons provided, Pete circled the shrimp basket, the gumbo, and the key lime bread pudding, and indicated that he wanted Richard-size portions. I chose a Charlene-size oyster basket. Diet Coke for me. A Carolina Blonde for Pete.

Dixie dining at its best.

"Let me guess," Pete said, when the drinks had arrived. "That call was from a journalist."

"The same rat bastard that snuck onto my site on Dewees."

"He's graduated to the crime beat?"

"Do I look like the little twerp's employment counselor?" I was still so angry it came out shrill. "But he's got far more information than he ought to."

"Must have an informant."

"Gee. You think?"

"Okeydokey." Pete took a swig of beer and leaned back in a posture suggesting conversation was terminated until I'd composed myself.

Through the screen, I watched gulls circle trawlers at the dock. Their buoyant, hopeful looping was somehow calming.

"Sorry," I said when our food was delivered. "I'm not annoyed with you."

"No problemo." Pete pointed a shrimp at me. "A lot of reporters monitor emergency frequencies."

"I thought of that. Winborne might have picked up police transmissions concerning the discovery of the body, but he couldn't have learned about the ID that way."

"An insider at the coroner's or sheriff's office?"

"Maybe."

"Morgue staff?"

"It's possible."

"Unless . . ." Pete let the word hang.

A hushpuppy stopped halfway to my mouth. "Unless what?"

"What about your friend Emma? She have an agenda you don't know about?"

I'd thought of that. I'd remembered how Emma spoke up for Winborne, argued that his presence on Dewees would do no harm.

I said nothing. But Pete had raised a very good point.

What about Emma?

We ate and chatted about other things. Katy. Pete's mother's hip replacement surgery. My family. A trip we'd made to Kiawah twenty years earlier. Before I knew it, my watch said 5:45.

Ooooookay.

Pete insisted on picking up the check. He paid in cash. No plastic at the ole Wreck.

"Want to help me go through Cruikshank's files?" Pete asked, pulling in at "Sea for Miles."

"Wish I could, but it's crunch time for my field school exams."

"They can't wait one more day?"

"Tomorrow is the deadline for grade submission, I have to write at least a preliminary report on the Dewees dig for the state archaeologist in Columbia, and who knows what else could pop up."

"Looks like I'm on my own." Sad Pete face.

I smiled and punched Pete's shoulder. "Use a lifeline. Call your buddy Rejewski."

Climbing to my room, I dialed Emma's number. Her machine answered. I left a message.

By eight I'd finished the last exam, calculated grades, and e-mailed the list to the department

154

secretary at UNCC. She'd agreed to walk the form over to the registrar for me.

Again, I tried Emma. Hearing the same recording, I hung up.

By ten I'd composed a brief statement concerning the Sewee burial site on Dewees, including my opinion as to its value as a cultural resource. I e-mailed the document to the Office of the State Archaeologist, and sent copies to the South Carolina Institute of Archaeology and Anthropology, to the South Carolina Department of Archives and History, and to Dan Jaffer at USC-Columbia.

Then I sat back, debating. Dickie Dupree? The man was a weasel. No. That probably wasn't being fair to weasels. But the site was on Dupree's land, and my evaluation could affect decisions he might have to make. And, God forbid, Dickie's bottom line.

Birdie was curled on the desk to my left.

"What do you think, Bird?"

The cat rolled onto his back and stretched all four legs as far as they would go.

"You're right."

Using the Internet, I found an e-mail address and fired a copy off to Dupree.

Pete and Boyd were again in the den. The tube was on, though neither appeared to be watching. This time it was an old Bob Hope film.

Pete was on the couch, bare feet crossed on the coffee table, the Helene Flynn file open in his lap. He was making notes on a large yellow legal pad.

Boyd lay flopped on his side, back paws resting on his master's knee.

The file carton and eighth box sat side by side on the window seat.

On-screen, a man was describing zombies as having dead eyes, following orders, not knowing what they do, not caring.

"You mean like Democrats?" Hope inquired.

Pete threw back his lead and laughed.

"Not offended?"

"Humor is humor," replied Pete the Democrat.

The chow opened a sleepy eye. Seeing me in the doorway, he slunk to the floor.

Pete jabbed his pen at the TV. "This movie has some of Hope's best one-liners."

"Title?" When Pete and I first met, and during the early years of our marriage, old films had been one of our passions.

"*Ghost Breakers.*"

"Wasn't that the Bowery Boys?"

Pete made a buzzer sound. "Nnnnt! Wrong. That was *Ghost Chasers.*"

I couldn't help but laugh. It felt so natural.

Seeing Pete at that moment, lamplight softening the lines of his face, it suddenly hit me. Though we'd been apart for some time, led largely separate lives, there wasn't a day I didn't think, at least fleetingly, about my husband.

The laughter died on my lips.

"What's the plot?" I asked, detached, forcing blasé.

"Paulette Goddard has inherited a haunted castle. Hope's lines are classic."

"Any progress with the code?"

Pete shook his head.

Crossing to the window seat, I collected Cruikshank's belongings and settled on the couch. With the box between my feet, I disengaged the flaps and began rifling.

The first thing I removed was a trophy featuring a tiny capped figure holding a bat. A plaque on the wood base read: LEAGUE CHAMPIONS, JUNE 24, 1983. I put the trophy on the coffee table.

Next, I pulled out a baseball, its outer surface covered with signatures.

I set the ball beside the trophy, wondering if the two items were related. My mind began drifting.

Cruikshank had played in a league. Where? What position? Had his team been consistently good, I wondered, or did the ball and trophy represent their one championship season? What had it been like on that June day? Hot? Rainy? Had the score been lopsided? Had Cruikshank's team won with one heart-stopping hit?

Did Cruikshank have the game ball because he drove in the winning run? Had his teammates pounded his back? Had they all gone for beer and rehashed the game?

Had Cruikshank relived that moment in the years that followed? Alone with his bourbon, had he seen the pitch, felt the bat's grip in his palms, heard the crack as the ball ricocheted from the sweet spot?

Had the man marveled at how life had gone so terribly wrong?

On-screen Hope was quipping, "The girls call me Pilgrim, because every time I dance with one I make a little progress."

Pete was chuckling as I pulled a pair of framed photos from among Cruikshank's belongings. The first showed five uniformed soldiers, smiling, arm-draping one another's shoulders. The photo's owner was last on the left.

I studied the small figure. Cruikshank's hair was short, and he was squinting, probably facing into the sun. The crags in his face were softer, but already foretold the older man he'd become.

More drifting.

Had Cruikshank done a hitch in the army? The National Guard? He'd been too young for Vietnam. Where had he served?

The second framed photo showed darkly uniformed men stacked in formal, straight rows. I guessed it was Cruikshank's police academy graduating class.

A round metal tin held other police memorabilia. Collar brass from the different units in which Cruikshank had served. Colored bars that I assumed were departmental recognition awards. A duplicate shield.

A corrugated brown folder held a police academy diploma, several certificates from specialty training courses, and more photos. Cruikshank shaking hands with some high police official. Cruikshank with three men in suits. Cruikshank and another cop standing in front of a church with Billy Graham.

I fished some more.

A Zippo lighter with a CMPD logo. A key chain, pocketknife, and tie tack with the same logo. A CMPD badge. Handcuffs. Keys. A frilly garter. An old Sam Browne belt buckle. A scuffed holster. A speed loader for a revolver.

Everything went onto the table.

At the bottom of the box lay a book and several envelopes. Choosing a large brown one, I unwound the string and dumped the contents into my lap.

Snapshots. Grainy and fading to sepia at the borders. Scooping them up, I worked my way through.

Every photo included the same blond woman. Upturned nose, freckles, a classic *Little House on the Prairie* face.

In some shots, the woman was alone. In others, she was with Cruikshank. In a few, the two were part of a larger group. Christmas party. Ski trip. Picnic. Based on hairstyles and clothing, I guessed the photos had been taken in the late seventies or early eighties.

I checked the back of each print. Only one had writing. In it Cruikshank and the woman wore swimsuits and lay side by side on a blanket, chins propped on their fists. I read the notation: *Noble and Shannon, Myrtle Beach, July 1976.*

I picked up the last photo. Noble and Shannon, smiling like the world would always be young. I was not smiling. My mind was circling to a very dark place.

This Kodak moment captured Cruikshank and Shannon facing each other, hands outstretched, fingers intertwined. She was wearing a short white sundress and flowers in her hair. He was in a pale blue jacket. Above their heads, a banner identified the Viva Las Vegas Wedding Chapel. In front of them, down on one knee and mugging for the camera, was a faux Elvis, complete with shades and sequined white satin jumpsuit.

I stared at the image, a frozen moment at the birth of a doomed marriage. Once a treasured memento, the picture had become nothing more than a memory packed away in an old brown envelope.

My eyes wandered to Pete. I felt my lids burn. I wrested my gaze back. It fell on Cruikshank's possessions. Small comfort.

These items represented a life, a man who had enjoyed friendship, served his country, been a cop, played baseball, married. A man who had, in spite of it all, chosen to end that life.

Or had he?

My eyes dropped to the Myrtle Beach photo. Shannon and Noble. A marriage lost. A life lost.

On-screen, someone asked Hope if he thought Goddard should sell the castle.

"My advice is to keep the castle and sell the ghosts."

The sound of Pete's laughter pierced the armor of my phony nonchalance. How many times had he laughed with me? Clowned for me? Bought flowers when we had no money? Done the underpants dance when I was angry? Why had the laughter stopped? When?

Looking down at the heartrending collection spread before me, I was overwhelmed by the ruin of Noble and Shannon. By the finality of Cruikshank's death. By the calamity of my own lost marriage. By the confusion of emotions churning inside me.

I lost it.

Chest heaving, I pushed from the couch.

"Tempe?" Pete. Confused.

I stumbled over Cruikshank's box and lunged from the room, mindless of where I was going.

Ocean air. Stars. Life.

I threw open the front door and raced down the steps.

Pete was right behind me. In the front yard, he grasped one of my shoulders, spun me, and wrapped me in a hug.

"It's OK. Hey, Tempe. It's OK." Stroking my hair.

At first I resisted, then I yielded. Pressing my cheek to Pete's chest, I let the tears come.

I'm not sure how long we stood there, me sobbing, Pete making comforting noises.

Seconds, maybe eons, later a vehicle rolled up Ocean Drive, paused, then turned in at "Sea for Miles." I looked up. Silvery white moonlight illuminated the interior enough to show that the driver was alone.

The vehicle came to a stop. Maybe a Jeep? A small SUV?

I felt Pete tense as the driver's door opened. A man got out and circled the hood. I could see that the man was tall and thin.

And something more.

Oh, God!

The man froze, a silhouette in the headlights.

My heart flew into my throat.

Before I could call out, the man retraced his steps, slid behind the wheel, threw the car into reverse, and gunned down the drive.

I watched the beams swing wide.

Tires squealed.

The taillights shrank to tiny red specks.

# 15

Heart banging, I double-stepped the stairs, raced into the house, grabbed my cell, and hit a speed-dial key.

The phone rang four times, then an answering service cut in.

And delivered a message in French and English.

I punched again, missed, fingers clumsy with agitation. Repunched.

Same result.

"Pick up, damn it!"

"Just tell me who he was." Pete was following as I paced from room to room. Boyd was trailing Pete.

I hit the *R* on my speed dial a third time.

A mechanical voice informed me that the subscriber I was attempting to reach was unavailable.

"Go ahead. Turn yourself off!"

I hurled the phone. It bounced from the couch to the floor. Boyd ran over to sniff the offending object.

"Talk to me." Pete was speaking in that tone psychiatrists use to calm hysterical patients. "Who was that?"

Deep breaths. Steady. I turned to face him.

"Andrew Ryan."

A moment of mental Rolodexing. "The cop from Quebec?"

I nodded.

"Why would he show up then split without saying a word?"

"He saw us together."

More cerebral linking. Synapse. "So you two are—" Pete raised both brows, pointed to me, then toward the driveway where Ryan had been.

I nodded.

"Looked bad?" he asked.

"What do you think?"

I dialed Ryan twice more. His cell remained off.

I performed my nightly toilette with robotic detachment. Cleanser. Moisturizer. Toothpaste.

We're not sophomores going steady, I told myself. We're adults. Ryan is a reasonable man. I'll explain. We'll both laugh.

But would Monsieur Macho allow me the chance?

Lying in bed, I felt the weight of doubt in my gut. I took a long time to fall asleep.

By nine the next morning I wanted to turn my own cell off.

No. I wanted to pulverize it, then flush the plastic and metal bits into the sewer system of some

164

remote Third World country. Bangladesh would do. Or maybe one of the Stans.

The first call came at 7:55.

"Morning, ma'am. Dickie Dupree."

That was it for Southern pleasantries.

"Just checked my e-mail."

"You're up early today, Mr. Dupree."

"Found this report of yours. Now I'm looking toward dealing with a pack of dimwit bureaucrats."

"You're welcome, sir. I thought you'd appreciate a copy."

"What I don't appreciate is your telling folks up at the state capital that I got priceless relics on my land."

"That's not exactly what I told them."

"Comes damn close. Report like this can cause me delays. And delays can cause me a world of hurt."

"It's unfortunate if my findings adversely affect your project," I said. "My job was to describe honestly what I found."

"This country's going to hell 'cause of crap like this. Economy's in the toilet. People are screaming there's no work, nowhere to live. I provide jobs, put up decent housing. What do I get for my efforts? Horseshit like this."

On Dewees, Dupree was putting up million-dollar beach homes for the overindulged. I didn't say it.

"Now some cracker-ass fool with more degrees than brains is going to come down here and declare my property some kinda heritage site."

"I'm sorry if my findings inconvenience you."

"Inconvenience? That how you see it?"

The question seemed rhetorical, so I didn't reply.

"Your meddling could hand me a damn sight more than inconvenience."

I used my steely voice again. "You might have requested a cultural resource assessment before agreeing to develop the land."

"We'll see who's inconvenienced, Miz Brennan. I, too, have friends. Unlike your pals, these boys ain't paper-pushing eggheads."

With that he was gone.

I sat a moment, considering Dupree's last statement. Was the little toad implying he might order someone to hurt me?

Right. Maybe send Colonel to gnaw me to death, though any harassment of me would be stupid and ineffective. It would not solve his problem.

I dialed Ryan. His phone was still off.

Throwing back the covers, I headed for the bathroom.

The next call came at eight fifteen. I was in the kitchen, drinking coffee and eating one of Pete's cranberry and pine nut muffins.

Cranberry and pine nut? My reaction, too, but that's what they were. I'd read the label twice.

Birdie was at his bowl crunching small brown pellets. Boyd was in begging mode, chin on my knee.

"Gullet here."

"Good morning, Sheriff."

166

Gullet, too, skipped preamble. "Just left Parrot. Took some memory jogging, but the gentleman finally recalled a box that might have gotten separated from the main stack."

"Might this box have contained a computer and camera?"

"Parrot's a little hazy on contents. Vaguely remembered some electronic equipment."

"And what might have happened to this errant box?"

"Seems his son might have accidentally carried it off."

"Kids."

"I gave Parrot an hour to discuss the matter with sonny. I'll call when I hear from him."

I dialed Emma. And got her recorded voice.

I dialed Ryan.

*"L'abonné que vous tentez de joindre . . ."* The mobile customer you are trying to reach . . .

I wanted to reach across the line and throttle the woman. In two languages.

I tried Ryan at eight thirty and again at eight forty-five. No go.

I clicked off, misgivings still firmly lodged in my innards. I wondered where Ryan had gone. Why he'd come here. Why he'd kept his visit a secret. Was it surveillance? Trying to catch me with Pete?

At nine, I called Emma a second time. I was on a voice mail roll. The same recording asked for my name and number.

Odd, I thought, rinsing then placing my cup in the dishwasher. I'd phoned Emma twice the night

167

before, at six and at eight, and twice this morning. It wasn't like her to ignore my messages. Especially now, when I was so concerned about her health.

I knew that Emma often monitored calls, dodged conversations she didn't want to have. But she'd never done that with me. At least, not that I knew of. But then, when wrapped up in normal life, I called so rarely. Was she now ducking my calls because proximity made me a threat? An annoyance? Was my worry causing her discomfort? Did she regret taking me into her confidence? Was she avoiding me to avoid the reality of her disease?

Or was she really sick?

I made a decision.

Crossing the house to Pete's bedroom, I leaned close to the door. "Pete?"

"I knew you'd come knocking, sugar britches. Give me a minute to light some candles and cue Barry White."

Pete. You gotta love him.

"I have to go see Emma."

The door opened. Pete was wearing a towel and a half face of shaving cream.

"Deserting me again?"

"Sorry." I considered telling Pete about Emma's NHL, decided that doing so would betray a confidence. "Something's come up."

Pete knew I was being evasive. "If you divulge the full story you'll have to kill me, right?"

"Something like that."

Pete cocked a brow. "Any word from the French Foreign Legion?"

"No." I switched topics. "Gullet called. Parrot's kid probably has Cruikshank's computer."

"Think he'll release it to us so we can check the hard drive?"

"Probably. The sheriff's not exactly a techie, and he says he's shorthanded right now. And, thanks to Emma, he views me as part of the team. Sort of."

"Keep me posted."

"Can you manage to charge and carry your cell?"

Pete had been the last person in the western hemisphere to obtain a mobile phone. Unfortunately, his bold advance into the world of wireless communication had peaked at the moment of purchase. His BlackBerry usually lay dead on his dresser, forgotten in a pocket, or buried in the center compartment of his car.

Pete gave a snappy salute. "Will secure and maintain apparatus, Captain."

"Show no mercy at God's Mercy Church, Counselor," I said.

Ill-chosen words, as things turned out.

Emma owned a property so "old Charleston" it should have been dressed in a hoopskirt and crinolines. The two-story house was peach with white trim and double porches, and sat on a lot enclosed by wrought iron fencing. A giant magnolia shaded the tiny front yard.

Emma had been negotiating to purchase the home when we met. She'd fallen in love with its woodwork, its gardens, and its Duncan Street location, just minutes from both the College of

Charleston and the MUSC complex. Though the house was beyond her means in those days, she'd been overjoyed when her bid was accepted.

Good timing. In the years that followed, Charleston real estate shot into the stratosphere. Though her little slice of history was now worth a small fortune, Emma refused to sell. Her monthly payments were stiff, but she made it work by spending money on little other than food and her home.

It had rained throughout the night, freeing the city from its premature skin of oppressive heat. The air felt almost cool as I pushed open Emma's gate. Details seemed magnified. The rusty squeak of old hinges. Buckled cement where a magnolia root snaked beneath. The scent of oleander, confederate jasmine, crepe myrtle, and camellia floating from the garden.

Emma answered the door wearing a bathrobe and slippers. Her skin looked pasty, her lips dry and cracked. Greasy stragglers hung from an Indian-print scarf knotted on her head.

I tried to keep the shock from my face. "Hey, girlfriend."

"You're more persistent than a Yahoo! pop-up."

"I'm not selling products to enlarge your man's penis."

"Already got a magnifying glass." Emma mustered a weak smile. "Come on in."

Emma stepped back, and I brushed past her into the foyer. The smell of pine and wood polish replaced the perfume of flowers.

The inside of Emma's house was exactly as promised by the outside. Straight ahead, double mahogany doors gave way to a wide hallway. A large parlor opened to the right. A bannistered staircase curved up to the left. Everywhere, Baluchi and Shiraz carpets topped gleaming wood floors.

"Tea?" Emma asked, exhaustion emanating from every part of her body.

"If you let me make it."

As I followed Emma, I scoped out the house.

One look told me where my friend's money was going. The place was furnished with pieces that had been crafted before the founding fathers inked up their pens. Had she needed cash, Emma could have sold off antiques through the next millennium. Christie's would have taken months just to write catalog copy.

Emma led me to a kitchen the size of a convenience store, and settled herself at a round oak table. While I started a kettle and got tea bags, I told her about Cruikshank's boxes. She listened without comment.

"Cream and sugar?" I asked, pouring boiling water into a pot.

Emma pointed to a china bird on the counter. I carried it to the table and took a carton of milk from the fridge.

As Emma sipped I brought her fully up to date. The missing computer. The images on the disc. The odd fractures on the two cervical vertebrae.

Emma asked a few questions. It was all very friendly. Then I changed the tone.

"Why are you ignoring my calls?"

Emma looked at me as you might a squeegee kid asking to do your windshield, uncertain whether to say "thanks" or "buzz off." A few seconds passed. Setting her mug carefully on the table, she seemed to make a decision.

"I'm sick, Tempe."

"I know that."

"I'm not responding to treatment."

"I know that, too."

"This latest round is knocking me on my ass." Emma turned her face away, but not before I saw the pain in her eyes. "I've been unable to do my job. First Monday, now today. I've got a skeleton I'm failing to get ID'd. You tell me I've got a dead former cop who might not have killed himself. And what am I doing? I'm home sleeping."

"Dr. Russell said you might experience some fatigue."

Emma laughed. There was no humor in it. "Dr. Russell's not here to see me heaving my guts out."

I started to protest. She cut me off with a raised hand.

"I'm not going to get better. I need to face that." Emma's eyes came round and dropped to her mug. "I need to consider my staff and the community I've been elected to serve."

"You don't have to make any major decisions right now." My mouth felt dry.

A wind chime danced outside the window, merry, oblivious to the anguish on the opposite side of the glass.

"Soon," Emma said softly.

I set down my mug. The tea was cold, untouched.

Ask?

The chimes tinkled softly.

"Does your sister know?"

Emma's eyes came up to mine. Her lips opened. I thought she was about to tell me to go to hell, to stop meddling and mind my own business. Instead she just shook her head no.

"What's her name?"

"Sarah Purvis." Barely audible.

"Do you know where she is?"

"Married to some doctor in Nashville."

"Would you like me to contact her?"

"Like she'd care."

Pushing from the table, Emma walked to the window. I followed, stood at her back and lay a hand on each of her shoulders. For several moments no one spoke.

"I love baby's breath." Emma was gazing at a stand of delicate white flowers in the garden outside. "The flower ladies sell baby's breath at the marketplace. That, too." She pointed at a cluster of green and white stalks topped by long, slender leaves. "Know what that is?"

I shook my head.

"Rabbit tobacco. Tea brewed from rabbit tobacco was once considered the best cold remedy in the Carolina Lowcountry. Rural folks still smoke it for asthma. Its other name is life everlasting. I planted it when . . ."

Emma took a deep, ragged breath.

Though my throat felt tight, I kept my voice low and even.

"Let me help you, Emma. Please."

A beat passed. Another.

Without turning, Emma nodded.

"But don't call my sister." She drew a deep breath, let it out slowly. "Not yet."

Driving from Emma's home, emotions battled in my head. Anxiety concerning my relationship with Ryan. Frustration with the Dewees and Cruikshank cases. Worry for Emma. Anger at my impotence in the face of her illness.

Moving through the sunshine of that glorious morning, I swallowed the fear and fury and doubt, and reshaped them into something new. Something positive.

I couldn't reach into my friend's marrow and restore the life her own cells were taking from her. But I could ply my trade and ease her professional concerns. I could work to give Emma the answers she wanted regarding the skeletons.

A stubborn resolve formed in my heart.

As it did so, the Lowcountry was again preparing to give up a secret. Another body would be discovered within twenty-four hours. This one would present me with more than dry bones.

# 16

My new resolve took me back to MUSC. Why? Lack of a better idea.

Finding a morgue attendant, I explained who I was and that I was acting on behalf of the coroner. I requested CCC-2006020277 and CCC-2006020285. When the gurneys arrived, I extracted the sixth cervical vertebrae from Cruikshank and from the Dewees skeleton, and carried both to the scope. A quick check confirmed that the fracture patterning was the same on each neck bone. OK. I was dead certain.

Cause?

Connection between the two cases?

As before, I gave the questions some thought. Then I moved on to the dirt that Topher had collected from the Dewees grave. Why? Lack of a better idea.

Placing a rectangular stainless steel pan in the sink with a screen positioned above, I retrieved one of three black plastic garbage bags lying at the foot of the Dewees gurney. Disengaging the bag's wire twister, I poured a layer of dirt and gently shook the screen.

The sandy soil filtered through the mesh, leaving behind pebbles, snail shells, bits of sand dollar, starfish, mollusk, and crab. After checking the debris with a magnifying glass, I dumped it and poured more dirt.

Same rocks and shards of marine life.

I was on my second bag when a minuscule sliver caught my eye. The thing was embedded in a broken snail shell, and so small I almost missed it.

A filament of some sort? A thread?

Using forceps, I extracted the snail and placed it in my gloved palm. The creature's shell was less than three centimeters long, brown and coiled, but rounder and more squat than those I was used to seeing on the beach.

I returned to the gurney and checked Topher's label. The bag I'd chosen held dirt from directly around the bones.

Moving to a side counter, I carefully tweezed the filament free from the shell, centered it on a slide, and covered it with a tiny glass plate. Then I placed the slide under the microscope, and leaned into the eyepiece.

The object appeared as a blurry curved line. Some knob fiddling brought it into focus.

The thing was an eyelash. A black eyelash.

I was thinking about that when my cell phone

sounded. The caller ID showed an eight-four-three area code.

Not Ryan.

Disappointed, I stripped off a glove and took the call.

"Tempe Brennan."

"Gullet here. Got us a Dell Latitude laptop PC and a Pentax Optio 5.5 digital camera."

"It was all an unfortunate misunderstanding."

"It was. Parrot senior was most apologetic. Parrot junior looked like he'd had better mornings."

"What now?"

"Camera's empty. Either Cruikshank left nothing on it, or Junior wiped it clean to cover his rear. The computer is password protected. We played with it some. Got nowhere."

"May I take a crack?"

There was a pause before Gullet spoke again.

"You got experience with these things?"

"I do." Said with more conviction than I actually felt. I'd always used passwords on my PC, but wasn't actually a Sherlock at cracking security codes. Fact was, I'd never hacked into a computer.

I listened to several more seconds of dead air. Then, "Can't hurt. Miz Rousseau trusts you, and my deputies have got other things filling their dance cards today."

"I'm at the morgue."

"Be by in an hour."

The remaining soil produced nothing of interest. I was retying the last bag when the sheriff arrived.

Gullet placed a plastic-wrapped bundle on a side

counter. Then he folded his shades and hung them by a bow from his breast pocket. For a moment, his gaze lingered on the two gurneys at my back.

"Miz Rousseau here?" he asked.

"She had something elsewhere that needed her attention," I said. "Have a look at this."

Gullet stepped to the scope. I inserted one fractured vertebra. Gullet observed it without comment. I switched to the other.

Gullet straightened and looked at me.

I explained that the first specimen had come from Cruikshank, the second from the unknown found on Dewees.

"Both cracked a neck bone." Gullet spoke with his flat, almost bored drawl.

"They did."

"How?"

"I don't know."

Inserting the eyelash slide, I indicated that he should take another look.

"What am I squinting at?"

"An eyelash."

Gullet peered through the eyepiece a few seconds longer, then again regarded me without expression.

"It came from the grave on Dewees," I said.

"Two billion people share this planet. That would make how many billion eyelashes?"

"This one came from eighteen inches below the ground surface, in dirt directly associated with the body."

Gullet's face didn't change.

"This eyelash is black," I said. "The man on Dewees had pale blond hair."

"Could it belong to one of your diggers?"

I shook my head no. "They're both too fair."

One bushy brow might have ascended a micromillimeter.

"Lashes good for DNA?"

"Mitochondrial," I said.

Gullet didn't react.

"A type of DNA that traces through maternal relatives." Oversimplified, but good enough.

Gullet nodded, walked to the counter, and withdrew an evidence transfer form from his bundle.

I joined him and signed my name and the date.

Gullet tore off and handed me my copy. Then he folded the form and shoved it into an inside jacket pocket. His eyes again wandered to the gurneys.

"You find anything tying these fellas together?"

"No."

"Except each managed to break his neck."

"Except that."

"If these boys are linked, we got us a double homicide. Hypothetically speaking, of course."

"Hypothetically speaking," I agreed.

"Serial?"

I shrugged "maybe." "Or the two might have known each other."

"Go on."

"Maybe they witnessed something that got them both killed."

Not a flicker in Gullet's face.

"Maybe they were involved in something."

"Such as?"

"Drugs. Counterfeiting. The Lindbergh kidnapping."

"Hypothetically speaking."

"Hypothetically speaking."

"My chief deputy of special ops nailed that building."

My face showed something. Confusion.

"Cruikshank's CD. The photos. My staffer says that brick building's a free clinic over on Nassau."

"Who runs it?" I asked, at last making the leap.

"GMC."

"Herron and his flock. Jesus! Could it be the one where Helene Flynn worked?"

"Now I understand your boyfriend's got an interest in those boys, but a law degree doesn't make him a cop in my town. If we're looking at murder, and I'm not yet saying we are, I don't want some wingtipped cowboy spooking potential suspects."

It seemed pointless to mention that Pete wasn't my boyfriend. Or that he owned not a single wingtip.

Gullet pointed a warning finger. "You keep that boy reined in. Things go sideways, I'm the one takes the heat."

"Will you check out the clinic?" I asked.

"Not much to justify that at the moment."

Gullet tapped the PC. "You come up with the password, you call. Otherwise we shoot this thing up to SLED." South Carolina Law Enforcement.

"Won't that mean queuing up for a long wait?" I asked.

Gullet repositioned his Ray-Bans. "You take your shot, ma'am."

When the sheriff had gone, I phoned Emma. She told me to leave the eyelash and snail and she'd have Lee Ann Miller pick them up and send them to the state crime lab.

After photographing the vertebral fractures, I bagged and delivered the lash and shell, and told the tech I was through for the day. The clock said two. I headed home.

On the way, I phoned Pete's BlackBerry. No answer. Big surprise.

I was so pumped about getting into Cruikshank's hard drive, I didn't stop for lunch. At "Sea for Miles" I took Boyd out to the road for a quick health break, threw together a ham and cheese sandwich, then settled at the kitchen table.

The laptop booted through the Windows opening sequence to a blue screen. There, a cursor blinked, awaiting clearance to load personal settings.

I started with commonly used passwords: 123123. 123456. 1A2B3C. Password. Open.

No go.

Cruikshank's initials? Birthday?

I got up and retrieved the AFIS printout that Emma had given me.

Noble Carter Cruikshank.

I tried NCC, CCN, and varying combinations of the man's initials, with and without his date of birth, forward and backward. I inverted each name, then rearranged groupings of letters. Then I substituted digits for letters and letters for digits.

The cursor didn't budge.

Charlotte Mecklenburg Police Department.

I tried every combination using CMPD in differing positions with the name and DOB.

Nope.

Shannon. I didn't have Shannon's middle or last name. When had they married? No idea. The beach photo was dated July 1976. I tried more combinations.

The cursor wouldn't buy it.

Baseball. I got the box and pulled the trophy. June 24, 1983.

DOB. Date of league championship. Combined. Scrambled. Inverted.

No sale..

I played with Cruikshank's address and every date on the AFIS sheet.

By four thirty I'd run out of ideas.

"I don't have enough personal information," I said to the empty kitchen.

Boyd shot to his feet.

"Still mad about the stingy walk?"

Boyd's mouth opened and his tongue drooped over one purple gum.

"You chows are a forgiving breed."

The chow cocked his head and tipped his ears forward.

"Let's switch to the files."

Shutting down the laptop, I moved to the den. Boyd padded along.

Cruikshank's file carton was still on the window seat. I took it to the coffee table and sat on the couch.

Boyd hopped up beside me. Our eyes met. Boyd dropped back to the floor.

The box held about forty manila folders, each with a handwritten date and name. Some files were fat, others thin. I ran through the tabs.

The files were organized chronologically. I could tell from the dates there were times Cruikshank was working multiple cases. There were also gaps, presumably his periods of heavy drinking.

I pulled the oldest file.

*Murdock, Deborah Anne. August 2000. C.*

Deborah Murdock's folder held the following:

Shorthand notes similar to those in Helene Flynn's file.

Canceled checks drawn on the joint account of Deborah and Jason Murdock. The last was written December 4, 2000.

Photos of a couple entering or exiting a restaurant, bar, or motel.

Letters addressed to Jason Murdock in Moncks Corner, South Carolina, and signed by Noble Cruikshank. The letters spanned the period from September to November 2000.

I was getting the drift. I read only one letter.

Yep. Deborah was the woman in the pics. The man wasn't Jason.

I moved on.

*Lang, Henry. December 2000. C.*

Same deal. Notes, checks, photos, reports.

Cruikshank spent six months on this one. Here it was hubby who was stepping out.

Next folder.

*Todman, Kyle. February 2001. C.*

This case involved an antiques dealer who suspected his partner of ripping him off. It took Cruikshank a month to nail the swindler.

I pulled file after file. The stories had a sad sameness to them. Cheating spouses. Missing parents. Runaway teens. Few had happy endings. What is it they say? If you acknowledge your suspicion, it's probably true.

I looked at the clock. Six fifteen. I wondered what Pete was doing.

I wondered what Ryan was doing.

I checked my cell. No messages. The battery was fine.

Of course it was.

Back to the files.

*Ethridge, Parker. March 2002.*

This was one of the fattest jackets in the carton.

Parker Ethridge, age fifty-eight, lived by himself. In March 2002 Parker's son went to collect him for a long-planned fishing trip. Ethridge wasn't home and was never seen again. Cruikshank spent over a year investigating, but to no avail. Ethridge junior fired him in May 2003.

*Franklin, Georgia. March 2004. C.*

In November 2003, a nineteen-year-old coed disappeared from her dorm at the College of Charleston. Four months later, dissatisfied with police progress, Georgia's parents hired Cruikshank to find their daughter. He did. Living with a Buddhist jewelry maker in Asheville, North Carolina.

*Poe, Harmon. April 2004.* Unemployed male. Last seen at the Ralph H. Johnson VA Medical Center. Reported missing by a friend.

*Friguglietti, Sylvia. May 2004. C.* Elderly female. Wandered from an assisted living center. Found floating in the harbor near Patriot's Point.

Again, I checked my watch and my cell.

Seven fifty-two. No calls.

Discouraged, I rolled my shoulders and stretched my arms overhead. Boyd opened sleepy lids.

"It wasn't a complete waste of time," I said.

Boyd rolled his eyes up at me.

"I've learned that *C* on a tab means the case was closed."

Boyd looked unconvinced. I didn't care. I was getting somewhere.

Dropping my arms, I picked up where I'd left off.

*Snype, Daniel. August 2004.* Disappeared while visiting Charleston from Savannah, Georgia. Return bus ticket unused. Reported missing by granddaughter, Tiffany Snype.

*Walton, Julia. September 2004. C.* Runaway housewife found living with her boyfriend in Tampa, Florida.

Some of the most recent files contained only newspaper clippings and a few shorthand notes. No checks. No photos. No reports.

I read several clippings. Each described a missing person.

"Were these cases Cruikshank was hired to investigate?"

Boyd had no answer to that.

"Or was he looking at MPs for some other reason?"

Or that.

Opening the last file, I read another clipping.

A name caught my interest.

# 17

Homer Winborne's byline graced the most recent article. Less than two column inches, the piece reported on the 2004 disappearance of a man named Lonnie Aikman.

*A Mount Pleasant woman is asking Charleston residents to keep an eye out for her son. Lonnie Aikman, 34, has been missing for two years, Susie Ruth Aikman told the* Moultrie News.

*"He just vanished," said Aikman. "He said, 'Catch you later, Mom,' and went off and never come back."*

*When police failed to locate Lonnie, Aikman consulted a psychic and was told her son was in the Charleston area. Aikman says seeing the psychic was a last resort.*

*"When you lose someone you're willing to believe in anything that will give you hope," she explained.*

*Aikman searched and put up posters asking anyone with information to call her, the Charleston police, or the sheriff's office. Aikman says her son suffers from schizophrenia and was taking medication at the time of his disappearance. She fears he may have been kidnapped.*

*"I'm afraid he's somewhere being held against his will," said Aikman.*

*Lonnie Aikman is 5'8" and weighs 160 pounds. He has green eyes and brown hair.*

The piece ran in the *Moultrie News* on March 14. Cruikshank had circled Aikman's age, the date of his disappearance, and the word "schizophrenia."

I checked several clippings. Similar information had been circled in each.

So Cruikshank was collecting stories on missing persons. These didn't appear to be client-initiated investigations. The files contained no checks. No reports. Why the interest?

Two of Cruikshank's files contained only handwritten notes. One was labeled *Helms, Willie,* the other *Montague, Unique*. Their placement in the carton suggested they'd been created shortly before Cruikshank's death. Why? Who were Willie Helms and Unique Montague?

Frustrated, I began a spreadsheet and went back through the folders, pulling out unsolved missing persons cases.

*Ethridge, Parker, white male, 58, 5 feet 7 inches, 135 pounds, gray hair, blue eyes. Last seen March 2002.*

*Moon, Rosemarie, black female, 28, 5 feet 3 inches, 105 pounds, red hair, brown eyes. Last seen November 2002. Known drug user and sex trade worker.*

*Watley, Ruby Anne, black female, 39, 5 feet 5 inches, 140 pounds, black shoulder-length hair, brown eyes. Last seen July 2003. Known drug user and sex trade worker.*

*Poe, Harmon, 39, white male, 5 feet 11 inches, 155 pounds, brown hair, brown eyes. Last seen April 2004. Known drug user.*

*Snype, Daniel, 27, black male, 5 feet 5 inches, 120 pounds, blond shoulder-length hair, brown eyes. Last seen June 2004. Known drug user and sex trade worker.*

*Aikman, Lonnie, white male, 34, 5 feet 8 inches, 160 pounds, green eyes, brown hair. Last seen spring 2004. Schizophrenic.*

The Dewees case matched none of the profiles. I added it to the spreadsheet.

*CCC-2006020277, white male, 35–50, 5 feet 10 inches to 6 foot 1 inch, blond hair. Fractured C-6 vertebra. Nicks on twelfth rib, twelfth thoracic vertebra, and upper lumbar vertebrae. Buried on Dewees.*

Winborne had written his article in March. Did Aikman's disappearance explain Winborne's behavior on Dewees? Did the reporter think we'd stumbled across Lonnie?

Cruikshank had clipped Winborne's story on or after March 14. Was Aikman's the last file he opened?

And why the Helms and Montague files? What was contained in the coded comments?

I was trying to make sense of my notes when Pete arrived.

"It is I, the great bearer of pizza," his voice boomed from the foyer.

I heard keys hit a tabletop, then Pete appeared in the doorway. He was in chinos and what looked disturbingly like a bowling shirt. A Hornets cap completed the ensemble.

Boyd shot over and circled the great bearer's ankles, nose sniffing the grease-stained box in his hands.

"I bought a large on the chance that you were here and hungry. Why are you working without lights?"

I'd been so intent on my spreadsheet I hadn't noticed the room dim. My watch now said eight twenty.

"Why is it dark so early?"

"There's a kick-ass storm moving in. The whole island's battening down hatches. Do we have hatches? Are they battened?"

I noticed Pete's cap. "Bad news, Pete. The Hornets moved to New Orleans."

"I like the colors." Pete took the cap off and admired the logo.

"Purple and turquoise?"

"Not turquoise, you boor. Teal. Hues chosen by Alexander Julian and envied all across the league."

"Designer hues or not, the team left Charlotte."

Tossing the cap to a sideboard, Pete tipped his head at the files stacked beside me. "What are you doing?"

A tickle from my lower centers. *Heads-up!*

What? Heads-up to what?

"Ground control to Tempe."

I snapped back.

"What are you doing?" Pete repeated.

"Going through Cruikshank's cases."

"Cruikshank's PC, I assume. Any luck with it?"

I shook my head. "Can't fathom a password. Where have you been all day?"

"Trapped in fiduciary hell. What's brown and black and looks good on accountants?"

Knowing it was a mistake, I raised both palms.

"Doberman pinschers."

"That's lame."

"But true. These guys must choose accounting because they lack the charisma to be undertakers."

"Did you quiz Herron about Helene Flynn?"

"The good reverend felt we should start with the books."

My brows drifted upward.

"Don't give me that look. Buck hired me to trace his money. In the process I was to learn what I could about the daughter."

"Did you tell Herron that Cruikshank is dead?"

"Yes."

"His reaction?"

"Shock, sadness, and a heartfelt wish for a peaceful rest. Find anything in the files?"

"Maybe."

We moved to the porch. The breeze was spinning the ceiling fan without aid of electricity.

I set out plates and napkins. Pete divvied up pizza. As we ate, I explained what I'd learned.

"A *C* on the tab means the case was closed."

"*Now* we're getting somewhere."

"That's what I told Boyd."

Boyd's ears shot forward. His nose never left the table edge.

"A lot of Cruikshank's recent files contained nothing but clippings on missing persons. I made a spreadsheet and started looking for patterns. What are these things?" I pointed to small black globs on my pizza.

"Dried currants. And?"

"Since 2002, Cruikshank opened jackets on two women and four men reported missing in the Charleston area. No checks or reports. He also had a couple that held nothing but notes."

"So he wasn't actually hired to look for those people."

"That's my take."

Pete gave the idea some thought. "Could the Dewees guy be one of Cruikshank's MPs?"

"He's not really a match for any of them."

"Who are they?"

"One male is black, three are white. Their ages range from twenty-seven to fifty-eight. One guy works in the sex trade. Two are drug users. One is schizophrenic. The women are black, twenty-eight and thirty-nine. Both are prostitutes and drug users."

"Think it could be some kind of serial killer, maybe a predator grabbing hookers and druggies? Fringe people no one will miss?"

"I don't know the exact date Aikman went missing. Or the Dewees man. But eight months elapsed between the disappearances of Ethridge and Moon, another eight between Moon and Watley. Then it's nine months until Poe. Two months later, it's Snype. If it's a serial, the progression is atypical."

"Aren't serial killers typically atypical?" Pete helped himself to more pizza.

"These profiles are all over the map. Men, women. Black, white. Ages range from twenty-seven to fifty-eight."

"Not restricted to teenage street boys? Or coeds with long, center-parted hair?"

"You're a profiler now?" Acknowledging Pete's references to victim types preferred by John Gacy and Ted Bundy.

"A mere savant. And bearer of pizza."

"Whose idea was the currants?" I asked.

"Arturo's."

For a few moments we listened to waves pound the shore. I broke the silence.

"The article on Lonnie Aikman was written by

Homer Winborne. It appeared in the *Moultrie News* on March fourteenth. So we know Cruikshank was alive then."

"Winborne's the guy who showed up at your site?"

I nodded.

"Did you call him?"

"I will."

"Any word from Monsieur—"

"No." I took another slice, plucked currants, and set them on my plate.

"A bit gastronomically rigid," Pete said.

"Currants and anchovies don't really mix. Tell me what happened with Herron."

"I never actually met Herron."

Pete described his day with the GMC accountants. He wasn't exaggerating. It sounded deadly. I remembered what Gullet had told me.

"Someone in the sheriff's office ID'd that brick building in the pictures on Cruikshank's disc."

"Oh, yeah?" Garbled by pizza.

"It's a free clinic run by GMC."

"Where?"

"Nassau Street."

Pete's jaw froze, then he swallowed. "That's where Helene Flynn worked. At least at one point."

"That was my guess. So it makes sense Cruikshank would stake the place out."

Pete wiped his mouth, balled his napkin, and tossed it onto his plate. "Is Gullet going to follow up?"

"Neither Dewees nor Cruikshank is topping the

sheriff's agenda. I showed him the two fractured vertebrae, but he's still not convinced either man was murdered."

"Maybe I should—"

"Gullet definitely does not want you making contact with anyone at that clinic. He was very clear on that."

"What could it hurt—"

"No."

"Why not?" Pete's voice had an edge. I knew that edge. My estranged husband was not a man who liked to be blocked.

"Please, Pete. Don't jam me up with Gullet. He's already letting you and me go where we have no business going. We've got Cruikshank's files and computer. We have a lot to lose. I don't want to risk it. I have to help Emma clear these cases."

"You've done what you can. Emma's the coroner here. Gullet's her battle."

My gaze drifted into the darkness outside the screen. The surf was a silvery white line beyond the lumpy black cutouts I knew were dunes.

I made a decision.

"Emma's sick."

"How sick?"

I told him about the non-Hodgkin's lymphoma, and about Emma's recent relapse.

"I'm sorry, Tempe."

Pete placed his hand on mine. We sat without talking. Outside, the ocean sounded a thundering ovation.

My thoughts were on Emma. Pete's? Good

question. I hadn't a clue what he was pondering. Helene Flynn? GMC cash flow? Cruikshank's code? Dessert?

Puzzled by the quiet, Boyd nudged my knee. I patted his head and got up to clear pizza debris. A change of topic seemed indicated.

"I found an eyelash when I screened the Dewees grave soil. It's black. The hair in the grave was blond."

"Aren't everyone's eyelashes black?"

"Not without mascara."

"Think it's from whoever buried the guy?"

"The students who dug him up both have light hair."

"Locard's exchange principle." Pete beamed a "savant" smile.

"I'm impressed," I said.

Pete had cited a concept well-known to criminalists. Locard stated that two objects coming into contact will each transfer particles, one to the other. A crook in a bank. A sniper on a tree branch. A murderer digging in sand. Every perp carries trace evidence from a scene and leaves some behind.

"You going to call this guy Winborne?" Pete asked.

I glanced at my watch. It was almost ten.

"Eventually. I may play around with Cruikshank's files a little longer."

"Why did the accountant cross the road?"

Pete was on an accountant roll. I just looked at him.

"Because the file said that's what they did last year."

I'd barely hit the couch when my eyes fell on Pete's cap. My restless subconscious whispered again. *Yo!*

What? NBA? Hornets? Turquoise?

Teal!

Jimmie Ray Teal.

When had I read that article? The last morning of the field school. Less than a week.

Pete was moving through the house, battening, I assumed.

I called out. "What day is garbage pickup?"

"Hell if I know. Why?"

I'd taken a load of papers to the front-yard Dumpster the previous Monday.

"Why?" Pete repeated himself.

I grabbed a flashlight and bolted out the front door and down the steps. Wind was now seriously whipping the palmettos. I could smell rain. The storm wasn't far off.

Flipping the Dumpster lid, I heaved out a blue plastic newspaper recycling tub.

I started at the bottom, hauling out papers, checking dates with my beam, holding the rejects down with one foot. Halfway through, I became aware of a car moving up Ocean Boulevard. I continued working through the stack.

The headlights drew closer.

Bingo! May 19. Front section. Gusts rippled the pages in my hands.

The car slowed. I ignored it.

197

I found last Friday's business review, classified ads, local and state news.

The car stopped opposite "Sea for Miles," twin beams angled toward the Dumpster.

I looked up, but could make out only the lights.

Ryan? I felt a flutter in my chest.

The car did not move on or turn into the drive.

I shielded my eyes.

The driver gunned the engine. Tires spit loose dirt and the car shot forward.

Something flew toward me.

Dropping the paper, I threw up my hands.

# 18

Something hard winged off my elbow. Pain fired up my arm. I felt liquid and smelled beer.

With my good hand, I swept my flashlight in an arc. The beam fell on a beer bottle angled against the Dumpster.

Thrown by whom?

Kids on a joyride?

Some joy.

Intentionally aimed? At me personally?

Last Friday's paper was now scattered across the yard with portions pasted by the wind to the outside of the Dumpster. I gathered sections and returned to the house. Pete had moved from the kitchen to the den, and was scribbling on one of his legal pads. Glancing up, he noticed me holding my arm.

"Lightning strike?" At least it wasn't another accountant joke.

"Some moron whipped a bottle out a car window."

Pete's brows dipped. "You OK?"

"Nothing a little ice won't heal."

I made light of the incident, but inside me a gnawing doubt was beginning to sprout. Pete had spotted a strange vehicle at the house early Sunday morning. Now this. Was someone trying to deliver a message? Joyriding vandals didn't ordinarily stop and survey a target. Or aim at people. Express dislike of something I had done? Dickie Dupree? I resolved to pay closer attention to my surroundings.

While icing my elbow, I reread the story in last Friday's *Post and Courier*, and entered Jimmie Ray Teal into my spreadsheet.

*Teal, Jimmie Ray, 47. Male. Last seen May 8 leaving Jackson Street apartment. Brother. Medical appointment.*

I was wondering about Teal's racial background when another thought struck me. The city councilman's son, Matthew Summerfield, was another missing person. But the kid didn't really fit the pattern of the other Charleston MPs. What pattern?

*Summerfield, Matthew IV, 18. White male. Last seen February 28 leaving Old City Market. Drug user.*

I fell asleep listening to Pete's kick-ass storm.

That night I dreamed disordered dreams. Ryan holding an infant. Gullet shouting words I couldn't

200

catch. A toothless man panhandling with a Hornets cap. Emma beckoning from a dark room. My feet wouldn't move, and she receded from me.

I was awakened by the sound of my cell. Reaching for it, I felt pain in my elbow.

"Gullet here." I could hear voices in the background. Phones. "We've got us another one."

My stomach tightened.

"Storm washed a barrel up south of Folly Beach. Couple of fishermen took a peek, found a body. The area's county, so my office caught the call. Miz Rousseau's indisposed again, said you should be included. Appears you're becoming de facto coroner, young lady."

At 7 A.M. the young lady was not up to a snappy retort. "Give me directions," I said, fumbling for pen and paper.

"Got no time for you getting lost. Meet me at the morgue in thirty minutes."

"What's the rush?" Bristly. But Gullet was right. I'd probably have trouble finding the place.

"Tide's coming in."

I yanked on jeans and a T, pulled my hair back, slapped on mascara, and hurried downstairs.

Pete was gone, I assumed to continued actuarial torture. Boyd and Birdie were in the kitchen, eyeing each other over an upended cereal bowl.

Birdie split when I appeared. Boyd sat. He had milk on his snout.

"You're busted, chow."

I placed the bowl in the sink, poured coffee, and checked my arm. A bruise was starting that would eventually grow to spectacular proportions. And colors.

When I unpegged his leash, Boyd went berserk. I ran him out to the curb. The yard was littered with palmetto fronds and other debris.

After watering the Dumpster, the mailbox, and a fallen branch, Boyd started up the road. I tugged him back to the house. He twirled the eyebrow hairs. Are you nuts?

"Payback for the Cheerios caper," I said.

The brow hairs went crazy.

I downed a granola bar and headed for MUSC. The sheriff was waiting by the morgue door.

Gullet took the James Island connector over the Ashley and headed south. Shortly, signs gave directions to Folly Beach.

As he drove, Gullet shared what he knew. It was little more than he'd told me on the phone. Fishermen. Barrel. Body.

I asked why the coroner had requested my presence. Gullet speculated that the corpse would be less than pristine.

I gazed out the window, letting houses, trees, and utility poles blur. Gullet initiated no further conversation. I noticed he kept sneaking glances at my elbow.

I remembered Pete's Sunday morning car. Last night's bottle. What the hell. If someone was bent on harassing me, it might help for the sheriff to know. I told him what had happened.

"You raise some hackles around here?" Gullet asked in his usual flat tone.

"I pissed off a reporter named Homer Winborne."

"Winborne's harmless."

"And a developer named Richard Dupree?"

"Surprised the State Department hasn't pressed ole Dickie into service. Man's a born diplomat."

"Is he harmless?"

Gullet hesitated. "Mostly."

Mostly? I let it go.

Fifteen minutes after crossing the Ashley River, Gullet veered onto a small road cutting through marsh. On both sides, spartina and needlerush arrowed from sparkling amber toward an immaculate blue sky. Lowering my window, I breathed a primeval perfume of growth and decay. Oysters. Fiddler crabs. A million invertebrates older than time.

Buoyed, I gave communication a go.

"Did you know that South Carolina has more marsh acreage than any other Atlantic Coast state?"

Gullet looked at me, then back at the road.

"The lab boys finished with Pinckney's wallet."

"Anything in it besides the license?"

"Nothing much. Bunch of coupons for buy-one-get-one-free meals, a grocery store discount card, a lottery ticket, sixty-four bucks, and a Trojan Magnum XL."

"Pinckney was an optimist."

"In more ways than one."

For the rest of the trip I observed egrets, bodies white amid the rippling green grass, spindly legs rising from the dark mudflats.

When Gullet pulled the Explorer to a stop, I had only a vague idea where we were. Ahead were two shacks shaded by an enormous yaupon holly. Beyond the shacks, a wooden pier jutted into what I guessed was either the Stono River or some tentacle of an Atlantic estuary.

Two vehicles were present. A cruiser with lights flashing, radio sputtering, and a black panel truck.

Red-winged blackbirds rose in a squawking gaggle as Gullet and I climbed from the Explorer. A uniform left the cruiser to greet us. I recognized the hawk nose and razor creases. Deputy H. Tybee.

"Sheriff. Ma'am." Tybee touched his brim to each of us. "Gentleman named Oswald Moultrie discovered the DOA while checking his crab pots this morning. Lives yonder." Tybee raised his chin to the first shack.

"Thought they'd stumbled on Blackbeard's lost treasure?" Gullet was staring past Tybee toward the pier.

"I don't know the answer to that, sir." Humor was not Tybee's forte. "Following your orders, we've secured the site and left everything as we found it."

"You got statements?"

"Yes, sir."

"Who lives in the other shack?"

"The one with the red awning belongs to Moultrie's brother, Leland."

I followed Gullet as he left Tybee and walked toward the water. I could see that the inlet was narrow, at points barely wide enough to allow the passage of two boats. The tide was out, leaving the pier high above the bank. The rickety wooden structure reminded me of the egrets, rising from the mud on long stick legs.

Two men sat smoking under Leland's awning. They looked like clones. Black. Wiry. Gray plastic glasses. The Brothers Moultrie.

Lee Ann Miller and another sheriff's deputy were at the shore end of the pier. Gullet and I joined them. Greetings were exchanged. The deputy's name was Zamzow. He appeared close to being sick.

As I walked to the pier, my nostrils picked up a sharp, rancid odor mingling with the smell of salt and decaying vegetation. Behind me conversation continued. Speculation on how the barrel had gotten up the creek. Suggestions concerning the best way to retrieve it.

Blocking the voices, I focused.

The pier was outfitted with a wooden platform for scaling and gutting fish. Flies were holding a jamboree on its surface. Two rusted crab pots lay to one side of the platform. A long-handled ax leaned against the other.

I looked down.

The water was dark green, the mud black and slime-slick. Tiny crabs darted this way and that, moving sideways, claws brandished like gladiator shields. Here and there, I could pick out the three-prong pattern of bird tracks.

The barrel lay half submerged, a dead thing beached by the storm. Boot prints led to and from it. The surrounding mud was chaos, churned by the Moultries' efforts to drag their booty up the incline.

A chain looped the barrel. Some links were corroded, most looked solid. I noted nicks in both the barrel and chain.

The barrel's lid lay on the mud, inner side up. A deep gouge buckled one edge.

Inside the barrel, I could see a hairless scalp, a face, the features eerily pale in the muddy brown water.

I was ready.

"Looks like an oil drum," I said, rejoining the others.

"Rusty as a coffin nail," Miller said. "Any logo or lettering is probably long gone."

"The barrel may be old, but the chain's not. Get close-ups and bag the ax. They probably hacked through the links with the blade, then knocked the lid off with the blunt side."

"Leland claims the thing popped open on its own," Deputy Zamzow said.

"Right," I said.

"How do you want to handle the body?" Miller asked. "I'm thinking we should take the whole shooting match."

"Absolutely," I agreed. "We don't know what's in that barrel."

Miller gave one of her mile-wide smiles. "When I heard 'barrel,' I brought the stinky van and an acre of plastic sheeting. I've hauled one or two of these babies in my time."

Gullet spoke to Zamzow. "Get your vehicle in here."

The man hurried off.

Gullet turned to Miller. "You got chains?"

"Rope."

"Waders?"

Miller gave a decidedly unenthusiastic nod.

"We'll run lines round the thing, haul her up the bank, then get her onto a hand truck."

Miller looked at the creek. "Could be snakes in there."

"Cottonmouths, maybe even a water-lovin' rattler or two." Gullet's voice held not a trace of sympathy.

Miller crossed to the van and returned with waders and two coils of yellow polypropylene rope. Dumping them at our feet, she began shooting scene photos.

With Zamzow hand-signaling, Tybee positioned the cruiser. Then Zamzow tied two lines to the bumper and ran each out to the end of the pier.

Tybee stayed at the wheel. Miller and Zamzow rejoined Gullet and me. No one made a move for the waders.

"This old gal's no water princess," Miller said.

"I'm a nonswimmer." Zamzow's face was the pale green of a Monet landscape.

The Moultries observed from their lawn chairs.

The day was heating up. The tide was turning. Behind us, flies were doing Riverdance on sunbaked fish guts.

Grabbing the waders, I yanked off my sneakers,

shoved my feet down the legs, and maneuvered the straps up onto my shoulders. Then I drew a deep breath, bellied over the pier, and dropped to the bank. Miller tossed me gloves and I tucked them under one arm.

The mud was slippery but firm. Stepping gingerly, I worked my way toward the barrel, crabs skittering from my path.

Gloving, I retrieved and pushed the lid into place. My stomach rolled. Up close, the stench was nauseating. After whacking the lid tight with a rock, I yanked off the gloves and signaled for a line.

Zamzow tossed down the first length of rope. I fashioned a noose, slipped it over the unsubmerged end of the barrel, rolled it down about eighteen inches, and tightened the knot.

Bracing against the barrel, I maneuvered toward its submerged end. As I moved, flecks of rust broke free and dropped to the mud.

At the water's edge I stopped and did a quick scan. Not a coiled body in sight.

Deep breath. Go.

The incline was steeper than I'd anticipated. One step and the creek covered my shins. Another and it was over my knees.

Slogging forward, I rounded the barrel. The water was now waist high, my legs lost to the murky gloom.

I signaled, and Zamzow tossed another rope. Forming another lasso, I placed the knot on top of the barrel, drew a deep breath, and squatted.

The water felt cold against my face. Eyes

squeezed, I tried wriggling the noose up under the submerged end of the barrel. Again and again it slipped. Again and again I came up for air, squatted, and struggled some more, clawing at the mud, forcing the line between the barrel and the bank. The effort made my battered arm ache.

The fourth time I surfaced, Gullet's voice boomed out: "Freeze!"

Clawing wet hair from my face, I looked up. Gullet's eyes were pointed at the opposite bank.

"What?" I panted.

"Stop. Moving." Low and even.

Instead of listening, I turned and followed Gullet's sight line.

My heart slammed into my throat.

# 19

Mondo gator. Six, maybe seven feet. I could see mud-caked scales, a yellow-white throat, jagged teeth jutting up from a powerful jaw.

A jaw that was pointed directly at me.

As I watched, the gator slipped from the bank and disappeared below the surface.

Heart banging, limbs pumping, I churned shoreward.

Gullet jumped from the pier and slip-slid across the mud. Balancing on the barrel with one hand, he extended the other. I grabbed on and pulled with all my strength. Pain jolted my bottle-battered elbow.

The oil-slick mud sent me slithering through Gullet's grasp. I fell back and muddy water closed over me. The waders filled and grew heavy.

Adrenaline fired through my system. Throwing one shoulder, I rolled and groped, enveloped in darkness.

Where was the barrel?

Dear God. Where was the gator?

Desperate, I frog-kicked, found the bank with my hands. Planting both feet, I surfaced. Gullet whistled and pointed to a rope he'd tossed into the water.

Miller was shouting, "Haul ass, darlin'! Haul ass!"

A Moultrie brother stood beside Miller. He had something in his hands. He and Zamzow were looking off to my left.

The engorged waders made movement a struggle, last night's nightmare in real time. Muscles straining, I slogged toward the rope, aware of the reptile behind me.

Was it behind me?

Something splashed to my left. I braced for teeth on my flesh.

"Pull!" Miller shouted.

Reaching the rope, I crooked one knee against the bank, hauled, and lunged upward. I felt Gullet's hands. I felt terra firma.

For a moment I stood doubled over, legs trembling, muddy water pouring from the waders. When I looked up Miller raised both thumbs and beamed.

"Didn't think gators liked salt water," I panted.

"This un ain't picky." Grinning, Moultrie scooped a chicken neck from his bait bucket and tossed it upstream.

Inverted V's rippled outward as the gator swam toward the poultry.

We waited twenty minutes on the pier, drinking coffee and watching the gator maintain a holding pattern ten yards up the creek, submerged save for its vertebrae and snout tip. It was unclear if the animal was looking back at us, protecting its dinner, or dozing.

"Tide's not getting any lower." Gullet tossed his dregs down onto the mud. "Who wants to wrestle Ramon?"

Oswald Moultrie had provided us with the gator's name, and the fact that he was a regular in the creek.

"Might as well be me. I'm already wet." Wet hardly covered it. Mud smeared every inch of my body.

"No need to prove you ain't afraid of gators," Miller said.

"I'm not afraid of gators," I said. True enough. I'm afraid of snakes. I kept that to myself.

"Got some heat now." Zamzow brandished a Remington shotgun that he'd retrieved from the trunk of his cruiser. "Critter starts moving this way, I'll park a bullet in his brain."

"No need to kill him," Gullet observed. "Shoot into his path and he'll turn back."

I handed Miller my Styrofoam cup. "Tell Moultrie to keep the Bojangles ready."

As before, I dropped from the pier, crossed the mud, then side-stepped around the barrel into the creek.

The sheriff was right. The tide was coming in.

The water had crept to a point just below the barrel's brim.

This time we had a plan. I would go underwater and maneuver the lasso under the bottom rim of the barrel. That accomplished, I would hold the up-side while Gullet and Zamzow heaved on two auxiliary lines attached to the down-side.

Though not without mishap, the plan worked. After three tries the second rope looped the barrel. Panting and dripping, I tightened both nooses and tugged, testing. The lines seemed secure.

I signaled to Gullet. Gullet signaled to Miller. Miller called to Tybee. Beyond the pier, the cruiser's engine turned over.

Slowly, the ropes grew taut. The barrel shifted, rocked back into place.

Gullet waved. Miller shouted. The cruiser's engine raced again. Holding my breath, I crouched down like a baseball catcher and pushed on the bottom of the barrel with my shoulders. Nothing budged.

Lungs burning, I pushed again and felt movement.

I surfaced to the sounds of sucking and scraping. The barrel was oozing from the water onto the mud.

With Gullet and me pushing and Zamzow guiding, the barrel crept up the bank, filthy water pouring from gashes in its sides.

One eon and we'd gotten above the high tide line. Another and we'd moved from mud to solid ground. When we finally crested the bank, Miller was waiting with her camera and a hand trolley.

Wordlessly, Leland Moultrie indicated a spigot beside his veranda. Thanking him, I moved to the house, stripped off the waders, bent at the waist, and ran water through my hair and over my face. Oswald Moultrie appeared from inside and offered me a towel. I almost hugged him.

When I returned from my cleanup, Miller was still snapping photos. I watched fluid ooze from the barrel, wondering about the person inside. Had he or she been dead decades? Years? One full moon? Was the body bloated and discolored from its time in the sea? Had scavengers slithered, crawled, or swum through fissures in the metal, long ago stripping the flesh from the bones?

If a full autopsy was impossible, would Emma ask that I examine the bones?

Did the queen like bad hats?

A sudden thought. Could the body in the barrel be one of Cruikshank's MPs?

A terrible thought. Could it be Helene Flynn?

A clapper rail called from some hidden perch. Its rattle snapped me back to the present.

Miller was snugging her trolley to the barrel. Gullet pushed, raising one side, and the prongs slid beneath. With Tybee and Zamzow spotting, Miller wheeled her cargo off to the coroner's van.

That was it. I'd done my part. Miller and the deputies could load the damn thing.

The clean, dry deputies.

Leaning on Tybee's cruiser, I laced on my sneakers. Then I crossed to Gullet's Explorer, dug out my pack, and dragged a comb through my hair.

I caught my image in the rearview. Mascara had been a really bad idea.

Tybee and Zamzow stayed behind to shoot video and walk the area, and to continue interrogating the Moultries. Gullet and I followed Miller to the MUSC morgue, a plastic sheet separating us from the Explorer's seats.

While I showered and changed into scrubs, Miller offloaded the barrel. Fifteen minutes after arriving, I rejoined her at the intake area just inside the rolling metal doors.

"Where's Gullet?" I asked.

"Got a call."

"From his couturier?"

Miller laughed. "Could be. Sheriff's mindful of his appearance, and that don't mean mud up his gumpy. I suspect he may also be detailing that SUV of his. You're to let him know what we find."

"You phone Emma?"

Miller nodded. "Coroner says open her up. Allocation's my call. Either you or one of our pathologists wins the cigar."

"You sticking around?"

"Wouldn't miss it."

Miller logged the case and prepared an ID marker, CCC-2006020299. I positioned the card while she shot close-ups of the barrel and chain.

"Chain's in good shape." Miller was squinting through her viewfinder. "Barrel's a bucket of rust."

"The two could be made of different metals."

"Or could be a new chain wrapping an old barrel."

A puddle spread across the cement as we worked, carrying with it the smell of decay. When Miller finished with photography, we both inspected the barrel's exterior. As she'd predicted, any words or logos were long gone.

"There must be lots of companies that manufacture fifty-five-gallon drums," I said.

"Dozens," Miller agreed.

After snapping a few Polaroid backups, Miller disappeared, returned with a crowbar and chain saw.

"OK, sweetie, how do you want to go about this?"

"No reason we can't just knock it open," I said.

"Worked for Larry and Moe." Miller pulled on big leather gloves, crowbarred one edge, then tried to lever the lid. The thing stayed put.

"You whacked this sucker pretty good," Miller said.

"I had a little adrenaline working."

After prying more edge, Miller inserted the crowbar and thrust down on the shaft. Half the lid popped free, sending wet rust particles cascading downward. Miller inserted her fingers, tugged at intervals along the lid's perimeter, then yanked upward. The metal disc came away in her hands.

An old, damp smell rose from the barrel. Rotten seaweed. Stale salt water. And more. The smell of death.

Setting the lid on the concrete, Miller picked up a flashlight, and we both leaned in.

The form was human, but not human, a grotesque reproduction in waxy white. It sat humped over, head between its knees.

Miller's nostrils narrowed. "You may be off the hook on this one, doc."

I wasn't so sure. In the presence of moisture, the hydrogenation and hydrolysis of body fat can lead to the formation of matter containing fatty acids and glycerol. This greasy, sometimes waxy substance is known as adipocere, or grave wax.

Once formed, grave wax can hang around a long time, forming a cast of the fatty tissues. I'd seen corpses in which adipocere preserved the body and facial features, while putrefaction turned the insides to soup.

"Body was put in feet first, then shoved down," Miller said.

"Or the victim was forced to climb in and squat," I said.

"Naked."

"Looks small." I spoke without thinking, caught up in the usual swirl of sadness and anger.

"Female?" Taut. Miller was swirling with me.

"I'd rather not speculate."

But I already knew. I'd seen too many ravaged wives, coeds, stepdaughters, waitresses, hookers. My gender was the little guy, the one who took the punches.

"Lots of sand," I said, refocusing my anger. "Probably used to weight the barrel."

"Rocks would have been a better choice," Miller said. "One whack with a boat propeller, one erosion point, sand's outta there. Probably why the thing became buoyant and washed up."

"Let's get her on a table," I said.

Together we lowered the trolley so it lay parallel to the concrete, moving carefully, as though afraid to jostle the occupant. Pointless. She was past caring.

Miller donned goggles, revved the chain saw, and cut the barrel lengthwise from rim to rim on two sides and the bottom, removing the section immediately overlying the body.

The remains were back-side down in the barrel's lower half, head tucked between tightly flexed legs. I could see abrasions in the adipocere where the knees and shins had scraped against the drum's inner surface.

While I'd showered and changed to scrubs, Miller had draped a gurney with plastic sheeting. Removing her goggles and leather gloves, she now wheeled it into position. Together, we shifted the gurney's removable tray to the floor beside the barrel. When we'd pulled on surgical gloves, I took the head and Miller took the buttocks.

"Ready?" Tense.

I nodded.

We lifted an inch, testing. The soapy flesh held.

"OK," I said.

We lifted another inch, then another, tugging gently at any resistance. Slowly, the barrel released its prisoner. We held a moment, allowing fetid liquid to drip. I nodded. Stepping sideways, we lowered the body and raised the tray. I circled the gurney.

Though the flesh was grotesquely distorted, the hair and skin sloughed, the genitals told me the victim was, indeed, female. Her time in the barrel had left her molded into a fetal curl.

Crazy, but the woman seemed to be shielding herself from the indignities her unnatural death would call down upon her. From me. From Miller. From the army that would gather to reconstruct the horror of her final moments, to detail the destruction wrought by her watery confinement.

Some part of me wanted to cover this woman, to protect her from the gowned figures, the glaring lights, the flashing bulbs, the gleaming instruments. But the rational part of me knew that would do her no good. Like the man on Dewees, and the man in the trees, the woman in the barrel needed a name.

I vowed to give that to her. To find the identity that would link her with the living. To end the anonymity that kept her from being mourned, from having her suffering recognized.

Working together, Miller and I eased the woman from her side to her back. I waited while Miller shot pictures. Then, using gentle pressure, we tried to manipulate the tightly clasped limbs.

"Poor gal's kinked like a cement contortionist," Miller said. "This may take muscle."

We increased our pressure. One by one, the arms yielded and we straightened them at the woman's sides.

We shifted to the legs. While Miller pushed on

the right knee, I pulled on the ankle. The rigor yielded.

As the woman's leg straightened, a glob slid from her belly and settled by her hip.

*Thup.*

Miller voiced my thought.

"Holy hell, what's that?"

# 20

"Let's lower the other leg," I said.

Miller took the knee. I took the ankle. Together we unlocked and straightened the limb.

The belly was a chasm of putrefied jelly, emitting a stench that could have emptied whole villages.

Breathing through my mouth, I circled the table.

The glob was the same greasy white as the woman's flesh, but covered with silky brown wisps.

I checked the woman's thighs. Brown wisps spiderwebbed her flesh.

Threads? Hair?

I poked the glob. It felt somewhat firm, but slough-prone, like overripe fruit.

Or flesh.

Sudden insight.

Using a fingertip, I scraped up and examined several wisps.

Fur.

As Miller watched, I dug into the glob and extricated one scrawny limb. Then another.

Miller's eyes widened. Wordlessly, she found the hind legs, and, together, we uncurled the small creature. Hairless, bloated, and marinated in decompositional runoff, its species was unrecognizable.

"Fido, Felix, or Flopsy?" Miller asked.

"It's not a rabbit. The face is flat and the fore and hind limbs are equal in length." I probed the nether regions and extracted a long, thin tail. "Let's check the teeth."

While I held the head, Miller pried the jaws.

"It's a cat," I said.

I pictured Birdie. I looked at this woman, dumped in a barrel with her pet like so much garbage.

I fought the urge to slam my fist into the stainless steel. I closed my eyes.

*Focus, Brennan. You will further the investigation only if you focus.*

"Let's find out who she is," I said.

Miller wheeled the gurney up the ramp and into the hospital. I followed and we ascended to an autopsy room. First off, I checked the fingers to see if we could recover any prints or print fragments. Not a chance.

Miller rang a tech to request X-rays. While the body was gone we both filled out forms. Neither of us spoke.

When the X-rays arrived Miller popped them onto wall-mounted light boxes. While she and the tech transferred the woman's body to an autopsy table, I moved along the row, examining gray and white images of her insides.

The brain and organs were mush. The eyes would yield no vitreous fluid. This case would be strictly skeletal. My baby.

I focused on the bones. I saw no obvious fractures or anomalies. No surgical implants, pins, or plates. No foreign objects. No bullets. No metallic trace.

No teeth or dentures.

"We won't be needing Bernie Grimes," I said. "She's edentulous."

"Senior citizen?" Miller asked.

"Middle-aged, not geriatric," I said, distracted by what I was seeing on the last two films.

Miller came up beside me.

"Gold star for diligence, Kyle," she threw over one shoulder to the tech who had shot the X-rays. "Good angles on the kitty."

"I wasn't sure—"

I cut Kyle off. "Look at this." I pointed to a white spot the size and shape of a small rice kernel, dead center below the cat's neck.

"That an artifact?" Miller asked.

I shook my head. "It shows up on both plates."

Double-checking the feline X-rays, I got a scalpel, returned to the gurney, and made an incision. Thirty seconds of probing produced a tiny cylinder. I held it on my palm for Miller and the diligent Kyle.

"I know you're going to tell me what that is," Miller said.

"Pet ID chip, properly known as a transponder."

Miller looked at me as though I'd said it was a snakebot designed to maneuver through space.

"The device consists of a miniaturized coil and memory circuit encased in biocompatible glass. It's implanted using a hypodermic syringe, just under the skin, between the shoulder blades."

"By controllers of the Matrix?"

"By veterinarians. The procedure takes less than a minute. My cat has one and he hasn't a clue."

"How's it work?" Miller sounded skeptical.

"The chip's memory circuit contains a unique preprogrammed identification number, which can be read by a scanner. The scanner sends a low-power radio signal to the coil, which sends a copy of the ID number back to the scanner. The number can be checked against a central databank, where the pet's ownership records are kept."

"So if Fluffy takes a powder, Fluffy's owner gets her back."

"If Fluffy is lucky enough to get bagged and scanned."

"Isn't that an irony. Easier to trace a cat than a human being. What's the shelf life?"

"Theoretically, the chip can function up to seventy-five years."

"Who's got these gizmos?" Dawning comprehension.

"Vets. Animal shelters. SPCAs. They're pretty common."

"So the dumb sonovabitch may have left the proverbial smoking gun."

I nodded. "As least as to an ID of the victim."

Miller produced a ziplock and I deposited the capsule. She turned to Kyle.

"Find me a vet who can scan this thing."

While Kyle disappeared in search of a phone, Miller and I resumed our examination of the body.

"Think she's white?" Miller asked, looking at what remained of the face.

"The cranial X-rays suggest Caucasoid skull and facial architecture."

"What's telling you middle-aged?"

"Moderate arthritis. Bony spicules where the ribs attach to the breastbone. Think you can harvest the pubic symphyses?"

"With guidance." Miller went in search of a striker saw.

I centered a rubber headrest behind the woman's neck. Her face provided scant clue to her appearance in life. The eyelids were gone, the orbits filled with the same waxy material that clung to her bones. No lashes, brows, or head hair remained.

Miller returned. While I snapped photos, she removed the pubic symphyses, then took them to find a soaking container. I was shooting a facial close-up when something caught my attention. Setting the camera aside, I leaned in.

A groove circled the woman's neck, penetrating a quarter inch into the crumbly flesh. The groove was narrow, less than half the width of my little finger.

Postmortem? An impression created by contact with something in the barrel? Damage due to marine scavengers?

Grabbing a magnifying lens, I ran a finger over the furrow. The edges were clean and well defined. No way the indentation had been caused by nibbling creatures.

I heard a door open, close, then footsteps. Miller said something. I didn't look up. I was following the furrow's path, checking its orientation. Checking the flesh above and below.

The groove was horizontal, with an irregular enlargement on the left side of the neck. Abrasions nicked the surrounding tissue.

"What's so intriguing?"

I handed Miller the glass. She studied the groove. Then, "This what I think it is?"

"Horizontal furrow. Defensive fingernail scrapes."

"Ligature strangulation?"

I nodded.

"What kind of ligature?"

"Smooth, round cross section, small diameter. Maybe a wire of some kind."

The grooved flesh jogged loose a memory. Cruikshank dangling from an oak in the Francis Marion National Forest.

Miller must have had the same thought. "What about hanging?"

"With hanging, the furrow rises to a suspension point. This one's horizontal all the way around."

I studied the woman lying in a puddle on stainless steel. The usual signs of asphyxia had been obliterated by decomposition and saponification. There were no petechia from increased venous pressure. No indicators of cyanosis. No tissue hemorrhage. No trachea, no esophagus, no muscle to section. Nothing that would allow a pathologist to definitively conclude that death had been caused by strangulation.

"When the bones are stripped I'll examine the larynx, especially the hyoid and thyroid cartilages. But, given what I see, I'm reasonably certain."

My brain flashed another snapshot image. The Dewees bones. Tiny nicks. When the woman's flesh was removed I'd also take a hard look at her vertebrae and ribs.

Miller changed the subject. "Kyle found a vet who can scan your capsule."

"Where?"

"Block and a half from here. Dr. Dinh." Miller stuck a yellow Post-it to one of the glass-fronted cabinets above the counter. "Says he'll be in his office until five thirty. Then he's off for the long weekend."

I'd totally forgotten. Monday was Memorial Day. The clock said four thirty. I had to hurry.

Crossing to the counter, I removed the pubic bones from the bowl in which Miller had placed them to soak. The cartilage detached easily, allowing me to see that both symphyseal faces were smooth, with some depression relative to their rims.

Miller watched expectantly.

"Yep. Just north or south of forty." I pulled off my gloves and lowered my mask. "Gotta catch Dinh before he heads out. When will the skeleton be fully cleaned?"

"Monday morning."

"I hate to ask you to work on a holiday weekend," I said.

Miller laughed. "Sweetie, I've got nothing planned but a Home Depot jaunt."

"You're a saint."

"Patron of spackle and Spic and Span. In the meantime, what do I tell Gullet?"

"Tell him she's a middle-aged white woman who was strangled and stuffed in a barrel with her cat."

Dr. Dinh shared a pink stucco strip mall with an electronics shop, a cell phone vendor, an insurance office, a dollar store, and a video rental outlet. Yellow lettering on the window identified the Animals Love Care Veterinary Clinic.

My exhausted mind started playing games. Animals love care? Loving care for animals? Love and care? Priced separately? Package deals upon request?

I really needed a bubble bath and dinner.

Luck was with me. On my second drive-through an SUV backed out of one of the dozen slots. I pulled in.

As I entered the clinic, a woman brushed past with a rat-size Chihuahua cradled in one arm. The rat kicked into, what? Yapping? Even yapping doesn't adequately capture the shrillness.

Dinh's waiting room was an extravagant eight by ten. Straight ahead was a faux-bamboo-fronted counter with a circa '83 PC on top. No one was working it.

Beyond the counter were two closed doors, each with a Lucite holder appropriate for depositing charts. Muffled voices floated from behind one door. A waiting file suggested a presence behind the other.

Painted wooden chairs lined the wall to one side of the counter. An old man occupied the farthest on the right. An old beagle slouched against his leg.

A woman occupied the farthest chair on the left, a turquoise pet carrier on the linoleum by her feet. Through the carrier's door I could see something with beady black eyes and whiskers. A ferret?

My watch said five fifteen. Things were looking bad for Dinh's five thirty exit.

Gramps and the beagle visually tracked me to a middle chair. The woman continued thumbing her BlackBerry. The ferret-thing retreated into shadow.

Taking up a cat magazine, I settled back.

I was two pages into an article on thwarting feline blanket sucking when a woman exited room one accompanied by twins and a golden retriever. Moments later a small man with a shiny brown head emerged through the same door. He wore silver-rimmed glasses and a blue lab coat labeled *Dinh*.

Dinh invited ferret woman to enter the space vacated by Mom and the boys.

I stood.

Dinh approached and asked if I was the one with the chip. I began to explain. Hand-flapping me quiet, he held out a palm. I gave him the ziplock, and he disappeared into examining room two.

I sat, wondering how long I'd be cooling my heels.

It went like this.

Five fifty-six. Woman and poodle exit room two.

Six oh four. Gramps and beagle enter room two.

Six twenty-two. Ferret woman exits room one.

Six forty-five. Gramps exits room two, sans beagle.

At 7:05, Dinh reappears and hands me a piece of paper. On it were written two names: "Cleopatra" and "Isabella Cameron Halsey." I assumed the former was the late feline, the latter its late owner. Below the names was a King Street address.

I thanked Dinh. Coolly. I'd long since passed the threshold for niceness. My request had probably taken the man five minutes. He could have done it first and sent me on my way. Instead he'd made me wait two hours.

Minutes later I was jammed up in traffic near the Old City Market. I'd been so irritated with Dinh I'd cut down the Peninsula, not up toward the bridge.

I made a turn. Another. The streets were narrow and clogged with tourists. I wanted to be home, not creeping along behind a horse-drawn carriage. I was annoyed with my own stupidity. I was tired, grubby, and wanted to cry.

I passed a gray stone church with a towering steeple. St. Philip's. OK. I was on Church Street. I had my bearings. Despite Old Dobbin, I was making progress.

The buggy slowed. Over the hum of my AC I heard the driver's muffled voice, presumably concocting stories about landmarks. My stomach growled. I added hungry to my list of complaints.

Finger-drumming the wheel, I looked out the passenger-side window. Tommy Condon's Irish Pub. Patrons dining on the porch. They looked happy. Clean.

My gaze drifted to Tommy's lot. Fell on a Jeep.

My fingers froze.

I checked the plate. My heart kicked in extra beats. I had to get out of the car.

My eyes darted from curb to curb. Not a chance of finding a spot on Church. Where was the entrance to Tommy's lot?

Dobbin was clopping along at the speed of mud. There was nothing I could do but follow.

Finally, I rounded the corner. One street up, I found a gap and jammed the car in.

Slamming the door, I broke into a run.

# 21

Ryan was at a porch table, smoking. In front of him were the remains of a cheeseburger basket and an empty beer mug. A small metal disc held multiple butts, suggesting he'd been at the pub for some time.

Not good. Ryan relapsed to cigarettes only when anxious. Or angry.

*Keep it light.*

"You from around here, handsome?" Light, bubbly, and strained as hell.

Ryan's face swiveled toward me. Something flicked in his eyes, then disappeared before I could read it.

I gestured at a chair.

Ryan shrugged.

I sat.

Ryan ground his cigarette into the disc.

"Snowbird migrating south for some sun and sand?" I persisted.

Ryan didn't smile.

"Why didn't you come inside at Anne's house Wednesday night?"

"I'd booked for the ghost dungeon walking tour."

I ignored that. "You're avoiding my calls?"

"Reception problems."

"Where are you staying?"

"Charleston Place."

"Nice."

"Thick towels."

"I'd prefer you bunk at Anne's."

"Pretty crowded."

"It's not what you think, Ryan."

"What do I think?"

Before I could answer a waitress appeared at our table.

"Hungry?" Ryan's offer was delivered with all the warmth of a supermarket cashier.

I ordered a Diet Coke and Ryan asked for a Palmetto Pale Ale.

OK. He wasn't jumping up to hug me, but he wasn't leaving. Fair enough. I knew my reaction had I driven fourteen hundred miles to find him cuddling his ex.

But I hadn't been cuddling Pete. Ryan was exhibiting all the self-assurance of a pimply eighth grader.

We sat in silence. The night was humid and windless. Though I'd changed to clean scrubs before leaving the hospital, these, too, were beginning to feel damp and clingy. Irritation started to surface.

Reason raised a restraining hand. When the waitress brought our drinks, I decided to approach from another angle.

"I had no idea Pete would be coming down or that we'd be here at the same time. Anne invited him. It's her house and I was scheduled to leave the day he arrived. That's probably why she didn't mention it. The place has five bedrooms. What could I say?"

"Keep your pants on?"

"That's not how it is."

Ryan raised a palm, indicating he didn't want to hear.

That gesture launched a resurgence of the irritation impulse.

"I've had a rough week, Ryan. You could cut me some slack."

"You and hubby devise some sort of calamity scorecard? One point for sunburn. Two for a bad Pinot. Three for ants during the picnic on the beach."

Occasionally, I give myself good advice. Example: Don't get irritated. Often I ignore that advice. I did so now.

"Haven't you just spent a week in Nova Scotia with your former lover?" I blurted.

"Pretend I just slapped my forehead in surprised realization of your concern."

Hot. Hungry. Tired. Lousy at diplomacy in the best of moods. I really lost it.

"I've just learned a friend is sick, probably dying," I snapped. "A reporter is hounding me and a developer is threatening me. I've been sucked into three homicides. I've spent the last seven days either in an ER, at a morgue, or slogging through muck in search of putrefied bodies." A bit of an exaggeration, but I was on a roll. "Wednesday night I suffered an emotional implosion. Pete was concerned and offered comfort, which I badly needed. Sorry for my timing. And sorry to bloody hell I bruised your fragile male ego."

Out of breath, I sat back and crossed my arms. In my peripheral vision I could see the couple to our right staring. I glared at them. They turned away.

Ryan lit up again, drew deeply, exhaled. I watched the smoke spiral up toward an overhead fan.

"Lily told me to piss off."

"What? What do you mean? When?" Stupid, but Ryan's segue to his daughter had caught me off guard.

"We got into an argument sometime after you and I talked on Sunday. Started over some dolt with studs sticking out of his face. Hell, I don't even remember. Lily stormed out of the restaurant, said I was ruining her life, hoped I'd leave and never come back."

"What does Lutetia think?"

"I should back off and give Lily space for a while." Ryan's face was a stone mask. "I spent all day Monday and most of Tuesday trying to talk to the kid. She wouldn't see me or take my calls."

I leaned forward and placed my hand on his. "I'm sure it'll be fine."

"Yeah." Ryan's jaw muscles bunched, relaxed.

"Lily needs time to get used to the idea of you as her father."

"Yeah."

"It's been less than a year."

Ryan did not reply.

"Do you want to talk about it?"

"No."

"I'm glad you decided to come here."

"Oh, yeah." Ryan gave me a mirthless smile. "*There* was a great idea."

"I was a head case Wednesday night. Self-pity, pity for others, tears, the whole bit. When you arrived, Pete was trying to settle me down. That's it. Nothing more. I'm sorry about my lousy timing."

Ryan didn't respond. But he didn't pull back.

"I wouldn't lie to you. You know me."

Still, Ryan remained silent.

"It was nothing, Ryan."

Ryan toyed with his cigarette ash, rolling it on the edge of the metal disc. A full beat passed. Another. Ryan broke the silence.

"After Lily's rejection, I was filled with guilt. I felt like a failure. The only person I wanted to be with was you. The decision was simple. I hopped in the Jeep and headed south. Then, after driving twenty hours, to see you there in the yard . . ."

Ryan left the thought unfinished. I started to speak. He cut me off.

"Maybe I overreacted Wednesday night, let anger rule the moment. But I've realized something,

Tempe. I don't know my daughter. OK. I buy the blame for that. But I don't know you, either."

"Of course you do."

"Not really." Ryan took a drag, released the smoke. "I know *about* you. I can quote your résumé. Brilliant anthropologist, one of a handful in your field. Undergrad at Illinois, Ph.D. from Northwestern. DMORT experience, U.S. military consults, genocide expert for the UN. Impressive bio, but none of that gives any hint of how you think or what you feel. My daughter's a blank canvas. You're a blank canvas."

Ryan slid his hand from under mine and picked up his mug.

"I've shared a great deal more than my résumé," I said.

"You're right." Ryan drained half his beer. To calm his anger? To collect his thoughts? "You married Pete the barrister at age nineteen. He was a cheat. You were a boozer. Your marriage went bust. Your daughter's a university groupie. Your best friend's a realtor. You have a cat. Like Cheetos. Hate goat cheese. Won't wear ruffles or stilettos. You can be caustic, hilarious, and a tiger in bed."

"Stop." My cheeks were on fire.

"I've pretty much run the list."

"You're not being fair." I was too exhausted mentally and physically to protest with much vehemence. "And it's deliberate."

Placing his forearms on the table, Ryan leaned close. In the still air I could smell male sweat, aftershave, and a hint of the cigarettes he'd smoked.

"We've been friends for a decade, Tempe. I know you feel passionate about your work. Otherwise, most of the time, I'm clueless about what you feel. I have no idea what makes you happy, sad, angry, hopeful."

"I follow the Cubs."

"See what I mean?" Slumping back, Ryan stubbed out his cigarette and chugged his beer.

Tight bands squeezed my chest. Anger? Resentment?

Fear of closeness?

I sipped my Coke. Silence roared between us.

The waitress looked our way but knew better than to interrupt. The couple beside us paid their check and left. Another horse clopped by on Church. Or maybe it was the same horse I'd followed in my car. My mind slid sideways.

Did the horse mind walking the same brainless loop? Did it dutifully obey day after day out of fear of the whip? Did it pass the time dreaming equine dreams, or did it know only the world between blinders?

Was Ryan right? Did I wall myself off? Had I put on emotional blinders? Barricaded myself against troubling memories and troubling issues of the present?

A sudden pang struck deep in my chest. Was Pete one of those issues? Was I being fully honest with Ryan? With myself?

"What is it you want?" My mouth felt dry, my throat constricted.

"Lutetia was very curious about you. I didn't have answers for most of her questions. That surprised her. I said the things she was asking about weren't important. She told me that might be true, but, nevertheless, I should know them.

"Motoring solo allows for a lot of introspection. On that long drive I came to understand that Lutetia is right. There are areas of non-communication, Tempe. Our relationship has borders."

Relationship? Borders? I couldn't believe I was hearing this from Andrew Ryan. The bad boy. The player of the field. The Don Juan of Montreal homicide.

"I don't intentionally keep things from you," I mumbled.

"It's not *what* a person shares, but *that* a person shares. Intentional or not, you often close me out."

"I don't."

"Why do you call me Ryan?"

"What?" The question threw me. "It's your name."

"My last name. My family name. Other cops call me Ryan. The guys in my hockey league. You and I have been as intimate as two people can be."

"You call me Brennan."

"When we're working as professionals."

My eyes remained fixed on my hands. Ryan was right. I didn't know why I did that. A distancing measure?

"What is it you want?" I asked.

"We could start with conversation, Tempe. I

239

don't need a busload. Just tell me things. Begin with family, your friends, your first love, your hopes and fears . . ." Ryan threw up a hand. ". . . your views on mind and anomalous monism."

I ignored the attempt at a lighter touch.

"You've met Katy. Anne. My nephew Kit."

Harry.

In the early years, when Ryan was inviting and I was declining personal involvement, my sister, Harriet, came to Montreal in search of Nirvana. She ended up sandbagged by a cult, and Ryan and I saved her ass. One night the two went missing, and, I suspect, did the biblical deed. I've never inquired. Neither Ryan nor Harry has ever explained.

"And Harry."

"How is Harry?" Ryan's voice sounded a fraction less taut.

"Living in Houston with a harpsichord maker."

"Is she happy?"

"She's Harry."

"Introduce me to your parents." Dr. Phil prompting a talk show guest.

"Michael Terrence Brennan, litigator, connoisseur, and good-time drunk. Katherine Daessee Lee, known to one and all as Daisy."

"Thus your unpronounceable middle name."

"Like Daisy, with a soft *s*."

"Daisy. I kind of like—"

"Don't even think of saddling me with that moniker."

Ryan flourished two scout's-honor fingers.

240

I swallowed and began.

"Michael's Chicago Irish, Daisy's old-line Charlotte. College sweethearts, they marry in the fifties. Michael signs on with a big Chicago law firm and the happy couple settle in Beverly, an Irish neighborhood on Chicago's south side. Daisy joins the Junior League, the Ladies' Auxiliary, the Rosary Society, and the Friends of the Zoo. Temperance Daessee, their firstborn, puts an end to Mrs. Brennan's social ambitions. Harriet Lee follows in three years. Three more, and it's Kevin Michael."

Almost four decades and the pain still sliced me in two. I was aware I was speaking in third-person present tense, but couldn't help myself. Somehow the ploy helped. Ask Freud.

"Nine months later, baby Kevin succumbs to leukemia. Devastated, Daddy sets a land speed record for the single-malt sprint into unemployment, cirrhosis, and an overpriced coffin. Mama retreats into debilitating neurosis, eventually slinks back to Charlotte with young Temperance and Harriet. The trio take up residence with Grandma Lee."

Ryan reached out and thumbed a tear from my cheek. "Thanks." Spoken so softly, I barely heard.

"Next installment, the Charlotte years." I arced a hand, suggesting a movie marquee.

Pub sounds swirled around us. Seconds passed. A minute. When Ryan's gaze met mine some of the tension had eased in his face.

Leaning back, Ryan raised his brows as though

seeing me for the first time. The man loved raising his brows. And it worked for him. Gave him an air of unruffled curiosity.

I imagined my appearance. Smudged mascara. Tear-streaked face. River-rat hair yanked up in a knot.

I knew what was coming. An unspoken question as to today's events. OK. Business. Familiar ground. Neutral.

"It's a long story," I said.

"Involving mud wrestling?"

"Involving a reptile named Ramon."

"Loved Henry Silva as the big-game hunter."

Blank stare.

"*Alligator.* 1980. Heartlessly flushed in his youth, Ramon grows to thirty feet and wants out of the Chicago sewer system. Great film. Classic B creature feature."

"Do you want to hear this?"

"I do."

"Can I have a cheeseburger?"

Ryan signaled the waitress, ordered, then chest-crossed his arms and thrust out his legs, ankles crossed.

"You know about the Dewees skeleton," I began.

"The one your students unearthed."

I nodded. "He was a white male, probably in his forties. Probably dead at least two years. I found an odd fracture on one of his neck vertebrae, and nicks on his twelfth rib and on several lower back vertebrae. He'd had dental work, but nothing popped when we ran his identifiers through NCIC.

Ditto for a match with local MPs. One item of interest. I found an eyelash with the bones. The Dewees guy is blond. The lash is black. Emma's sent it to the state lab for DNA testing."

"Emma?"

"Emma Rousseau is the Charleston County coroner." I couldn't handle discussing Emma right then.

"The Dewees skeleton is body number one."

"Yes. Pete's in Charleston doing a financial investigation and searching for a client's daughter. Helene Flynn disappeared over six months ago while working at a street clinic operated by God's Mercy Church, the brainchild of a local televangelist named Aubrey Herron.

"When Helene vanished, her father, Buck Flynn, hired a private investigator named Noble Cruikshank. Two months into the investigation, Cruikshank pulled his own vanishing act. Cruikshank drank. He'd been on benders before where he just disappeared for a time, so no major search was launched. Last Monday, kids found a body hanging from a tree in a national forest just north of town. We got prints, ran them through AFIS. Bingo. The dangler was Cruikshank, who, by the way, was carrying the wallet of a guy named Chester Pinckney, a local swamp rat."

"Why?"

"No idea. Pinckney says his wallet was stolen. More likely, he lost it."

My cheeseburger arrived. I added lettuce, tomato, condiments.

"Cruikshank was male, white, forty-seven. He had a neck fracture like the man on Dewees. Same vertebra, same side, though the noose was knotted at the back of his head."

"Nicks in the ribs and lower back?"

"No."

I took a moment to devour a significant portion of my burger.

"Gullet, that's the Charleston County sheriff, got Cruikshank's belongings from the guy's landlord. Among them was a disc of photos showing people coming and going from the clinic at which Helene Flynn worked. Another box held files. Some contained the stuff you'd expect on a PI's cases. Notes, canceled checks, copies of letters and reports. There was one file on Helene Flynn. Others held nothing but clippings on missing persons. Still others held only handwritten notes."

"Get much from the notes?"

"Zilch. They're in code. We also have Cruikshank's PC, but so far no password."

"OK. Cruikshank is body number two. When do we get to Ramon?"

I told him about the woman and the cat in the barrel.

"She's white, approximately forty, and probably died of ligature strangulation. The cat was registered to one Isabella Cameron Halsey. I plan to follow that up tomorrow."

"Anything to connect the three cases?"

"The deceased are all white and middle-aged. The two men have identical neck fractures. The woman's been strangled. Beyond that, not really. But I haven't finished with the barrel lady. Her bones won't be fully cleaned until Monday."

Ryan dropped his eyes to the little metal disk filled with cigarette ash. But he wasn't really seeing it. He looked like he was focusing on some thought, coming to grips with some realization.

"You really have pulled the plug on Pete?" he asked.

"I moved out on the man how long ago?" Words chosen carefully.

Ryan's gaze came up and settled on mine. The blue eyes, the sandy hair, the lines and creases in all the right places. Looking like that must be breaking six state laws and a dozen federal guidelines, I thought. What was I doing? Why hadn't I simply said yes to Ryan's question about Pete? Would I now get a brotherly kiss on the cheek and a fond good-bye? My fingers remained tight on the handle of my mug.

Then Ryan smiled.

"Startovers?" he asked in a quiet, calm voice.

"Olee ocean free," I answered, relief flooding through me.

Ryan held out a hand. We shook. Our fingers lingered, then separated slowly.

"My dear old Irish mother gave a lot of thought to choosing my Christian name," Ryan said.

"Don't push it, bucko," I said.

"I'll keep trying."

"Fair enough."

"I'm a detective," Ryan said.

"I know."

"I detect things."

"A special skill."

"I could, if properly persuaded, place my years of experience at your disposal."

"With Isabella Halsey?"

"And the cat. I love cats."

"What sort of persuasion?"

"Persuasive persuasion." Ryan ran one finger across my hand and up my wrist.

I signaled the waitress.

When the bill arrived we both went for it. Ryan won. As he dug out his credit card, I rose and circled the table.

Arm-wrapping Ryan's shoulders, I laid my cheek on the top of his head.

Ryan agreed to move into the house.

# 22

Ryan and I were eating Cap'n Crunch when we heard Pete's bedroom door open.

"Lucy, I'm home!" Desi Arnez boomed across the house. "What's that Jeep"—Pete bounded into the kitchen—"ers creepers."

Boyd jumped up. Ryan did not. The cop and the chow did the eyebrow thing. The counselor shot his to the hairline. Like Desi.

"And who's this nice young man?" A smile tweaked the corners of Pete's mouth.

I made introductions. Ryan half rose and the men shook hands.

Pete was in running shorts, a sweatshirt with the sleeves and neck cut off, and Nikes. Turning his back to the counter, he palmed himself up and sat facing us, lower legs dangling.

"Interesting time at GMC yesterday?" I asked.

"Not as interesting as yours." Pete's gaze slid to

Ryan, back to me. The corners of his mouth again twitched.

I narrowed my eyes in a "don't you dare" warning.

Pete's face went Lucille Ball innocent.

Ryan's attention remained focused on the Cap'n.

"Money in. Money out," Pete said. "I'm of the growing opinion that Daddy Buck needs an accountant, not an attorney."

"Did you speak to Herron?"

"Damndest thing. The rev had to make an unscheduled trip to Atlanta. Unavoidable. So sorry. The staff will do everything they can to help."

"Everything except talk about Helene."

"They talk. What they say is, she was here, she's gone, we don't know, we haven't heard. Maybe California." Pete's feet were swinging, his heels thunking the under-counter cabinets. "Oh. And pray God she's well."

"Have they offered insight on how one of their brethren vanishes leaving no trace?"

"They're sticking with the gospel according to California. There are dozens of street clinics in the land of fruit and nuts, many operated, not surprisingly, by fruits and nuts. They suspect Helene may have abandoned the gospel for the teachings of crazoids and slipped outside the system."

*Thunk. Thunkety-thunk-thunk* went the Nikes.

"It's possible to effectively disappear if she's in some communal living arrangement, using no credit cards, paying no bills, car insurance, taxes, or social security."

"Which would explain the truncated paper trail. Cruikshank reported to Daddy Buck that he'd found nothing postdating last November. At least nothing up until his own disappearance. Anything new on Cruikshank?"

*Thunk. Thunk.*

I shook my head. "Stop banging Anne's cabinetry."

Pete's legs went still for a full ten seconds. He turned to Ryan.

"You drive that Jeep all the way from Canada?"

"Her name's Woody."

"Long trip."

"Tough on her. Her heart's back in the Adirondacks."

Blank stare.

"Must be a tree thing."

"Funny." Pete's face came back to me. "He's a funny guy."

Now I gave Ryan the eye squint warning.

"Did you learn why Cruikshank had that other guy's wallet?" Pete asked.

*Thunk. Thunk.*

"Chester Pinckney. No, we didn't."

"Good day yesterday?"

I described the recovery of the woman in the barrel.

"A gator's no match for you, sugar pants."

"Do not call me that."

"Sorry."

*Thunk. Thunk.*

I told Pete about the strangulation, the cat, the chip, and Dinh. Ryan listened and watched. I knew his philosophy. People speak two languages, only one verbal.

"How's Emma?" Pete asked.

"She took a pass."

"Still bad?"

"I've got to call her."

Pete hopped down, raised a heel to the counter, and began stretching. Ryan fluttered his lashes at me, a swooning deb. I repeated my eye squint.

"What's your next move?" I asked Pete.

"Beach run with Boyd. Then golf."

"Golf?"

Pete switched legs. "Tomorrow is Sunday, Herron will be back for the big show. That's when I climb into the ring for some divine intervention."

"Your metaphor is mixed."

"My results won't be."

"You're feeling pretty cocky."

"Relax, I'm wearing a jock strap." Lowering his leg, Pete winked in my direction.

Major league eye roll.

Seeing the leash unpegged, Boyd went wild. Pete squatted, hooked his collar, then rose and pointed in my direction.

"Have a really special day."

Pete and chow disappeared.

From beyond the door. "Sugar britches."


We took Ryan's Jeep into Charleston. He drove. I

directed. On the way, I told him about my long friendship with Emma, about the curious rapport that kept us bonded, despite long periods of noncommunication. I shared the secret of Emma's lymphoma. He suggested a visit after we'd been to Isabella Halsey's house.

I also told Ryan about Dickie Dupree and Homer Winborne. He asked my level of concern, on a one-to-ten scale. I gave the developer a five, the journalist a minus two.

I remembered a comment from our discussion the night before.

"What's anomalous monism?"

Ryan gave me a look of feigned disappointment at the gap in my schooling. "It's a type of dualism in the philosophy of mind and action. Mental processes have genuine causal powers, but the relationships they enter into with physical entities can't be explained by the laws of nature."

"Like our relationship."

"There you go."

"Hang a left here. Why Woody?"

Ryan shot me a questioning look.

"When did you name your Jeep Woody?"

"This morning."

"You made that up."

"Inspired by GI Joe."

"Pete was a Marine. And don't say ridiculous things to him. I don't want him thinking you're a clown."

Isabella Halsey lived on King Street, deep in the heart of old Charleston. As usual, that district was crowded with people who looked like they'd arrived on the Donald Duck parking shuttle. Women in designer sundresses, or in shorts that barely covered their cheeks. Men with large bellies and mesh baseball caps blankly gazing, or talking on cell phones while wearing golf shirts and eighteen-hole tans. Sunburned kids. Hand-holding newlyweds, or weds-to-be.

The Old City Market was a hive of activity. Ice cream peddlers jangling their bicycle bells. Black ladies selling flowers and sweetgrass baskets, or offering to cornrow your hair. Husbands shooting footage of Mom and the kids. Retirees puzzling over walking-tour maps. Teens pointing throwaway Kodaks at each other. Vendors hawking beans, pralines, and peach preserves.

Halsey's address was just off the Battery, a harbor-front commons complete with statues, cannons, and a Victorian bandstand. The little park always strikes up a Sousa march in my head.

It also strikes up memories of fourth grade history with Sister Mathias. It was from the Battery, in April of 1861, that Charlestonians watched Confederate soldiers battle Union troops holed up across the water at Fort Sumter. *Bonjour*, Civil War. Some historical preservationists have yet to say *adieu*, and fight to preserve the Confederate flag and to sing "Dixie."

After parking, Ryan and I headed south on East Bay. Past Rainbow Row, we took Tradd three blocks inland to a narrow brick-paved portion of Church.

Unlike Cruikshank's humble digs, Halsey's home would have warranted the name "Magnolia Manor." Window boxes overflowed with flowers, and the side yard was crowded with the spreading breadth of the grand old trees.

Though realtors would use the terms "authentic," "original," and "uncorrupted" to describe the house itself, "handyman's delight" popped into my mind. The beige stucco, black shutters, and wrought iron fencing all needed paint. The walkway and courtyard pavers were green with infiltrating moss.

Approaching the gate, Ryan and I were enveloped in the fabled blossom scent.

"Washington log some Z's here?" Ryan asked in a low voice.

"The general did sleep around."

Through the magnolias, I could see a woman sitting at a side yard table, her white hair dappled with sunlight. The woman was knitting. Though her jaw, neck, and arms had the loose, wrinkled tissue of the elderly, her hand movements were strong and confident.

"The lady in the barrel was around forty," I said. "If the victim is Halsey, that could be her mother."

Ryan laid a hand on my shoulder. I looked at him. The Viking blues held an expression I couldn't read. A recognition of my caring? An acknowledgment that I did, indeed, feel things deeply?

Ryan nodded encouragingly.

"Excuse me," I called into the courtyard.

The woman's head came up, but she didn't look our way.

"Sorry to bother you, ma'am." I hesitated, unsure what words to use. "We're here about Cleopatra?"

The woman turned toward us. Sunlight on her glasses masked the expression in her eyes.

"Ma'am? May we speak with you a moment?"

The woman hunched forward and her mouth tightened into an inverted U. Setting her knitting on the table, she waved us into the yard. As Ryan and I crossed to her, the woman pulled smokes from a pocket and lit up.

"Join me?" The woman offered a pack of Davidoff mini-cigarillos.

Ryan and I declined.

"Lord in heaven with all his angels and saints." The woman flapped a blue-veined hand. "You young folk run from tobacco, take the caffeine outa your coffee, the cream outa your milk. Sissies. That's what I call y'all. Sissies. Want some sweet tea?"

"No, thank you."

"Cookie?"

"No, thank you."

"'Course not. Might be real butter in those cookies. From a real cow." To me. "You a model, buttercup?"

"No, ma'am." Why was I always targeted for nicknames?

"Oughta be. You're skinny enough." The woman placed her free hand under her chin and

254

smiled up through lowered lids, Lana Turner posing for a studio shot. "Miss Magnolia Blossom, 1948." Chuckling, she drew a cigarillo hit. "A few of my parts sag a touch now, but this old gal had every chin in Charleston wagging back then."

The woman pointed at a wrought iron bench. "Set yourselves."

Ryan and I sat.

"Lemme guess. You and this young man are researching the lifestyles of Dixie's rich and famous?"

"No, ma'am. I—"

"I'm pulling your leg, buttercup. Get to it. Why are you and handsome asking after dead Egyptians?"

"I'm speaking of a cat."

The wrinkled eyes narrowed, then widened behind their lenses.

"You referencing my Cleo?"

"Yes, ma'am."

"You found my wandering cat?"

Leaning forward, I placed a hand on the old woman's knee. "I'm so sorry to have to tell you this. Cleo is dead. We located your address through an ID chip implanted beneath her skin." I took a deep breath. "Cleo's body was found with that of a woman. We suspect the dead woman was Cleo's owner."

A glint came into the wrinkled old eyes. I braced for tears.

"Isabella Halsey?" the woman asked.

"Yes."

I expected heartbreak, anger, disbelief. I got none of those.

The woman chuckled again.

Ryan and I glanced at each other.

"You think this old gal's shuffled off."

I sat back, confused.

"You're right and you're wrong, buttercup. Poor Cleo may be pushing up daisies with her mistress. But that unfortunate soul sure as the Lord in heaven isn't me."

Déjà vu. Wadmalaw Island. Chester Pinckney.

Twice in one week? I felt my face redden.

"*You* are Isabella Cameron Halsey?" I guessed.

"Alive and kickin'." Pulling wadded tissue from her décolletage, Halsey blotted her cheeks. "Or at least knittin'. About all that's tolerable on a scorcher like this."

"Cleopatra was your cat?"

"She surely was."

"You had the chip implanted?"

"I surely did." Theatrical sigh. "Sadly, Cleo loved another."

"What do you mean?"

"Hard as I tried, that cat was never content with me. Just had to roam, the furry little slut." Halsey eyed Ryan coyly. "Pardon my French, sir."

"*Pas de problème, madame.*" No problem. Ryan's accent was over-the-top Parisian.

Halsey fluttered her lashes. Ryan beamed her a smile.

"What happened to Cleopatra?" I asked.

"I tired of unrequited love. One day, I just

opened the door and set her free."

"Do you know what happened to her?"

"She took up with another."

"Do you know who?"

"'Course I do. I used to see them together at the park."

The name provided our first big break.

# 23

"One doesn't cross paths with a whole passel of Uniques in one's lifetime. Name like that stays to mind."

I felt a ripple of excitement. Two of Cruikshank's files contained only coded scribblings. One of those bore the name Unique something.

"What was Unique's surname?" I asked, voice neutral.

"The lady was not on my Christmas card list." Halsey's spine stiffened ever so slightly. "Unique was Cleo's friend. I suppose the two formed a bond, both loving the streets and all."

"What can you tell me about her?"

"Speaking frankly, which I always make it my habit to do, that kitty's brain was centered in her southern parts, if you take my meaning."

"I meant Unique."

"Of course you did. Let's just say our perspectives differed. Our life experiences."

"Oh?"

Halsey lowered her voice, a well-bred lady dissing one who is not of her class. "Poor thing pushed her belongings around in a supermarket cart, bless her heart."

Another Southernism. Hitch the phrase "bless her heart" to its bumper, and any slur becomes mannerly.

"Are you saying Unique was homeless?" I asked.

"Most likely. I never pried. That would be rude." Halsey grinned at Ryan. "Are you certain you wouldn't like a nice sweet tea? Maybe some Snapple?"

Ryan grinned back.

"No, thank you," I said. "When was the last time you saw Unique?"

Halsey tapped her chin with one finger. The joints were knobby, the skin nicotine yellow. "Been a while since I've noticed. These people do change neighborhoods like other folks change socks."

I didn't reply to that.

"Four, maybe six months? My sense of time's not what it once was."

"Did you ever speak with Unique?"

"Once in a blue moon. On occasion I gave the poor creature food."

"How did you learn Unique's name?"

"Asked a neighbor, seeing as the lady had my cat and all. Said he encountered her now and again over to the Catholic cathedral."

"How old was Unique?"

"Old enough she should have been cutting that

hair. Long just doesn't work on women of a certain age. But there I go again, judging other folks." Halsey turned to Ryan. "But you know what? I'm eighty years old, and pretty damned good at it."

Ryan nodded understanding.

"A certain age?" I asked.

"Hard to tell for certain. The gal was a bit unkempt. But she wasn't a beneficiary of the youth charities, that's a sure fact."

"Is there anything else you remember?" I asked.

"She had no teeth, bless her heart."

My heart kicked into high gear as Halsey kept talking.

"To be honest, I probably resented Unique, Cleo being so fond of her and all." Halsey's shoulders slumped. "There's simply no telling the feline heart. Cleo could have lived in high cotton with me. Didn't matter a twit. Off she went."

"I have pets. I know that must have made you sad."

"Unique did give Cleo a lavish of love. Strapped that cat to her chest with one of those contraptions young mamas use for toting their babies."

Catching Ryan's attention I shifted my eyes toward the gate. Ryan nodded.

"Thank you so much for your time, Mrs. Halsey."

"It's Miss. Never married."

"Sorry," I said.

Halsey mistook my meaning. "Don't be. You can't imagine how little I care."

Ryan and I rose. Halsey pushed to her feet and

accompanied us across the courtyard.

"If this dead woman is my Cleo's Unique, it truly grieves me. Isabella Halsey's not one for grudges." The wrinkled face broke into a smile. "Except for that ingrate cat."

Repeating my thanks, I exited the gate. Ryan followed. As I secured the latch, Halsey spoke again.

"Forgiveness is the fragrance that the violet sheds on the heel that has crushed it. Isn't that the loveliest thought?"

"It is," I said.

"Do you know who penned those words?"

I shook my head.

"Mark Twain," Ryan said.

Halsey smiled up at Ryan. "You must be a Southern boy."

"Canadian," I said.

Halsey's smile melted into puzzlement. We left her to ponder the wonders of cross-border literacy.

"What do you think?" Ryan asked when we were back in the Jeep.

"Privilege can be inordinately selfish."

"But graciously genteel. Especially here."

"We Southerners pride ourselves on manners."

"You think your barrel lady is this street woman Unique?"

"Cleo was with her. The unknown was edentulous. Unique was edentulous. But there's more." I told Ryan about Cruikshank's two files that contained nothing but notes.

"What was that Unique's last name?"

261

"I don't remember."

"What was the name on the other file?"

I shook my head. I was dialing my cell phone.

"Calling Macho Gazpacho?"

Eye roll.

Pete answered on the third ring.

"Sugar br—"

"Are you still at Anne's house?"

"I'm great, thanks for asking. The workout was terrific. Boyd says to say hi."

"I want you to find something in Cruikshank's files."

"Am I allowed to know why?"

I outlined what we'd learned from Isabella Halsey, and described what to look for among Cruikshank's folders. Pete said he'd check and call back. Minutes later my cell rang.

"Unique Montague and Willie Helms."

"Thanks, Pete."

I clicked off and gave Ryan the names.

"Worth a visit to the cathedral?" he asked.

"It's just up at Broad."

Leaving the Jeep on Legare, Ryan and I crossed to the church. As we climbed the steps, Ryan indicated one of two stained glass windows above the front entrance.

"The papal coat of arms."

I indicated the other window. "The seal of the great state of South Carolina."

"High cotton." Ryan held the *i* at least four beats.

"You just learned that phrase from Halsey."

"It's a good one."

"Don't abuse it."

John the B's was quintessential cathedral. Carved oak pews and white marble altar. Windows depicting the life of Christ. Organ the size of the international space station.

Air that smelled of flowers and incense.

Flashback. Sunday Masses. Gran and Mama in chapel veils. Harry and I thumbing mother-of-pearl First Communion missals.

"—try the good father over there."

Ryan's voice brought me back. I trailed him toward the altar.

The priest was small, with high cheekbones, almond eyes, and softly accented speech that employed no contractions. Though he identified himself as Father Ricker, I suspected an Asian connection somewhere up the family tree.

After introductions, I inquired about Unique Montague.

Ricker asked the reason for my interest.

I told him that a woman's body had been found, and that it might be that of Unique Montague.

"Oh, dear, dear me. I am so sorry." Ricker crossed himself. "I am parochial vicar here at St. John the Baptist. Unfortunately, my knowledge of individual parishioners is limited. But I did occasionally speak with Miss Montague."

"Why was that?"

Embarrassed grin. "Miss Montague had a cat. I, too, am a lover of cats. But then, perhaps our brief meetings were part of God's greater plan."

Ryan and I must have looked confused.

"Perhaps the good Lord directed me to Miss Montague so I could later help with her mortal remains."

"Can you describe Miss Montague?"

Ricker's description fit.

"When did you last see her?" I asked.

"It has been awhile. This past winter sometime."

"Do you know if Miss Montague has family in Charleston?"

"I believe she has a brother." Ricker's eyes went from me to Ryan, then back to me. "I am sorry. We spoke only infrequently, when I was on the grounds and she needed water for her cat."

Ricker was friendly enough, but cautious, always taking a few seconds before responding.

"Would the church have records?" I asked. "An address? Next of kin?"

Ricker shook his head. "Miss Montague was not an official member of this congregation. I am sorry."

"Thank you, Father." Digging a card from my purse, I jotted my cell phone number and handed it to him. "Please call if you think of anything."

"Yes. Of course. So sad. I am so sorry. So sorry. I will pray for her soul."

"Think Ricker's sorry?" Ryan asked as we walked toward Broad.

"Fivefold. Though I may have missed a few before starting my tally."

"What's a parochial vicar?"

"A provincial parson?"

"The Vicar Ricker."

Ryan unlocked the Jeep. I got in and buckled up. The inside temperature was at least seven thousand degrees.

"What next?" Ryan slid behind the wheel.

"AC."

"Yes, ma'am." Ryan cranked the knob. "I jus' love driving Miz Tempe."

"How about this? We buy take-out and have an early lunch with Emma. I shoot the names Unique Montague and Willie Helms to Gullet. While the sheriff works that angle, you and I take another look at Cruikshank's files."

"Sounds like a plan."

Only things didn't go that way.

Gullet was out. I left a message with his switchboard.

Emma didn't answer her home phone. After tracking her down at the coroner's office, I went into my now familiar harangue about stress and rest.

"Relax. I'm limiting myself to non-life-threatening paperwork. Lee Ann filled me in on your encounter with Ramon the Reptile."

"Did she mention Cleopatra the Cat?"

"She did. Lead go anywhere?"

I told Emma about the trail from Dinh to Isabella Halsey to the homeless woman named Unique, and described Cruikshank's unsolicited missing persons files.

"So the Helms and Montague files didn't even contain news clippings?"

"Nothing but handwritten notes."

"Why was Cruikshank investigating Helms and Montague if there were no media reports on their disappearances, and no one hired him to do so?"

"Interesting question."

"Let me get this straight. You think the barrel lady could be Halsey's Unique, and that that Unique could be Cruikshank's Unique Montague."

"Two-part question, Madam Coroner. As to Part A, what are the odds on the cat? As to Part B, Unique's not exactly a common name."

"Worth following up," Emma said.

"I've already started. A priest at St. John the Baptist thought Halsey's Unique had a brother somewhere in the Charleston area. I'll feed that to Gullet. In the meantime, could one of your people take a crack at locating dental records for Willie Helms?"

"Why?"

"Cruikshank was looking into two missing persons completely on his own. He didn't even have news stories of their disappearances. Montague was one, and Helms was the other. I'm thinking Helms could be our Dewees unknown."

"It's a long shot, but I'll get Lee Ann on it. She's superb at sweet-talking dentists."

"You could have been the recipient of crab Rangoon and shrimp lo mein."

"Got a Moon Pie and a Pepsi."

"Probably why you're sick."

"Have a good one."

We did. On the patio at Poogan's Porch. Shrimp and grits for me, chicken Charleston for Ryan. My cell phone rang as we were leaving.

"Dr. Brennan?"

"Yes."

"Father Ricker. At St. John the Baptist."

"Yes, Father."

"Sullivan's Island."

"I'm sorry?" Jesus. It was catching.

"Miss Montague's brother lives on Sullivan's Island. I kept trying to recall her words that day. I remembered that something in our conversation made me think of my childhood. I prayed, and God answered. Sullivan was the name of my very first cat. Sullivan's Island."

"Thank you, Father. That's very helpful."

"The Lord does work in mysterious ways."

"Yes."

Ryan tried Lily as I tried Gullet. He had no luck. I did. This time, the sheriff was in.

I relayed Ricker's information. Though not enthused, Gullet said he'd have an investigator canvass the Montagues on Sullivan's Island.

When I'd disconnected, Ryan asked, "Did you tell me Cruikshank was staking out some treatment center?"

"A clinic operated by GMC. Helene Flynn was working there when she vanished."

"Cruikshank had Unique Montague's name on a file."

"He did."

"Cruikshank was surveilling a free clinic."

267

"Not a verb. But, yes, he was."

I saw where Ryan was going.

"The clinic provides medical care to the poor and homeless. Unique Montague was poor and homeless." Excited, I twisted toward Ryan. "Maybe that's the connection that interested Cruikshank."

"Maybe."

I couldn't escape the feeling that there was more to it than that.

"This may sound crazy, but something in my gut tells me my two unknowns are linked to each other and to Cruikshank. Maybe even to Helene Flynn."

"I see the Cruikshank–Flynn–clinic link, with maybe a Montague tie-in, but how would the Dewees man fit in?"

"I'm not sure."

"This linkage theory is based on what?"

"Intuition?"

Ryan shot me a "give me a break" look.

I threw up my hands. "Doesn't that define gut feeling?"

Chest-crossing my arms, I slumped back. Ryan was right. Nothing really hooked all four cases together. Cruikshank and Dewees both had the peculiar neck fractures. That linked them. Maybe. Maybe it was coincidence.

The Dewees skeleton had nicks, Cruikshank didn't. I'd sure as hell check the barrel woman's ribs and vertebrae on Monday.

The woman in the barrel was probably Unique Montague. Cruikshank had Montague's name in his files. He had Helene Flynn's name in his files. That connected Flynn and Montague to Cruikshank.

Cruikshank had Willie Helms's name in his files. Could the man on Dewees be Willie Helms? If so, he was linked to Flynn and Montague via Cruikshank.

Was the man on Dewees linked to Cruikshank by the odd neck fractures? If so, was he linked to the others by association with Cruikshank? Was the similarity in fracture patterning simple coincidence? Lots of "if"s swirling around without any "then"s.

I didn't believe in coincidence. What did I believe in?

Hard evidence. Demonstrated facts.

Problem. We had none. Or none that established links. Bone nicks. Neck fractures. An eyelash in a snail shell. Hand-scribbled notes.

A computer disc.

"There are photos of people entering and leaving that clinic," I said. "Cruikshank saved them to CD."

"Was Helene Flynn in any of the images?"

"No," I said. "But Unique could be."

"Where's the disc?"

"Gullet's office."

Suddenly, I was in a froth to revisit that disc.

# 24

JPEG thirty-three showed a woman exiting the brick building. She had oddly puckered lips and hair tangled wildly around her face.

She also had an infant carrier strapped to her chest.

I couldn't believe I'd forgotten the image.

We were in the sheriff's office. I'd introduced Ryan, explained that he was a cop, and vouched for his discretion. Gullet had been cordial but cool. Or maybe he wasn't listening. It was impossible to read the guy.

This time we were using my laptop to view the CD. Gullet was peering over my shoulder. Ryan was seated on the far side of the room.

"What's that?" Gullet pointed to a shadow curving from the lower end of the baby carrier.

I enlarged the image to full screen and zoomed in. Though the shadow became a hodgepodge of tiny rectangles and squares, it was clear that something solid was snaking from the carrier.

"Cleopatra's tail," I said.

"You sure?" Gullet monotoned behind me.

"Look at the alternating bands of light and dark. I know cats. Those are stripes ringing a cat's tail."

"I'll be jigswiggered."

I peeked over the monitor at Ryan. His brows lifted ever so slightly. I lowered mine. *Don't say it.*

"What's the story on this Montague woman?" Gullet asked, still studying the patterned curl that was Cleopatra's appendage.

"You know what we know." I began clicking through the rest of the pictures. "Any luck locating the brother?"

"We've found seventeen Montagues in the metro area, none on Sullivan's. We're working the list. Saying we find this guy, will Miz Rousseau manage to pull DNA from the barrel DOA?"

"Yes."

Gullet said nothing. Jigswiggered speechless?

"Who runs this clinic in the images you're viewing?" Ryan asked.

"God's Mercy Church," I said.

"I mean on a day-to-day basis. Who's there on the ground?"

Behind me, I felt Gullet reorient toward Ryan. "My apologies, but your affiliation again, sir?"

"Lieutenant-detective, Major Crimes, Quebec Provincial Police," Ryan said.

Gullet was silent a moment, as though thinking about that. Then, "Oh. Canada."

271

"We stand on guard for thee."

I jumped in.

"I work with Detective Ryan in Montreal. He's visiting in Charleston this week. As long as he's here, I thought I'd get his view of things, just in case I was missing something obvious."

"Homicide?" Gullet asked Ryan.

"Yes. We just change the pronunciation."

"May I ask what brings you to Charleston?"

"Got some time. Thought I'd drop by, help you streamline the department."

Gullet's eyes narrowed maybe the breadth of a hair. Mine narrowed considerably more.

"You been working the murder squad long?"

"Yes, I have."

"You choose that?"

"Yes, I did."

"You know why?"

"Yes, I do."

"Lieutenant Ryan is regarded as one of the best homicide detectives in Quebec," I said. "His input could help. Bring a fresh perspective."

Gullet's body language told me he wasn't buying it. I laid it on thicker.

"I've seen Detective Ryan crack cases that had been stalled for months. He has an uncanny ability to read crime scenes and to penetrate the minds of perps."

"Miz Rousseau good with his involvement?"

"She is."

"Hell's bells, we're going to have more guests than regulars 'fore I know it."

Silence filled the room. I was about to break it when Gullet spoke again. To me.

"He screws up, it's on you. And the coroner."

"I trust him."

"I'm not signing your check, sir. Your input's strictly unofficial."

"And exceedingly discreet," Ryan said. "All homicides interest me, Sheriff, and if I can help without getting in your way, I'd like to."

"Long as we understand each other." Gullet showed not a trace of expression. "Might as well come on around, Detective. Have yourself a look."

Ryan got up and joined us. I set my computer to slide show mode. Gullet spoke as Ryan viewed the images.

"Clinic's on Nassau. GMC owns the building and equipment, provides an operating budget, hires and fires employees, but otherwise stays pretty much hands-off. Place is open Tuesday through Saturday, handles mostly colds and minor injuries. Anything more serious gets routed to a hospital ER. The staff is small, one full-time nurse, one drop-by doc, some cleaning and clerical personnel."

"Who are they?" I asked.

Gullet crossed to his desk, picked up and opened a manila folder.

"Doc's name is Marshall. Nurse is Daniels. Woman named Berry handles paperwork and supplies. Guy named Towery does cleaning."

I was about to ask a question when a woman appeared in the doorway.

"Sheriff, you said you wanted a heads-up on complaints from the Haeberles. Marlene's cater-wauling on 911. Says John Arthur's whacking on her again."

"She OK?" Gullet asked.

"John Arthur's on another line. Says Marlene's blinded him in one eye with a wooden spoon."

"They drinking?"

"Does my hound Tyson scratch his fleas?"

"Merry hell." Gullet looked at his watch. "Tell Marlene and John Arthur I'm riding over there myself. And I best not find they've got tequila on board."

The woman withdrew.

"We serve and protect," Gullet deadpanned to Ryan and me. "Even our own blockheaded trailer-trash in-law kin."

"May I save these images?" I asked, pointing to my laptop.

Gullet nodded.

After creating a folder, I uploaded Cruikshank's pictures to my hard drive. As my computer shut down, I changed topics.

"Did you find anything on Willie Helms?"

"I've got an officer asking around at the shelters. Refresh me. What's our interest in this boy?"

"While investigating Helene Flynn, Cruikshank was gathering information on Willie Helms, Unique Montague, and a number of other MPs. I believe he was pursuing something on his own."

"Uh-huh." Skeptical.

"Emma's looking for a dentist who might have

treated Helms," I said. "The man on Dewees had a lot of fillings."

"It's one hellacious long shot."

A lot of folks were pointing that out.

"*One* of the best detectives in Quebec?"

"Don't believe anything I said in there. It was all hype."

"Jigswiggered?"

"You knew what he meant."

Ryan pulled into traffic. For a Saturday afternoon, there was quite a bit. "Is that a bad thing? To swigger a jig?"

"Under certain circumstances."

"Or were plural jigs wiggered? Perhaps he really meant to swig a jigger."

I punched Ryan's arm.

"That's an assault."

"Arrest me."

"Now what?" Ryan asked.

"Cruikshank, Flynn, and Montague all tie in to that clinic, but Gullet doesn't want any wingtipped cowboys harassing the staff."

"I'm strictly a loafer man."

"He meant Pete."

"The cute little tyke."

Twenty minutes later we were back on the Peninsula, in a run-down section between the historic district and the Cooper River Bridge. The *quartier* featured low brick and frame bungalows, sagging porches stacked with rusted appliances, here and there a plywood-boarded window or door.

Ryan spotted the redbrick building first. Pulling to the curb, he cut the engine.

The clinic was a plain box with rusty ACs jutting from the windows and abandoned lots on both sides. In keeping with the hood, there were no shutters, no signs, not an architectural frill of any kind. The interior blinds were closed, as on the day Cruikshank's photos were snapped.

As we watched, the front door opened, glinting late-afternoon sunlight from the tinted plate glass. An old woman emerged and began picking her way along the walk.

Shielding my eyes with one hand, I scanned up and down Nassau, following sight lines out from the clinic door. Half a block north was a bus shelter. Half a block south was a phone booth. Through the dingy glass I could see the receiver dangling by its cord.

"Pics were probably shot from the phone booth and the bus stop," I said.

Ryan agreed. We got out and crossed the street.

The building looked seedier on actual viewing than it had on the disc. I noticed a window crack patched with gray duct tape. The tape was curled at the edges, suggesting the patch had been there awhile.

Ryan held the door and we both entered. Inside, the air was warm and smelled of alcohol and sweat.

The reception area held rows of Kmart vinyl chairs, two of which were occupied. A woman with a black eye. A kid with one of those unfortunate goatee things on his chin. Both were coughing and sniffing. Neither bothered to look our way.

The receptionist did bother. She was about my age, tall and muscular, with mahogany skin and up-slicked frizz that was black at the roots and bronze at the tips. I assumed this was Berry, CEO of paperwork and supplies.

Running through Cruikshank's images, I spotted Berry in my mind's eye—JPEG 7. The tall black woman with the blond hair.

Seeing us, Berry straightened and set her jaw. Perhaps she'd already given last call. Perhaps our appearance suggested we weren't there for Pepto.

Ryan and I crossed to the reception desk. I smiled at Berry. Her face remained hard as a Hell's Angels logo. She wasn't fingering brass knuckles, but it was close.

I introduced myself. "I'm Dr. Brennan. This is Detective Ryan. We're working with the Charleston County Coroner's Office, investigating the possible death of a woman who may have been Unique Montague."

"Who?"

I repeated the name.

Berry's eyes were black-brown, the whites yellow as stale beer. I watched them rove down, then back up my body. The movement nudged the jittery little temper trigger in my brain.

"We have reason to believe Miss Montague was a patient at this clinic," I said.

"Do you?"

"Was she?" I tried but failed to keep the irritation from my voice.

"Was she what?"

I turned to Ryan. "Are my questions unclear, Detective? Maybe too ambiguous?"

"I don't think so," Ryan said.

I turned back to Berry. "Was Unique Montague a patient at this clinic?"

"I'm not saying she was, not saying she wasn't."

Again, I turned to Ryan. "Maybe it's my manner. Maybe Miss Berry doesn't like the *way* I'm asking the questions."

"You could try being more polite," Ryan said.

"Friendlier?"

Ryan shrugged.

Swinging back to Berry, I smiled the friendliest of smiles. "If it's not too inconvenient, would you mind sharing with us what you know about Miss Montague?"

Berry's eyes bore into mine. I definitely disliked what I saw in them. I also disliked the fact that she was right. Ryan and I had no official jurisdiction, and Berry had no reason to cooperate with us. Nevertheless, I maintained my bluff.

"Do you know what's really, really fun?" I gave Berry another big smile. "Visits to the police station. The officers give you free soft drinks, doughnuts if you're lucky, and a cozy little room all to yourself."

Flipping her pen onto her appointment book, Berry sighed dramatically. "Why do you want to know about this Montague person?"

"Her name has surfaced in connection with a police investigation concerning a dead body."

"Why her name?"

"I don't think that's relevant." To Ryan. "Do you think that's relevant, Detective?"

"I don't think so."

Leaning back, Berry crossed tree-trunk arms on a double-D chest. "You work for the coroner?"

"I do."

"Better haul out a body bag."

"Why is that?"

Berry looked to Ryan. "You two are such a scream I might die laughing right here in this chair."

"That's a very old line," I said.

"I'll hire new writers."

"Let's start over. Unique Montague may have come in with a cat on her chest."

"Lots of our patients have parasite problems."

Obviously, this wasn't working. Mention Helene Flynn? Noble Cruikshank? Bad idea. If a connection existed, such questions could raise the alert Gullet wished to avoid.

"I'd like to speak with Dr. Marshall," I said.

"He won't talk about patients." Realizing her mistake, Berry corrected herself. "If this Montague *was* a patient, which I'm not saying she was."

"She was."

We all three swiveled toward the woman with the shiner.

# 25

The woman was watching us from under half-mast lids, one swollen and discolored. Her skin was sallow, her cropped black hair spiked out in clumps.

"You're acquainted with Unique Montague?" I asked.

The woman raised two palms. Her nails were chewed, her inner elbows welted with sinewy scars. "I said she come here. Nothing more."

"How do you know that?"

"I spend half my life waiting at this dump." The woman glared at Berry. "Don't matter if you're dying."

"You're not dying, Ronnie." Berry's tone was cold and unfeeling.

"I got the flu."

"You're a junkie."

I intervened. "You spoke to Unique Montague here at this clinic?"

"I don't waste no breath on whackos. Heard this whacko talking to a big brown cat. Called herself Unique."

"You're sure?"

"I heard you askin'. I laid down an answer."

"When was she here?"

One bony shoulder hitched.

"Do you know where she lives?"

"Whacko told the cat they was going to some shelter."

"Which shelter?"

"I look like a fucking social worker?"

"Language," Berry admonished.

Ronnie's mouth clamped into a thin, tight line. Kicking out her feet, she laced her fingers on her belly and lowered her eyes.

Goat-chin spoke without raising his head from the wall. "Someone gonna see me, or should I just go home and mail my snot to y'all in a baggie?"

Berry was about to respond when a door opened, footsteps clicked, and a man entered from a hallway to the right of her desk. The man held two charts.

"Rosario. Case."

Hearing his name, goat-chin asked, "You the doc?"

"No."

A smirk crossed the kid's face. "Nurse Nancy?"

"Daniels. Corey Daniels. You got a problem with male nurses?"

When goat-chin opened his eyes, the smirk evaporated. For good reason.

If Berry was big, Daniels was bigger. I'm not talking NBA tall and skinny. This guy looked like Sasquatch in scrubs. His hair was pulled back in a sumo knot, and a line of tattoos snaked from his biceps to his wrist.

"Sorry, man." Goat-chin lost all interest in eye contact. "I feel like shit."

"Uh-huh." Daniels shifted to Ronnie. "You living out another dose, sunflower?"

"I got a fever."

"Uh-huh. Both of you follow me."

"Mr. Daniels," I said, as Ronnie and goat-chin pushed to their feet.

"Yo." Surprised, as though noticing Ryan and me for the first time.

"They're asking about some woman named Unique Montague." Berry's voice seemed a bit louder than necessary.

"And they are?"

"Coroner and a cop."

"Got ID?" Daniels asked Ryan.

OK. The nurse was more shrewd than the secretary. Or not. I produced my UNCC faculty card. Ryan flashed his badge. Daniels barely glanced at either.

"Wait while I situate these patients."

Whatever "situating" involved, it took twenty minutes.

When Daniels returned, he again spoke only to Ryan. "Dr. Marshall wants you to come back in an hour so he can talk to you personally."

"We'll wait," Ryan said.

"Could take longer." Daniels kept his eyes steady on Ryan.

"We're patient people."

Daniels gave Ryan a "suit yourself" shrug. When he'd gone, I took a shot at a ceasefire.

"May I ask how long you've been with this clinic, Miss Berry?"

Sullen stare.

"How many patients do you treat each week?"

"If this is a job interview, I'm not applying."

"I'm impressed with GMC's commitment to the poor."

Berry put a finger to her lips and shhh'ed me. The gesture jiggled that limbic switch.

"You must be very devoted to the organization's aims to do this type of work."

"I'm a saint."

I wondered how saintly she'd be with my boot up her ass.

"Have you worked at other GMC clinics?"

Eyeing me coldly, Berry pointed at the Kmart chairs.

"What? Am I speaking in a rude manner again?" Barely holding my temper in check.

Again, Berry jabbed the sit command.

The little bundle of axons triumphed. The switch engaged.

"How did it work? You got the front desk when poor Helene vanished?"

Berry turned away.

I was conjuring an even more stupid quip when Ryan laid a calming hand on my shoulder. I had done exactly the sort of thing Gullet had warned against. Gratuitously disclosed information without getting anything in return. Chagrined, I settled into the chair next to Ryan.

Berry got up and locked the front door, then returned to her desk and busied herself shuffling paper.

Ten minutes dragged by.

Goat-chin appeared clutching a small white bag. Berry let him out. A short time later it was Ronnie.

Now and then I'd glance up and catch Berry watching us. Her eyes would flick away and paper would rustle. The woman seemed to have a lot of paper.

At seven, I rose, paced, resumed my seat.

"You think Marshall slipped out the back?" I asked Ryan under my breath.

Ryan shook his head. "The pit bull's still guarding the front."

"Did I?"

Ryan gave me a quizzical look.

"Slip out. Leave. Daniels acted like I wasn't here."

"The pit bull noticed you."

I glared at Ryan.

"OK. The staff lacks some people skills."

"GMC should look for a twofer, get their up-front tag team sensitivity training."

"I thought you weren't going to ask about Flynn," Ryan said with just a hint of reproach.

"I wasn't. Daniels pissed me off. Berry pissed me off. And it occurred to me that if they worked here

284

together, Berry and Flynn might have confided in each other."

Ryan looked dubious.

"They could have been friends." More petulant than I intended.

Slumping back, I chewed a thumbnail. Ryan was right. It was unlikely Berry and Flynn had much in common. And, to be honest, I hadn't really thought it through that far. It was an impulse question, sparked by anger. Maybe I'd tipped our hand needlessly.

"You want to take Marshall?" I asked.

"My involvement is strictly unofficial." Ryan mimicked Gullet's monotone drawl.

"You think this is a waste of time, don't you?"

"Maybe. But I sure enjoy seeing you kick ass."

"I'm certain it was Montague in that barrel. I just want to get a take on the clinic staff."

"I apologize for keeping you so long."

Ryan and I looked up to see a dark-haired man in the hallway entrance. Though of average height, he was heavily muscled, and wore a white lab coat, gray slacks, and Italian shoes that probably cost more than my car.

"Dr. Lester Marshall. Sorry, but my nurse failed to get your names."

Ryan and I stood. I made introductions, leaving our affiliations vague. Marshall didn't ask. Apparently Daniels had covered that for us.

"My nurse tells me you're inquiring about Unique Montague. May I ask why?"

Behind us all paper-shuffling ceased.

"We believe she may be dead."

"Let's discuss this in private." To Berry, "Corey has left, Adele. You may go, too. We're through for the day."

The first-floor layout suggested the clinic had started life as a private home. As Ryan and I followed Marshall down the hallway, I noted two examination rooms, a kitchen, a large supply closet, and a bath.

Marshall's office was at the rear of the second floor, perhaps once a bedroom. Four other doors opened off the upstairs corridor. All were tightly shut.

The doctor's space was small and outfitted spartanly. Battered wooden desk, battered wooden chairs, battered filing cabinets, window AC barely keeping up with the heat.

Marshall seated himself at the desk. On it lay a single folder. No photo of the wife and kids. No funny plaque or carving. No paperweight or mug from a medical conference.

I checked the walls. No framed pictures. Not a single certificate or diploma. Not even a state medical license. I thought doctors were required to display those. Perhaps Marshall's hung in an examining room.

Marshall gestured Ryan and me into chairs with a flourished palm. Up close I could see that his hair was styled, not cut, and receding fast. He could have been anywhere from forty to sixty.

"You know, of course, that rules of confidentiality prohibit the sharing of patient information by a health care provider." Marshall showed teeth that were even and brilliantly white.

"Miss Montague was a patient at this clinic?" I asked.

More perfect teeth. Caps?

I pointed to the folder. "Am I correct in assuming that's Miss Montague's file?"

Marshall aligned the bottom of the folder straight with the desk edge. Though his fingers were thick, the nails were manicured. His lower arms suggested time spent at a gym.

"I'm not requesting the woman's medical history," I said. "I'm simply asking for confirmation that she was treated here."

"Would that fact not constitute a part of one's medical history?"

"It's highly likely Miss Montague is dead."

"Tell me about that."

I gave him the basics. Found in the water. Decomposition and saponification. Nothing confidential there. Not my fault if he thought it was an accidental drowning.

Still Marshall didn't open the folder. In the small, warm room I could smell his cologne. It smelled pricey. Like his nurse and receptionist, the guy was annoying as hell.

"Perhaps you'd prefer a warrant, Dr. Marshall. We could alert the media, get lots of airtime for GMC, maybe score you some national coverage."

Marshall made a decision. Or perhaps the decision had been made earlier and the good doctor had been buying time to assess.

"Unique Montague did present here for care."

"Describe her, please."

Marshall's description matched the DOA in the barrel.

"When was Miss Montague's last visit?"

"She came infrequently."

"Her last visit?"

Marshall opened the folder and carefully flattened the flap with one palm.

"August of last summer. The patient was given medication and told to return in two weeks. Miss Montague failed to follow up as advised. Of course, I can't—"

"Do you know where she lived?"

Marshall took his time perusing the file, turning pages and aligning each even with the edges of the others. "She provided an address on Meeting Street. Sadly, it is a familiar one. The Crisis Assistance Ministry."

"A shelter."

Marshall nodded.

"Did she name next of kin?"

"That line is blank." Marshall closed the file and used the same palm motion to press the crease. "That is often the case with our clientele. Unfortunately, I haven't the time to become personally involved with my patients. It's my one regret about the practice I've chosen."

"How long have you been with the clinic?"

Marshall smiled, this time baring no teeth. "We've finished discussing Miss Montague, then?"

"What else can you tell us?"

"The woman loved her dear cat."

Marshall recentered the two halves of his tie. It was silk, probably by a designer I didn't know.

"I am generally present at this clinic for some part of each Tuesday, Thursday, and Saturday. On alternating days I see patients elsewhere." Marshall stood. We were being dismissed. "Feel free to contact me if I can offer further assistance."

"I don't think he liked us." Ryan started the Jeep.

"What was your take?" I asked.

"The guy's a hand washer."

"He's a doctor."

"In the Howard Hughes sense. I'll bet he double-checks locks, counts paper clips, arranges his socks by color."

"I arrange my socks by color."

"You're a girl."

"I agree. Marshall's overly neat. But do you think the poser knows more than he's saying?"

"He admits he knows more than he's saying. He's a doctor."

"And the others?"

"Big."

"That's it?"

"Big and surly."

Reaching out, I cranked the AC.

"And Daniels has done time."

"Why do you say that?"

"Jailhouse tattoos."

"You're sure?"

"Trust me. I'm sure."

289

Maybe it was the heat. Maybe frustration at my inability to produce results. Even Ryan was irritating me.

Or was I irritated at myself for losing my cool? Why had I asked about Helene Flynn? Had mentioning her been a good move or a gaffe? Would word get back to GMC? To Gullet?

My visit could stir things up, maybe force a response from Herron, motivate GMC to cooperate in the investigation of Flynn's disappearance.

On the other hand, my little drop-in could cause problems for Emma. Infuriate the sheriff, and push him to cut me out of the loop.

At least I hadn't divulged details of Unique Montague's death.

No cool. No results.

I leaned back to ponder. I was doing that when my cell phone sounded.

No results? Oh, baby, did we have results.

# 26

Emma sounded more energized than she had in days. When I asked how she felt, it was back to "hellcat."

"Thirty-four calls. Bingo. Lee Ann hits on a dentist holding a Willie Helms chart. Dr. Charles Kucharski. I paid the old codger a visit."

"That's how you limit yourself to paperwork?"

Emma ignored that. "Kucharski was so glad for a visitor I thought he might handcuff me to a wall in a homemade bunker."

"Meaning?"

"I doubt his patient load is overwhelming."

"Uh-huh." I sounded like Daniels.

"Kucharski remembered Helms as a tall pale guy, mid to late thirties, with a lot of tics. Helms's last visit was in April of 1996."

"What kind of tics?"

"Erratic neck and hand movements. Kucharski had to secure Helms's head and wrists to the chair while he drilled and filled. Kucharski thought it could have been Tourette's."

"Did Helms provide contact information? Address? Employer?"

"Helms's father, Ralph Helms, paid the bills. Willie listed that number in his record. When Lee Ann called, the phone was no longer in service. Turns out Helms senior died in the fall of ninety-six."

"Thus the termination of the regular checkups."

"Helms gave his employer as Johnnie's Auto Parts, off Highway 52. Guy named John Hardiston buys junkers, deals in scrap metal, that kind of thing. Hardiston says he hired Helms out of friendship with Ralph, let him live in an old trailer at the back of the yard. Helms took care of the dogs, acted as a kind of security guard. Worked for Hardiston almost ten years, then, one day, just took off."

"When was that?"

"Fall of 2001. Hardiston says Helms was always talking about going to Atlanta, so he didn't think much of it, just figured the guy finally packed up and went. Hardiston says Helms turned out to be a good employee, was sorry to lose him."

"But he didn't try to find him."

"No."

"If Helms died in 2001, that fits with my estimated PMI."

"Our bug guy suggests an outer limit of five years. That was my other news. You want me to read his preliminary report?"

"Summarize."

There were pauses as Emma pulled phrases from the text. "Empty puparial cases. Multiple soil-dwelling taxa. Beetles represented by cast skins and dead adults."

I heard the shuffling of paper.

"Helms's antemortem dental X-rays showed mucho mouth metal, so I picked up the post-mortems and dropped both sets by Bernie Grimes's office. He'll call as soon as he can break free to do the comparison."

Emma paused for effect.

"There's more. Buried in the mound on my desk I also found a fax from the state forensics lab."

"The eyelash yielded DNA?"

"Pleeze. They've only had it since Thursday. But a malacologist looked at the shell."

"Malacologist?" That was a new one on me.

"Expert in clams, mussels, and snails. The thing is"—pause—"*Viviparus intertextus.*" I could tell from Emma's cadence she was reading from the fax. "*Viviparus intertextus* is moderately common in swamps in the South Carolina Lowcountry, but is never found at the beach, in estuaries, or anywhere near salt water."

"So that snail shouldn't have been in that grave," I said.

"The species is strictly freshwater."

"Oooohkay." My mind thumbed through the possibilities. "The vic was killed elsewhere then transported to Dewees."

"Or the body was buried elsewhere, dug up, and moved to Dewees."

"Or the snail dropped from the gravedigger's clothing or shovel."

"All reasonable explanations."

We both mulled the list. Neither of us proposed a reasonable top candidate.

Emma shifted topics. "What's happening with the barrel lady?"

I described our visit to the GMC clinic.

"Gullet's not going to like it."

"No," I agreed.

"I'll take care of it," she said. "And I'll prod him on Helms, though I doubt much will happen over the long weekend."

"You really are feeling better?"

"I am."

"Get some sleep," I said.

After clicking off, I outlined the conversation for Ryan.

"So you and Emma could be three for three on IDs. Cruikshank. Helms. Montague. Know what's called for?"

I shook my head.

"Crab Rangoon."

"Sa-Cha shrimp?"

"Definitely. Shall we offer to feed Clod Clodersocks?"

Orbital roll. "Pete's real name is Janis."

Ryan looked at me.

"Latvian. You sure you don't mind?"

"Wouldn't want an athlete of Janis's stature eating unhealthy fried food."

I called Pete. He was home and hungry.

The idea proved lucrative for Cheng's Asian Garden in Mount Pleasant. Despite my protests, Ryan paid, once again confirming the old adage that women are doomed to perpetual attraction to the same type of man. My current lover and my estranged husband are clones in numerous respects, particularly with regard to picking up the tab. Neither lets me pay. Neither underbuys.

When we arrived at "Sea for Miles," Pete had the kitchen table set, chopsticks and all. Boyd was centered under it. Birdie was observing from the high ground of the refrigerator top.

Pete looked relaxed, his face tanned from hours on the golf course. Ryan and I looked like people who'd spent a long hot day in a Jeep.

"Never know when it could turn chilly," Pete said, nodding fake approval at Ryan's gabardine pants. Though I shot him my usual eye squint warning, I had to agree, wool looked out of place.

"Trip south was spur of the moment. Gotta hit the Gap." Ryan tipped his head at Pete's cargo shorts. "Those are natty."

"Thanks."

"Had some just like that," Ryan said.

Pete started to smile.

"Outgrew them in my teens."

The smile dissolved.

And so on.

As we worked through the shrimp, the Rangoon, and a dozen other selections, I brought Pete up to date on Montague, Helms, and the clinic. He told us he'd arranged for an accountant to help him with the GMC books.

The rest of dinner was a pas de deux of veiled digs. By the time it ended I felt like I'd been in the ring with Ali and Frazier. Nevertheless, when I explained that Ryan and I planned to revisit Cruikshank's belongings, Pete offered to help.

We were clearing the table when my cell rang. It was Emma.

"It's positive. The man on Dewees is Willie Helms."

"Yowza!"

Pete and Ryan both turned, little white cartons in hand.

"So the questions become what happened to Willie Helms, when, and why was he buried out on that island?"

"That's Gullet's department," Emma said.

Closing the cell phone, I told Pete and Ryan about Helms. They both said "yowza."

Ten minutes later it was the sheriff himself.

"Thought I told you not to stir things up at that clinic." As usual, Gullet jumped right in.

"You specified wingtipped cowboys."

"In the context of the girl who run off."

"Helene Flynn vanished. That doesn't mean she's run off."

There was a pause. Then, "Helene Flynn was unstable."

"What?"

"I'm going to discuss this with you once. Then we're going to drop it because that girl's disappearance did not take place within my jurisdiction." Gullet paused again. "When that young lady went missing, her daddy made a life's work of calling my office, demanding an investigation. I talked to Aubrey Herron personally at the time. Before her departure, Helene Flynn had taken to harassing both Marshall and Herron. In the end GMC had to ask her to leave."

"This is the first I've heard of this."

"Herron doesn't like to criticize former members of his flock."

"What was Helene harassing him about?"

"She was convinced Marshall was playing loose with the finances. Herron says he looked into it, found nothing amiss. The young lady just expected too much for the kind of operation his organization could support. Now you forget that clinic. I don't have time to be appeasing irate doctors."

"Marshall called you?"

"Of course he called me. Man was fuming. Said you'd been bullying his staff."

"Our visit hardly constituted bully—"

"And I don't have time to be running herd on you and your boyfriends."

*Easy, Brennan. Let it go. This is not the man to argue with.*

"I think I've got our two remaining MPs ID'd. The barrel DOA is probably the street woman I phoned you about, Unique Montague. Descriptions I obtained from the dead cat's previous owner and from a priest at St. John the Baptist match the profile I constructed from the bones."

297

"Miz Rousseau just called with that news."

There was a burst of static. I waited it out. "Unique Montague was a patient at the GMC clinic."

"So are a lot of folks."

"Flynn and Montague had ties to the clinic. Cruikshank was staking it out."

"'Course he was, he was looking for Flynn. And some bag lady dropping in is hardly grounds for a warrant, that being the point of the place. Talk about this other ID Miz Rousseau discussed."

"The man buried on Dewees is our long shot, Willie Helms. Lee Ann Miller found the dentist. Bernie Grimes did the comparison." I told the sheriff about Helms's father and employer. "Hardiston last saw Helms in the fall of 2001."

I braced for another monotone rant. Gullet surprised me.

"One of my deputies found a vagrant thought he'd swapped a few swigs with a Willie Helms."

"Could he describe the guy?"

"The good citizen lacks his full share of neurons. But my deputy managed to get out of him that Helms was a tall twitchy guy with blond hair and a serious love of hootch."

"That fits with the dentist's recollection. When was the man's last encounter with Helms?"

"Gentleman's oddly coherent on that point. Says it was the day the buildings went down."

I thought a moment. "The Twin Towers?"

"Nine-eleven. Says he and Helms watched coverage in some bar down by the port. Claims he never saw Helms again." Gullet cleared his throat. "Listen, nice work on Montague and Helms. Now back off that clinic. No sense rousing the dogs unless we got cause."

"What's cause?"

Long pause.

"Two patients."

"You don't think—"

"These are not suggested guidelines I'm serving up. Back off, Doc. That clinic's not my jurisdiction. I would have to present the evidence to the city police."

"Cruikshank, Helms, and Montague all turned up dead on your patch."

Gullet said nothing. Of course he knew that. Nevertheless, I pressed my point. "You're saying that if I tie another MP to that clinic, your department will interrogate Marshall and his staff? Or bring in the city police to do it?"

"Right now you've got a disgruntled employee who's probably run off, and the gumshoe her daddy hired to find her. That's not enough. You find some other patient's gone missing, you got my attention. And another thing. You've had that gumshoe's laptop long enough. I'll be collecting it first thing Tuesday."

Dial tone.

Pete and Ryan had been listening to my half of the conversation. I provided Gullet's.

"Why's the sheriff so freaked about the clinic?" Pete asked.

"Gullet strikes me as a letter-of-the-law type,"

Ryan said. "No warrant, no entry. No smoking gun, no warrant."

"Or he's in bed with Herron," I said.

"Maybe GMC's a big contributor to Gullet's campaign chest," Pete said.

Maybe, I thought. Or just a prominent corporate citizen pulling weight.

When the plates had been cleared, I brought Cruikshank's carton to the table and Pete took Helene's file and settled on the couch. As I showed Ryan my spreadsheet, Boyd shifted between the kitchen and the den. Birdie remained on his Sub-Zero mesa.

After adding Unique Montague and Willie Helms to the spreadsheet, I pulled Cruikshank's clientless cases.

"The Helms and Montague files contain only notes," I said.

Ryan glanced through each.

"Others contain only news clippings and notes."

I opened Lonnie Aikman's file, and Ryan and I skimmed Winborne's article.

Ryan thought a moment. "Kucharski thought Helms may have had Tourette's."

"Symptoms fit."

"So he may have been under a doctor's care."

"Maybe."

"Aikman was schizophrenic and on meds," Ryan noted.

"So the article says."

"Prescribed by a doctor."

I got Ryan's meaning. "You think Helms or

Aikman could have been treated at the GMC clinic?"

"It's something to gnaw on. Willie Helms was a long shot and that panned out."

I wasn't really listening. I was remembering. Another MP. Another article. Retrieved by Dumpster-diving in a storm. Name?

Grabbing the tablet on which I'd drawn my spreadsheet, I fanned the pages. A small rectangle fluttered to the tabletop. *Post and Courier,* Friday, May 19.

I read aloud, picking out the salient points for Ryan.

"Jimmie Ray Teal is a forty-seven-year-old male who disappeared on May eighth," I said. "He was last seen leaving his brother's Jackson Street apartment heading for a medical appointment."

Bolting from the table, I dug out a phone directory and thumbed through the *T*'s. There was a Nelson Teal listed on Jackson. I dialed. The phone went unanswered for ten rings. I dialed again, with the same result.

Ryan and I looked at each other.

"Aikman's mother lives in Mount Pleasant," Ryan said.

I went back to the directory.

"No Aikmans in Mount Pleasant, but there's one on Isle of Palms, another in Moncks Corner, and a couple in Charleston."

Ryan dialed the suburbs, while I took Charleston proper. Amazingly, everyone answered. Sadly, no one knew or had heard of Lonnie or his mother.

"I've met the journalist," I said.

"Got his number?"

I scrolled through calls received on my cell. Winborne's number was still there. Phoning him appealed to me about as much as a case of shingles. But at least the bozo hadn't written anything on Cruikshank.

I checked my watch: 10:07. Drawing a deep breath, I dialed.

"Winborne." Distorted, as though through half-chewed caramels.

"It's Dr. Brennan."

"Hold on."

A pop-top whooshed. I heard swallowing.

"OK. Shoot."

I repeated my name.

There was crinkling, then the sound of more chewing. "The lady dug the site on Dewees?"

"Yes."

"Got more than you bargained for on that one, eh, Doc?" Plankton was as annoying on the phone as he'd been in person.

"Mr. Winborne, this past March you wrote an article for the *Moultrie News* concerning the 2004 disappearance of a man named Lonnie Aikman."

"How 'bout that. The chick reads my stuff."

The chick fought the urge to disconnect.

"May I ask why you did a story so long after Aikman's disappearance?"

"You're phoning to tell me that skeleton was ole Lonnie."

"No, I am not."

302

"It is, though, isn't it?"

"No."

"Bullshit."

I waited.

"You still there?"

"I'm here."

"The Dewees stiff's really not Aikman?"

"The remains were not those of Lonnie Aikman."

"But you know who it is."

"I'm not at liberty to release that information. Mr. Winborne, I'd like to know the reason for your interest in Lonnie Aikman."

"You know the drill, Doc." Garbled by spitty mastication. "You scratch my back, I scratch yours. Suddenly, I'm feeling a mite itchy."

I hesitated. What to give the little reptile?

"The man on Dewees has been positively identified through dental records. While I lack the authority to release his name, I promise to encourage the coroner to share that information with you once next of kin notification has been completed."

"That's it?"

"I also promise that if the Dewees skeleton turns into breaking news—"

"Did you actually say breaking news? Like on CNN? Like I could do a spot with Anderson Cooper? Maybe Wolf would invite me to the Situation Room?"

"Mr. Winborne, I—"

"Breaking news! I think I may wet myself."

Winborne's cackling set my nerves on edge.

"I would simply like to know what you learned about Lonnie Aikman."

"Why?"

"The information may be relevant to a death investigation." Through barely parted teeth.

"Whose?"

"I can't tell you that."

"How's Cruikshank fit in?"

"What?"

"The PI found swinging in the Francis Marion. How's he fit in?"

"You reported that Aikman's mother lives in Mount Pleasant, yet I can't find a listing."

"Cruikshank?"

This was going nowhere. I had to give him something.

"Noble Cruikshank's death is being viewed as a probable suicide."

"Probable?"

"The coroner's investigation is ongoing."

"What was he looking at?"

"Cruikshank specialized in missing persons."

"Like Lonnie Aikman?"

"I have no reason to suspect that Cruikshank's death is connected to the disappearance of Lonnie Aikman. Now I'm itching, Mr. Winborne."

"Fair enough. Susie Ruth Aikman remarried. Phone's in her new husband's name."

"May I have the number?"

"Doc, you know better. Giving that out would be violating a confidence, exposing an informant to who knows what."

All my molars were now tightly clamped. "Would you call Mrs. Aikman and ask her to phone me?"

"Sure, Doc. This is going well, don't you think?"

Twenty minutes later he phoned back.

"Four days ago a car was hauled from a creek bed off Highway 176, northwest of Goose Creek. A woman was behind the wheel."

Winborne sounded shaken.

"Susie Ruth Aikman is dead."

# 27

"Cops on the scene found no signs of foul play, figured Susie Ruth fell asleep or konked out and veered off the road."

"How old was she?"

"Seventy-two." All jollity had left Winborne's voice.

"Was she ill? Heart problems? Dementia?"

"Not that anyone knew."

My mind was racing. An unexplained traffic fatality would normally call for a coroner's investigation. Susie Ruth Aikman's body was found on Tuesday. Emma and I had spent that whole day together. Why hadn't she mentioned the old woman's death? She was too ill? Forgot? Didn't see the relevance?

"Look, I wasn't bucking at the bit to crash your dig. That was my editor's brilliant idea. But when you found those bones . . ." Winborne hesitated, as though weighing how much to reveal, how much to hold back. "I've been poking at something for a couple months now."

I waited out another, longer pause.

"I don't want to do this over the phone. Meet me tomorrow."

"Tell me when and where."

"Unitarian Church, corner of Clifford and Archdale. Follow the brick walkway to the path connecting to King. I'll be there at nine. I'll wait ten minutes."

"Do I come solo and dress in black?"

"Yeah, come alone. Wear what you want."

I was treated to another dial tone. Lately that was happening a lot.

While preparing for bed, I told Ryan about my upcoming rendezvous with Winborne.

"Hang a flag on the balcony?"

"Oh, yeah," I agreed. "Very Deep Throat."

Ryan removed my panties and draped them on the deck.

At nine the next morning I was passing through the Unitarian churchyard gates. Ryan was next door at St. John's Lutheran. Bells were gonging at the cathedral, First Baptist, Emmanuel A.M.E., Bethel United Methodist, St. Michael's Episcopal, and First Scots Presbyterian. Really. It's no fluke Charleston's nicknamed the Holy City.

The Unitarian churchyard was like a hothouse gone feral. Lush trees ruled the path. Crepe myrtles, lantana, and daylilies held sway at the cemetery.

307

Winborne was at the spot he'd described, five-o'clock shadow making his face resemble an unwashed ashtray. My guess? Plankton looked unshaven long before stubble was cool.

Winborne watched me approach, a guarded smile on his lips.

"Good morning."

"Good morning," I replied. *This better be good*, I held back.

"Look, I know we got off on the wrong foo—"

"I appreciate your holding the Cruikshank story."

"My editor killed the piece."

I should have known. "What is it you have to tell me?"

"I've been digging into something."

"So you said last night."

Winborne glanced over his shoulder. "Something's rotten in this town."

Did the little twerp really say "rotten in this town"?

"What is it you've been investigating, Mr. Winborne?"

"I'm looking at Cruikshank. I already told you that. What I didn't tell you is that March's story on Lonnie Aikman wasn't my first. I did a piece when the guy first went missing in 2004. Cruikshank dug it up and tracked me down."

"You met with Cruikshank? When?" I wanted to ask how he'd learned of the Cruikshank ID, but put that off until later.

"Last March. Cruikshank came asking about

Lonnie Aikman. You know me, first thing, I gotta know why. Cruikshank wouldn't give, so I had to use my powers of persuasion."

"Itchy and scratchy."

"Name of the game. And I got a nose." Winborne tapped a finger to one nostril. "I see a PI bird-dogging a lead, I figure maybe there's a story. So I start sniffing down the same hole."

An old man shuffled up the path, grunted hello as he passed. We both nodded. Winborne watched the man's retreat, looking as relaxed as a vegan in a stockyard.

"Cruikshank tells me he's looking for some church lady or clinic worker or something went missing last fall, thinks she may have known Aikman. So I tell him about Lonnie, but I'm suspicious, see. Lonnie vanished in 2004. How could this chick have known him? So I follow him, and sure enough, Cruikshank doesn't go places a nun would be hanging."

"Meaning?"

"One night, he parks in a tavern on King's. Real sleaze joint. Second night he's cruising the titty bars, schmoozing the working girls, if you take my meaning."

That made no sense. Cruikshank was hired to find Helene Flynn. Was he doing that? Or sliding into a binge?

"How do you know Cruikshank was on the job?" I asked.

Winborne shrugged.

"Did you confront him?"

Winborne's eyes slid to his shoes, came back to a spot somewhere over my shoulder. "Third night out he spotted my tail."

I could picture that scene, Winborne with his Nikon, Cruikshank threatening to make liver mush of him.

"I played it cool, told him I thought he was feeding me a line, said I'd keep on him until he came clean."

"Cruikshank told you to scram or he'd beat the crap out of you," I interpreted.

"OK. I backed off. So what? You ever meet the dude?"

I'd seen Cruikshank's photo, and had to confess. Though not big, the guy looked wiry and mean. He'd have frightened me, too.

"When was this?"

"March nineteenth."

"What did you tell Cruikshank about Lonnie Aikman?" I asked.

"What his mother told me. Guy was weird, thought government agents had implanted some kind of device in his brain. Used to e-mail everyone from the dog catcher right up to George W. Thirty-four years old, unemployed, lived with his mom. Nice lady, by the way."

"In your article you described Aikman as schizophrenic. Did he take medication?"

"On and off, you know how that goes."

"Do you know where he was treated?"

"Subject never came up."

"You didn't ask?"

"Didn't seem important." Winborne crossed hairy arms over an ample chest. "Susie Ruth worked her whole life for some tailoring service. Maybe she had insurance that she was able to keep him on because of his disability."

"Was she employed at the time Lonnie went missing?"

"She'd been retired for years." Digging into a back pocket, Winborne unfolded a copy of his 2004 article and handed it to me. "Mama Aikman's little boy."

The text provided nothing beyond what had appeared in Winborne's follow-up story. It was the photo that caught my attention.

Lonnie Aikman's eyes were dark and luminous, his mouth wide, his lips parted, revealing widely gapped teeth. Shoulder-length hair. Studded ears. Aikman looked about seventeen.

"How old was this print?" I asked.

"The guy was under the delusion that the CIA was monitoring his brain. Wouldn't let anyone take his picture, trashed every old one he could find. That was copied from a high school shot Susie Ruth kept hidden." Winborne curled the fingers of both hands. "Now you. Give. What's the deal with Cruikshank?"

I weighed my words carefully. "From his files, it appears Cruikshank was looking at MPs in the Charleston area. Some were addicts or sex trade workers, others were not."

"Hookers and druggies drop out of sight all the time." Winborne sounded like Cleopatra's jilted

311

owner, Isabella Halsey. "Gimme a who's who."

Pulling out a paper, I read the names I'd copied from my spreadsheet, leaving out Unique Montague and Willie Helms. "Rosemarie Moon. Ruby Anne Watley. Harmon Poe. Parker Ethridge. Daniel Snype. Jimmie Ray Teal. Matthew Summerfield."

"And the church lady. Who was she again?"

"Helene Flynn."

"One of those storm-trooping to save everyone's butt from fiery retribution, right?"

"GMC."

"Creeping Christians are a pain in the ass, you ask me. Jimmie Ray Teal and that councilman's kid, Matthew Summerfield, got coverage lately, so I'm hip to those names. The others . . ." Shrugging, Winborne pooched out his lips.

I offered him the paper on which I'd jotted the names. "Do you remember any more details about Aikman?"

"It wasn't exactly the story of the year."

Impulse. "Ever hear of a guy named Chester Pinckney?"

Winborne shook his head. "Why?"

"Cruikshank might have known him." I didn't share the fact that Pinckney's wallet had been found in Cruikshank's jacket. "Call me if you think of anything else," I said, wondering why this conversation had warranted a clandestine meeting.

I was two steps up the path when Winborne's voice stopped me.

"Cruikshank did let one thing slip."

I turned.

"Said he'd stumbled onto something bigger than a missing church worker."

"Meaning?"

"I don't know. But within months Cruikshank's found hanging from a tree." Again Winborne glanced over his shoulder. "And now Susie Ruth Aikman's found dead in her car."

As soon as Ryan and I got home I booted my laptop and opened the file in which I'd saved Cruikshank's CD images. Pete joined us as we were cruising through the JPEGs. I could feel the two of them on either side of me, each as truculent as an elk in rut.

Though a few of those pictured bore a vague resemblance to Lonnie Aikman, no one entering or leaving the clinic was a dead ringer match. Big surprise. Susie Ruth's photo was at least fifteen years out of date, and the detail in Winborne's photocopy was lousy. In addition, many of the subjects in Cruikshank's shots were turned away from the camera. Those faces that were visible became unrecognizable blurs when enlarged.

As we searched, Pete and Ryan matched sarcasm for sarcasm, the air of politeness never leaving their voices. After an hour I tired of their jousting and went to my room to try Nelson Teal's number again. My efforts were unrewarded.

In my absence Pete made sandwiches and Ryan phoned Lily. His daughter's mobile continued to ignore him. A call to Lutetia confirmed that Lily was fine, but still refusing contact with her father.

At noon we reconvened in the kitchen, and the mental cut and thrust between the men started anew. Halfway through lunch, I'd had it.

"You two are acting like escapees from a school for the criminally immature."

Two faces went puppy dog innocent.

"How about we all take a sabbatical. It's a holiday weekend, a time-out will be rejuvenating." I couldn't believe I was saying this. But the constant bickering was grating on my nerves.

"Pete, go play another eighteen holes. Ryan, let's drive into town and ambush Emma for a day at the beach."

I got no arguments.

It took twenty minutes of urging, but Emma finally gave in.

The sun was hot, the sky ceramic blue and unmarred by a single cloud. When we arrived, weekend sun worshippers were already out in force, baking on towels, lazing in sand chairs, destroying epidermis.

Emma and I alternated between floating on air mattresses and walking the beach, waves cresting into froth around our ankles. High up, pelicans drifted in formation. Now and then a squadron member would tuck its wings and plunge seaward. The lucky ones would surface with fish, the unlucky with water streaming from their beaks.

As we strolled, I described my conversations with Gullet and Winborne, and asked if I could work at the morgue in the morning. Emma assured me she'd again arrange clearance. Though tempted, I didn't inquire about Susie Ruth Aikman. Nor did I query the thorny cruise ship fatality that I'd read about in Winborne's article on Aikman.

Ryan passed the hours reading a Pat Conroy novel in the shade of an enormous umbrella we'd dragged from under Anne's house. Now and then he'd venture forth, swim alternating laps of the crawl and some French Canadian form of the backstroke, then towel off, lather up, and resettle in his chair.

By the time we headed back to "Sea for Miles," Emma's color was approaching normal. Ryan's had gone from chicken white to lemonade pink.

After I showered, the three of us hit Melvin's for barbecue, then Ryan and I drove Emma home. It was a frivolous, tranquil, and altogether soothing afternoon.

And well timed. Holiday weekend or not, I was about to hit Gullet's trifecta.

# 28

At eight thirty the next morning Ryan and I were on our way to MUSC. He looked relaxed for the first time since arriving in Charleston. The night before he'd had another conversation with Lily's mother. Though his daughter still felt angry and hostile toward him, Lily had agreed to speak with a counselor. Lutetia was setting up a series of appointments.

Or maybe it was the sunburn. Or the post-barbecue nooky. Whatever the cause, Ryan seemed much less tense.

Lee Ann Miller met us at the morgue door. After a virtual replay of Ryan's early morning comments concerning the rainbow bruise on my arm, she went to retrieve the barrel lady from the cooler. In her absence, I again tried Nelson Teal. This time the line was engaged.

Possible progress. A busy signal meant someone

316

was home, unless another incoming call was tying up the line.

Having delivered the remains to the autopsy room, Miller took off to do paperwork. Ryan settled in a chair with his Conroy book.

I gloved, then laid out the skeleton. Based on my experience with Cruikshank and Helms, my impulse was to go straight to the vertebrae. Instead, I followed protocol, methodically moving from the head toward the feet, examining each bone under magnification.

The skull showed no signs of violence. The jaw was undamaged. I found nothing on the hands, nothing on the arm or shoulder bones. The sternum and upper cervical vertebrae were intact.

Then everything changed.

"Look at this," I said to Ryan, a cold dread sprouting in my gut.

Ryan squinted into the scope.

"You're looking at the left transverse process of C-6. The fractures are identical to those I found on Helms and Cruikshank. Same vertebra, same side."

"Hyoid broken?" Ryan referred to a U-shaped throat bone that's often fractured during manual strangulation.

"No."

Ryan straightened. "Hanging?"

"The fracturing is limited to one side."

"Sudden wrenching?" Ryan was going through the same mental checklist I'd considered.

"Maybe." I pointed to the vertical hinge fracture on the anterior lamina of the transverse process.

"This is where the anterior scalene muscle originates." I moved the tip of my pen to a bony prominence beside the fracture. "This little bump is called the carotid tubercle, because it's the pressure point for the carotid artery. Sudden wrenching could cause compression of the carotid sheath. If compression was severe enough it could cut off blood flow to and from the brain, and that could result in death."

"Half nelson?" Ryan referred to the wrestling hold in which one arm is passed under the opponent's armpit from behind and brought around to the back of the neck.

I raised both palms in frustration. I'd been thinking about this since first seeing the fractures on Willie Helms's vertebra. I still hadn't figured it out.

"I understand the physiology of the injury, it's the mechanism that confuses me. The hinge fracture suggests quite a bit of force was applied. A sufficiently severe back and crosswise wrench of the head against the contraction of the anterior scalene usually tears or loosens the anterior tubercles of the fourth through the sixth vertebrae. So how could so much force be delivered yet only a single bone be broken?"

Ryan delivered a "don't look at me" look, then settled back with his book.

I returned to the bones.

And minutes later found the first nick. L-3. Belly side. Like Helms. The dread expanded into my chest. I continued my examination.

It took less than an hour. When done, I summarized my findings for Ryan, indicating each area of trauma with a pen.

"Hinge fracture on the left transverse process of the C-6 vertebra. A total of eight cut marks on the belly surfaces of lumbar vertebrae two, three, and four. That's it. No other damage to the skeleton."

"Think she was gut-stabbed?" Ryan asked.

"If this is a stabbing, the perp was cranked. The blade would need to have penetrated her entire abdomen to nick the vertebrae on their anterior sides."

"Any idea of tool type?"

"The cuts are tiny, V-shaped in cross section, with clean edges and no striations. All I can say is that it's an implement with a very sharp, non-serrated blade."

"Defense wounds?"

I shook my head. "The hand and lower arm bones are undamaged."

"So Cruikshank had the fractured neck vertebrae, but not the nicks. Helms and Montague had both." I could tell Ryan was thinking out loud.

"Yes. If they were killed by a common killer, they may have been killed for different reasons."

Neither of us came up with a good explanation. But Ryan's earlier comment had tickled a memory. Years back a colleague had reported on unilateral midneck fractures. Who? And where? Was it a presentation at a professional meeting? A published article? In what journal?

I needed to get online.

Driving back to Isle of Palms, I again called Nelson Teal. This time a woman answered. I introduced myself and explained my reason for phoning. The woman gave her name as Mona Teal.

"Jimmie Ray, that be my husband Nellie's kin. You find him?"

"No, ma'am. I'm sorry." As I listened, the missing piece in Jimmie Ray's biological profile clicked into place. The cadence of Mona's speech told me the Teals were of African-American descent.

"Well, you ain't calling to say he's passed, so praise the Lord for that."

"Does Jimmie Ray live with you?"

"Lordy, no. Jimmie Ray jus' kinda floats around down by the docks. He's not real good in the head."

I was confused. "If Jimmie Ray lives on the streets, how do you know he's missing?"

"I make that poor lamb fried chicken every Monday, see it as the Lord's work. Monday back one, Jimmie Ray come early, said he wanted to shower 'cause he's goin' to the doctor. He does that now and again, uses our place to clean his self up.

"Jimmie Ray starts telling me about a rash he's sufferin'. Lord, I didn't want to hear about that. He's barely here, then off he goes. Never come back. That ain't like Jimmie Ray. Boy's set in his ways, don't cotton to nothing altering his routine. When he misses two Mondays runnin', I know something's amiss. Jimmie Ray sure do like my chicken."

"Do you know where Jimmie Ray was going for his appointment?"

"Weren't no appointment. Jimmie Ray couldn't afford no private doctor."

"Oh?" *Calm.*

"Uses the free clinic over to Nassau, same as Nellie and me."

"The GMC clinic?" *Calm.*

"Tha's it. No appointments there. You sit your bottom down, wait your turn."

I gave Ryan a thumbs-up. Taking a hand from the wheel, he returned it, knowing I'd just tied Teal to the clinic.

"Thank you, Mrs. Teal."

"You find Jimmie Ray, you tell him his chicken's waiting."

I clicked off and raised a palm. Ryan high-fived it.

"And then there were three," I said, dialing Gullet.

My jubilation was cut short when Gullet's receptionist said her boss was absent until Tuesday. I stressed the importance of my contacting him. She said the sheriff had gone fishing and could not be reached.

Call Emma? I decided to wait until I'd researched the meaning of the neck fractures.

Pete was out when Ryan and I got back to "Sea for Miles." A blessing. Their alpha male routine was getting real old.

I went straight to my laptop and got online. Suspecting I'd be occupied for some time, Ryan set

321

off in search of climate-appropriate clothing.

I started with the *Journal of Forensic Science*, bombed, moved on through a dozen more forensic publications. Two hours later I was out of ideas. Though I'd learned a lot about injuries due to traffic accidents, hockey, diving, and "spear-tackling" in football, nothing fit the pattern I was seeing. Try as I might, I couldn't remember where I'd encountered the report I was remembering.

I stared at my computer screen, frustrated, wondering for the billionth time if anything really connected these cases. Cruikshank, Helms, and Montague all exhibited unilateral neck fractures on the sixth cervical vertebrae. Helms and Montague had nicks in their lower back area. Montague was a patient at the GMC clinic. Jimmie Ray Teal was a patient at the GMC clinic. Helene Flynn had worked there.

Montague, Helms, and Cruikshank were dead. Teal and Flynn were missing.

Lonnie Aikman was missing. Susie Ruth Aikman was dead. Had mother or son been a patient at the GMC clinic? Were the Aikmans tied in at all? Were Cruikshank's other MPs?

It had to be the clinic.

Helene Flynn had complained about the clinic to her father before terminating contact with him. And to Herron. Cruikshank had been observing the place.

Or had Cruikshank been observing the people?

On impulse, I Googled the name Lester Marshall. I learned about an Arabian horse breeder and a guy who teaches qigong energy therapy, whatever that is.

When I added "Dr." to the name I was piped into a physician research service. For $7.95 the site promised to cough up everything but a doctor's grandmother's favorite recipe.

Why not?

My eight bucks got me the following.

Lester Marshall's address and phone number at the Nassau Street clinic. Now there was a buy.

Marshall's MD was earned at St. George's Medical School in Grenada.

Marshall's area of practice was family medicine, though he held no board certification in any medical specialty.

Marshall had done no residencies or fellowships.

Marshall had been on staff at a hospital in Tulsa, Oklahoma, from 1982 until 1989. He'd hired on with GMC in 1995.

Marshall had been the subject of no state or federal disciplinary actions.

I was printing my results when I heard the front door. From the swishing and crinkling I assumed shopping had been a success.

"Any luck finding your article?" Ryan asked, kissing the top of my head.

"No. But I did a little research on Lester Marshall." I handed Ryan my report.

"Grenada? That a real med school?"

"I think so. Though it's not exactly Johns Hopkins."

"Patchy employment history," Ryan said.

"Exactly. Where was Marshall from eighty-nine to ninety-five?"

"Wonder why he left Oklahoma."

"If Marshall got into trouble in eighty-nine the site wouldn't provide that information. They don't collect data on malpractice or lawsuits, and they don't report disciplinary actions older than five years."

"Did you try the pit bull and Daniels?"

I shook my head.

While Ryan took his purchases to the bedroom, I Googled Corey Daniels and Adele Berry. Nothing relevant came up. When I tried the Charleston white pages, I found a Corey R. Daniels on Seabrook Island.

A nurse living on Seabrook? That was odd. Seabrook and Kiawah islands were some of the priciest real estate in the Charleston area. Nothing low end.

I was thinking about that when Ryan reappeared. He was wearing a black cap with the brim turned backward, black Teva sandals, black shorts, and a black T depicting a devil clobbering an angel with a flashlight. The message read: *Electricity comes from electrons, morality comes from morons.*

"Nice," I said. Black, I thought.

"I found the message inspirational."

I found it unintelligible, but didn't say so.

"Didn't want to go too preppy," Ryan said.

"Black works with the pink skin," I said. "Hope the babes can resist."

"That can be a problem."

"Want to take a shot at hacking into Cruikshank's computer?"

"Not my strength. But I'll lend moral support."

"Morality's for morons." Pointing at Ryan's shirt, I heard a "psst" in my mind.

What? Electricity? Flashlight? Angel?

Wham-o. It was the Pete's-Hornets-cap-Teal synapse all over again. My mind catapulted the name from somewhere deep in storage.

"Larry Angel!"

"How I love him, how I tingle when he passes by." Ryan mimicked the Carpenters into an imaginary hand mike.

"Not Johnny Angel, Larry Angel. He was a physical anthropologist at the Smithsonian for years. It wasn't a journal article, it was a book chapter."

Ryan followed me to the den and watched as I dug a volume from the stack I'd used as a mini-lending library for my field school students.

And there it was. A black-and-white photo of a sixth cervical vertebra showing a hinge fracture through the anterior lamina and a hairline crack through the posterior lamina of the left transverse process.

"Whoa," Ryan said.

"Yowza," I said.

Together, Ryan and I skimmed the text.

I went cold all over.

I knew how Montague, Helms, and Cruikshank had died.

# 29

"I busted a hit man who popped his vics with a Spanish windlass." Ryan was using the slang term for the weapon described in Angel's chapter. "Saint-Jean-sur-Richelieu boy, old school. Hated guns.

"He'd slip a wire noose over the vic's head, loop one side around a solid object, piece of pipe, maybe a screwdriver. Twist the side loop, the noose tightened. Simple but effective means of strangulation."

Exactly as Angel described.

I was almost too repulsed to speak. "That explains why only a single vertebra was fractured, and on only one side. The wire concentrated the force. The side loop was on the left."

I pictured the groove circling Unique Montague's neck, the claw marks left by her desperate struggles for breath.

"It also explains cause of death," I said. "C-6 and C-7 are angled five to ten degrees, so pressure applied to the carotid tubercle from the front would have been directed downward and backward." I swallowed. "Circulation to the brain would have been compromised and air would have been cut off from the lungs."

"You're sure it's the same injury on all three?"

I nodded.

Ryan pierced me with the ice blues. "So your drunken PI didn't kill himself after all."

"Cruikshank, Helms, and Montague were all garroted."

"Why?"

"Don't know."

"Helms and Montague were stabbed, or jabbed, or pierced in some way. Cruikshank wasn't. Why?"

"Don't know."

"Helms was buried in a shallow grave. Montague was dumped at sea in a barrel. Cruikshank was strung up."

"Don't say it."

Ryan did not query a third "why."

Firing to my feet, I grabbed my cell phone. "It's that clinic. It all goes back to that clinic." Ryan watched me punch numbers. "Gullet wanted three? I got him three. But where is he? Off snuffing bass with his buddies."

Gullet's receptionist replayed her earlier message. The sheriff was unreachable. I repeated that my need for contact was urgent. Unreachable. When I asked for the sheriff's home or cell phone number, the woman disconnected.

"Sonova—"

"Calm down." Ryan, reason itself. "Call Emma."

I did. She was impressed with my findings, but suggested that nothing would change overnight.

"Terrific. You're as concerned as that bonehead sheriff. People are vanishing, turning up dead, but what the hell. Bad timing! It's Memorial Day!"

Ryan folded his arms and dropped his chin.

"Tempe—" Emma tried to break into my tirade.

"Throw some steaks on the barbie and crack out the beer! Jimmie Ray Teal may be rotting somewhere with a noose around his neck, maybe Helene Flynn, too. Who knows? Maybe a couple of hookers, a schizophrenic? But damn, it's a holiday!"

"Tempe—"

"Cruikshank, Montague, and Helms were garroted, Emma. Some cold-blooded maniac put a wire around their necks and squeezed the life out of them. And God knows what else was done to Helms and Montague."

"Tempe."

"Am I the only one who cares about these people?" Even to me I was sounding shrill, and somewhat irrational. If Teal and Flynn were dead somewhere, no urgent action would restore their lives.

"I want you to call my sister."

"What?" That caught me completely off guard.

"Will you do that for me?"

"Yes. Of course." Dear God, what had happened? "Why?"

"The discord between us has continued too long."

I swallowed hard. "Did you see Dr. Russell today?"

"I'll see her tomorrow."

"Why the change of heart?"

"Find Sarah. Say that I'd like her to visit."

"Shall I—"

"Yes. Tell her I'm sick."

"Give me the number."

Embarrassed hesitation. "I don't know it."

With my newly acquired skills in doctor-digging it took little Internet time to locate Mark Purvis, a cardiologist on staff at two Nashville hospitals. Unlike Marshall, Purvis was boarded up the wazoo.

Another few sites and I'd learned that Mark Purvis was married to Sarah Rousseau, an '81 graduate of South Florence High School in Florence, South Carolina. A number of Sarah's classmates really wanted to get in touch with her. Imagine.

I'd also acquired the Purvis's home number, address, and a map to their house. God bless the electronic age.

The Purvis's housekeeper informed me that the doctor and his wife were in Italy until the first week of June.

I practically slammed down the phone. Was the whole world suddenly unreachable?

Seeing my agitation, Ryan suggested a beach stroll. Boyd backed the plan. While walking, we all

329

agreed that the only forward motion to be made that day would have to involve Cruikshank's boxes and laptop.

Back at "Sea for Miles" we all had a drink, then went straight to the den. Ryan and I took the couch. Boyd settled at our feet. Birdie joined us, but chose to observe from the hearth.

"Want to take a crack at Cruikshank's code?" I asked.

"What do you think, Hootch?" Ryan addressed Boyd with the nickname he'd given him upon their first meeting.

Boyd raised his head, twirled the eyebrow hairs, then laid his chin back onto his paws.

"Hootch says no problemo."

"I'll finish this last box." I didn't mention the reason a few items had remained unexamined. Why stir memories of my Wednesday night meltdown and cuddle with Pete?

As I was opening the flaps, the subject of the Wednesday night driveway incident appeared in the flesh.

"What's cookin', good lookin'?" Pete called from the foyer.

Ryan's jaw muscles bunched.

Boyd shot from the room. I heard a thunk, then the rattle of golf clubs. Seconds later Pete appeared, the chow cavorting around him.

"Counselor." Ryan nodded a greeting to Pete.

"Detective." Pete nodded to Ryan.

"Tempe." Pete nodded to me. Adults, being polite. Then a smile curled Pete's lips.

"Sugar britches."

Don't start, I squinted.

"What's the latest?" Pete asked, all innocence.

I brought him up to date.

"I'm going through these last few things. Ryan is taking a shot at the notes."

"The detective may succeed where the lowly attorney has failed." Pete's voice had taken on an edge. He turned to Ryan. "Hoping to find the key to the killer, Andy?"

"No, info on troop movements in Iraq, Pete."

"Forgot." Pete pointed a finger at Ryan. "Andy's one mirthful fellow."

"You probably garner a few laughs on the links."

Pete fired a shot from his finger pistol. "Detect your asses off, people. I'm going to shower."

Boyd followed Pete to the doorway.

"Pete?"

He turned. "Yes, sugar britches?"

"Have you picked up any vibes at GMC as to why Cruikshank might have been killed?"

"None whatsoever." To Ryan. "By the way, good choice. Black goes with everything. Never needs laundering."

I watched Pete leave, feeling what? Annoyance? Pity? No. Mostly the sadness of loss.

Setting aside the trophy, the baseball, the police paraphernalia, and the photos, I dug out the book and the two envelopes I'd yet to open.

The book was titled *The Chronicle of Crime*, and promised details on "the most infamous criminals of modern times and their heinous crimes." Tall order.

I flipped to the table of contents. All the usual suspects were there. Lizzie Borden. Ted Bundy. Dr. Crippen. Jeffrey Dahmer. Albert Fish. Charlie Manson. Jack the Ripper. Peter Sutcliffe.

Something tingled below my sternum. Why was Cruikshank researching serial killers? Personal interest? Or was he looking for insight into Charleston's MPs?

I put the book on the coffee table and opened Cruikshank's first envelope. The contents consisted of a single photocopy and pages printed from the Net. The latter looked familiar. Very familiar.

"Cruikshank was looking at Lester Marshall," I said. "Visited the same physician credential checking sites that I did."

"Makes sense. He was observing the place where Marshall practices medicine. Cruikshank get anything beyond what you found?"

"Not really. But some of his searches had to do with another doctor. Dominic Rodriguez graduated St. George's the same year as Marshall, 1981, did a surgical residency at the University of California–San Diego, then practiced medicine there until 1990. The site lists nothing beyond that."

I picked up the photocopy.

"Looks like Cruikshank obtained a list of residency appointments for St. George's grads spanning the years eighty to eighty-five. Doesn't appear to have come from the Net."

I was talking as I read.

"Lot of foreign names. Some impressive appointments. Neurology—University of Chicago; internal medicine—Georgetown; emergency medicine—Duke. No Lester Marshall, but the name Dominic Rodriguez is circled. Do you suppose Cruikshank was looking at this guy because he and Marshall were classmates? But why Rodriguez? He's a cutter, Marshall's family medicine."

Ryan thought about that.

"Marshall dropped out of sight in Tulsa in eighty-nine, reappeared in Charleston in ninety-five. You're saying Rodriguez slipped under the radar in San Diego in ninety. That's curious."

I was replacing the first envelope when I noticed a flyer lying flat up against the side of the box. I took it out. The thing was a one-page travel brochure touting the benefits of a health spa in Puerto Vallarta, Mexico.

"Maybe Rodriguez was Mexican," I said, holding the ad up. "Started pining for the homeland."

"Right." Meaning, not a chance.

"It happens. Surgeons burn out. Maybe Rodriguez went to Puerto Vallarta in ninety to practice medicine in a less stressful environment."

"A spa?"

"The text promises medically trained personnel offering options found in few clinics worldwide."

"Such as?"

"There's a number you have to call."

"Maybe Cruikshank had the ad because he was looking for a detox program south of the border."

"Why?"

"The guy was a drunk."

"Why Mexico?"

"Good burritos."

Orbital roll. "Making progress with the code?"

"Yes."

"Really?"

"Yes."

"What?"

"Patience, fair maiden."

Tossing the flyer into the box, I opened the second envelope.

Again, the contents were photocopies and print-outs. There were six, maybe seven in all, some single sheets, others composed of multiple pages.

I started reading. At first, I was confused. As comprehension grew, the room receded around me, and a dark feeling took root inside me.

When I'd finished the articles, I checked the table of contents in the crime book. There it was. Fingers cold with dread, I turned to the chapter. A yellow Post-it marked the page, suggesting that particular case had been the focus of Cruikshank's interest.

Every neuron in my mind screamed *no!* The explanation was just too macabre. But it all fit. The clinic. The disappearances. The cut marks on Helms and Montague.

Had Helene Flynn been murdered because she'd learned about this? Had she stumbled on the truth while searching for evidence of financial wrong-doing? Had Cruikshank also found out?

I opened my lips to share the horrific idea with Ryan. I never spoke.

The next few moments exploded so quickly that in my memory there was no sequence. My later attempts to reconstruct the chronology yielded only jumbled images.

Pete moving toward the kitchen. Boyd rocketing from the den. Boyd barking. The kitchen light shooting arrows onto the corridor wall. A gunshot ringing out. Me on the floor, Ryan pressing my head to the carpet. Ryan's weight leaving my back. Me scrambling toward the kitchen, crouching, terrified. The barking more frenzied.

My blood freezing in my veins. Pete facedown on the floor, red mushrooming from some unseeable wound.

# 30

An ambulance arrived. Ryan held me in his arms as two paramedics worked on Pete. Boyd whined and scratched on the far side of the pantry door. I shared his fear. The kitchen seemed awash in blood. Could anyone survive the loss of so much?

Though I asked question after question, I was repeatedly ignored. After furious manipulation involving tubes and wound packing, Pete was strapped to a backboard, placed on a stretcher, and whisked away.

Two Isle of Palms uniforms arrived and asked a lot of questions. Their name tags read CAPER and JOHNSON. At one point Caper asked about the bruise on my arm. I described the previous Thursday's bottle-throwing incident. Caper put it in his notes.

Ryan told the cops he was on the job, showed his badge, and tried to deflect the interrogation. Caper and Johnson said they understood, but needed to file an incident report.

Tersely, I outlined what Pete was doing in Charleston. Caper wanted my thoughts on who might have shot him. I suggested he interrogate Herron and the GMC clinic staff. Caper's expression suggested that was unlikely to happen.

"Probably a beach prank," Johnson said. "Damn kids sneak Daddy's gun, get wasted, start firing bullets into the air. Happens every long weekend."

"Someone get drilled every long weekend?" Ryan asked.

I too knew that explanation was stupid, but I wasn't in the mood to argue. I was anxious to follow the ambulance.

An hour after the shooting Ryan and I were in the emergency room waiting area at the MUSC hospital. This time we'd entered on the Ashley Street side. The life side. I prayed Pete would be exiting through the same door.

An hour crept by. Another. Pete was in surgery. That's all they would tell me. He was in surgery.

The ER was chaos, the staff pushed to its limits by the full onslaught of an American holiday. A family of six burned in a barbecue grill explosion. A child pulled from a backyard pool. A drunk trampled by a horse. A woman beaten by her husband. A man shot by his lover. Drug overdoses. Dehydration. Sunburn. Food poisoning. It was a relief to be moved to the surgical waiting area upstairs.

We were entering our third hour when a doctor

approached, face tired, scrubs spattered with blood. My heart seized. I tried but couldn't read the doctor's face.

Ryan took my hand. We both stood.

"Dr. Brennan?"

I nodded, afraid to trust my voice.

"Mr. Petersons is out of surgery."

"How is he?"

"I removed the bullet and fragments. There's some damage to his right lung."

"Don't lie to me."

"He lost a lot of blood. The next twenty-four hours will be critical."

"Can I see him?"

"He's been moved to the ICU. A nurse will take you."

The ICU was a sharp contrast to the bedlam downstairs. The lights were low, the only sounds the squeak of an occasional heel or the hushed murmur of a distant voice.

Exiting the elevator Ryan and I followed our guide to a configuration of four glass-walled units. A nurse sat in the middle, monitoring the occupant of each bed.

Tonight, the glass quadrangle held three patients. Pete was one of them.

If the sight of Emma in the ER had caught me off guard, that paled in comparison with the shock of seeing post-surgical Pete. Despite his six feet, powerful shoulders, and boundless energy, the Latvian Savant looked ashen and shrunken in his bed. Vulnerable.

Tubes ran from Pete's nose and mouth. Another from his chest. A fourth from his arm. Each was taped with adhesive. An IV tree at the head of his bed dangled several bags. Machines surrounded him, pumping and whirring and sucking. A monitor displayed an undulating series of peaks and valleys, and blipped a constant rhythm.

Ryan must have heard my sudden intake of breath. Again, he enveloped my hand in his.

I felt my knees buckle. Ryan's arm went round my waist.

Pressing a palm to the glass, I closed my eyes and conjured up a long-abandoned childhood prayer.

Disregarding hospital regs, I called Katy's cell. Got a recording. What message to leave? "Katy, it's Mom. Please call me as soon as you can. It's very important."

Go or stay? The nurse assured me Pete would neither hear nor see during the night. "Go get some rest. I'll call if anything develops."

I took her advice.

Lying in bed that night, Ryan voiced the questions I'd been asking myself.

"Do you think Pete was the target?"

"I don't know."

"That bullet might have been meant for you."

I didn't say anything. I thought the shooter had been close enough to distinguish male from female, but perhaps he'd aimed at a silhouette.

Ryan pushed his point. "No one was thrilled to

339

see us at that clinic. If you're closing in on something, folks could be getting antsy."

"The IOP cops weren't impressed. It's America. It's Memorial Day. People fire guns."

"What's that developer's name?"

"Dickie Dupree." Ryan was thinking along lines I'd considered. "A strange car shows up. Someone beans you with a beer bottle. All around the time you're digging Dupree's site."

"The bottle could have been totally unrelated to the shooting."

"Dupree threatened you."

"Dupree could be a bottle thrower, but not a shooter or employer of shooters. That's too big-time for him. Besides, my report to the state was already in. What does he gain in having someone take a shot at me? Everything happened after we found Willie Helms's bones on Dewees. Maybe Helms is the triggering factor."

"Maybe it's Montague."

"Maybe it's that clinic." I sat bolt upright. "Oh my God. I was so upset about Pete I forgot."

Throwing back the covers I dashed downstairs, Boyd at my heels.

The contents of Cruikshank's second envelope lay scattered across the den. Snatching up the papers and the crime book, I raced back upstairs, Boyd matching me tread for tread.

"Ever heard of William Burke and William Hare?" I asked when I was once again under the blankets.

Ryan shook his head.

"Burke and Hare were responsible for sixteen murders spanning a period of less than a year."

"When and where?"

"Edinburgh, 1827 to 1828. At that time, under British law, only the bodies of executed criminals could be used for dissection. Demand exceeded supply for the fresh corpses needed to teach anatomy and surgery, and grave robbing became common."

"Gotta admire those Scots. Entrepreneurial. Even the criminal set."

"Bad news, Ryan. Burke and Hare were Irishmen who moved to Scotland to work on the Union Canal. Both ended up living in a boarding-house owned by Maggie Laird. Helen MacDougal also roomed there, and the four became drinking buddies.

"In 1827 one of Laird's boarders fell ill and died owing back rent. On the day of the funeral Burke and Hare robbed the coffin and sold the man's body to Robert Knox, an anatomy professor at the Edinburgh Medical School."

"How much?"

"Ten pounds seven shillings. Big bucks back then. Seeing an income stream of easy money, the dynamic duo made a career change into the cadaver supply business. When another boarder fell ill, Burke and Hare suffocated him by pinching off his nose and mouth. That became their MO, and the origin of the modern term "burking."

"Next came a relative of Helen's, a street busker, a string of prostitutes. Eventually, Burke and Hare grew lazy, or complacent, and started taking victims close to home. The neighbors began to notice that locals were disappearing, and Dr. Knox's students began to recognize faces on their tables. The downfall came with the murder of a hooker named Mary Docherty.

"When arrested, all four turned on each other. Burke and Helen MacDougal were charged and tried, Hare and Maggie Laird turned king's evidence. Helen won a verdict of not proven, Burke was found guilty and sentenced to death. Before his hanging, Burke admitted to a total of sixteen murders."

"Why risk murder? Why not read the obits and buy a good shovel?"

"These guys were slugs. Digging a grave was too labor intensive."

"Cruikshank was collecting articles on Burke and Hare?"

"Lots of them." I held up the papers.

Ryan considered this for several seconds.

"You think someone at the GMC clinic is knocking patients off for their corpses?"

"Cruikshank must have been considering the possibility."

"OK. Suppose that's it. Why? Where's the profit?"

"I'm not sure. Wait. Maybe they were harvesting skeletal parts to sell for medical purposes. Remember that scandal involving a funeral home and a number of tissue procurement companies?"

Ryan shook his head.

"The funeral home was removing bone from corpses without permission, and replacing it with polypropylene pipe. Alistair Cooke was reported to be one of the victims."

"You're not serious."

"It was all over the news. The stolen bone was sold to companies that supply hospitals with tissue. Cadaveric bone is routinely used for grafting."

"But bone doesn't make sense. Helms was buried. Montague was tossed into the ocean. Their skeletons were intact."

"Maybe their bones turned out to be unsuitable for some reason."

"Such as?"

"I don't know. OK. Maybe it wasn't a problem with the bones. Maybe the perp got spooked, the drop-off was spotted, the cleaning apparatus broke down. A thousand things could have gone wrong."

"What about the cut marks?"

What about the cut marks? Lower back. Pelvic and abdominal area.

*Think outside the box, Brennan. Outside the bones.*

My mind tossed up a gruesome possibility.

"But you're right about one thing," Ryan was saying. "Helms lived in a scrap-yard trailer. Montague was homeless. Aikman was mentally ill. Teal was unstable and lived on the streets. Who else is missing? Hookers. Druggies. Those on the fringe, those no one notices. The same people who fell victim to Burke and Hare."

It couldn't be. The idea was too terrible to contemplate.

"But there's no proof anyone's dead except Helms and Montague." Ryan's voice was barely registering. "So what have we learned? Cruikshank was digging into Burke and Hare. Cruikshank was staking out the GMC clinic. Helene Flynn worked there. Montague and Teal were patients there. But we don't even know that Teal is dead."

"Cruikshank sure is," I said. "Because he uncovered something that got him killed. Ryan—"

"Shh."

"No. Listen."

Clicking off the light, Ryan pulled me to him. When I tried to protest, he hugged me tighter. I fell silent and we lay together in the dark. Sometime later, Birdie hopped onto the bed. I felt him circle, then curl at my side.

Tired as I was, sleep wouldn't come. My mind kept offering up the same dreadful suspicion. Kept repeating the same horrified response: *It can't be.*

I refused to think about my appalling hypothesis. To calm myself I chanted silently. Tonight, rest. Tomorrow, pursue.

It didn't work. My thoughts raced from topic to topic. I kept seeing the rigging and tubes pumping to keep Pete alive. I relived mopping Anne's kitchen floor, pictured my tears falling and mingling with his blood. I went cold at the prospect of telling Katy that her father was dead. Where was Katy?

I remembered my recent call to Emma, dreaded the awful conversation I would have upon her sister's return from Italy.

I considered Gullet. Was his attitude toward me resistance, or merely indifference?

I thought of Dupree and his threats. Were they threats? What could he really do? All developers bitched to their friends in government about archaeologists interfering with progress.

Faces strobed in unending spirals through my brain. Pete. Emma. Gullet. Dupree. Lester Marshall. Corey Daniels. Adele Berry. Lonnie Aikman. The gargoyle features of Unique Montague. The fleshless skull of Willie Helms. Pete again.

The digits on the bedside clock glowed orange. Outside the ocean rolled, a soft, murmuring whisper. Minutes passed. An hour. Beside me, Ryan's body hadn't relaxed. His breathing hadn't steadied into the rhythm of sleep.

Share my suspicion with Ryan?

No. Wait. Dig. Be sure.

"You awake?" I whispered softly.

"Hm."

"Thinking about Lily?"

"Among other things." Ryan's voice was dusky.

"What?"

"Cruikshank's code."

"You crack it?"

"Except for the Helms file, I think it's mostly initials, dates, and times."

"*C* means case closed."

"Breakthrough noted."

I jabbed Ryan with an elbow.

"CD is Corey Daniels. AB, Adele Berry. LM,

Lester Marshall. Not sure about some of the others. The dates are obvious. I think the numbers after each set of initials indicate the times that person entered or left the clinic."

"It's that simple?"

"There's more to it, but I think basically Cruikshank was keeping track of when people came and went."

"Staff only?"

"I think some were patients. Helms is another story. Those notes must have to do with research rather than surveillance since Helms disappeared before Cruikshank was hired to find Helene."

"If Cruikshank's system is so easy, why didn't Pete get it?"

Earlier, Ryan wouldn't have missed an opportunity for a dig. Not tonight. "When Pete was working it he didn't have the names of the clinic staff. Or Willie Helms. What time is it?"

I looked at the clock. "Three ten."

"Doesn't matter. I don't think the notes will yield much." Ryan pulled me to him. "You sleepy?"

"I'm not in the mood, Ryan."

"I was thinking of Cruikshank's laptop."

"Gullet wants it back tomorrow."

"Want to take one last run at the password?"

"Yes." And there was something else I wanted to check into. Could it be?

"Did you find Cruikshank's police ID number?" Ryan asked.

"There's a badge, but the Charlotte PD doesn't number them."

"Did Cruikshank keep any other police equipment? A holster? Handcuffs? A handcuff key?"

"Yeah. Why?"

"Contrary to our glamorous public image, we in law enforcement aren't all that complex. Old cop trick: use your ID number as your password. Older cop trick: scratch your ID number onto your belongings."

Boyd and I set a land speed record bolting down the stairs. Ryan followed at a more dignified pace. By the time he'd joined us I'd hit pay dirt.

"Cruikshank scratched digits beside the keyhole." Thrusting the handcuffs at Ryan, I dashed to the desk, opened and booted the Dell. "Read them off."

Ryan did. I hit the keys. Black dots appeared in the little white window, then the screen changed to the Windows desktop.

"We're in!"

"Mailbox first?" Ryan asked.

I spent ten minutes poking around.

"The PC's set up for wireless, but there's no e-mail. I doubt Magnolia Manor's plugged in, so Cruikshank probably used coffee shops or libraries to access the Net. He's got hundreds of downloads. You might as well go back to bed."

"You sure?"

"This is going to take a while."

Ryan kissed my head. I heard footfalls on the carpet, then his tread on the stairs. Boyd stayed at my feet.

Everything faded from my consciousness but the

softly lit monitor of a dead man's PC. Beyond its glow, Anne's picture window was a shiny black rectangle of glass. As I read file after file, a hard knot formed in my gut.

When I finally sat back, the window had gone gray, and the vast Atlantic was emerging from an early morning mist.

The hunt for explanations was over.

My guess had been correct. I knew. And the reality was as ruthless as any I'd imagined. But that would have to wait.

I had my own reality to contend with. I called the ICU. No change. No obvious improvement, but Pete was stable.

Try Katy again? No point. She'd get my message if she had her cell on. If she didn't, another call would just result in another message. If I didn't hear from her within a few hours, I'd call the university and ask for help in locating her.

I stretched out on the couch.

# 31

"You awake?" I whispered.

"I am now."

"People are being murdered for their organs."

"Uh-huh." Ryan stretched out a hand. I took it.

"Cruikshank figured it out."

Ryan propped himself up onto one elbow. His hair was tousled, and the baby blues were heavy with sleep.

"The idea crossed my mind, but it seemed so far out there I didn't even mention it."

"It's true."

"A drugged traveler wakes in an ice-filled bathtub? A college student comes to sporting stitches after a wild party?" Ryan's tone was beyond skeptical. "Organ theft stories have been making the rounds for years."

"What Cruikshank stumbled onto is far worse than any urban myth. People are being choked to

349

death, Ryan. Their organs are being carved from their bodies."

"No way in hell."

I ticked off points on my fingers. "Inexplicably dead MPs. Skeletons with cut marks." Ryan started to speak. I blew past him to ring man. "Cut marks consistent with scalpel nicks. A sketchy doctor in the United States, with a med school classmate who's dropped off the map. A mysterious health spa in Mexico."

Ryan scooted up and put a pillow behind his head. "Show me."

Crawling under the covers, I sat Indian style, opened Cruikshank's laptop and rested it on my crossed ankles.

"Cruikshank spent a lot of time researching transplantation, black marketeering in organs, Charleston MPs, and a place called Abrigo Aislado de los Santos near Puerto Vallarta."

"The Mexican resort in the brochure?"

"Yeah," I snorted. "Last resort."

I nibbled a cuticle, debated how to take Ryan through this since I'd just begun to comprehend most of it myself.

"Since the early fifties, transplantation has become relatively common. A kidney or a portion of liver can be given by a living donor, even a single lung, though that's rare. Heart, cornea, double-lung, or pancreas transplants have to come from cadaverous donors.

"The problem is there aren't enough organs to go around. If you can use a live donor, you're better off. You might be compatible with a family member, a friend, or a charitable donor, though those are few and far between. If you need a cadaverous donor, you could sit for months, or even years."

"And die waiting."

"In the United States, those needing cadaverous donors become part of OPTN, the Organ Procurement and Transplantation Network, operated by an independent nonprofit organization called UNOS, the United Network for Organ Sharing. UNOS maintains a database of eligible transplant recipients, as well as information on all organ transplant centers throughout the country. UNOS also establishes policy with regard to priority and who gets which organs."

"How does a patient get into the network?"

"You have to find a transplant team qualified with UNOS. That team decides if you're a good candidate, physically and mentally."

"Meaning?"

"It's complicated, but drug and alcohol abusers and smokers are usually disqualified, for example. UNOS also ranks potential recipients based on health, urgency of need, compatibility, length of time on the list, that sort of thing. They want available organs used where they are likely to do the most good."

Ryan cut to the core. "So those rejected and those tired of waiting go outside the system."

"So-called brokers arrange sales of human organs to patients who can pay. Usually the sellers are willing participants. Kidneys are the most commonly traded, and, in most cases, it's poor people in developing countries selling their organs to the wealthy. The cost can run over one hundred thousand dollars, with the donor receiving only a fraction of that."

"This is widespread?"

"Cruikshank had tons of research on his computer. Some of his sources describe the kidney trade as a global phenomenon. Nancy Scheper-Hughes, a Berkeley anthropologist, has established an NGO called Organ Watch, which claims to have documented organ harvesting in Argentina, Brazil, Cuba, Israel, Turkey, South Africa, India, the United States, and the United Kingdom. Cruikshank also found information on Iran and China."

I clicked a few keys, and Ryan and I skimmed a report on the use of executed criminals as donors in China.

"You can actually purchase package deals." I opened a series of files and we both read in silence.

An Israeli-led syndicate offered transplant tours to Turkey and Romania for $180,000 U.S. A New York woman bought a kidney from a Brazilian donor, then traveled to South Africa for surgery at a private clinic at a total outlay of $65,000 U.S. A Canadian went to Pakistan in a cash-for-kidney deal costing $12,500 Canadian.

"Check out this Web site."

I clicked to another download. A Pakistani hospital described itself as a fifty-bed private facility in operation since 1992. The site offered a package that included three weeks' lodging, three daily meals, three presurgical dialysis sessions, donor expenses, surgery, and two days' post-discharge medication for $14,000 U.S.

*"Tabarnac!"* Ryan sounded as appalled as I felt.

"Most countries outlaw this, but not all. In Iran, for example, it's legal but regulated." I opened another file. "The U.S. National Organ Transplant Act of 1984 prohibits payment to those providing organs for transplantation. The Uniform Anatomical Gift Act allows individuals to specify that some or all of their body may be donated after their death. Nineteen eighty-seven revisions to the act prohibit the taking of payment for donated parts."

"OK. Cash for kidneys. But murder?"

I opened several downloads.

South Africa. June 1995. Moses Mokgethi was found guilty of the murder of six children for their organs.

Ciudad Juárez and Chihuahua, Mexico. May 2003. Hundreds of women had been killed since 1993, and bodies continued turning up in the desert. Federal investigators claimed to have evidence the women were victims of an international organ trafficking ring.

Bukhara, Uzbekistan. No date. A family named Korayev was found with the passports of sixty missing persons, an enormous sum of money, and bags of body parts in their home. Their company, Kora, promised visas and overseas jobs. Instead, according to police, the Korayevs killed their clients and, working with a doctor, pipelined their organs to Russia and Turkey.

"Jesus."

"Theft from fresh cadavers is even more common," I said. "And not just in the Third World. Organ Watch has also reported on U.S. cases in which families of brain-dead patients have been offered as much as a million dollars to give organ harvesters access to the bodies immediately upon death."

The room was brightening. I got up and slid open the glass door. The smell of the ocean made me think of boogie-boarding with my kid sister, Harry, beach blanket gossip with high school best friends, sand castle construction with Katy and Pete.

Pete. Again, that pang deep in my chest.

I wanted to go back to one of those long summer days, to forget putrefied bodies, and scalpels, and wire nooses.

"So you believe someone at the GMC clinic is snuffing street people to harvest their organs." Ryan's voice brought me back. "And that Cruikshank was about to blow the whistle."

"I think Cruikshank was killed to keep him quiet. And I'm wondering about Helene Flynn, too."

"Suspects?"

"I'm not sure. The operation would have to involve several people, and a clinic has to be at the core. The average guy on the street can't just yank out a kidney."

Returning to bed, I opened another file.

"Removing an organ isn't all that complicated. In the case of a heart, for example, the vessels are clamped, and a cold, protective solution is pumped inside. The vessels are then severed, and the heart is placed in a bag filled with preservative. The bag is packed in ice in an ordinary cooler and flown or driven to its destination."

"How long do you have?"

"Four hours for a heart, eight to ten for a liver, three days for a kidney."

"Tight schedule for a heart. But plenty of time for transport to kidney recipients."

"Waiting in pre-op at some sterile facility tucked away in the hills." I clicked some more keys. "Cruikshank was looking into Abrigo Aislado de los Santos. Know what that means?"

Ryan shook his head.

"Isolated health shelter. Read the language on their Web site."

The more he read, the more deeply Ryan frowned. " 'Unique therapeutic regimes available to individually qualified customers.' What the hell does that mean? You need a pedigree to get a pedicure?"

"It means call us. Provide background. If your story and portfolio check out, we'll get you a kidney."

"I'm guessing putting organs in isn't as simple as taking them out."

I looked Ryan directly in the eye. "Implantation requires a surgeon working in a relatively sophisticated facility."

Ryan's expression told me he was careening along the same deductive pathways I'd followed, speeding toward the same appalling finish. After a full minute, he spoke.

"You've got the GMC clinic on this end, serves druggies, crazies, the homeless. A few patients disappear now and then, no one notices. You would need a small plane, a cooler, a pilot who doesn't ask a lot of questions. Or maybe the mule's actually in the loop. You've got an experienced surgeon operating in an isolated location, catering to those needing organs and willing to pay a substantial price."

"Lester Marshall and Dominic Rodriguez attended the same med school, dropped out of sight around the same time," I said. "Rodriguez is a surgeon."

Ryan picked up the thread. "Two old classmates hook up, hatch a cash-for-organs scheme. Marshall comes here. Rodriguez goes to Puerto Vallarta, sets up a clinic disguised as a spa."

"Or Rodriguez might have left San Diego to practice medicine in Mexico. Could be Marshall got into some kind of trouble, went south, and the two reconnected," I said.

"Marshall takes the organs out, Rodriguez puts them in. Donors don't complain because they've been paid or because they're dead. Recipients don't complain because what they've done is illegal. A hundred thousand a pop buys a lot of margaritas."

"Illegal drugs are flown to the U.S. from Mexico

all the time," I said. "Why not organs going the other way? They're small, easy to transport, and the payoff is huge. It explains the nicks, the garroting, the hidden bodies."

"The Burke and Hare script taken to a different level."

A gull touched down on the deck railing. Boyd lunged toward the screen, tail wagging. The bird took flight. The chow turned and looked at us. Ryan and I looked at the chow, thinking the same thought. Ryan voiced it.

"What we've got is speculation. We need to background Rodriguez, find out if the guy's in Mexico. We need to know where Marshall spent those missing six years. And why. And we need info on pilots and planes in the Charleston area. And boats."

Ryan looked confused.

"Willie Helms's body had to have been taken by water to Dewees Island. Unique Montague was dumped in the ocean. I doubt the killer used a ferry for either of those jaunts."

"Doesn't everyone and his granny own a boat in this town?"

I thought a moment. "Let's review Cruikshank's notes some more. You think some of the letters represent initials. You're probably right. What if we check those letter combinations against other Charleston MPs?" I was thinking out loud. "If we find a match it probably puts that MP at the GMC clinic."

"From the dates I saw in the notes, Cruikshank

was only staking the place out during February and March of this year."

My mind was cranking now. "OK. I have the MP files from Emma. I think they cover the period of Cruikshank's investigation. I'll check the date each MP was last seen and compile a list. Maybe we can cross-check the list against flight plans logged by small-plane pilots."

"That would be a major law enforcement undertaking, particularly if it involved more than one Charleston-area airport. Also, smugglers rarely log flight plans."

"OK. The disappearances could coincide with times a plane was taken from an airfield."

"Assuming the plane's not kept in a barn somewhere. If they're not filing flight plans, they won't be logging in or out of an airport."

Sudden thought. "What about GMC? They've got a plane. Is it possible this thing goes higher than Marshall? Herron and his staff refused to respond to Helene's complaints. Then she went missing."

"I thought Helene was suspicious about the mishandling of funds."

"That's always been Herron's version. But he and his people refused to help Cruikshank find her, then Cruikshank dies. Stonewalled Pete, too, for that matter, then Pete is shot. Could someone high up at GMC be involved? Oh my God, Ryan, GMC operates clinics throughout the Southeast!"

"Let's not get carried away. When's Gullet coming by?"

"He wanted Cruikshank's computer first thing

this morning." Ryan threw back the covers. I grasped his wrist. "Gullet hasn't been busting a gut helping me out. Do you think he could be protecting Herron?"

Pulling my hand to his lips, Ryan kissed the knuckles. "I think Gullet's solid."

"You're probably right. But do we have enough to convince him?"

"Call Emma. Explain our thinking. Helene's complaints to her father and to Herron, then her sudden disappearance. Cruikshank's link to Helene. Cruikshank's files on Burke and Hare, UNOS, the organ trade, Rodriguez, and the Puerto Vallarta clinic. The evidence of garroting on Cruikshank, Helms, and Montague. The scalpel nicks on Helms's and Montague's vertebrae and ribs. Find out when Emma expects a DNA report on the eyelash you found with Helms's bones."

"Planning on snatching some discarded chewing gum?"

"Saw that on TV. Slick. But I'm a used-soda-can man myself," Ryan said.

"The snail shell that held the eyelash came from a freshwater species, yet it was found with Helms's body on a saltwater beach. We should find out if Marshall lives near a freshwater swamp or beside a stream or river."

"You dazzle, Dr. Brennan."

"And think about Dewees. The island population is less than that of Mayberry. There's no bridge or connector and the ferry is only for residents and their guests." I was pumped. "Where does a perp typically dispose of a body? Within his or her comfort zone."

"Incandescent!"

"Thank you, Detective Ryan."

"Here's a plan. Call the hospital, find out how Pete's doing. Then pull out your spreadsheet and make a list of dates MPs were last seen. In the meantime, I'll make a few calls. When I finish, we'll do some digging on Marshall and the gentle folk of Dewees."

Ryan grabbed his surfer shorts.

"Deputy Dawg Gullet won't know what hit him."

# 32

The charge nurse told me that Pete was awake and talking, and that his vitals were stable. The doctor would see him this morning and decide how long he needed to stay. I thanked her and asked her to be sure to tell Pete I'd called.

I phrased my e-mail message to Katy very carefully. "Your father will be in the hospital for a few days. He received a gunshot wound from a home intruder at Anne's house on Isle of Palms. *Do not panic.* He is recovering nicely. He is at the Medical University of South Carolina hospital in Charleston. He will be released before you could get there, and will tell you all about it when you next see him. Love, Mom."

Then I turned to my MPs. The chronology went back five years. I was finishing when Ryan came into the kitchen. After pouring coffee, he joined me at the table. One cocked brow told me I wasn't looking my best.

"Don't say it, Ryan."

"You owe a fellow named Jerry a whole lot of scotch."

"And Jerry would be?"

"Buddy at Quantico. NCIC search turned up zip for Dominic Rodriguez. But Jerry found him by other means." A smile played Ryan's lips. "Jerry's devious."

"Don't toy with me, Ryan." Grabbing my hair, I yanked it up into a knot.

"Likes Glenlivet."

"Noted."

"Rodriguez is a Mexican national. Born in Guadalajara." Titillating pause as Ryan took a long, appreciative sip. "Currently employed as chief of wellness therapy at Abrigo Aislado de los Santos in Puerto Vallarta, Mexico."

"Get out! Why did Rodriguez leave San Diego?"

"Jerry soldiers on, even as we speak. Now. Lester Marshall."

I waited out more coffee intake.

"Name lit up the marquee."

"You're kidding." My heart was plowing in my chest. "What did Marshall do?"

"Good doctor got a little liberal with pharmaceuticals."

"Self-prescribing?"

"And overprescribing for patients. Making a handsome living writing scrips for controlled substances. Colleague dropped a dime. Marshall got his license suspended, but apparently wasn't all that contrite. After a second complaint and investigation, Marshall's license was revoked. Tulsa prosecutors weren't amused, brought criminal charges. Marshall did eighteen months, vamoosed."

"Where was Marshall between Tulsa and Charleston?"

"Jerry's checking. Got your dates lined up?"

I showed Ryan my list. He did some mental math.

"The Abrigo Aislado de los Santos opened its *puertas* in ninety-two. Marshall stopped practicing medicine in Oklahoma in eighty-nine, left the state in ninety-one after doing his time in stir, resurfaced here in ninety-five." Ryan tapped my list. "If this drinking buddy that Gullet's deputy interviewed is correct, Helms disappeared after nine-eleven, 2001, these others after that. Either Marshall and Rodriguez took a long time to gear up, or a number of cold cases need reopening. Heard from Gullet?"

I shook my head. The topknot failed.

"Wonder if the bass were biting." Ryan tucked a few strands behind my ears.

I picked up my cell phone. This time Gullet's receptionist put me through. I wasted no time on pleasantries.

"Marshall is killing people to steal their organs."

"That's a mighty serious accusation." Flat. "Heard about the shooting. May I inquire how the counselor is faring?"

"Recovering nicely, thank you for asking."

"IOP PD calling the plays?"

"Yes."

363

"How they reading it?"

"They're inclined to view the incident as accidental."

"Hmm."

I didn't know what that meant, but I wasn't in the mood to pursue the discussion.

"The marks on Helms's and Montague's bones are consistent with cuts from a scalpel blade."

After getting another "hmm," I told Gullet what I'd found on Cruikshank's computer. When I stopped speaking, he made a noise I took to mean "go on." I outlined what we'd discovered about Marshall and Rodriguez.

"You're talking Helms and Montague," Gullet monotoned.

"So far. An MP named Jimmie Ray Teal was also a patient at the GMC clinic. Who knows how many others? I think someone killed Cruikshank to shut him up before he could go to the authorities. Probably Helene Flynn for the same reason."

"Uh-huh."

"A schizophrenic named Lonnie Aikman disappeared in 2004. A journalist reran a story about him back in March. Aikman's mother was found dead in her car this past Tuesday. Someone may have killed her so Jimmie Ray wouldn't trace back to GMC."

"One buried, one in the ocean, one hanging from a tree, one dead in a vehicle. Not exactly a signature."

"Whoever is masterminding this is smart. Probably varied his MO so the murders wouldn't link up if the bodies were found. But one thing is sure. We have three garrotings."

"Where's this Mexican clinic?"

"Abrigo Aislado de los Santos, in Puerto Vallarta."

I heard Gullet's desk chair swivel. Then, "What is it you want done?"

"I need any information you can gather on the ownership or leasing of private planes in this area, especially any use by GMC or Marshall. And a list of all locally registered private aircraft, if that's possible."

"I'll put a deputy on it."

"And insight into who might be comfortable using Dewees as a body dump."

"I pulled a list of homeowners when you found Helms. Only a handful stay on the island full-time. Most properties are second homes, many purchased for use as tourist rentals. It'll take time to check rental records going back through 2001. Private owners who do their own renting often don't keep much by way of records."

"Do it. Where does Marshall live?"

"Hang on."

Ryan's cell rang while I was holding. He answered. I heard a lot of "yeah" and "uh-huh" as he took notes.

"Marshall's got a place on Kiawah Island." Gullet was back on the line. "Vanderhorst Plantation."

"Pretty high end for a pill pusher working part-time at a charity clinic. Does he own a boat?"

"I'll look into it." Gullet delivered the admonition I was expecting. "Now don't you and your one still active boy pal go pestering Marshall again. If you're right about any of this, no sense provoking him into a sprint."

"If?" I'd been up all night and my Southern gentility, never my strongest point, was eroding. "Marshall's a sleaze. Two patients and a former clinic employee have disappeared. God knows where Flynn's body is!"

"You tell me Rodriguez has no criminal record. He's Mexican and he's left California to practice in Mexico. No one has shown me any connection to South Carolina. I have no basis to ask Mexican authorities to make inquiries. You know as well as I do probing a man based on his heritage is considered harassment. Ethnic profiling."

"There could be a hundred reasons Rodriguez—"

Flapping a hand for attention, Ryan slid me his tablet. I read the notes.

"Rodriguez isn't in the NCIC database because he hasn't committed a crime in the United States. Rodriguez lost his license in California for having sex with patients."

I threw Ryan a questioning look. He nodded confirmation.

"How does that add up to a crime in South Carolina?"

I couldn't believe this deadass was still unconvinced. "Do I have to dump a five-gallon Hefty full of kidneys on your desk?"

Ryan mouthed, "Good one."

"I have found, miss, that in law enforcement, runaway conjecture is a poor substitute for evidence. You might give that some thought. I'm coming to collect that computer." Gullet's tone actually conveyed sentiment now. Distaste. "Sit tight."

"Let me guess," I said, returning Ryan's tablet. "From the multitalented Jerry."

"Jerry's the bomb."

"Gullet's on his way. He's listening, but not persuaded. Thinks I'm a hysteric."

"What will it take?"

"A guilt-riddled recipient baring his soul on Jerry Springer."

Two hours later we had something better, thanks to the enigmatic but assiduous Jerry. I hit Gullet as he walked through the door.

"James Gartland, Indianapolis, Indiana. End-stage renal disease. Three years on dialysis. Traveled to Puerto Vallarta in 2002. Paid a hundred and twenty thousand dollars for a kidney and a sojourn at the Abrigo Aislado de los Santos.

"Vivian Foss, Orlando, Florida. End-stage renal disease. Eighteen months on dialysis. Flew to Puerto Vallarta in 2004. Vivian's spa getaway cost a hundred and fifty grand." I thrust Jerry's information at Gullet. "The lucky recipients will not be crazy about testifying, but God bless subpoenas."

Gullet took a long time reading what Ryan had written during his third conversation with Jerry.

"This contact is FBI?"

"Yes," Ryan said.

"He spoke with Gartland and Foss personally?"

"Yes."

"How'd he get the names?"

"Persuaded a very nice Spanish-speaking agent in Quantico to speak to a very nice Mexican lady at the Abrigo."

"Money talks?"

*"Sí."*

"Why'd these people open up?"

"Jerry's a very charismatic guy," Ryan said.

Gullet kept staring at the tablet. I guessed he was organizing facts in his head. When he looked up, his face was a sculpture in stone.

"Feds thinking of jumpin' in on this?"

"Right now it's just Jerry doing me a favor. This plays out the way we're thinking, I'm sure the Bureau will be nose to the glass."

"Still, Gartland and Foss without more don't demonstrate a crime."

I threw up my hands.

"However." Gullet inhaled then exhaled through his nose. Hitched his belt. "Marshall keeps a twenty-three-foot Bayliner at the Bohicket Marina. According to the dock manager, the boat went out Saturday, hasn't come back."

"Ryan and I talked to Marshall on Saturday," I said.

"You mention any of this?" Gullet waved Ryan's tablet.

I shook my head. "But I asked about Unique Montague and Helene Flynn."

Gullet checked his watch. Ryan and I checked ours. It was 9:47.

"Let's see if we can locate the gentleman and speak some more. The clinic may not be my jurisdiction, but two bodies are."

Ryan and I followed Gullet to the clinic. On the way we barely spoke. I was wired, yet exhausted from my night without sleep. I could only guess what was going on inside Ryan.

Two deputies met us outside on Nassau. The crime unit arrived as Gullet was instructing his backup team. A search warrant had been granted. Once it was served, the CSU would toss the clinic from top to bottom. On the way in from Isle of Palms, Gullet had reconsidered and phoned Mexico. I hoped that a similar scene was playing out at the spa in Puerto Vallarta.

My heart pounded in my chest. What if I'd made a mistake? No. I couldn't be wrong. It had to be Marshall. The man was evil and a predator for profit.

One uniform circled the block to cover the rear of the clinic. Ryan and I trailed Gullet and the other uniform through the front door. Berry was at her desk. Her eyes widened as she took in the sheriff and his deputy, hardened when she spotted Ryan and me.

Gullet strode to the desk. The uniform lingered at the entrance. Ryan and I stepped to either side of the room.

Three patients waited in the vinyl chairs, an

elderly black woman, a punk in sweats, and a man who looked like a high school tennis coach. The old woman watched us through large, square glasses. The punk and the coach headed for the door. Gullet's deputy stepped aside to let them pass.

"Where's Dr. Marshall?" Gullet asked Berry, all business.

"Examining a patient." Hostile.

Gullet moved toward the corridor down which Marshall had led us three days earlier. Berry charged from her desk and spread her arms across the entrance, a pit bull defending her patch.

"You can't go back there." Still hostile, but now a note of fear.

Gullet kept going. We all followed.

"What do you want?" Berry backed down the hall, arms spread-eagle, still trying to block our progress. "This is a clinic. People are sick."

"Please clear the way, miss." Gullet's voice was Southern steel.

I was so pumped I almost pushed Berry aside myself. I wanted Marshall in the sheriff's presence quickly, before he could dial his Mexican counterpart.

Then the doctor appeared, exiting his office, chart in one hand. "What's the commotion, Miss Berry?"

Berry's arms dropped, but the glare held. She started to speak. Marshall cut her off with the flick of a manicured hand.

"Sheriff Gullet," said Marshall, looking perfectly composed in his white lab coat and impeccably coiffed hair, Marcus Welby calming an unruly patient. He nodded in my direction. "Dr. Brennan. The name is Brennan, is it not?"

My heart was racing. I wanted to get the goods on this bastard and see him pay for what he'd done.

"Dr. Lester Marshall, I have a warrant to search these premises for information concerning patients who have vanished under suspicious circumstances." Gullet's voice was typically deadpan.

Marshall's lips curled into a reptilian smile.

"Now why would such disappearances concern me, Sheriff?"

The words were out before I could stop them. "You know there's stuff in here that may tell us why and how they died."

"Is this a joke?" Marshall spoke to Gullet. "If so, I assure you, I am not amused."

"Sir, I am going to ask you to step aside while we conduct our search." Gullet's tone remained expressionless. "I'd prefer to make this as painless as possible for both of us."

"What should I do?" Berry asked, her voice pitched higher now.

Marshall ignored her. "What is this insanity, Sheriff? I'm a doctor. I help the poor and the sick. I don't victimize them. You are making a mistake." Marshall spoke to Gullet, his icy calm in stark contrast to the rising agitation of his receptionist.

"Sir." Gullet never took his eyes from Marshall.

Marshall handed the chart in his hand to Gullet. "You will regret this, Sheriff."

"Tell me what to do!" Berry barked.

"Please see to the patient in exam room two, Ms. Berry."

Berry held a moment, eyes darting from Gullet, to Marshall, to me. Then she lumbered up the hall and disappeared through one of the doors.

Gullet motioned Marshall to the waiting area. "We'll just stand easy until the warrant arrives."

Marshall's eyes locked on to mine. In them I saw unconcealed hatred.

As the deputy led Marshall past me to a vinyl chair, I caught a whiff of the pricey aftershave, noticed again the creamy silk, the soft glow of the tasseled leather. My fingers curled into fists of anger. I felt repulsed by the arrogance, by the pompous indifference of the bastard.

Then I spotted it. Marshall's right temple. A vein pulsed like an engorged snake.

Marshall was terrified.

# 33

We waited outside, drinking coffee from Styrofoam cups. A small crowd gathered on the sidewalk, attracted by the cruisers and the crime scene van. When the DA arrived with the warrant, the CSU moved in. Gullet asked Ryan and me to sit tight while the team tossed the clinic and he and his deputy interrogated the staff.

An hour passed. Slowly, the gawkers drifted off, disappointed that no body had appeared.

Just before noon, Gullet strode across Nassau to where Ryan and I were leaning on the Jeep.

"Finding anything that could lead to charges?" I asked.

"Got a couple things you might want to see."

Ryan and I followed Gullet into the clinic. Berry was being questioned at her desk. Daniels was sitting in one of the vinyl chairs. Neither appeared to be enjoying the day. Marshall had gone out to wait in his car.

"What if he uses his cell phone?" I asked Gullet.

"I can't really prevent that, but I can sure trace any calls he makes."

Gullet led us to a second-story treatment room. The place looked standard-issue. Chair. Stool. Gooseneck lamp. Dome-topped trash can. Paper-draped examination table.

As I crossed the linoleum, my eyes roved the cabinets and walls. Plastic cups, tongue depressors, eye test chart, baby scale.

"No bloody scalpel?" Ryan asked behind me.

"Just this."

I turned. Gullet was holding a clear plastic evidence bag. Inside was a noose made of quarter-inch wire. Seeing the side twist, I knew the loop's deadly purpose.

I pictured Unique Montague hopping up onto the treatment table, alone, unwell, trusting the kindly doctor to make her better. I pictured Unique in that rusty barrel, decomposing in salt water. I imagined sea creatures probing the metal to get inside to her rotting flesh. I felt the beginnings of rage.

"Where was it?" Ryan asked.

"Stashed in an under-counter cabinet."

"Prints?" I asked, seeing powder on the wire.

Gullet shook his head.

"He probably wore surgical gloves. Though it sure as hell wasn't to protect the patient." I couldn't keep the loathing from my voice.

"Follow me," Gullet said.

The two remaining upstairs doors led into one large chamber, probably created by removing walls between what had been small bedrooms and a bath. The chamber had been outfitted with a refrigerator, a double stainless steel sink, and counters and cabinets identical to those in the examining room. An IV pole stood in one corner. An operating table held center stage.

Lining one wall were four bright blue coolers, the kind you buy at Wal-Mart to haul lunch to the beach. Each had been tagged with a red-and-yellow evidence sticker.

"A do-it-yourself surgery," Ryan said.

"Complete with blackout curtains and state-of-the-art OR lighting." Gullet swept an arm around the room.

Evidence bags covered the table. I crossed to them.

Surgical clamps. At least twenty scissors of various types. Hemostatic, mosquito, and tissue forceps. Scalpel handles and boxes of disposable blades. Shipping labels stamped BIOLOGICAL SUPPLY HOUSE SPECIMEN. Sterile pouches. Stacked instrument trays.

Liquid mercury boiled in my chest.

"What about patient files?" I asked, finding it hard to keep my voice neutral.

"Berry will be producing all paper records," Gullet said. "We've confiscated the computer."

"Does patient information go up the chain to GMC?"

Gullet shook his head. "Clinic is a self-contained operation, records never leave. After six years, they're destroyed."

"What's Berry's story?" Ryan asked.

"Never saw a thing out of the ordinary. Dr. Marshall is a saint."

"How about Daniels?"

"Never saw a thing out of the ordinary. Dr. Marshall is a saint."

"The cleaning guy?"

"O'Dell Towery. Comes in nights. Mildly retarded. Got a deputy talking with Towery now. Doubt that's going anywhere."

"What's happening in Mexico?" I asked.

"Soon's I hear, you'll know."

"What about Marshall's office?"

"CSU bagged one thing you'll like." Gullet thrust both hands into his pants pockets, came out empty, patted his shirt. "Hold on."

I heard the sheriff clomp down, then back up the hall. Reentering the OR, he held out a small evidence bag. "From a hollow below the pen rack in the desk drawer. CSU sucked it out with some kind of vacuum thingy."

I felt jubilation elbow the abhorrence in my gut.

The bag held a small brown shell. Like the small brown shell I'd found in Willie Helms's grave.

"If you folks will excuse me a moment," Gullet said, "I must inform the good doctor that he is under arrest for suspicion of the murder of Unique Montague, and arrange for his custody and transportation."

After a quick lunch, Ryan and I stopped by the hospital. More good news. Pete was conversing normally and regaining a little color. According to the surgeon, the Latvian Savant had suffered muscle tearing and some arterial bleeding and would need rehab, but should mend without permanent damage.

I was surprised by the choking sensation in my throat.

I knew I'd be relieved and grateful, but was stunned by the intensity of emotion that swept through me. Looking at Pete with his tubes and tape and machinery, I felt tears break from my lids. A few inches more toward the midline, and that bullet could have killed him. Disguising the gesture as a hair tuck, I wiped my cheeks.

Ryan took my hand and squeezed. I looked up. The confusion on his face told me he'd seen.

Emma had also had a reasonably good report. Her blood count wasn't up, but neither was it down. Dr. Russell had adjusted her regimen and dosage, and though still exhausted, she was no longer tossing *all* of her cookies.

At our request, Emma called the malacologist. If Ryan and I came to Columbia, would he examine the shells that day?

He would. We were cookin'!

The drive took less than ninety minutes. A man named Lepinsky met us in the lobby of the state crime lab building. Lepinsky was tall and brawny, with a shiny bald head and a loop in one ear, more Mr. Clean than my image of a biology prof.

"Thanks for coming in," I said.

Lepinsky shrugged one overmuscled shoulder. "No classes today, campus is a spit from here."

Lepinsky took us to a small lab containing cabinets with zillions of long, narrow drawers. Black-topped counters held work trays, glove boxes, glass slides, and microscopes.

"Let's see what you got," Lepinsky said, holding out a hand the size of one of those foam things fans wave at sporting events.

I produced the evidence bag.

Lepinsky tweezed out the shell, placed it under a scope, sat, and adjusted focus.

Seconds ticked by. A full minute. Five more.

Ryan and I exchanged glances over Lepinsky's hunched back. Ryan raised his brows and palms. What could be taking so long? I shrugged.

Lepinsky flipped the shell.

The air was close and hot and smelled of disinfectant and glue. Beside me, Ryan shifted his feet. Checked his watch.

I gave him the look my mother gave me when I wiggled in church.

Ryan cleared his throat, turned, and checked out the cabinets.

Lepinsky again rotated the shell. Changed magnification.

Ryan crossed his arms. I knew a comment was coming.

"Cases hold reference collections?" he asked.

"Mm," Lepinsky said.

"Cost a lot of clams?"

Lepinsky didn't answer.

"Must have been a bear to mussel them up here."

I rolled my eyes.

"Mussels and clams are not the same thing," Lepinsky said, deadpan as Gullet, then looked up. The scope light made the hairs curling from his T look like small, white wires.

"And what are you kiddies hoping Santa will bring?"

"A freshwater snail named *Viviparus intertextus*," I said.

"You've been good boys and girls."

"So mussels and clams don't attend the same family reunions," Ryan said, merging onto I-26. "Go figure."

It was after six, and we were on our way back to Charleston. We'd stopped at Maurice's Piggy Park. The man's politics are offensive, but Maurice Bessinger makes primo barbecue sauce.

Exhausted from my all-nighter, and gorged on pork, fries, and sweet tea, I wanted to collapse against the headrest and drift off. Instead, I called to tell Gullet about Lepinsky's ID.

"The snails were the same freshwater species I found buried with Helms."

"You're going to love this."

Did I actually hear a note of something in Gullet's voice? Pleasure? Satisfaction?

"When they finished the clinic, the DA got a second warrant and CSU tossed Marshall's home. The doctor is one fastidious little toad. Place was like a monastery, antiseptically clean, few personal items. But Marshall was a collector."

"Shells!" No question about *my* tone. Elation.

"Hundreds, all labeled and lined up in neat little boxes."

I heard a voice in the background.

"Hang on." Gullet put me on hold.

While waiting, I told Ryan about Marshall's hobby.

"Hope he didn't put clams and mussels in the same tray."

When Gullet reengaged he had more news.

"Marshall's Bayliner's in Key Largo, Florida."

"That was fast."

"Sent out an APB on the boat's make and registration number. Key Largo cops spotted her about twenty minutes ago. Name's the *Flight of Whimsy*."

"Flight, yes, whimsy, no. How'd she get to the Keys?"

"Gentleman named Sandy Mann claims to have purchased her in Charleston, made the run south on Sunday. Time line tallies. According to witnesses, the *Flight of Whimsy*'s been docked at the marina since sometime on Monday."

"What's Mann's story?"

"He's on his way in to tell it."

"Rodriguez?"

"The Puerto Vallarta police hit the Abrigo whatever about the time we were busting Marshall. Found pretty much the same setup, though more sophisticated on that end. Spa's a front."

"Rodriguez?"

"Not at the spa, his home, or his club. One vehicle missing. Girlfriend thinks he may have driven to Oaxaca to visit friends."

"He's skipped."

"Most likely."

"Marshall must have tipped him."

"They'll nail him. Though the Mexican cops aren't certain what the charges will be."

"The man sold organs ransacked from murder victims."

"I suspect Dr. Rodriguez's lawyer will paint a different picture. If he has bogus records for the sources of the organs he implanted it may be hard to make a case. We need to show delivery of a victim's organ and knowledge on his part."

"Doctor." I snorted in disgust. "The man is a moral invalid and should be locked up. No one who promotes death deserves to be called doctor. Same goes for Marshall."

"Marshall's not going anywhere. Magistrate's holding him on a charge of murder one."

"What's he saying?"

"'I want a lawyer.'"

"Statute gives him the right to a hearing before a judge within forty-eight hours. Marshall will be out on bond by Friday."

"If so, we'll be on him like white on rice. My deputy's going through clinic files now."

"You've got my spreadsheet?"

"First set of names we checked. Nothing. Marshall probably destroyed all records for patients he killed."

"He still had Montague's file."

"True."

When we'd disconnected, I updated Ryan. Then I leaned back and closed my eyes. Though dog tired, I felt good. Really good.

Marshall was behind bars and evidence was being collected that would nail him for homicide and countless other charges.

We'd shut down an international ring trafficking in human organs. Though Rodriguez had slipped the net for now, I was sure he'd be caught and prosecuted.

I'd fulfilled my vow to help Emma. The man on Dewees, the man in the trees, and the lady in the barrel could now rest in peace.

Gullet was working with the Charleston PD, and I was sure other MPs would eventually be tracked. Maybe Aikman, Teal, and Flynn. If international laws were broken, the FBI would undoubtedly sign on.

When Ryan pulled in at "Sea for Miles," I checked the dash clock: 7:42. We were climbing the steps when my cell phone sounded. I clicked on, hoping it was Gullet with news Rodriguez was in the bag.

"Dr. Brennan." The voice was male, but otherwise, nothing clicked.

"Who's calling, please?"

"Dr. Lester Marshall. I need to see you."

"There is absolutely nothing—"

"Quite the contrary. And perhaps I misspoke." Marshall paused. "It is *you* who need to see me."

"I doubt that."

"Doubting me would be unwise, Dr. Brennan. Come tomorrow. You know where to find me."

# 34

Marshall was being held at the detention center on Leeds Avenue in North Charleston. Ryan and I went to see him the next morning. We'd discussed the pros and cons before falling asleep. Ryan was con. I was pro. Gullet and the DA took my side, saying there was nothing to lose.

To be honest, I was curious. Marshall's ego was the size of a planet. Why would he lower himself to call me? Did he want to make a deal? Pointless. Plea bargaining was a matter for the DA.

In addition to curiosity, I had another purpose. I'd seen Ryan interrogate suspects. Given Marshall's arrogance, I felt there was a chance the creep might incriminate himself.

At the detention center, Ryan and I passed through security and were led to a second-floor interrogation room. Marshall and his lawyer were already there, seated at a gray metal table. Marshall tensed visibly at seeing Ryan. Neither man rose.

"Who's this?" the lawyer asked.

"Bodyguard," I said.

"No," the lawyer said.

Shrugging indifference, I turned to go.

Marshall raised a hand. The lawyer turned to him. Marshall gave a tight nod. The lawyer gestured that we should sit.

Ryan and I took chairs opposite the two men. The lawyer introduced himself as Walter Tuckerman. He was short and balding, with heavy-lidded eyes flecked with tiny red veins.

Tuckerman spoke first, looking at me. "Dr. Marshall has a statement to make. You, and *only* you, may ask questions pertaining to that statement. Should any question go outside the bounds of that statement, I will terminate this meeting. Is that understood, Miss Brennan?"

"It's 'Doctor.' " Icy.

Tuckerman gave me an oily smile. "Dr. Brennan."

Who the hell was this guy? Marshall was taking up *my* time. Though my impulse was adios, I remained seated.

Tuckerman patted his client's sleeve. "Go ahead, Lester."

Marshall folded manicured hands on the tabletop. He was looking significantly less natty today in his washed-too-many-times faded blue prison garb.

"I have been set up."

"Really."

"There is nothing concrete to connect me to

385

these murders." Marshall kept his eyes fixed on me.

"The DA thinks otherwise."

"What has been concocted is purely circumstantial."

"Unique Montague, Willie Helms, and Noble Cruikshank were all strangled with a wire noose. The police found such a noose at your clinic. In harvesting the organs of Helms and Montague, you left scalpel cuts on their bones."

"Anyone can buy a scalpel."

"Your clinic is outfitted with a makeshift OR. Odd for a facility specializing in aspirins and Band-Aids."

"It was hardly an OR. I am occasionally called upon to excise a boil or do simple suturing. I require good lighting."

When Gullet, the DA, and I had deliberated the advisability of my visiting Marshall and had decided that I would, indeed, talk with him, we'd also discussed what approach I would take. The DA had suggested that I appear open, create the impression I was tipping my hand, while at the same time revealing nothing that the accused didn't already know. Ryan had agreed that the tactic could prove fruitful.

"The Puerto Vallarta police raided your buddy's 'spa.'" I finger-hooked quotation marks. "We know Rodriguez trained as a surgeon, and have statements from patients who received kidneys at his facility. We know that you and Rodriguez attended med school together, and that both of you were sanctioned for abusing your medical licenses." The DA had already shared with Marshall her awareness of all this.

"Very true. But the scenario you've fabricated is entirely speculative."

"Enjoy malacology, Dr. Marshall?" Marshall knew about the eyelash, but we weren't certain if he knew about the shells. We'd decided I would bring them up in order to gauge his reaction.

Marshall ignored the question.

"Your collection missing a few specimens? *Viviparus intertextus* maybe?"

"Hardly relevant," Tuckerman said.

"The *Viviparus intertextus* shell found with Willie Helms was identical to a shell found in your office desk. Willie Helms was buried on a beach on Dewees. *Viviparus intertextus* is a freshwater species."

"Ask yourself, Dr. Brennan, why in the world would I carry shells on my person while disposing of a body? Surely you see that that is pure stage management."

"You're suggesting someone planted the shells on Helms's body and in your desk to throw suspicion on you?"

"I am. Originally, not to throw suspicion on me. Just to introduce a spurious factor so that if the body was discovered there would be evidence it came from some other area. But after your visit to the clinic, the killer decided to point the finger toward me by planting a shell in my desk. I never took shells to the clinic."

"And who would this killer be?"

"Corey Daniels."

"Where did Daniels get them?"

Marshall snorted derisively. "He could have gathered them from any swamp. Think about it. If you want to throw suspicion on a true collector, why choose a species that's as abundant in this general area as a common housefly? Anyone with half a brain would have chosen a much more exotic form. This is typical of Daniels. The man is a dullard."

"I discovered an eyelash inside that shell. Black. Willie Helms was blond. Enjoy the mouth swab, Dr. Marshall? That lash should yield some interesting DNA."

Marshall let out a long breath and stared at the ceiling, a teacher displeased with an ill-prepared student. "Even if the lash is mine, I worked with Daniels every day. He had easy access. Body hairs are shed routinely."

I did not reply.

"Let me ask you this." Marshall's eyes came back to me. "Was evidence found with any of these other victims?"

"I am not at liberty to discuss that." I knew the DA had not shared that finding with Marshall and his lawyer. No way I'd provide the defense with a statement of what we didn't know.

"The answer is no. Otherwise I would be charged with those crimes. Think about the flaw in your reasoning." Marshall's tone was pure disdain. "I am sufficiently vigilant to leave not a single clue with any other victim, yet I drop a shell and an eyelash with Willie Helms? Then I leave another shell in my desk?"

The question seemed rhetorical, so I didn't answer.

"Are you so blinded by hatred of me that you cannot consider the possibility that I am being framed?" Marshall spread his fingers.

"By Corey Daniels."

"Yes."

I shook my head in disbelief. "A nurse wouldn't have the skills to extract live organs, and to do it under your nose without your knowledge."

"Extraction is not that difficult, particularly if you're not concerned about the welfare of the donor. Check Daniels out. He's got a record."

"Let me get this straight. You're claiming Corey Daniels was killing *your* patients and selling organs to *your* former classmate?"

"What I'm claiming is that I'm being framed." The vein in Marshall's temple was pumping a geiser.

"Why did you dump your boat?" Ryan asked.

Tuckerman's hand shot up. I could see nicotine stains on his fingers.

Marshall cut Tuckerman off before he could object to Ryan's participation in the interview.

"That sale had been in the works for months. A sport fisherman named Alexander Mann made me an offer last fall, then his loan fell through. It took him until now to arrange financing."

Ryan said nothing. It was a technique I'd seen

him employ many times. When faced with silence, most suspects feel compelled to resume talking. Marshall did that now.

"You can verify my account by speaking with the man."

Ryan and I gave Marshall more silence.

"Pen and paper," Marshall demanded of Tuckerman.

"Lester—"

Marshall flicked an impatient hand.

Tuckerman took a ballpoint and a yellow legal pad from his briefcase. Marshall wrote calmly, then tore off a sheet and handed it to me.

"That's Mann's bank. Call them."

Wordlessly, I folded the paper and placed it in my purse. "Your pilot should tell an interesting tale."

Marshall looked momentarily flustered. "Pilot?"

I kept my eyes steady on Marshall.

"What pilot?"

"I didn't come to trip you up, Dr. Marshall." That was exactly the reason I'd made reference to the pilot. Gullet had yet to track down a plane or any information on the means by which organs were smuggled to Mexico. "I came to hear you out."

"What you're saying is absurd." Marshall wet his lips. "I have no pilot."

Marshall closed his eyes. When he opened them something cold and hard had come into his gaze. He fixed it on me.

"The situation is simple. Daniels has framed me.

Thanks to you, Gullet and his moronic DA have fallen into the trap of believing ridiculously circumstantial evidence. I am not amused. These false accusations are ruining my good name."

"Is that what this is, Doctor? Name calling? Sticks and stones?"

"I break no bones. I am a healer."

I shook my head, too disgusted to answer.

Marshall retwined his fingers.

"I know you loathe me for many things. I have failed to uphold my Hippocratic oath. Years ago I abused drugs. All that has changed."

Marshall clasped his fingers so tightly the flesh blanched.

"I accepted my present position with GMC to compensate for the waste I have made of my talents and my life. I served time in prison. Undoubtedly you have discovered that. During those years of confinement, I met people whose existence I could never have imagined. I saw violence. I saw despair. I vowed upon my release to place my medical skills at the service of the disadvantaged."

I heard shifting in the chair beside me. No way Ryan was buying it.

"I know I appear guilty. And I *am* guilty of many things. But not this. Despite my past failings, I am and have always been a healer. I did not kill these people."

Raising the clasped fists to his chin, Marshall breathed deeply. "But perhaps I misjudge my tormenter."

Marshall let out the breath.

"If not Daniels, someone else is setting me up."

"Good one on the pilot," Ryan said as we were leaving the detention center.

"I thought Marshall might let something slip."

"He's cunning as a fox."

"He is that. So why did he want to talk to me?"

"You're cuter than Gullet, and the DA probably told him to kiss off."

"Think there could be anything to it?"

"Yeah, right. And hot pants were a high point in fashion."

"I had hot pants," I said.

Ryan did a Groucho brow flash. "Seeing that might have altered my opinion of the seventies."

"If Marshall's on the level, you were right about Daniels doing time."

"Whaddya know."

It was a short drive to the sheriff's department. Exiting the Jeep, I noticed Adele Berry thundering down the front walk. Past her I could see Gullet's dog sleeping under a row of boxwoods bordering the building.

Berry's updo was wilted, her black skin glistened, and her red polyester blouse was mottled with sweat. Though it was close, the retriever took best in show.

Berry hesitated. I thought she'd circle to avoid us, but instead she bore down like a swimmer firing off the block.

"Why you doing this?" The fleshy face was

welded into a mask of anger. "Why you trying to ruin a good man?"

"Dr. Marshall murdered innocent people," I said.

"That's crazy talk."

"The evidence is overwhelming."

Berry ran a palm across her forehead and wiped it on her skirt. "I got blood pressure could launch a missile. My job's gone, but my bills sure as hell gonna keep on comin'. Anyone getting killed, it's you and the police killing me." She pronounced it "poe-lice."

"How long did you work at the GMC clinic?"

Berry shot a hip and planted an enormous hand on it. "You've got no right to ask me nothin':"

"No, I don't. But I find it curious you wouldn't want to share anything that could help the investigation."

Again Berry palmed away perspiration. "Five months. So why bust my ass? And Daniels. They're grillin' that man like a cheese sandwich."

"Daniels may have seen or heard something."

"They're learning nothin'."

"What does that mean?"

"Means there's nothin' to learn."

With a last parting glare, Berry strode toward the parking lot.

"I still think she dislikes us," Ryan said, holding wide the glass door.

Daniels was cooling his heels in an interrogation room. Gullet was watching him through two-way glass.

I described our meeting with Marshall. Gullet listened, hands in his pockets. Ryan studied Daniels.

"Think there could be anything to Marshall's claim he's been set up?" I asked.

Gullet turned back to the glass. "Not by this guy. He's dumb as a bag of hammers."

"What's his story?"

"Born in seventy-two, no juvie record. Enrolled in College of Charleston in ninety, premed major. Story goes there was some great-great-grand-something picking up the tab. Daniels took up with a woman who didn't make grade, the Golden Goose cut the eggs, Daniels buggered off to Texas. He did nursing school in El Paso while the girlfriend worked and picked up the bills."

"Why Texas?"

"Girlfriend's home turf. Daniels got his RN in ninety-four, started working at the same hospital he did his training."

"Where's that?"

"Some branch of UT. I can check."

"How did he end up back here?"

"Relationship went south, lot of domestic calls by the neighbors, girlfriend eventually threw him out, got a restraining order, he violated, whole thing came down to a brawl, she's down the stairs with a broken collarbone. Daniels got tagged for six, did three. Dropped out of sight for a while, busted up a hand, slunk back to Charleston in 2000 for R and R. Started at the clinic in 2001. Guy's no braintrust."

"Or he could be one hell of a con," Ryan said.

"Sir?" Gullet's tone was pure cynicism.

"Never rule out the improbable."

"Trust me. There's no Phi Beta Kappa key in this guy's drawer."

"Daniels earned an RN," I said. "He can't be that stupid."

Gullet blew air through his nostrils. "Lord save me from conspiracy theories. Marshall is dirty and looking for a fall guy."

"What's Daniels's take on Marshall?"

"Let's just say he's not eager to talk about the boss."

"Why are you still holding him?" Ryan asked.

"Lousy attitude. Providing quiet time for the boy to ponder respect for the law."

We watched Daniels probe a molar with a thumbnail. I was surprised when Ryan asked permission to question him.

"Now why would I let you do that, Detective?" Gullet's tone was almost amused.

"I think I've spotted a basis for rapport," Ryan said.

Gullet shrugged, hands still pocketed. "Use the recorder."

# 35

Gullet and I watched Ryan enter the interrogation room. Daniels looked up, then stretched out his legs and slouched, one arm on the table, one draping the chair back.

"Remember me, Corey?" Ryan asked.

"Detective Do-right."

"Close enough."

"I need a cigarette."

"Tough," Ryan said.

Daniels looked momentarily surprised, went back to bored.

*Rapport?* I thought.

"Do you object to having this interview taped?" Ryan asked.

"Would it matter if I did?"

"It's for your protection and mine."

Ryan turned on the machine, tested, spoke his name, the name of the witness, the time, and the date.

"Your boss is in a lot of trouble," Ryan began.

"What's that got to do with me?"

"What were your duties at the GMC clinic?"

"I'm a nurse."

"What did you do, exactly?"

"Nurse people."

"Easy enough to find out."

"Do what you gotta do."

"I'm getting the impression there's a lack of enthusiasm for this conversation, Corey."

"What? I should say I like getting busted by the heat?"

"Some of that heat could be turned onto you."

"You'll never make a case for me offing those people."

"Who says anyone wants to do that?"

"Marshall's not trying to put this on me?"

"Actually, he is."

"I been hassled before. I can deal." Daniels shot a hand through his hair. "I really need a smoke."

"Why nursing?"

"What?"

"You're what? Six-five, two-eighty? Tough guy like you. Why nursing?"

"Good money. High demand."

"Write your own ticket."

"Yeah."

Ryan indicated Daniels's tattoos.

"Where'd you do your stretch?"

"Huntsville."

"What was the bump?"

Daniels snorted. "Bitch claimed I smacked her

around, coonass judge bought the whole crock."
Daniels made a finger pistol of his right hand and
shot it at Ryan. "Don't mess with Texas."

I glanced at Daniels's tattoos. Skulls, a skewered
heart, spiders in a web, entwined snakes crawling
the forearm. Classy. I was beginning to wonder
when the rapport would kick in when Ryan thumb-
jabbed Daniels's belt buckle.

"I see you're a Harley guy."

"So?"

"I had a ninety-five Ultra Classic Electra Glide.
Loved that bike more than my own mother."

For the first time Daniels looked directly at
Ryan. "You shitting me?"

"Man lies about some things. His height. His
dick. Never his bike."

Daniels slapped a hand to his chest. "Two
thousand and four Screamin' Eagle Fat Boy."

"A softail man."

"Touring bikes are for wimps," Daniels scoffed.

"No feeling in the world like flying with the wind
in your face."

"You got that right."

"Ever been gunning along, suddenly you're
eating cement?" Ryan asked, grinning.

"No shit." Smiling broadly, Daniels placed both
arms on the table, palms up. One wrist was circled
by a crescent-shaped scar. "A nun." Daniels shook
his head in disbelief. "Clipped by a nun in a
Hyundai. Next thing I know I'm in an ER and she's
setting up a hotline to God. Hospital scene was
worse than the fucking wipeout."

"When I got nuked the prick never stopped."

"This nun still follows up, feels guilty as hell. I tell her forget it. Price of the ride, man, price of the ride."

"Permanent damage?"

"Pussy left hook, but who needs it? My right's the annihilator." Another incredulous head shake. "A nun."

Ryan nodded understanding, fellow bikers baffled by the foibles of fate. Daniels was the first to speak.

"Look, man, I'm sorry those people got greased. But I had nothing to do with it."

"We're not trying to get in your face, Corey. This is information gathering. We just need to know if you ever noticed Marshall do or say anything weird."

"It's like I told that Nazi sheriff. Marshall was a psycho about two things. Keeping the place clean, and keeping out of his office."

"What was the purpose of the large room upstairs?"

Daniels shrugged. "Beats me. Never saw anyone in it but the cleaning guy."

"You never found that odd?"

"Look. I came in, I did my job, I left."

"Notice anything off about Marshall?"

"We've been over and over this shit. I wouldn't want to get naked with the guy, but Marshall was an OK boss, all right?"

"How about Helene Flynn?"

Daniels slouched back again. "Shit, I don't

know. She was like this nun I'm talking about. Classy. Real nice to the patients. I tried feeling her out, you know, dropped a few lines, chick shut me down cold. I don't need to go begging for it, you know what I mean?"

"Did Helene get along with Marshall?"

Daniels's finger was working the tabletop, making a soft squeaking noise.

"Corey?"

Daniels shrugged. "I dunno. At first, yeah. Later, she seemed jumpy when the doc was around. I figured maybe he was hitting on her, too."

"Do you know why she left?"

"Marshall said she quit, hired Berry." Daniels was still fingertipping the table. "Don't ask, don't tell. That's my motto."

"Did Marshall ever work late?"

"Sometimes he let Berry and me leave early."

A second passed. Daniels's finger froze.

"Fuckin' A, man. I see what you're saying." Daniels overnodded as he spoke. "Something's wrong there. The guy's a doctor. Locking up was Berry's job."

From the sheriff's department, we went to the hospital. Pete was in a private room on the med-surge floor. Ryan waited in the lobby while I went up.

The Latvian Savant was awake and cranky. His Jell-O was green. His nurse was deaf. His gown was too small and his cheeks were catching cold.

Though Pete's carping was annoying, annoyance was a relief. My heart felt light. He was healing. Katy had called finally and I'd been able to assure her of her father's imminent recovery.

Lily phoned Ryan late that afternoon. She was with friends in Montreal and wanted to see him. Ryan promised to be there by Friday. His vacation was over, he had to return to work on Monday. Leaving two days early meant he could spend the weekend with his daughter. He was grinning when he delivered the news. I hugged him. We held each other a very long time, each lost in thoughts of another. A nonsevered spouse. A newly realized child.

Ryan and I decided to splurge that night. My work in Charleston was done. Emma's unknowns were ID'd, and Marshall was looking at a lot of hard time. Maybe worse. Pete was improving rapidly. Lily was reaching out. We dined on steak and lobster at 82 Queen.

Throughout dinner Ryan and I circled cautiously, stuck to neutral topics, restricted ourselves to present and past tense. He didn't ask about the future. I didn't offer reassurance. I couldn't. I was still puzzled and confused by the strength of my reaction to Pete's proximity. To his near brush with death.

There was a lot of self-congratulation, much laughter, frequent clinking of glasses. At times I wanted to reach out and take Ryan's hand. I didn't. In the time since, I've often wondered why.

Ryan left after breakfast on Thursday. We kissed

good-bye. I waved until his Jeep disappeared, then went back into Anne's house, empty again save for a dog and a cat. I was staying in Charleston until Pete could return to Charlotte. Beyond that, I had no plans.

Boyd and I spent Thursday afternoon with Emma. When she opened her front door, Boyd jumped up and nearly knocked her down. I felt like *I'd* taken a blow to the chest. All the sparkle was gone from Emma's face. Her skin was pallid, and though the day was warm and moist, she wore a sweat suit and socks. I had to struggle to keep my smile pasted in place.

Gullet had already told Emma of Marshall's arrest. Sitting in porch rockers, we reviewed my conversations with the doctor and his nurse. Her reaction was immediate and uncompromising.

"Daniels running an international organ ring and framing his boss? Give me a break. You've seen the evidence. Marshall is a turd and he's guilty as hell."

"Yeah."

"What? You're not convinced?" Emma's skepticism ran planetary rings around Gullet's.

"Of course I am. But there are a couple things that bother me."

"For instance?"

"There wasn't a single personal item in Marshall's office. So why that one shell?"

"A million reasons. He meant to take it home but forgot about it. One escaped from a container,

402

rolled out of sight in his desk drawer, and he never knew it was there."

"Helms was killed in 2001. That shell was in Marshall's drawer all that time?"

"We're not talking conch shells, Tempe. The things are tiny."

"True."

Seeing a squirrel, Boyd shot to his feet. I put my hand on his head. He twirled the eyebrow hairs at me, but held.

I pressed my point. "But Marshall is smart. Why would he carry shells when burying a corpse?"

"Maybe the shell got wrapped up with Helms's body and Marshall didn't notice."

Boyd's head movement told me he was tracking the squirrel.

"Gullet said it himself," I said. "Marshall is fastidious. It just doesn't fit the guy's personality."

"Everyone slips up eventually."

"Maybe."

I tapped Boyd's head and pointed to the floor. Reluctantly, he settled back down at my feet.

Emma got iced tea, then the two of us rocked in silence.

A man passed outside the fence, a woman with a stroller, two kids on bikes. Occasional chow whines suggested ongoing interest in Rocky.

"What do you think the final body count will be?" I asked.

"Who knows?"

I remembered some of the names in my spread-sheet. Parker Ethridge. Harmon Poe. Daniel

Snype. Jimmie Ray Teal. Matthew Summerfield. Lonnie Aikman.

"Can I ask you something, Emma?"

"Sure."

"Why didn't you tell me about Susie Ruth Aikman?"

"Who?" Emma sounded genuinely baffled.

"Lonnie Aikman's mother was discovered dead in her car last week. Wouldn't that be considered a suspicious death?"

"Where was she?"

"Highway 176, just northwest of Goose Creek."

"Berkeley County. That's not my jurisdiction. But I can find out about her."

Of course it wasn't. I felt like an idiot to have doubted my friend. Ask about the cruise ship incident Winborne had referenced in his article on Aikman? Forget it. None of my business.

By four thirty Emma was fading. We went inside, and I made spaghetti with sauce from her freezer. Boyd prowled the kitchen, getting in my way.

Watching Emma rearrange rather than eat her dinner, I remembered my call to her sister. I told her that Sarah would be returning from Italy in the next few days, and promised to try her again. Emma insisted I let it go.

At six Boyd and I headed home. While I drove, the chow worked a loop in the rear, moving from window to window, periodically stopping to lick my right ear and cheek.

Boyd was in midcircuit when I turned into the drive at "Sea for Miles." Suddenly, he stopped, and a low growl rose from his throat.

My eyes jumped to the rearview mirror. An SUV was riding my bumper.

Fear rippled through me.

"Easy, boy." Reaching back, I finger-wrapped Boyd's collar.

Boyd tensed and gave a full-out bark.

Eyes on the rearview, I hit a button on the armrest. The automatic locks clicked shut.

The SUV driver's door opened. I saw a logo.

Boyd barked again.

I let out my breath. "It's OK, tough guy."

It was. I recognized the figure barreling toward me.

For once, I could read the expression on Gullet's face.

The sheriff wasn't happy.

# 36

Wordlessly, Gullet handed me a copy of today's *Post and Courier*. I scanned the front page.

Winborne had struck again. Only this time the story wasn't buried with the local news. Cruikshank, Helms, the clinic raid, Marshall's arrest. The piece was accompanied by a photo of the Reverend Aubrey Herron, fist raised heavenward in his trademark gesture of petition. The story wrapped up with the usual titillating teases about possible leads, final body count, and danger to the public.

I felt momentary confusion, then my emotions distilled into a searing white anger.

"That slimy little worm!"

The sheriff watched me, face stony as one of the Battery statues. Sudden realization.

"You don't seriously believe *I* tipped Winborne?"

"You told me you know him." Gullet's face deepened into a glower.

"You told me he's harmless." I glowered back.

"I don't like my investigation hung out like some cheap episode of reality TV. Herron's livid, the media are sharpening their knives and forks, and our phones are clamoring like church bells on Sunday."

"Look in your own backyard."

"You suggesting there's a leak in my department?"

"I don't know what to suggest. The story on the Cruikshank ID sure as hell didn't come from me. Winborne's been looking into Cruikshank's disappearance for a couple of months." I rolled the paper and thrust it at Gullet. "I never told him we had Cruikshank's body."

"Herron's got powerful friends."

"Of course he does. He's best buddies with God."

"With or without God he can make life hellacious for a local elected official, including the county sheriff."

Boyd's muffled bark cut across our raised voices.

I crossed to my car and opened the door. Boyd shot out and ran from bush to bush, squirting and back-flinging dirt with his paws. Bounding back, he shoved his snout into Gullet's crotch.

I wanted to high-five the dog.

Gullet chucked Boyd's ears.

Boyd licked Gullet's hand.

*Traitor*, I thought, turning my glare on the chow.

"Winborne had the vics and the arrest info, but nothing as to motive," I said.

"Agreed." Gullet rolled the paper and tapped it against one palm. "If he'd known about Rodriguez or the organ theft he'd have printed that."

"How much could Winborne have gotten by scanning police frequencies?"

"Some." Gullet did a slow eye crawl of my face. "But not all this. The radio traffic wouldn't have told him we'd identified the forest hanger as Cruikshank. He got that some other way."

As it turned out, there was a modest upside to Winborne breaking the Cruikshank story.

Early Friday a call came in to the sheriff's switchboard. Barry Lunaretti owned a King Street dive named Little Luna's. Reading Winborne's article, the name "Cruikshank" triggered an itch in Lunaretti's head. Hours later the synapse fired. Searching his lost-and-found, Lunaretti came up with a jacket holding a wallet belonging to Noble Cruikshank.

When Gullet called I did a little synapsing of my own.

"Is Little Luna's ever called the Double L?"

"Believe it is."

"That was the one bar Pinckney remembered. Cruikshank must have mistakenly grabbed Pinckney's jacket and left his own. Pinckney was undoubtedly drunk that night, hungover the next morning. He forgot about his outerwear and focused on his wallet. Does Lunaretti remember when the jacket was left?"

"Says it's been a couple of months."

Beyond satisfying my curiosity and tying off a loose end, the information didn't seem particularly dramatic. We already believed Cruikshank had been alive until a couple of months ago.

Gullet also had a progress report on the phone record dumps at Marshall's house and the GMC clinic.

"Over the past three months, calls to and from Marshall's home involved the exotica of car repairs, haircuts, and dental appointments."

"Popular guy."

"Got a little problem at the clinic, however."

I didn't interrupt.

"It'll take a while to work through all the numbers, but one pattern is clear. As a rule no one phoned in or out after closing. Four thirty, five o'clock, the place went dark." I heard Gullet's breath on the mouthpiece. "One odd one, though. On March twenty-fourth at seven oh two P.M. a ninety-second call was made to Noble Cruikshank's home."

"No! Marshall?"

"Call was dialed from his office."

"So what's the problem?"

"On March twenty-fourth Marshall was at a muscular dystrophy fund-raiser in Summerville. Witnesses confirm his presence from six thirty until ten."

My fingers tightened on the handset as a dark suspicion began to emerge.

So who called Cruikshank?

A murderer luring his victim to a rendezvous?

Wait. Think. Follow the chain. Where's it going? The call. Cruikshank's death.

"Everything points to late March for Cruikshank's DOD," I said. "He never cashed Flynn's February check. Credit card action ended around that time. Winborne saw Cruikshank on March nineteenth. I'm thinking Cruikshank died before noticing he had the wrong jacket, otherwise he'd have retrieved his wallet. He was probably killed the same night he and Pinckney crossed paths at Little Luna's. Pinckney filed a police report. Can you pull it?"

"I'll get on it."

Gullet called back in twenty minutes.

"Pinckney reported his wallet stolen on March twenty-sixth. Said it was swiped the night before."

"Someone phones Cruikshank from the GMC clinic on March twenty-fourth. Cruikshank's probably dead on March twenty-fifth. That can't be coincidence."

"So who made the call? An informant? The cleaning person?"

"What if Marshall is telling the truth? What if someone is framing him?"

"Daniels?" Gullet sounded like I'd said Milosevic had been nominated for a peace prize.

"I know it sounds nuts. A lot of signs point toward Marshall, and we followed them, but some of what he's saying is true. The surgery, the noose, the victims being patients. That's all circumstantial. Daniels worked at that clinic, too. What do we know about him?"

"Daniels doesn't explain Marshall's ties to Rodriguez. Or Marshall dumping his boat. Marshall was a shell collector. A shell from his desk matched a shell found with Willie Helms's body. Let's not waste our time. Marshall's dirty and that lash will prove it. Good thinking on this Pinckney thing, but I've got to go deal with an army of journalists camped on my doorstep."

"Any news on Rodriguez?"

"No."

"Found any connection to a pilot or plane?"

"No. It's the DA's baby now. Your job's done."

Gullet left me listening to dead air.

At nine o'clock Friday morning Lester Marshall and Walter Tuckerman appeared before a judge. Tuckerman argued that his client was a physician and a respected member of the community. The prosecution argued that he was a flight risk. The judge ordered Marshall to turn in his passport and set bail at one million dollars. Tuckerman was arranging bond. Marshall would be out before nightfall.

Gullet was right. I was through. What remained was detective work and assembling the pieces for a prosecution. It was up to deputies, the crime lab, and the DA. Phone records. Patient files. Hard drives. Time lines. Flight plans. Witness accounts. Television portrays police investigation and criminal prosecution as métiers of heart-stopping exhilaration, joie de vivre glamour, and slicker-than-snot technology. They're not. Solid cases are built upon hours and hours of mind-numbing thoroughness. Follow every angle. Sift through mounds of data. Miss nothing.

My contribution had been made. Nevertheless, I couldn't let it rest. The same thought kept winging through my brain: What if Marshall was on the level? What if we had the wrong man?

I should have been happy that the murders had stopped, more relaxed than I'd been in weeks. Instead, I was wired as a hophead on a full load. I couldn't read, nap, sit still. The same doubts kept slamming me again and again. What if Marshall is telling the truth? Is there a killer still at large and planning a sudden holiday in Mexico?

I ran Boyd on the beach. Showered. Made a sandwich. Ate a bowl of Chunky Monkey. Turned on the news. Listened to an anchorman breathlessly report Marshall's bail hearing.

Agitated, I clicked off and tossed the remote onto the couch. Dear God! What if we'd made a mistake?

At one, I gave up. After rechecking Daniels's address in the white pages, I grabbed my keys and was out the door. I didn't know what I expected to learn. Something from his manner, something from his expression?

Apparently Daniels wasn't into sand and surf. His condo was in a golf course complex complete with overgroomed foliage, tennis courts, lagoon, and pool. Each unit looked like its roof had been sliced lengthwise, with the surviving half left pointing skyward. Trés avant-garde.

Daniels lived in 4-B. Leaving my car, I slipped on shades and a sun hat. Now who'd seen too many *Columbo* episodes?

I checked a few numbers, decided I was headed for a cluster of villas to my left. The path wound through beds mounded with pine needles and planted with marigolds and crepe myrtle bushes that would one day be trees. Water sprayed from unseen spigots, sparking sunlight and magnifying the scent of flowers and earth.

Traversing the grounds, I noticed Beemers, Benzes, and high-end SUVs nosed up to individual units. Oiled bodies tanned on poolside chaises. Though not oceanfront, Daniels obviously wasn't sitting in the cheap seats. My reaction was the same as when I'd first found Daniels's Seabrook address in the telephone directory. How does a poverty clinic nurse afford such digs?

I had no plan. When I found Daniels's unit I would do what felt right.

What felt right was to knock. So much for *Columbo.*

No answer.

I tried again, with the same result. Leaning in, I peeked through a tall, thin window paralleling the door.

Daniels liked white. White walls, white wicker mirror, white bar stools, white kitchen cabinets and countertops. A white staircase shotgunned straight to a second floor. That's all I could see.

"Looking for Corey?"

I spun at the sound of the voice.

Red suspenders. Straw hat. Bermuda shorts. U.S. Postal Service shirt.

"Didn't mean to startle you, ma'am."

"No," I said, my heart settling back down. "I mean yes. Is Corey here?"

"Pretty predictable, that one. If he's not working, he's out fishing." The postman smiled up at me, one hand on his pouch, the other holding a folded magazine. "You a friend?"

"Mmm." Fishing? Boat? I did a little fishing of my own. "Corey does love his boat."

"Man's got to get away sometimes. Funny world, isn't it? Big boy like that's a nurse while tiny little girls are fighting in Iraq."

"Funny world," I agreed, my mind fixing on what I'd just learned. Daniels owned a boat!

Climbing three steps, the postman held up the magazine bundle. "Stick that in the slot?"

"Sure."

"Good day, ma'am."

I waited until the postman was moving down the path, then re-crossed the porch and rifled through Daniel's mail. *Boating* magazine. *PowerBoat*. The rest of the stack consisted of envelopes and fliers, all addressed to Corey R. Daniels. With one exception. A standard white envelope with a frosty little window. Probably a bill. The addressee was Corey Reynolds Daniels.

Shoving the mail into the slot, I headed back to the car.

The boat slips nearest to Daniels's condo were at Bohicket Marina, just past the entrance to Seabrook Island. Seemed like a good place to start.

I was there in minutes. A woman leatherized by way too much sun and wearing way too little swimsuit directed me to a sportfish cruiser on pier four.

Lines ticked masts as I walked out onto the dock. Or was it sheets? Sheets to the wind? My mind was really on a rip.

Daniels's boat wasn't one of the largest, maybe a thirty-five-footer. It had a pointy bow with a metal rail shooting to midship, a covered center console, a platform off the stern, and a cabin that looked like it could probably sleep four.

My eyes roved, taking in detail. Fighting chairs. Outriggers. Rod holders. Fish box. Bait station. Live well. The craft was definitely outfitted for fishing. But not today. Everything was secured and Daniels was nowhere to be seen.

Condo minimally a half million. Boat probably another three hundred thousand. How did he do it? The guy had to be dirty.

Sometimes it's a sight, a smell, a spoken word. Sometimes there's no trigger at all. Something just goes *boing!* and that cartoon strip bulb goes on.

My eyes fell on the boat's name.

*Boing!*

415

# 37

The *Hunney Child*.

*Some great-great-grand-something picking up the tab.*

*My nephew's living here now and he's got a dandy of a boat.*

Corey Reynolds Daniels.

Althea Hunneycut Youngblood. Honey.

Honey had married into the Reynolds family. She had a nephew who'd returned to Charleston. She had given that nephew her boat.

Honey lived on Dewees Island.

Willie Helms had been buried on Dewees Island.

Corey Daniels was Honey Youngblood's nephew. He knew Dewees Island.

Was Marshall right? Had we really arrested the wrong man? Did Daniels have the ruthlessness and brainpower to be the main guy?

Call Gullet?

No. I needed more.

I needed to get to a different marina. Throwing myself behind the wheel, I headed to Isle of Palms.

The *Aggie Gray* took ten minutes to chug in. The crossing back to Dewees Island took another twenty. It seemed a lifetime.

Luck was with me. There was an unattended golf cart at the ferry dock. Jumping in, I sped toward the administrative center.

Miss Honey was in the nature museum, cleaning an aquarium at the sink. A box of fist-size shells rested at her elbow.

"Miss Honey, I'm so glad I caught you."

"Caught me? Land's sake, girl, where else on the Lord's green earth might I be?"

"I—"

"Cleaning house for the hermit crabs." Honey nodded toward the box. Here and there I could see a curled appendage cautiously testing the outside world.

"Miss Honey, you mentioned your nephew last time we spoke."

The gnarled hands slowed, but continued scrubbing the tank. "Corey being mischievous again?" She gave the second of four syllables a very hard *e*.

"We're looking into some patient care questions at the GMC clinics and how they are staffed and all, and I'm curious about Corey's training."

"Being a nurse doesn't mean he"—the old woman hesitated—"isn't right."

"Of course not. Such stereotypes are absurd."

Honey was scouring so hard her curls were bouncing.

417

"Corey was going to be a doctor. Followed his heart instead. Boys grow up. What can you do?"

"Corey trained in Texas?"

"He did."

"Where?"

"University of Texas. He called it UTEP." *Pfft.* "What kind of name is that for a school? Sounds like a spray for foot fungus."

Honey ran water into the aquarium.

"What caused him to return to Charleston?" I asked.

"Got into trouble, lost his job, got hurt, got broke."

The old woman looked up, and the pale eyes crimped into the tiniest of frowns.

"My nephew would have made a fine doctor."

"I'm sure he would have. What were his nursing specialties?"

"ER at first, then neurology." *New*-rology. "Before he came back he'd worked his way into the OR. Did surgical nursing for two years. Mite messy for my taste. But you can't tell me slicing and sewing folks is an easy job. Yep. For my money, Corey turned out just fine."

I was barely listening. Two more disparate facts had clicked into place.

I was now concerned that we really had arrested the wrong man. The killer was looking more like Daniels.

And Daniels was still out there.

I felt cold all over.

I had to phone Gullet. No. I had to speak to Gullet. Against all logic, I was coming to believe Marshall's story that Daniels was setting him up. Persuading the sheriff to consider the idea would require face-to-face effort.

Friday afternoon traffic was bloated by weekenders pouring into the city. The drive to North Charleston took almost forty minutes.

Gullet was in his office. He looked as tense as I'd ever seen him.

"I want you to hear me out on something very important," I said, positioning a chair directly opposite the sheriff's desk.

Gullet checked his watch, then exhaled in resignation. The message was clear. This better be good. And short.

"Marshall claims he's been set up by Daniels."

Gullet studied me. "Everyone from the governor on down is using me for a dartboard. You telling me you think I've jailed the wrong man?"

"I'm telling you it's a possibility."

"We've got enough to fry Marshall three times and back."

"Marshall says our evidence is all circumstantial."

Gullet started to object. I forged ahead.

"To an extent, he's right. The evidence collected so far proves that patients were murdered at that clinic. The wire noose could have been stashed by anyone. The shell could have been planted in Marshall's desk. You know that's what the defense will argue."

"What they'll argue and what a jury will believe may differ considerably."

"You said yourself there's a problem with the phone records," I pressed on. "Someone called Noble Cruikshank from Marshall's office on a night Marshall wasn't even there."

"Cruikshank was investigating. Someone could have been snitching."

I could see Gullet didn't want to believe. He'd arrested a man, a physician. He wanted his case to be airtight. I'd urged him to that conclusion. The DA had agreed. Now I was waffling.

"Daniels's full name is Corey Reynolds Daniels, but I'm sure you already know that. What you may not know is that Daniels has an aunt living on Dewees Island. That aunt gave Daniels a boat."

"Having a boat and knowing Dewees doesn't make him a killer."

"Following nursing school, Daniels was employed by a hospital for three years. He didn't always work in a public service clinic."

"Not enough." The chair puffed as Gullet dropped back against the leather.

"He was a surgical nurse. For two years he scrubbed in, watched operations, had plenty of opportunity to learn procedure."

"Handing out instruments is a long way from being a surgeon."

"It wouldn't have taken a surgeon on this end. There was no concern with keeping patients alive. All that was needed was a knowledge of how to remove organs so as to preserve them.

"Think about timing. Daniels arrived back in Charleston in 2000, started working at the clinic in 2001. Willie Helms disappeared in September of 2001."

Seeing the first glimmer of doubt in Gullet's eyes, I hammered home the last nail.

"Cruikshank was downloading articles on organ trafficking. I read quite a few when I was checking his hard drive, but didn't realize the relevance of one in particular. Until now.

"Since 1993 almost four hundred women and girls are known to have been killed in Ciudad Juárez and Chihuahua, Mexico, another seventy have been reported missing. Students, store clerks, assembly plant workers, some as young as ten years. Bodies have been found buried in shallow graves in the desert, and at construction sites and railroad yards around the city.

"In 2003 the Mexican attorney general's office took over several cases. Federal investigators said they had evidence some victims may have been killed by an international organ trafficking ring. One AP article Cruikshank found quoted an organized crime prosecutor as saying a witness had identified an American man as part of that ring."

I drilled Gullet with a look.

"Daniels trained and worked in El Paso, Texas. Ciudad Juárez is directly across the border from El Paso."

"You saying Daniels was involved?"

"I'm saying he *could* have been involved. Even if he wasn't involved, he was in El Paso. He'd have heard about the killings. He might have made contacts. Or he might have taken the idea and come here to set up his own franchise."

Gullet ran a hand over his jaw.

"Daniels lives on Seabrook and owns a very pricey boat."

"You say he's a Reynolds."

"Which may or may not be relevant. I know, taken alone, none of these facts looks suspicious. Familiarity with Dewees Island. Owning a boat. Access to the GMC clinic and its patients. Surgical training. Presence in El Paso. Expensive lifestyle. Unexplained phone call from Marshall's phone. But added up . . ." I left the inference unstated.

Gullet's eyes locked onto mine. No one spoke.

The phone broke the silence. One ring. Four. Gullet ignored it.

Some moments indelibly imprint the memory, encrypting sensory input unnoticed in real time. That was such a moment.

I remember a tiny red square blinking on the phone. A voice in the corridor calling someone named Al. Dust particles dancing, sunlight slashing the blinds. A tic jumping the corner of Gullet's right eye.

Seconds passed. A minute. A woman poked her head through the door, the same woman who'd sent Gullet to calm his in-laws, the battling Haeberles.

"Thought you might want to know. Marshall's out. And he just held a press conference. Lawyer did the talking. Marshall worked on a nomination for best performance by a persecuted innocent in a nonspeaking role."

Gullet gave a tight nod.

"Tybee thinks he might have something on a pilot."

"Tell him I'll be right there."

I checked the time. Daniels could be leaving town, could be hundreds of miles from Charleston already. The thought of him slipping free sent a chill through my marrow.

"Would you consider picking Daniels up?" I asked.

"For what?"

"Beating his dog. Spitting on the sidewalk. Peeing off the bow of his boat. I don't care. Get him downtown, get warrants, and do the same kind of premises search, auto search, and review of phone records you did on Marshall. You may hit on something."

"Media's on me like a wolf pack on spareribs. Herron's livid over the publicity." Gullet flapped a hand at the phone. "Spent my morning getting reamed by the mayor and the governor. Last thing I need is another shaky arrest."

"At least get warrants to search his house and his boat."

"Authorized on what basis? Suspicion there might be something we missed? I do that, the press will crucify me."

"As a possible aider and abetter. A co-conspirator. Use all the same stuff you used to get the Marshall warrants. Look, I know it's hard to think of Marshall as anything other than a greedy bastard who murdered sick, helpless people."

"You surely did press that point. Now you're defending the man?"

"I'm saying I'm not sure." My throat felt dry. I swallowed. "In the interest of duty you should at least explore the possibility that the killer is Daniels. You should pick him up if you have even the slightest doubt."

"I'm unfamiliar with the legal niceties where you ply your trade, Doc, but that's not how it works here. I can't arrest people over doubts. Besides, I don't have doubts. You do. I think Marshall's guilty as shit." It was the first time I'd heard Gullet use profanity.

"If Daniels is out there he can kill again." It came out more forcefully than I intended.

Gullet's jaw muscles bulged, relaxed. "Kill who? There won't be any more surgeries at that clinic."

"I was thinking of Marshall. He's free. If Daniels offs Marshall the investigation could end. People could assume a friend or relative of a victim took Marshall out, and Daniels walks."

Never taking his eyes from me, Gullet finger-jabbed a phone button. A staticky voice came across the speakerphone.

"Zamzow."

"Marshall left the courthouse?"

"About forty minutes ago."

"What's he doing?"

"He was with a suit. Stopped by an office on

Broad, suit stayed behind, now Marshall's heading south on seventeen."

"Probably going home. Stay on him."

"Discretion needed?"

"No. Let him know you're there."

Gullet punched the button and the line went dead.

"You really should get Daniels," I pressed.

"You're right about one thing. What's pointing to Marshall is largely circumstantial. But what you're giving me on Daniels isn't any better." Gullet stood. "Let's see what Tybee's got."

Deputy Tybee was at one of two computers in a second-floor squad room, stacks of printouts spread around the keyboard.

"Whaddaya got?" Gullet asked as we entered the room.

Tybee turned to us, his face more hawklike under fluorescents than it had been outside.

"When the phone dumps on Marshall's home and the clinic were going nowhere, I thought to myself, Where was this guy making contact? A pay phone? What pay phone?" Tybee tapped a finger to his temple. "I dumped the booth on Nassau, checked outgoing calls placed around DLC for the most recent MP." Tybee was an acronym man. Date of last contact. Missing person.

"Jimmie Ray Teal?" I asked.

"Yeah. Teal's DLC was May eighth. Started working the list, checking numbers against names. Fortunately, Nassau isn't the most popular booth in the city. Halfway through, I hit on something.

"May sixth, nine thirty-seven A.M. Someone dialed a cell phone belonging to Jasper Donald Shorter. Call lasted four minutes. The same number was dialed on May ninth at four oh six P.M. Lasted thirty-seven seconds."

"Two days before and one day after Teal's DLC," Gullet said. "You run a check on Shorter?"

"You're going to love this." Tybee shuffled through the printouts. "Shorter has a sheet. Did six years in the air force, was dismissed from service after drugs were found in a package he was shipping to the States from Da Nang. Dismissal of an officer is equivalent to a dishonorable discharge for an enlisted man. Makes future employment a real bear."

Tybee held out a paper.

Gullet and I scanned the contents. The document was a photocopy of Shorter's military record.

Jasper Donald Shorter had been a pilot in Vietnam.

# 38

"Shorter was a flyboy," Gullet said.

"Still is." Tybee dug out another paper. "Owns a Cessna 207, tail number N3378Z."

"Drug-runner favorite," Gullet said.

"Yes, sir," Tybee agreed. "Single-engine. Can fly low and land in a field. But the 207's a poor choice for long-haul stealth flights. Can't go from here to Puerto Vallarta without refueling. And there's another problem. Every plane that flies in the United States has to be registered, and Shorter's tail number would be traceable straight to him. But drug runners often steal planes or purchase them from prior owners, paint over the tail numbers, then stencil on bogus ones."

"Find the plane. If you spot Shorter, stay with him and call me."

"Yes, sir."

Gullet turned to go. I had one last question for Tybee.

"Where does Shorter live?"

"Seabrook."

I felt a buzz of excitement. "Where on Seabrook?"

Tybee typed a few keystrokes and a list came up on the screen.

"Pelican Grove Villas."

The buzz became a rush. I whipped around to Gullet.

"Daniels lives at Pelican Grove Villas."

Gullet stopped, hand on the doorknob.

"Same complex?"

"Yes! Yes! That can't be coincidence. Marshall must be on the level. It's got to be Daniels!"

Something shifted in Gullet's expression. He gave a tight nod. "I'll bring him in."

"I want to go with you," I said.

Gullet regarded me, stone-jawed. "I'll let you know when we've got him."

With that he was gone.

There was nothing to do but go home. And wait.

After walking Boyd, I zapped a frozen dinner and turned on the news. An appropriately concerned anchorwoman was reporting on a fire in a public housing block. Her air became subtly but fittingly shocked when she launched into coverage of the Marshall story. Footage showed the clinic, a younger Marshall, a clip of Herron leading a stadium in prayer, Marshall and Tuckerman leaving the courthouse.

I hardly heard. I kept going over every fact I

knew. Kept checking my watch. Each time only minutes had passed.

Was it Daniels? It had to be Daniels. Had Gullet found him? What was taking so long?

I watered Anne's cactus collection. Collected a load of wash. Emptied the dishwasher.

My thoughts were in collision, but there was no one with whom to discuss my doubts, weigh the probability of Daniels versus Marshall. I needed to talk to Ryan, to get his perspective. I thought of calling, decided he should be free to focus on Lily. Birdie was occupied with a catnip frog. Though keenly interested, Boyd was a lousy conversationalist.

Pete called around six thirty, bored and cranky. I told him I'd come by and fill him in on the events of the past four days.

Pete was reading Friday's *Post and Courier* when I arrived. Crumpling the paper, he complained about the food, itchy dressings, his first physical therapy session.

"Aren't we a black hole of need," I said, kissing the top of Pete's head.

"It's called venting. But you're not really listening."

"No," I admitted.

"Tell me what's happened."

I laid it all out. The makeshift OR. The organ theft. The wire noose. The shells. Unique Montague. Willie Helms. The other MP's. Rodriguez. The Abrigo Aislado de los Santos in Puerto Vallarta.

I told Pete that Rodriguez and Marshall were med school classmates, and that both had been sanctioned, Marshall for drug abuse, Rodriguez for sexual misconduct, and that Marshall had actually done a short stretch. I added that Marshall had sold his boat immediately after Ryan and I questioned him at the clinic, and ended by describing Marshall's arrest and subsequent release on bond.

"You should be proud of yourself," Pete said.

For a minute I was persuaded again. But, no, it had to be Daniels.

"I think I may have talked Gullet into arresting the wrong man."

"Don't believe everything you think."

I slapped Pete's wrist. He cringed in exaggerated pain. I checked my watch.

"No one talks Gullet into anything," Pete said.

"Maybe not, but I pushed him hard. And now Gullet's taking heat."

"From whom?"

"The press. Herron. The rev's powerful friends." I worried my right cuticle with my left thumbnail. "What if we're wrong? Gullet will have a lot to explain in the next election."

"The evidence sounds pretty convincing to me."

"It's all circumstantial."

"Sufficient circumstantial evidence can carry the burden of proof if the jury believes it." Pete reached over and separated my hands. I checked my watch. Where the hell was Gullet?

"If Marshall's not guilty, is there another candidate?" Pete asked.

I laid out what I'd learned about Corey Daniels.

Boat. Familiarity with Dewees Island. Surgical scrub nurse. Presence in El Paso during a period of grisly murders, some of which may have been linked to organ trafficking. Calls made from Marshall's phone when Marshall wasn't at the clinic. Residence in the same complex as a pilot of tarnished reputation. A pilot who was contacted immediately before and after the disappearance of Jimmie Ray Teal. Contacted from a pay phone just yards from the clinic.

"Maybe Marshall and Daniels are in it together," Pete said when I'd finished.

"Possible. But I keep thinking about my conversation with Marshall. I dislike the man, but some of his points make sense. Leaving shells lying around his office doesn't fit his personality. He's alibied out for the night Cruikshank's home was phoned from his line. The history of the boat sale can easily be checked. If they're in it together, why finger Daniels unless Marshall is trying to do a plea deal and get to the DA first?"

"Is either Marshall or Daniels stockpiling money?"

"Gullet says no evidence of that, though one can easily hide cash. Daniels lives way beyond what I'd expect a nurse could afford." I described the *Hunney Child* and the Seabrook condo, and explained Daniels's family connections.

"The Reynolds aluminum clan."

"Exactly. But that could mean nothing."

My eyes flicked to my watch. Five minutes had passed since my previous time check.

"It took some convincing, but Gullet's gone to pick Daniels up." I went back to picking. The cuticle was now a bright angry red. "But the case against Daniels is also circumstantial. I'm hoping some searches and some phone records will turn up gold."

"What about the eyelash?"

"DNA takes time."

"Capitaine Comical gone back to the tundra?"

"Yes."

"Miss him?"

"Yes." I'd caught a trace of Ryan's scent on my pillow that morning and felt a loneliness more intense than I'd anticipated. An emptiness. A sense of impending closure?

"How's Emma?" Pete pulled my hands apart and held on to one.

I shook my head.

Ten minutes later my mobile sounded. Gullet's number glowed on the screen. Heart thumping, I clicked on.

"Daniels wasn't at Bohicket or at his condo. Boat's in the slip. Sent out an APB on his vehicle."

"Any progress on Shorter?"

"No sign of him, but the plane's kept at a private airstrip out Clement's Ferry Road. Small operation. No tower, but they sell fuel. Watchman says Shorter flies a group of businessmen up to Charlotte every Saturday morning, comes Friday evenings to do routine maintenance. Tybee will be waiting when Shorter shows up."

"What's Marshall doing?"

There was a pause. In the background I could hear Gullet's radio sputter.

"Zamzow lost him."

"Lost him?" I couldn't believe it. "How could he lose him?"

"Eighteen-wheeler jackknifed not far in front of his position. Involved two cars. I diverted him to that."

"Jesus Christ!"

"It's temporary. Tuckerman's called a press conference for ten tomorrow morning. Marshall will be putting on a puppy face for his public, and we'll resume our tail then."

When we'd disconnected, I looked at the patient. Mercifully, Pete was dozing.

Glancing back at my phone, I noticed the little icon indicating voice mail waiting. I listened to the message.

Emma, 4:27 P.M. "Call me. I have news."

While talking to Tybee, I'd left my purse in Gullet's office. Emma must have phoned then.

I hit *E* on my speed dial. Emma's machine answered after four rings.

"Damn!"

I was about to disconnect when Emma's live voice cut in over her recorded voice.

"Hang on."

The message ended, and a long beep sounded. I heard a click, then a change in sound quality.

"Where are you?" Emma asked.

"At the hospital."

"Staff catches you on a cell phone they'll break out the rubber hoses. How's Pete?"

"Sleeping," I said, just above a whisper.

"You and Gullet have been busy."

"Emma, I think we've made a mistake."

"Oh?"

I got up, closed the door, and gave Emma a condensed version of everything I'd told Pete. She listened without interrupting.

"Don't know if my news will resolve anything. Got DNA results today. It's Marshall's eyelash."

"You're right. That could go either way. But it narrows the possibilities. Either Marshall disposed of the body, or participated in the disposal, or was being set up even at the time the body was buried. But why a setup back then? That kind of contingency planning seems something of a stretch. And an eyelash, for God's sake? Sounds like a TV plot where the cops find one skin cell in an acre of shag carpet. What are the chances an eyelash will be found?"

"Who's your pick?"

"Daniels. He's dim enough to think something like that would work."

"Mine, too. Keep me in the loop."

"I will."

I set the phone on vibrate mode. Minutes crept by. I was gnawing a cuticle when it signaled.

Gullet.

"IOP PD just spotted Daniels's vehicle at the Dewees marina."

"He's gone to see his aunt? If so, why? And why not take his own boat?"

Gullet ignored the questions. Rightly so. They were irrelevant.

"I'm checking with Dewees to see if Daniels is out there. Posted deputies on his condo and at Bohicket. We'll get him."

"Please call when you do. The guy gives me the creeps."

Pete was snoring. Time to go.

I was clearing the newspaper from Pete's bed, trying not to rustle, when my eyes fell on the grainy black-and-white of Aubrey Herron. Herron was caught in a posture of supplication, face tipped, eyes closed, arm stretched above his head.

Left arm.

The thought struck like a tsunami. Unbidden. Unforeseen. Shocking.

"Damn," I whispered, fingers clenching in distress. "Damn, damn, damn."

The paper trembled as visions screamed through my mind.

A trio of sixth cervical vertebrae, all fractured on the left.

A wire noose with a side loop for applying deadly force.

Corey Daniels beyond one-way glass. A hand shooting through hair. A finger working a desktop. An arm draping a chair back. A scar circling a wrist.

Lester Marshall leafing through pages in a

patient chart. Jotting words on a legal pad.

Kaleidoscope images fused into realization.

Daniels spoke of permanent damage from a motorcycle accident. He had strength only in his right hand.

Marshall rummaged Montague's file with his left hand. He wrote with his left hand.

Daniels was right-handed. Marshall was left-handed.

A Spanish windlass is slipped over a victim's head from behind.

On Montague, Helms, and Cruikshank, the force had been applied to the left side of the neck. They had been strangled by a lefty.

I'd sent Gullet after Daniels.

The killer couldn't be Daniels.

Where was Marshall now?

# 39

Dropping the paper, I grabbed my phone and dialed Gullet.

No answer.

*Damn!*

I dialed the sheriff's department switchboard. The operator told me Gullet was unavailable.

"I need to contact him. Now."

"Are you calling to report a crime?"

"Gullet's on his way to arrest a man named Corey Daniels. Get through to him. Tell him to call Brennan before proceeding."

"Is this a reporter?" Wary.

"No. This is Temperance Brennan. I'm working with the coroner's office. I have information the sheriff will want. It's very important to get through to him."

A beat of hesitation.

"Your number?"

I provided it. "How can I contact Deputy Tybee?"

"I can't give that out."

"Please contact Tybee." I had to restrain myself from screaming at the woman. "Tell him to call me. Same number. Same message."

Totally frustrated, I disconnected.

I looked at Pete. He was well past dozing and into REM. I thought about leaving, decided to hold. What if Gullet or Tybee called while I was in the elevator with no signal?

I began pacing, working the cuticle with my teeth.

*Call, damn it!*

Not a ripple from the phone.

*Call!*

How could I have been so stupid? So gullible? Marshall had played me like a fish at a time when I should have been adding the missing pieces to the puzzle.

*Calm, Brennan. Nothing's lost. Marshall has been charged. He'll have to stand trial. Daniels can be released.*

As usual, I ignored my own advice. I was pumped with anxiety, angry at my own stupidity. The cuticle looked like raw flank steak.

My higher centers tried reason.

*Gullet has grounds to pick Daniels up. He can also release him as new facts emerge. That happens. No one will die.*

Die?

I froze as another kaleidoscoping chain winged toward another terrible realization.

Marshall was the killer, yet the case against him was circumstantial. Who could nail it down?

The pilot, that's who.

If Shorter was indeed Marshall's mule, Marshall had a major loose end. If the DA got to talk to Shorter, he might deal. If Shorter flipped, his testimony could bury Marshall and Rodriguez.

Marshall was ruthless. Marshall had eluded Zamzow and was running free. Marshall would understand the risk represented by Shorter. He would try to eliminate that risk. If he succeeded, it could prevent a conviction.

I was jabbing keys on my cell when a nurse opened the door. Lips pursed, she pointed at my hand and shook her head no.

Pocketing the phone, I hurried from the room and down the hall. Dingy lighted panels marked the elevator's creeping upward progress.

*Come on!*

The doors opened. I rushed in, practically bowling over the occupants before they could draw back. We descended, all pointlessly watching the blinking floor numbers.

*Come on!*

The lobby was deserted. Heading out the doors, I dialed Gullet.

Still no answer.

*Damn!*

What was happening at the marina? On Dewees? At Daniels's condo? Bohicket?

What was happening at the airstrip on Clement's Ferry Road?

Tybee was the greater concern. He had no clue Shorter might be a target. Shorter wouldn't be expecting an attack from Marshall. The doctor had little to lose, everything to gain by eliminating his pilot. Marshall had no idea Daniels was being followed, probably planned to make Shorter's murder look like Daniels's work. Was Marshall a shooter? Had he shot Pete? IOP police still had nothing on the shooting. The searches of Marshall's office and home hadn't turned up a gun.

Breathless, I threw myself into my car. Turned the key. Hesitated.

IOP? Gullet?

Clements Ferry Road? Tybee?

Tybee could be at risk.

Marshall had killed how many people? If Tybee blundered upon a hit on Shorter, Marshall wouldn't hesitate to kill him, too. Of the two, Tybee was the one more likely to be caught by surprise. The cruiser would be easy to spot. Tybee would be unprepared for an assault.

Fingers trembling, I dialed the sheriff's department. Same operator. I gave my name. She started to speak. I stopped her in midspiel, told her to tell Gullet and Tybee it was urgent I hear from them.

"Sheriff Gullet and Deputy Tybee are out of contact at the moment."

"Radio. Phone. Carrier pigeon." It was almost a shriek. "However you do it, get my message to them."

I heard a sharp intake of breath.

"Tybee could be in danger."

I rang off.

What next? Gullet had been emphatic about my noninclusion in Daniels's apprehension. I didn't even know Gullet's location. Tybee would be at the airstrip by now, but I wasn't exactly sure where that was. Best to wait this out at the house. Surely one of them would call shortly.

I hadn't remembered to leave a light on. "Sea for Miles" was dark, though a partial moon cast a shadowy glow against the exterior walls, as though from a dimmed lantern.

Boyd barked as I turned the key, then cavorted in circles around me. I set down my purse and checked the house phone. No messages.

The place felt eerie. No Pete. No Ryan. Too many rooms and too much quiet for one person. Thank God for the dog and the cat. I stroked them both in turn.

I turned on a TV and watched *Headline News* for a while, but I wasn't tuned in mentally. Why weren't Gullet and Tybee calling? Marshall and Daniels were both at large, and deputies were pursuing the wrong man. The killer could be positioning himself to strike again. There was urgency here.

Or was there?

Marshall had been charged, arraigned, and released on bond. More evidence of his guilt wouldn't cause a rearrest. The urgency was to call off the arrest of Daniels. What if he tried to flee and was injured? What use would Marshall's lawyer make of Daniels's arrest at tomorrow's news conference?

*Call, damn it. Call now!*

Feeling agitated, I took my cell and a Diet Coke and walked out toward the beach. Boyd was indignant that I shut the door in his snout, and scratched at it angrily, but I didn't want to lose track of him in the dark.

The tide was high, leaving little room between the dunes and the water's edge. No late-evening walkers slogged the surf's white curls. I took a sand chair from the gazebo and carried it to the water's edge.

Settling down, I dug my toes into the sand, sipped my drink, and waited for the phone to ring. The moonlight made fluorescent patterns on the waves. The wind rolled off the water. It was lulling, calming. I began to unwind. Almost.

Pete and Ryan. Ryan and Pete. Why the ambivalence? Forgotten feelings were surfacing and creating discomfort. Strange. And surprising. But no action was required. Would the concern persist? I would see.

A lone walker approached from my left. Unconsciously, I took note. Hooded sweatshirt. Odd. The night wasn't chilly. Muscular build. The walker angled so as to pass between my chair and the dunes.

Suddenly, I was choking. The phone and the drink flew from my hands.

I was shocked at how fast the man had moved. And at his strength.

I grabbed at my throat. I was gasping and could barely speak.

"Stop!" It came out a hoarse whisper.

"Enjoy the view, you arrogant, ignorant, meddling bitch," hissed a voice I had heard before. "It's the last you'll ever see."

Desperate, I clawed my flesh.

"Flynn and Cruikshank tried to bring me down and I dealt with them, but you stumbled onto things that weren't your business and you ruined *my* business. I provided a valuable service. I took the few good parts those throwaway people had and sent them where they could be put to better use. Too bad I can't take yours."

The thing around my throat tightened. I couldn't breathe. Couldn't cry out. My vision blurred.

"You caused me great harm. It's payback time, Dr. Brennan. Say good-bye."

The voice was barely registering in my tortured brain. My lungs burned, and every cell in my body screamed for air. The world began to recede.

*Fight!*

With all my strength I lunged upward and backward. The top of my head struck him under the chin, knocking him backward. His grip loosened.

I dove toward the water, trying to dash into the waves. He caught a handful of hair and yanked me back.

I lost my balance and went down, legs straight out in front. Before I could roll to either side, the hand that held my hair shoved me down hard, forcing my chin against my chest. The other hand went to my neck.

Then, inexplicably, the hands released. I struggled to my knees, but couldn't stand. As I tried to push up with my palms, the pressure on my neck eased and I heard a second voice. A voice I had also heard before.

"Set me up for this one, you demented prick bastard."

Blood pounded in my ears. Or was it the surf?

I lifted my head enough to see Corey Daniels, his massive left arm around Marshall's throat, his right arm holding Marshall in a hammerlock. Marshall's face was contorted in pain.

That was good.

# 40

Saturday night the heat broke, giving way to one of those glorious Lowcountry Sunday mornings. By ten, Pete and I were at the gazebo, flip-flops kicked, working through every newspaper I'd managed to score at the island Red and White.

I was perusing the *Charlotte Observer* sports section, when a slow-moving shadow crossed the page. I glanced up. A V of pelicans was wind-slipping overhead.

After pouring a refill from the coffee thermos, I put my feet on the railing and surveyed my surroundings. Beyond the dunes the tide was receding, yielding additional beach footage with each low, lazy swell. To the southwest, Lilliputian kites danced the sky over Sullivan's Island. In the shrubs beside the boardwalk, birds twittered in intense midmorning dialogue.

On the way home from MUSC the previous afternoon, Pete had announced that one of his law partners was coming Monday to drive him to Charlotte. Buck Flynn and his pals had retained accountants to continue probing Aubrey Herron's books. Based on what he'd seen prior to having his lung rearranged, Pete doubted GMC was doing a soft shoe with donor bucks.

I didn't argue with Pete's plan. The Latvian Savant was healing well. I knew he was anxious to get back to his clients.

I'd spoken with Tim Larabee, the Mecklenburg County medical examiner, and with Pierre LaManche, the chief of medico-legal in Montreal. A skull and a pair of mummified infants had come into the Charlotte facility. Two partial skeletons had arrived at the LSJML. Both pathologists had assured me the cases could wait, allowing me to remain in Charleston for Emma.

And for one final task.

I was opening the *Atlanta Journal-Constitution* when I felt more than heard footsteps rumble the boardwalk. Turning, I saw Gullet striding our way. He wore Ray-Bans, khakis, and a denim shirt without an embroidered name. I assumed the ensemble was the sheriff's idea of civvies.

"Mornin'." Gullet nodded at Pete, then me.

Pete and I said, "Mornin'."

Gullet settled onto the gazebo bench. "Glad to see you're improving, sir."

"I am. Coffee?" Pete tapped the thermos.

"Thank you, no." Planting his feet, Gullet leaned forward and rested one beefy forearm on each beefy thigh. "Had a nice little chat with Dickie

Dupree. Seems Dickie has an employee who's long on ambition and short on brainpower. George Lanyard." Gullet tipped his head at me. "Dickie read his copy of the report you'd sent to the state archaeologist and went ballistic. Lanyard misread his boss's remarks about wanting your hide. I'm paraphrasing there."

"Lanyard thought Dupree was suggesting that someone should shoot me?" I couldn't keep the disgust from my voice.

"Not shoot you. Harass you. Lanyard's admitted to pegging the beer bottle at the Dumpster and firing at the house. Says he never intended to hurt anyone." Gullet turned the Ray-Bans on Pete. "You stepped into the kitchen at the wrong time."

"Dickie wasn't personally involved?" I asked.

"Dupree got madder than hoppin' hell when Lanyard came clean about what he'd done. Thought I was going to have another homicide right there on the site." Gullet took in a long breath and let it out. "I believe him. Dupree may step outside the bounds of decorum now and again, but the man's no criminal."

"What's happening with Marshall?" Pete asked, showing no interest in Lanyard.

"DA cut a deal. Marshall provides the name and location of every one of his victims, the state agrees not to stick a needle in his arm."

I snorted derisively. "The state should at least insist on taking one lung and one kidney."

"I'll pass that along." Did Gullet almost smile?

"I expect the suggestion will be well received, but doubt it will be acted upon."

"He's talking?" Pete asked.

"Like a teen with a cell phone."

I already knew. Gullet had called following Marshall's disclosure to the DA Saturday morning. I felt the familiar blend of sadness and anger when I thought of the carnage.

Marshall's first victim was a prostitute named Cookie Godine, murdered in the summer of 2001. Willie Helms was killed that September. Both bodies were buried on Dewees Island. Missing their kidneys and livers.

Marshall knew Corey Daniels's history, and hired him in part for that reason, shortly before the first murder. From the beginning, Marshall planned to plant some trail signs to divert suspicion toward Daniels, just in case the clinic was ever implicated. But digging graves was strenuous physical labor and not to the doctor's liking. When the Godine and Helms disappearances passed unnoticed, Marshall became bolder and switched his MO from burial in a shallow grave to burial at sea.

Rosemarie Moon and Ethridge Parker were killed in 2002, Ruby Anne Watley in 2003, Daniel Snype and Lonnie Aikman in 2004. The final victims were Unique Montague and Jimmie Ray Teal. Barring a fluke such as the storm that brought Montague's barrel up the Moultrie brothers' creek, recovery of additional remains was highly unlikely.

Though it gave me no satisfaction, I'd been right about Helene Flynn and Noble Cruikshank. Flynn started working at the GMC clinic in 2003. What triggered her distrust of Marshall was suspicion over finances. Not understanding how minimally GMC funded the clinic, Helene became irate over what she perceived as a major disconnect between conditions on Nassau and Marshall's lifestyle. In order to confirm her misgivings, she began snooping into the doctor's private life. Though unable to secure proof of financial wrongdoing, she complained to her father and to Herron.

Marshall found out Helene was observing him. Fearing she'd eventually stumble onto the truth, Marshall strangled her, dumped the body in the ocean, sent the key and rent money to her landlady, and fabricated the California story. Ironically, Helene never learned of the murders or of Marshall's organ theft activities.

Cruikshank also had to go, but he was a PI, a former cop, and his client was Buck Flynn. He might be missed, so a more elaborate plan was needed. After researching Cruikshank's past, Marshall settled on suicide, but the mechanics of it had the potential to be difficult.

"I'm curious," I said. "Cruikshank wasn't big, but he was tough. How did Marshall manage to take him out?"

"Marshall tracked Cruikshank to Magnolia Manor and began trailing him when Cruikshank went out in the evenings. He discovered that

Cruikshank liked to drink, and that Little Luna's was one of his haunts.

"One night Marshall was in Little Luna's and noted that Cruikshank was particularly sloshed. Marshall went to a pay phone near the door and dialed the bar. When the bartender answered, Marshall described Cruikshank's appearance and asked if he was there.

"The bartender got Cruikshank to the phone. Marshall identified himself as Daniels, and said he had important information on Helene Flynn and the clinic. He agreed to meet Cruikshank at Magnolia Manor."

"And Cruikshank was in such a hurry to get to the meeting place that he grabbed the wrong jacket on his way out."

"Exactly. He had his car keys in his pants pocket so he didn't notice the switch. Cruikshank was driving so erratically Marshall feared he'd be pulled over before he got home. No such luck for Cruikshank.

"Cruikshank had difficulty parking, which gave Marshall time to scope out the scene as he walked toward his victim. Marshall had taken to carrying his garrote on his surveillance outings, just in case an opportunity presented itself.

"Cruikshank was fumbling trying to lock his car. Marshall saw no one around, and the street was dark. He stepped up behind Cruikshank and had the loop over his head before Cruikshank sensed danger."

"How did he get the body to the national forest?"

"As soon as he'd strangled Cruikshank, Marshall draped one of Cruikshank's arms around his neck and slid his own arm around Cruikshank's waist. If anyone saw them, it would look like someone was hauling a drunken companion home. Marshall managed to maneuver the body into the front passenger seat of his own car and drove off. When he passed an unlit church parking lot, he pulled in and transferred the body to the trunk.

"Then he went home, collected two lengths of rope, and drove into the Francis Marion. Parking at the same spot where we all gathered on the day of the body recovery, Marshall took Cruikshank from the trunk and dragged him travois style into the woods. At the tree, he looped one rope under Cruikshank's armpits, threw the other end over the limb, and hoisted until Cruikshank's feet just cleared the ground. He'd dragged the body on a collapsible stepladder, which he then used to affix a second rope around Cruikshank's neck and tie it to the limb. Then he cut away the torso rope, collected his ladder, and left."

"And Cruikshank's car?"

"Marshall got the keys after he strangled Cruikshank. It must have given him a start when he found a wallet with another name, but he eventually decided he had the right man but the wrong jacket. That probably struck him as a piece of good fortune. The day after he strung Cruikshank up, he drove the car to the airport long-term parking lot. Used a briefcase to hide the license plate and decals that he removed. Then he took a cab from the airport back into the city. About a month later, the police removed the car to an abandoned car lot. By that time, Marshall must have been feeling downright invincible."

"How did Friday night play out?" Pete asked.

"Marshall cut to the ocean using the public access lane yonder, intending to approach your house from the beach." Gullet indicated a pathway several lots down. "Imagine his delight at seeing Doc Brennan parked right there on the sand."

Unconsciously, my hand went to my throat. "Why was Daniels following Marshall?" I asked, fingers tracing the welt Pete had dubbed my "organic necklace."

"Daniels's experiences with law enforcement have been less than optimal. Distrustful of cops, and worried that Marshall was working to set him up, Daniels decided to collect proof of his own. He intended to dog Marshall until he found hard evidence the guy was dirty."

"Why didn't Daniels use his own car?"

"Figured Marshall might spot it. Miss Honey keeps a vehicle on the mainland, so Daniels took auntie's and left his own at the marina."

"And prior to Marshall's arrest and his own interrogation, Daniels never suspected a thing?" I still found that incredible.

"I told you. RN or not, the guy's got the IQ of okra."

"Why was he so hostile at his interview?"

Gullet shrugged. "Hates cops."

"What about Herron and his cronies at God's Mercy Church?"

Gullet shook his head. "Long as he stayed on budget, Marshall had total autonomy running the clinic. Appears the GMC folks hadn't a clue what their physician was up to."

"Any word on Shorter?" I'd already learned that the Cessna was gone when Tybee arrived at the airfield Friday night.

"Lubbock PD bagged him at ten forty P.M. yesterday. That's what I'm here to tell you."

"Shorter flew to Texas?" I asked.

"He's got an ex living in Lubbock."

"Is he cooperating?" Pete asked.

Gullet did a "so-so" hand waggle. "Shorter claims he operates a legal shuttle and charter service. Admits to making deliveries for Marshall, but denies knowledge of the cargo. Way it worked, Marshall called one or two days in advance, then brought a cooler to the airfield at a prearranged time. Shorter flew to Mexico, landed in the desert outside Puerto Vallarta, and handed the cooler over to a Mexican named Jorge. Marshall paid ten thousand dollars cash per trip. Shorter says he didn't ask questions."

"Why the quick bolt on Thursday?"

"Shorter says Marshall's arrest spooked him, given his past legal problems."

We were quiet for a moment, considering that. I spoke first.

"Given Shorter's history, the most likely scenario has him running organs from Charleston to

453

Mexico, and drugs from Mexico into the States."

"Lubbock's on the same page, so they contacted the feds. DEA's tossing the plane. Shorter so much as waved a joint over a wingtip, they'll nail him. Besides, his story won't hold up. There's evidence that the tail of the plane has been painted over several times, probably to put on phony registration numbers for the illegal flights. And the Mexican authorities don't have him logging in to enter Mexican airspace."

"Has Marshall described how the scheme worked on the other end?" Pete asked.

"Marshall would phone Rodriguez when he found a clinic patient who was a match for one of Rodriguez's recipients. The victim was always homeless, or someone whose disappearance wouldn't be noticed.

"On the Mexico end, Rodriguez would place his call, and the recipient would hop a flight to Puerto Vallarta. On the Charleston end, Marshall would make his hit, and Shorter would overnight express the organ south."

"How did Marshall hook up with Shorter?" Pete asked.

"Shorter lives in the same complex as Daniels. The two popped an occasional beer, swapped stories. Daniels shared some of Shorter's history with Marshall, or maybe Marshall overheard Daniels talking about a pilot with a record. In either case, Shorter sounded like a good candidate for the new enterprise. Marshall researched the guy, dropped bait, Shorter bit."

"Daniels never learned that his neighbor was muling for his boss?"

"Hadn't a clue."

"How much do you think Shorter really knew?" I asked.

"Marshall's version pretty much confirms Shorter's claim that he was simply a courier. Says Shorter never asked about the contents of the coolers."

"Right," I said. "The honorable pilot never suspected he was running contraband."

Gullet shrugged. "Ten thousand smackers buys a lot of disinterest."

"What about Rodriguez? Was he in the loop on how Marshall was obtaining the organs?"

"Big-time. According to Marshall, the two were hatching plans as early as ninety-five."

"Rodriguez and Marshall graduated med school in eighty-one. How did they reconnect?"

"The two kept in touch. Knowing his old classmate had also become persona non grata in the medical profession, after his release from jail in ninety-one, Marshall called the only other crooked doctor he knew, then headed to Mexico. Rodriguez had been working at the Puerto Vallarta spa for a couple of years by then, and running a small private practice on the side. One thing led to another, and the two cooked up what they thought would be a low-risk money machine. They'd limit themselves to a handful of supplementary donors per year, score one or two hundred thousand per organ, lay low the rest of the time.

"The only question was where would Marshall work his end of the venture? Within months, GMC posted an opening for its Charleston clinic, and, given the salary, the organization wasn't too fussy about applicant credentials. Marshall managed to produce some forged documents and got a medical license in South Carolina. Rodriguez began buying used surgical equipment south of the border. Within a few years, they were ready to roll."

"Has Rodriguez been located?" I asked.

"Not yet. But the *federales* will get him."

"And charge him with what?"

"The Mexican authorities are putting considerable thought into that."

"Rodriguez will deny knowledge of the murders, claim he was assured the organs were legally obtained."

"Marshall is saying Rodriguez masterminded the whole scheme. Also claims he wasn't Rodriguez's only supplier."

"Marshall pled guilty to eleven counts of murder," I said. "How do we know there weren't more victims?"

Gullet leveled the Ray-Bans at me. "My gut tells me there were. Marshall's probably giving us the MPs we know about, and tossing in Godine for credibility."

A couple of details still bothered me.

"Lester Marshall is a painstakingly meticulous man. How could he have been so careless with those shells?"

"I suspect he's going to ponder that question

frequently in the coming years." This time Gullet actually did grin. "Marshall says he bought a bag of shells the day he murdered Willie Helms. Was hoping to find something good among the assortment. Best as he can figure, one shell found its way into a cuff or pocket, maybe at the market, maybe while walking back to the clinic. That one ended up with Helms. He remembers viewing the shells under a scope, then leaving them in his desk drawer for a short time. He thinks the packaging must have been torn."

"So one shell drops from Marshall's clothing onto Helms's body. Another rolls into a desk hollow. Marshall doesn't notice either."

Gullet nodded. "Marshall was more shocked than anyone that those little buggers turned up. Had to do some fast thinking to weave shell planting into his Corey Daniels setup scenario."

"Foiled by a mollusk," Pete said.

"Who dialed Cruikshank from Marshall's office?" I queried detail number two.

"O'Dell Towery."

"The cleaning man?"

Gullet nodded. "Towery's slow, but he remembers because it was outside his ordinary routine. Says Marshall instructed him to use his office phone at a specified time. Said he was expecting a message and wouldn't be able to make the call himself at that time. Told Towery that if no one answered, he should just hang up and give the slip with the number back to Marshall the next day. Marshall had an alibi elsewhere for that time. If

457

problems arose, the call would at least muddy the picture, at best throw suspicion on Daniels."

Silence.

Gullet's eyes dropped to his hands. "I understand Miz Rousseau's pretty sick."

"She is," I said. My mind wandered.

Emma had been running a fever when I'd visited on Thursday. That night, her temperature shot to 102, and the sweats, headache, and nausea became violent.

Suspecting infection, Russell had hospitalized Emma on Friday. I'd called Sarah Purvis on Saturday morning. Though just home from Italy, Sarah had immediately set out for Charleston.

Before her sister's arrival, Emma and I had had plenty of time to talk. I described all that had happened since Thursday. She reported that the Berkeley County coroner had ruled Susie Ruth Aikman's death as natural. The old woman had died of a massive coronary.

Then Emma had told the strange tale of the cruise ship incident.

A male passenger died while at sea. When the ship anchored in Charleston, the man's widow authorized cremation, signed the paperwork, then left with the urn. Days later a woman appeared at Emma's office claiming to be the wife of the deceased and wanting the body. Documents showed that lady number two was, indeed, the missus. Lawsuits were pending concerning disposition of the gentleman's ashes.

"This philandering cad had two women fighting

over his remains, Tempe. He was one of the lucky ones." Emma swallowed. I could see that conversation was becoming an effort. "I'm dying, of course. We all know that."

Fighting a tremor in my chest, I'd tried to shush her. She continued to speak.

"My death will not go unnoticed. I have people in my life. I'll be remembered, maybe even missed. But Marshall and Rodriguez preyed upon society's outcasts. Those dwelling alone on the edge, those with no one to mourn their passing. Cookie Godine's disappearance wasn't even reported. Ditto for Helms and Montague. Thanks to you, Tempe, those bodies did not remain anonymous."

Unable to speak, I'd stroked Emma's hair, one gulping, heaving breath away from full-out sobbing.

Gullet resumed speaking after his own brief reverie. "Doesn't seem right."

"No," I agreed. "It doesn't."

"She's a fine woman, and a true professional."

Gullet stood. I stood.

"Guess it's best not to question the good Lord's ways."

There seemed no reply to that, so I gave none.

"You did a crack-up job, Doc. I learned some things working with you."

Gullet held out a hand. Surprised, I shook it.

The last missing piece went from me to Gullet.

"The leak to Winborne didn't come from your office, Sheriff. At Emma's urging, Lee Anne Miller stirred the pot at the MUSC morgue. Winborne's informant was a second-year autopsy tech." Emma had also told me that on Saturday.

Gullet started to speak. I cut him off. If he was about to offer an apology for having accused me of sabotaging the investigation, I didn't want one.

"*Was*," I emphasized. "The gentleman is currently unemployed."

Gullet thought for a long moment, then turned to Pete.

"My best wishes to you, sir. Do you want to be kept informed as to charges against Lanyard? I expect he'll plead."

"This is your patch, Sheriff. What's acceptable to you and the DA is acceptable to me. When it's done, you might tell me the result, if you don't mind."

Gullet nodded. "I'll do that."

To me, "Seven A.M. Tuesday?"

"I'll be ready," I said.

# Epilogue

Dawn broke with a cool gray drizzle that continued throughout the morning. The sky went from charcoal to slate to pearl, but the sun remained only a dull white smudge.

By eight we were on the back of Dewees Island, in a stand of maritime forest five yards in from the high-tide beach. An occasional gust whispered in the glistening wet leaves. Drops ticked the plastic sheeting as I exposed it with my trowel. Miller's boots squished as she circled, Nikon capturing the melancholy mural.

Gullet stood above me, face impassive, errant breezes puffing his nylon jacket. Marshall watched from a golf cart, manacled arms crossed, a deputy at his side.

Beyond the rain and the wind and the camera, there was a stillness about the scene that seemed fitting. Solemn and somber.

By noon Miller and I were able to free Cookie

Godine from her makeshift grave. A mild stench rose, and millipedes skittered back toward darkness as we lifted the sad bundle and carried it to the waiting van.

In my peripheral vision, I noticed Marshall raise a hand to cover his nose and mouth.

Friday morning I rose at nine, put on a dark blue skirt and crisp white blouse, and drove to St. Michael's Episcopal. Leaving my car in the lot, I walked to the Old City Market, made a purchase, then returned to the church.

Inside, the crowd was larger than I'd expected. Emma's sister, Sarah Purvis, silent and pale. Sarah's husband and children. Gullet and a number of his staff. Lee Anne Miller and Emma's employees from the coroner's office. There were also several dozen people I didn't recognize.

I watched the mourners throughout the service, but didn't sing or join in the spoken prayers. I knew I'd weep if I dared open my mouth.

At the cemetery I stood back from the grave site, observing as the casket was lowered and the attendees filed by, each tossing down a handful of dirt. When the group had dispersed, I approached.

For several long moments I stood over the grave, tears streaming down my cheeks.

"I'm here to say good-bye, old friend." A tremor shook my chest. "You know you will be missed."

With trembling hands, I dropped the bouquet of baby's breath and everlasting life onto Emma's coffin.

It is now Friday night, and I am lying alone in my too empty bed, aching with regret that Emma is gone. Tomorrow, I will take Birdie and Boyd and return to Charlotte. I will be sad to leave the Lowcountry. I will miss the smell of pine, and seaweed, and salt. The ever-changing play of sunlight and moonlight on water.

In Charlotte, I will help nurture Pete back to health. I could not do that for Emma, could not will good cells into her body or drive out the *Staphylococcus* that finally took her life. I will still think about my husband's unfaithfulness, and about my perplexing continued attachment to him. I will try to separate those feelings from the feeling of tenderness engendered by the child who is as much him as she is me.

In a few weeks I will pack my bags, drive to the airport, and board a flight to Canada. In Montreal, I will pass through customs, then take a taxi to my condo in centre-ville. The next day, I will report to my lab. Ryan will be eleven floors down. Who knows?

One thing I do know. Emma is right. Whatever the outcome, I am among the lucky. I have people in my life. People who love me.

# From the Forensic Files of Dr. Kathy Reichs

At times I scratch my head in puzzlement. After years of obscurity, my field of endeavor is suddenly hot.

When I completed my grad studies, it was the rare cop or prosecutor who'd heard of forensic anthropology, and the rarer one who used it. My colleagues and I formed a tiny club, known to few, understood by fewer. Law-and-order professionals knew little about us. The general public knew nothing.

Awareness and utilization have increased over the years, but there are still only a handful of board-certified practitioners in North America, consulting to law enforcement, coroners, and medical examiners. The military employs a platoon or so.

Suddenly, though, notoriety has overtaken us. Popular literature came first: Jeffery Deaver, Patricia Cornwell, Karin Slaughter, and, of course, Kathy Reichs. Then came television: The break-through forensic sleeper *C.S.I.* attracted millions of viewers, and forensic science was in the air. And on the air. *Cold Case. Without a Trace.* We'd had *Quincy* in the seventies, but pathology now dazzled. *Crossing Jordan. DaVinci's Inquest. Autopsy.* All over the airways scientists were slicing and scoping and simulating and solving. And now there is *Bones*.

*Bones* is TV's newest forensic show and the nickname of the series' lead character, Temperance Brennan, the fictional forensic anthropologist I created ten years ago in my first book, *Déjà Dead*. In the series, Tempe is at an earlier point in her career, employed by the Jeffersonian Institute, and working with the FBI. And rightly so. The bureau was one of the first agencies to recognize the value of forensic anthropology, calling on Smithsonian scientists for help with skeletal questions way back at the beginning of the twentieth century.

Things were looser then, unstructured. Not so today. Forensic anthropology gained formal recognition in 1972, when the American Academy of Forensic Science created a Physical Anthropology section. The American Board of Forensic Anthropology was formed shortly thereafter.

Throughout the seventies, forensic anthropologists expanded their activities to the investigation of human rights abuses. Labs were set up and mass graves were unearthed in Argentina and Guatemala; later Rwanda, Kosovo, and elsewhere. Our role also grew in the arena of mass disaster recovery. We worked plane crashes, cemetery floods, bombings, the World Trade Center site, and most recently the tragedies of the tsunami and Hurricane Katrina.

Now, after decades of anonymity, we are stars. But the public remains confused concerning the labels. What's a pathologist? What's an anthropologist? What does forensics mean?

Pathologists are specialists who work with soft tissue. Anthropologists are specialists who work with bone. Freshly dead or relatively intact corpse: pathologist. Skeleton in a shallow grave, charred body in a barrel, bone fragments in a wood chipper, mummified baby in an attic trunk: anthropologist. Using skeletal indicators, forensic anthropologists address questions of identity, time and manner of death, and postmortem treatment of the corpse. "Forensics" is the application of scientific findings to legal questions.

And no one works alone. While TV glamorizes the individual heroics of the lone scientist or detective, real police work involves the participation of many. A pathologist may analyze the organs and brain, an entomologist the insects, an odontologist the teeth and dental records, a molecular biologist the DNA, and a ballistics expert the bullets and casings, while the forensic anthropologist pores over the bones. Numerous players place pieces in the jigsaw puzzle until a picture emerges.

My training was in archaeology, with a specialty in skeletal biology. I first found my way into forensic anthropology through a request for help in a child homicide investigation. The tiny bones were identified. A five year old girl, kidnapped, murdered, and dumped in a forest near Charlotte, North Carolina. The killer was never found. The injustice and brutality of that case changed my life. A little girl's life cut short with vicious indifference. Abandoning ancient bones for those of the recent dead, I switched to forensics and never looked back.

I like to think that my own novels played some small part in raising awareness of forensic anthropology. Through my fictional character, Temperance Brennan, I offer readers a peek into my own cases and experiences. *Déjà Dead* is based on my first serial murder investigation. *Death du Jour* derives from work I performed for the Catholic Church, and from the mass murder–suicides that took place within the Solar Temple cult. *Deadly Décisions* stems from the many bones that came to me thanks to les Hells Angels du Québec. *Fatal Voyage* is based on my disaster recovery work. *Grave Secrets* was inspired by my participation in the exhumation of a Guatemalan mass grave. *Bare Bones* sprang from moose remains I examined for wildlife agents. *Monday Mourning* grew from three skeletons discovered in a pizza parlor basement. *Cross Bones* draws on my visit to Israel, weaving strangely unreported Masada bones, a burial box purported to be that of Jesus' brother James, and a recently looted first-century tomb into a modern murder plot.

*Break No Bones* is a bit of a departure from my usual modus operandi in that the story arises not from a single or a pair of cases but from disparate professional encounters and experiences. Prehistoric burial sites excavated early in my career. An archaeological field school taught at UNCC. A coroner case hand-carried to me in a large plastic tub. Cut marks analyzed for a homicide investigation. Vertebral fractures examined for the reconstruction of a pedestrian hit-and-run. A suicide victim found skeletalized, hanging from a tree.

As with all my books, this latest Temperance Brennan novel draws on decades of personal involvement at crime labs and crime scenes. Add a pinch of archaeology. Stir in an urban legend or two. Toss in media reports of stolen body parts. Season with summers on the beach at Isle of Palms. Voila! *Break No Bones*.

Read on for an exclusive extract from the
new Temperance Brennan thriller

## *Flash and Bones*

Coming in September 2011 from
William Heinemann

# 1

Looking back, I think of it as Raceweek in the Rain. Thunderboomers almost every day. Sure, it was spring. But these storms were over the top.

In the end, Summer saved my life.

I know. Sounds bizarre.

This is what happened.

Bloated, dark clouds hung low to the ground, but so far no rain.

Lucky break. I'd spent the morning digging up a corpse.

Sound macabre? Just part of the job. I'm a forensic anthropologist. I recover and analyze the dead that present in less than pristine condition – the burned, mummified, mutilated, dismembered, decomposed, and skeletal.

OK. Today's target wasn't actually a corpse. I'd been searching for overlooked body parts.

Short version. Last fall a housewife vanished from her rural Cabarrus County home. A week ago, while I was away on a working vacation in Hawaii, a trucker admitted to strangling the woman and burying her body in a sandpit. Impatient, the local cops had sallied forth with shovels and buckets. The bones were delivered to the Mecklenburg County Medical Examiner's office in a Skippy peanut butter carton.

Yesterday, my aloha tan still glowing, I'd begun my analysis. A skeletal inventory revealed that the hyoid, the mandible, and all of the upper incisors and canines were missing.

No teeth, no dental ID. No hyoid, no evidence of strangulation. Dr. Tim Larabee, the Mecklenburg County Medical Examiner, asked me to have a second go at the sandpit.

Correcting screw-ups usually makes me cranky. Today, I was feeling upbeat.

I'd quickly found the missing bits and dispatched them to the MCME facility in Charlotte. I was en route to a shower, a late lunch, and time with my cat.

It was one fifty p.m. My sweat-soaked T was pasted to my back. My hair was yanked into a ratty knot. Sand lined my scalp and undies. Nevertheless, I was humming. Al Yankovitch, 'White and Nerdy'. What can I say? I'd watched a YouTube video and the tune lodged in my head.

Wind buffeted my Mazda as I merged onto southbound I-85. Slightly uneasy, I glanced at the sky, then thumbed on NPR.

Terry Gross was finishing an interview with Kay Ryan, the US poet laureate. Both were indifferent to the conditions outside my car.

Fair enough. Philadelphia is five hundred miles north of Dixie.

Terry launched into a teaser about an upcoming guest. I never caught the name.

Beep! Beep! Beep!

'The National Weather service has issued a severe weather warning for parts of the North Carolina piedmont, including Mecklenburg, Cabarrus, Anson, Stanly, and Union Counties. Severe thunderstorms are expected to move through the area within the next hour. Rainfall of one to three inches is anticipated, creating the potential for flash flooding. Atmospheric conditions are favorable for the development of tornadoes. Stay tuned to this station for further updates'

Beep! Beep! Beep!

I tightened my grip on the wheel and goosed my speed to seventy-five. Risky in a sixty-five mph zone, but I wanted to reach home before the deluge.

Moments later Terry was interrupted again, this time by a muted *whoop-whoop*.

My eyes flicked to the radio.

Whoop!

Feeling stupid I checked the rear view mirror.

A police cruiser was riding my bumper.

Annoyed, I pulled to the shoulder and lowered my window. When the cop approached, I held out my license.

'Dr. Temperance Brennan?'

'Looking somewhat worse for wear.' I beamed what I hoped was a winning smile.

Johnny Law did not beam back. 'That won't be necessary,' indicating my license.

Puzzled, I looked up at the guy. He was mid-twenties, slim, with an infant mustache that appeared to be going nowhere. A plaque on his chest said R. Warner.

'The Concord Police Department received a request from the Mecklenburg County medical examiner to intercept and divert you.'

'Larabee sent the cops to find me?'

'Yes, Ma'am. When I arrived at the recovery site, you'd left.'

'Why didn't he call me directly?'

'Apparently he couldn't get through.'

Of course not. While digging, I'd locked my iPhone in the car to protect it from sand.

'My phone is in the glove compartment.' No need to alarm Officer Warner. 'I'm going to take it out.'

'Yes, Ma'am.'

The numbers on the little screen indicated three missed calls from Larabee. Three messages. I listened to the first.

'Long story, which I'll share when you're back. The Concord PD received a report of a body at the Morehead Road landfill. Chapel Hill wants us to handle it. I'm elbow deep in an autopsy. Since you're in the area, I hoped you could swing by to check it out. Joe Hawkins is diverting that way with the van, just in case they've actually got something for us.'

The second message was the same as the first. Ditto the third, but more terse. It ended with the inducement: You're a champ, Tempe.

A landfill in a storm? The champ was suddenly not so chipper.

'Ma'am, we should hurry. The rain won't hold off much longer.'

'Lead on.' I could not have said this with less enthusiasm.

Warner returned to his cruiser, whoop-whooped, then pulled into traffic. Inwardly cursing Larabee, Warner, and the landfill, I palm-slapped the gearshift and followed.

Traffic on I-85 was unusually heavy for mid-afternoon. As we approached Concord, I could see that the Bruton Smith Boulevard exit ramp was a parking lot.

And realized what a nightmare this little detour of Larabee's would be.

The Morehead Road landfill is back fence neighbor to the Charlotte Motor Speedway, a major stop on the NASCAR circuit. Races would be held there this weekend and next. Tomorrow's qualifying would determine which lucky drivers would make the cut for Saturday's All Star Shootout.

Two hundred thousand avid fans would pour into Charlotte for Race Week. Looking at the sea of SUVs, campers, pick-ups, and sedans I guessed that many had already hit town.

Warner rode the shoulder. I followed, ignoring the hostile glares of those cemented in the logjam.

Lights flashing, we snaked through the bedlam on Bruton Smith Boulevard, past the dragway, the dirt track, and a zillion fast food joints. On the sidelines, the tattooed and tank-topped carried babies, six-packs, coolers, and radios. Vendors sold souvenirs from folding tables beneath improvised tents.

Warner looped the surrealistic geometry of the speedway itself, made several turns, then rolled to a stop outside a small structure whose siding might once have been blue. Beyond the building loomed a series of mounds resembling a Martian mountain range.

A man emerged and issued Warner a yellow hardhat and neon orange vest. As they talked the man pointed at a gravel road rising sharply uphill.

Warner waited while I received my safety gear, then we proceeded up the slope. Trucks rumbled in both directions, engines churning hard going in, humming going out.

When the road leveled I could see three men standing by an enormous dumpster. Two wore coveralls. The third wore black pants and a long-sleeved black shirt over a white T. Joe Hawkins, long-time death investigator for the MCME. All three featured gear identical to that lying on my passenger seat.

Warner nosed up to the dumpster and parked. I pulled in beside him.

The men watched as I got out and donned my hardhat and vest. Fetching. A perfect complement to my current state of hygiene.

'We gotta quit meeting like this.' Joe and I had parted at the sandpit barely an hour earlier.

The older man stuck out a hand. 'Weaver Molene.' Molene was flushed and sweating, and filled his coveralls way beyond their intended capacity.

'Temperance Brennan.'

I'd have skipped the handshake, given the black moons under Molene's nails, but didn't want to be rude.

'You the coroner?' he asked.

'I work for the medical examiner,' I said.

Molene introduced the younger man as Barcelona Jackson. Jackson was very thin and very black. And very, very nervous.

'Jackson and I work for BFI, the company that manages the landfill.'

'Impressive pile of trash,' I said.

'Site's got a capacity of over two and a half million cubic meters.' Molene ran a dingy hanky across his face. 'Friggin' weird Jackson stumbled onto the one square foot holding a stiff. Or maybe not. Probably dozens out there.'

Jackson had mostly kept his eyes down. At Molene's words, he raised then quickly dropped them back to his boots.

'Tell me what you found, sir.'

Though I spoke to Jackson, Molene answered.

'Probably best we show you. And quick.' He pocket-jammed the hanky. 'This storm's coming fast.'

Molene set off at a pace I would have thought impossible for a man of his bulk. Jackson scampered after. I fell into line, paying attention as best I could to the uneven footing. Warner and Hawkins brought up the rear.

I've excavated in landfills, am familiar with the aroma of *eau de dump*, a delicate blend of methane and carbon dioxide, with traces of ammonia, hydrogen sulfide, nitrogen, hydrogen chloride, and carbon monoxide added for spice. I braced for the stench. Didn't happen.

Good odor management, guys. Or maybe it was Mother Nature. Wind swirled dirt into little cyclones and tumbled cellophane wrappers, plastic bags, and torn paper across the landscape.

Our course took us the length of the active landfill, down a slope, then around a series of what appeared to be closed areas. Instead of raw earth, the tops of the older mounds were covered with grass.

As we walked, the rumble of trucks receded and the whine of fine-tuned engines grew louder. Based on the changing acoustics I figured the speedway lay over a rise to our right.

After ten minutes, Molene stopped at the base of a truncated hillock. Though tentative grass greened the top, the side facing us was scarred and pitted, like a desert butte gouged by eons of wind.

Molene said something I didn't catch. I was focused on the exposed stratigraphy.

Unlike the sandstone or shale making up metamorphic

9

rock, the mound's layers were composed of flattened Pontiacs and Posturpedics, of squashed Pepsis, Pop-Tarts, Pringles, and Pampers.

Molene pointed to a crater in a brown-green layer eight feet above our heads, then to an object lying about two yards off the base of the mound. His explanation was lost to a clap of thunder.

Didn't matter. It was obvious Jackson's 'stiff' had dropped from the mound, probably dislodged by the previous day's storm.

I crossed to the thing and squatted. Molene, Warner, and Hawkins clustered around me but remained standing. Jackson kept his distance.

The object was a drum, approximately twenty inches in diameter and thirty inches high. Its cover lay off to one side.

'Looks like a metal container of some kind,' I said without looking up. 'It's too rusted to make out a logo or label.'

'Flip it.' Molene shouted. 'Jackson and I turned the thing bottom-up to protect the stuff inside.'

I tried. It weighed a ton.

Hawkins squatted and, together, we muscled the drum upright. Its interior was filled with a solid black mass.

I leaned close. Something pale was suspended in the dark fill, but the pre-storm gloom obscured all detail.

I was reaching for my MagLite when lightning sparked.

A human hand flashed white in the electric brilliance.

Dissolved to black.

DON'T MISS KATHY REICHS'
FABULOUS NEW FORENSIC SERIES

# *Virals*

## Kathy Reichs

Tory Brennan is as fascinated by bones and dead bodies as her famous aunt, acclaimed forensic anthropologist, Tempe Brennan. However living on a secluded island off Charleston in South Carolina there is not much opportunity to put her knowledge to the test. Until she and her group of technophile friends stumble across a shallow grave containing the remains of a girl who has been missing for over thirty years.

With the cold-case murder suddenly hot, Tory realises that they are involved in something fatally dangerous. And when they rescue a sick dog from a laboratory on the same island, it becomes evident that somehow the two events are linked.

On the run from forces they don't understand, they have only each other to fall back on. Until they succumb to a mysterious infection that heightens their senses and hones their instincts to impossible levels. Their illness seems to have changed their very biology – and it's clear that the island is home to something well beyond their comprehension. It's a secret that has driven men to kill once. And will drive them to kill again . . .

**WILLIAM HEINEMANN: LONDON**

# Spider Bones

## Kathy Reichs

Dr Temperance Brennan spends her working life amongst the decomposed, the mutilated, and the skeletal. So the two-days-dead body she is called to examine holds little to surprise her. Until she discovers that the man is John Lowery, an ex-soldier who was apparently killed in Vietnam in 1968. So who is buried in Lowery's grave?

The case takes Tempe to an organisation dedicated to bringing home the bodies of unidentified soldiers where she must examine the remains of anyone who may have had a connection to the drowned man. It's a harrowing task, but it pays off when she finds Lowery's dog tags amongst the bones of a long-dead soldier.

As Tempe unravels the tangled threads of the soldiers' lives and deaths, she realises there are some who would rather the past stayed buried. And when she proves difficult to frighten, they turn their attention to the one person she would give her life to protect . . .

arrow books

ALSO AVAILABLE IN ARROW

# *206 Bones*

## Kathy Reichs

**'You have an enemy, Dr Brennan. It is in your interest
to learn who placed the call . . .'**

A routine case turns sinister when Dr Temperance Brennan is
accused of mishandling the autopsy of a missing heiress. Someone
has made an incriminating accusation that she missed or con-
cealed crucial evidence. Before Tempe can get to the one man
with information, he turns up dead.

The heiress isn't the only elderly female to have appeared on
Tempe's gurney recently. Back in Montreal, three more women
have died, their bodies brutally discarded. Tempe is convinced
there's a link between their deaths and that of the heiress.
But what – or who – connects them?

Tempe struggles with the clues, but nothing adds up. Has she
made grave errors or is some unknown foe sabotaging her? It soon
becomes frighteningly clear. It's not simply Tempe's career at risk.
Her life is at stake too.

arrow books

# *Devil Bones*

## Kathy Reichs

**An underground chamber is exposed in a seedy, dilapidated house with sagging trim and peeling paint . . .**

In the dark cellar, a ritualistic display is revealed. A human skull rests on a cauldron, surrounded by slain chickens and bizarre figurines. Beads and antlers dangle overhead.

Called to the scene is forensic anthropologist Dr Temperance Brennan. Bony architecture suggests that the skull is that of a young, black female. But how did she die? And when? Then, just as Tempe is working to determine the post-mortem interval, another body is discovered: a headless corpse carved with Satanic symbols.

As citizen vigilantes, blaming Devil-worshippers, begin a witch-hunt, intent on revenge, Tempe struggles to keep her emotions in check. But the truth she eventually uncovers proves more shocking than even she could have imagined . . .

arrow books